The Cactus Navy

USS Bull Shark Naval Thriller, Book 3

Scott W. Cook

The Cactus Navy

USS *Bull Shark* Naval Thriller, Book 3

© Copyright 2021 by Scott W. Cook

All rights reserved.

Book Cover and Formatting by Trisha Fuentes

No part of this book may be reproduced in any form or by any electronic or mechanical means, including information storage and retrieval systems, without written permission from the author, except for the use of brief quotations in a book review.

Contents

Preface vii
The Theater xi

Part One
Thumbing Back the Hammer

1. SOLOMON ISLANDS, NEW GEORGIA SOUND - 9°8' S, 159°38' E 3
   10 miles northwest of Savo Island
   – July 2, 1942 – 2341 ship's time

2. Naval Air Station Midway – Midway Atoll 28°12' N, 177°12' W 21
   July 6, 1942 – 0730 local time

3. USS Bull Shark 31
   – 975 miles south, southwest of Wake Island

4. USS Bull Shark 41
   – 3 miles west of Wake Island

   Chapter 5 55

6. Strike Carrier Sakai – July 25, 1942 67
   The Slot – Between Guadalcanal and Tulagi

7. USS BULL SHARK – AUGUST 1, 1942 – 1830 SHIP'S TIME 77
   12°18', 161°47'
   – 112 miles south, southeast of Guadalcanal

8. Honolulu, Hawaii 87
   – 1755 local time

   Chapter 9 99

10. Southern Coast of Guadalcanal 111
11. Between Guadalcanal and San Cristobal Islands 121
12. Bank of the Nombor River 133
13. Off the northeastern coast of Guadalcanal 147
    – 1945 local time
14. Hours earlier... 10 miles northeast of Aola Bay, Guadalcanal .. 159
    – 1930 local time

15. Several hours earlier – *the Guadalcanal interior*	169
16. 10 miles off Aola, Guadalcanal – *2225 local time*	181
17. Deep in the jungle	193
18. Honolulu, Hawaii – August 3, 1942 – *1130 local time*	209
Chapter 19	221
20. USS Bull Shark – Northwest of Florida Island *August 4, 1942 – 0830 local time*	231
21. The jungles of Guadalcanal – several hours earlier	247
22. New Georgia Sound	261
23. Palapao Village – Guadalcanal – *1940 local time*	271
Chapter 24	283
25. Vushicoro – August 5, 1942 – *0815 local time*	295
26. Bottom of New Georgia Sound – August 6, 1942 – *0115 local time*	307
27. Operation Watchtower – 120 miles W, SW of Guadalcanal *Thursday, August 6, 1942 – 1622 local time*	323
28. Honolulu, Hawaii – *2230 local time*	337

Part Two
Pulling the Trigger

29. D-Day – August 7, 1942 – *0600 Guadalcanal time*	353
Chapter 30	367
31. USS Bull Shark – *Eastern New Georgia Sound*	381
32. Beach Red, Guadalcanal - *0919*	393
Chapter 33	407
34. D-Day+1 August 8, 1942 – 0800 *USS Bull Shark – 130 miles northeast of the Florida Islands*	417
35. USS Bull Shark 1940	431

Chapter 36   443
37. Guadalcanal   459
   – *August 9, 1942*

EPILOGUE   473
Brisbane, Australia
– August 13, 1942

A Word from the Author   481
Other books by the Author...   483

Preface

In the first six months of World War II, Japan enjoyed tremendous success in seizing territory from the Indian Ocean to the South Pacific as well as the North Pacific around their home islands. This was done in order to consolidate much-needed natural resources and to gain strategic advantages in order to secure their large oceanic empire. It was for the latter reason that the Japanese attacked outlying islands, including Wake, Midway, New Britain (specifically the port of Rabaul), Tulagi and others. Their goal was to establish forward bases of operation to hinder and even cut off shipping and lines of communication between the United States and Australia.

Early in 1942, Japan invaded Bougainville, technically part of the Solomon Island chain but politically part of New Guinea. The air and naval bases they began constructing on Bual and Buan, islands that were part of Bougainville, were to reinforce their seizure of Rabaul, a major base of operation in the area. In order to further strengthen their position and weaken that of the Allies, the Japanese embarked on a plan to seize control of the entire Solomon Island chain, a nine-hundred-mile-long archipelago that would allow them to control important sea lanes between the U.S. and Australia.

Preface

Having already taken Tulagi during the Battle of the Coral Sea in May of 1942, the Japanese quickly established footholds on the nearby islands, including Guadalcanal.

Guadalcanal is a mostly tropical jungle island about ninety miles long and twenty-five wide. Rugged mountains and valleys mark the interior, yet on the northern side, there are drier flat grassy areas. One of these is Lunga Point, a promontory on the northeastern coast. It was here, in July, that the Japanese began the construction of an airfield that would be capable of servicing a large number of ground-based aircraft, as the base at nearby Tulagi was only able to support seaplanes. When an American reconnaissance flight spotted this construction, it became clear that something must be done.

After much debate and wrangling between the Navy and the Army, a plan was put forward to invade the Guadalcanal region, seize control of the new airfield and turn the tables on the Japanese plan. This operation, code-named Watchtower, would be the first offensive move of the Pacific War and the beginning of a years-long campaign of island hopping to retake the vast Pacific holdings from the Japanese Empire.

Thus, on August 6, 1942, a huge Allied fleet of 82 ships made its way into the waters south of Guadalcanal. The fleet consisted of aircraft carriers, warships and transports and bore over 19,000 Marines who would be tasked with taking and holding Guadalcanal, Gavutu, Tanambogo, Florida Island and Tulagi. It was the beginning of what was to be a six-month-long campaign and one of the most grueling endeavors of the war.

The deeds of courage, endurance, fortitude and sacrifice that marked the Solomon Islands Campaign cannot be overstated. So incredible are the stories of the Navy and especially the Marines that no fiction can do them justice. In this story, we'll experience some of these true-life epics through the witness of our old friends, the crew of the USS *Bull Shark*. The Marine Raiders, Melanesian heroes who assisted the American forces, the courageous coast watchers who made it all possible and the brave men of the Navy and Marine

Preface

Corps. In this book, your humble scribbler will attempt to illustrate the glories and the horrors of war in a way that brings a vital moment of our history to living, breathing life.

Once again, I wish to state that this is a work of fiction. And although real people do appear in this book, they are used fictitiously. As with other books in this series, I do take some dramatic license... since Captain Turner and crew are entirely fictional, it's impossible not to do so. Yet, I do this only to entertain. For example, near the end of the book, you'll be briefly introduced to Chesty Puller... yet in truth, Lt. Colonel Puller doesn't arrive on Guadalcanal until several weeks after I suggest he does... but it's all in fun!

For more accurate and in-depth reading about the struggle for Guadalcanal, I suggest one of the many fine books written on the subject. In particular, I recommend *Midnight in the Pacific* by Joseph Wheelan. This book is a detailed history and includes many personal accounts from those who served in what was a true living hell.

Once again, this book is dedicated to the greatest generation. Those who went to war and changed the world for us. The brave men of the silent service, the United States Marines and of course Merrit A. "Red Mike" Edson's First Marine Raiders as well as Evans F. Carlson's Second Marine Raiders.

The Theater

The Solomon Island chain is the largest archipelago in the South Pacific. Stretching over 900 miles and incorporating over 900 islands and atolls, the chain lies directly in line between Hawaii and Australia, with its center roughly a thousand miles west of the international dateline. Guadalcanal, the focus of this narrative, would seem to be a tropical island paradise. Located some three-hundred and fifty miles south of the equator, the island is, in fact, a soldier's nightmare. Receiving more than one hundred inches of rain annually, the island's dense jungles are always damp and dripping with runoff. Frequent rains turn roads and tracks into mud bogs and continually overflow the rivers and creeks near the coasts.

As if the weather weren't bad enough for our Marine heroes, the island boasts a prodigious number and diversity of fauna. Huge saltwater crocodiles, tarantulas, fire ants, centipedes, leeches, ringworm, enormous wasps and spider's as large as a man's fist abound. Of course, the malaria-infected mosquito was ever-present as well. There aren't many poisonous snakes, though... for that, the First and Fifth Marines were no doubt grateful... on the other hand, it wasn't uncommon to find sea snakes in the sea and at the beaches nearby. As if this weren't bad enough... sharks were to be found in the areas around Guadalcanal due to the fact that local islanders often floated their dead out to sea. This was unfortunate, especially during the disastrous Battle of Savo Island, wherein thousands of sailors died when four cruisers were obliterated by Japanese vessels in a horrific night action between Savo Island and Guadalcanal.

So many ships, both allied and IJN alike, went down between Guadalcanal and the islands of Tulagi, Gavutu and Florida Island that the area would quickly come to be known as Iron Bottom Sound.

As if jungle rot, blood-thirsty insects, ravenous giant lizards and meager rations weren't enough for the Marines to contend with... there were the Japanese as well. Soldiers who were so fearsome and vicious that even their wounded would contrive to stab, shoot or blow you up should you get close enough. Not even medical corpsmen were immune to the Japanese dedication to killing. Over and over again, from the air, the sea and the land, the Japanese tormented the Marines, airmen and sailors stationed at the captured Japanese airfield. Renamed for a Marine pilot who'd gone down during the Battle of Midway, Henderson Field would be the focal point for some of the most incredible acts of bravery and savagery in the entire war. Guadalcanal's operational code name was "Cactus." It was this moniker that lent itself to the nickname that the occupation force adopted for itself – the Cactus Airforce. This, after their first nickname, based on the hastily prepared and under-supplied way in which Watchtower was conceived... the Marines called it Operation Shoestring.

Part One

Thumbing Back the Hammer

"It is well that war is so terrible that we should grow too fond of it."

— Robert E. Lee

Chapter 1

Solomon Islands, New Georgia Sound - 9°8' S, 159°38' E

10 miles northwest of Savo Island – July 2, 1942 – 2341 ship's time

Lieutenant Commander Arthur Turner enjoyed the first watch. In the summertime, especially in tropical regions, he came on watch just in time to enjoy the sunset. He could bask in the pleasant cooling-off period when the sun's heat dissipated and the breeze over the ocean slowly lowered to match the temperature of the sea. While it was true that only a few hundred miles south of the equator in July, that temperature was almost ninety, it was still pleasant as compared to what had come before.

Turner relished the moonrises, too. The way the sky slowly changed color as it darkened after Sol eased himself into the sea. The azure blue of the western horizon, often still dotted with fluffy clouds, dark gray on their eastern sides and bright cotton-candy pink where the rays of the invisible sun still caressed them. And in the east, a rapidly deepening royal blue, then navy, then indigo and finally a blackness that sprouted thousands of tiny pinpricks of unimaginably distant suns.

Were there planets orbiting some of those suns? Were there men on them, sailing on their seas and gazing back at him, too?

Sailing tranquilly among all that vastness and more, the brilliant

– July 2, 1942 – 2341 ship's time

face of Selene smiled down on him as she rose silently above the world, casting her silvery reflection upon the waters. It was almost enough to make Turner forget about the fact that half the world was clawing at the throats of the other half.

The impression wasn't just illusory; it was as tenuous and insubstantial as wisps of the finest gossamer. For, after all, he was standing on the bridge of the most sophisticated killing machine ever devised, was he not?

USS *Bull Shark* **SS**-333, *Balao*-class American fleet submarine, drove herself through the night on two engine speed at a sedate ten knots. For several hours now, starting just about the time the sun's lower rim had appeared to touch the rim of the world, the submarine had been running on her four mighty diesels. The two after engines sending two and a half million watts of power into the four General Electric motors that drove her, and the two forward General Motors engines sending their two and a half million watts of energy into the boat's two massive Sargo battery banks.

It was quiet on deck, in spite of the six men posted there. The three lookouts in the periscope sheers were attentively scanning their sectors, and only occasionally would a smattering of quiet conversation drift down to their captain who was standing his watch. The boat's executive officer, Elmer Williams, recently and thankfully back from completing PXO School, was arranged on the after cigarette deck with his sextant taking the opportunity of a clear night to perform a lunar observation to triple-check their position. Beside Turner on the bridge was the quartermaster of the watch, the ship's chief of the boat, Paul "Buck" Rogers.

Turner inhaled deeply, sampling the heavy night air. On it wafted a variety of scents that lent an enriching headiness to the atmosphere. There was the ubiquitous taste of salt and iodine that marked life at sea. There was the tantalizing aroma of green things from the islands only just over the horizon. Chlorophyll. Earthy loam and even a tinge of volcanic sulfur. Then, of course, there was the

Solomon Islands, New Georgia Sound - 9°8' S, 159°38' E

smell of hamburgers, French fries and popcorn that rose in an invisible pillar from the open bridge hatch behind the watchstanders.

The snick of a lighter and the sudden sharp tang of burning tobacco overrode all the other scents for a moment and made Turner smile. He reached into the pocket of his shorts, pulled out his pack of Lucky Strikes and then cursed under his breath.

"Left 'em back in the machine again eh, Skipper?" The COB asked before chuckling softly.

"Aww, you know how it is Buck..." Turner rejoined. "I'm the captain. Got all kinda stuff on my mind. I can't be expected to remember to snitch a new pack of smokes *every* time. Sides... you'll let me cadge a pill, right? Buddy? Pal?"

Rogers leaned against the railing and took a long drag on his Camel, "Ahhhhh... that's cool and refreshing..."

Turner laughed, "Really, Buck? I can put you on report for this, you know."

"What's the charge?" Rogers asked wryly.

"Failure to give out with your smokes," Turner replied.

"Probably a hangin' offense, I'd imagine."

Rogers laughed and held out his pack to his captain, "Well... when you put it like that, sure you can grab a pill, sir. When they do hang me, I'll be damned if it's gonna be for something so trivial."

The two men shared a chuckle and a smoke together. They'd known one another for most of their adult lives. Certainly Turner's, as Rogers was two years older than Turner's thirty-two. In that time, more than a dozen years, they'd served off and on together and were as close as any enlisted man and officer could be, and then some.

"What're you two conspiring about?" Elmer Williams's voice asked from behind as he strode forward.

"Oh, just thinking of new ways to torture the new guy," Turner said.

Rogers snorted, "Yeah, after you bailed on us a while back, Mr. Williams... and who you left in your place... I'd watch my back, if I was you sir."

– July 2, 1942 – 2341 ship's time

Williams chuckled, "Hey, I was just following orders. Can't hold me responsible for those two clowns. I know it's... well, it's disrespectful to speak ill of the dead... but..."

"If you're an asshole in life, being dead doesn't change that, Elmer," Turner said, a hint of strain in his voice. "What happened to Pendergast... and I suppose Begley... was brought on entirely by themselves. It's a shame, really... but it's in the past. Now we've got our cuddly Mr. Williams back, huh, Buck?"

"That's right, sir," Rogers said with a broad toothy grin. "And yet another new assistant engineer. A guy who seems like he's a much better fit for this outfit, too."

Williams chuckled, "Yup... real nice guy. A little loud, at times. A bit larger than life... not unlike Pat, if you think about it."

Turner laughed, "Yeah, except for that Foghorn Leghorn accent of his. How are the men taking it, Buck? After our last experience with new officers..."

Rogers shrugged, "Lt. Porter Hazard seems to be gaining traction with the troops, sir. He knows his stuff, is a good submariner and for all his bluster is a friendly guy who's always ready with a kind word or to shoot the shit with the crew. His being a former Marine makes him an object of curiosity, I think."

"For us too," Turner admitted. "A bit strange, a guy nearly forty still a J.G. and who switched horses well into his career. Was in Nicaragua, I think. Haven't heard the full story yet, but we'll get it outta him sooner or later."

"*Bridge, conning,*" the voice of the communication's officer, Ensign Andy Post, emitted from the tinny bridge transmitter. Post was standing his watch in the control room as junior officer of the deck. "*Possible enemy contact on sugar jig. Bearing three-five-zero, range twenty-four thousand yards.*"

"Right down the slot," Rogers mused.

Turner met the other men's eyes, and even without looking, he knew that the forward port lookout would be training his 7x50 Bausch and Lomb binoculars in that direction. At twelve miles and

Solomon Islands, New Georgia Sound - 9°8' S, 159°38' E

from their height, the lookouts would probably not spot a ship unless it was foolish enough to be burning a mast light.

"Well, well, well..." he said, rubbing his hands together in absent enthusiasm. "The Jap finally decides to show his yellow kisser... conning, bridge... how many contacts and what're they up to?"

A pause and then, "*Indeterminant, sir. I think two and suspect more. Speed seems to be ten knots, though. I'll need a minute to get a comparison to determine their track.*"

"Understood, Andy," Turner said. "Secure the sugar jig, wait one and then do another sweep. Get a plot started."

Post acknowledged, and the men above waited in silent anticipation. For nearly a week now, *Bull Shark* had been prowling about the New Georgia Sound between Guadalcanal and Bougainville. Most of their patrol route was nearer the southern and eastern area of the sound, closer to Guadalcanal and Tulagi. Both recently invaded by and currently occupied by the Japanese.

Thus far, there had been no significant surface activity. A destroyer once during daylight hours and a variety of aircraft from Bougainville and the seaplanes that berthed in the Tulagi harbor. Certainly nothing by night.

"*Bridge, control,*" Post reported. "*Definitely two contacts with a possible third. Speed still ten and heading appears one-five-zero.*"

"Interesting..." Williams stated, rubbing his chin. "Not on a direct course for Tulagi..."

"Yeah, unless I'm off my mark, that'll take them toward the northeastern shore of Guadalcanal," Turner stated. He thumbed the transmit button. "Andy, sound general quarters. Battle stations torpedo. Order the helm to come right to zero-two-zero, current speed. Standby to dive once we're fully manned."

Turner cast his eyes off to the west, where the blanket of stars was being partially obscured by a line of dark clouds. A late evening rain squall. Hardly rare in the Solomons. He'd noticed it earlier as well, having appeared not half an hour before, and it seemed to be moving in their direction.

– July 2, 1942 – 2341 ship's time

Turner, his officers and the entire crew were eager to do some real submarining. To do the job that their boat had been built for. To go out on war patrol, interdict Japanese merchant ships and blast them into flotsam. There was something almost mundane about the concept when compared to their first two missions. Not that hunting down secret Nazi ships or a top-secret Japanese monster submarine wasn't interesting, of course. The four swastikas and two rising sun flags painted on the conning tower were certainly something to be proud of.

"Got 'em, sir!" one of the lookouts shouted. "Looks like two ships just visible over the horizon."

"We gonna attack on the surface, Art?" Williams asked.

Turner considered this for a long moment. Current submarine doctrine wasn't written that way. The old-guard skippers weren't in favor of it, stating that night surface attacks were too risky and exposed the boat to far too much danger. Their feeling was that a submarine should get out in front of a convoy, wait for it to pass by and send all your fish at them and then dive and evade.

While this was certainly preferred during daylight attacks, especially when a convoy was being escorted, things were different at night. At night, a submarine could use all of her advantages. She could use her more than twenty knots of speed to work into an attack approach that best suited her. She could use her radar, which, even over seven months into the war, was still almost entirely an allied tool. The younger new-guard skippers such as Art Turner were proponents of this type of attack, a far more aggressive way to fight from a submarine.

However, with the ships still only just coming up over the hill, Turner didn't yet know what was really out there. At ten knots, they'd likely be transports or cargo vessels... yet that wasn't necessarily true. They could be military ships moving slowly or at least moving slowly as an escorting force. With the moon so bright and the storm still coming up, Turner's best position would silhouette

Solomon Islands, New Georgia Sound - 9°8' S, 159°38' E

his boat nicely, and one of those ships might indeed possess a radar set.

"No, XO," Turner finally decided. "I want to get a close look at them. Clear the bridge!"

Turner pulled the dive alarm twice and the familiar and exhilarating *ah-ooooga, ah-oooga* blared through the boat. The lookouts quickly scrambled down from their perch and vanished down the hatchway. Williams went next, followed by the COB and finally Turner, who hauled on the lanyard as he descended the ladder. He dogged the hatch and took his place at the periscopes, pleased to see Pat Jarvis already at the TDC and Andy Post working at the small chart desk on his plot.

"All stop," the captain ordered. "Standby to answer bells on batteries. Rig out dive planes, close main induction. Open the main vents. Flood safety, flood negative and flood bow buoyancy."

Williams continued down into the control room, where he and the plotting party would work upon the target plot at the master gyrocompass table. Turner preferred this, as the table allowed for more room and a more expansive plot. However, he also wanted the AOOD with his maneuvering board at the chart desk working up his own track as both a backstop and as exercise.

"Green board," Lieutenant Frank Nichols stated from below. "Motors ready on battery, Captain. Keep in mind, we're only at about seventy percent... long dive today. We could still run with the snork, though, sir."

Turner looked down the hatch into the control room, "Not with that moon. I've got a feeling about this, Enj. We'll do it the old-fashioned way. Periscope depth, if you please. Helm, all ahead two-thirds. Andy, give me a course to put me dead ahead of that convoy. Say... four thousand yards. I want time to look them over."

"Sir, maneuverin' answerin' two-thirds," the helmsman, Richard "Mug" Vigliano, reported. "Bendix log indicates five knots."

"Very well," Turner replied.

– July 2, 1942 – 2341 *ship's time*

"Sir, at five knots... I recommend zero-three-five," Post stated after a moment.

"You heard the man, Mug," Turner stated. "Got that downstairs?"

"Aye-aye," Williams replied.

"Time to intercept will be sixty-four minutes," Andy reported.

"Very well. Pat, order both rooms to open their outer doors," Turner stated.

"Set depth on all fish to four feet for now. Speed fast."

"Forty-five feet," Nichols announced from below.

"Close vents," Turner ordered. "Blow negative to the mark."

The dive had been handled expertly, as always. So well did his officers and men work the ship that Turner hardly needed to give the orders. The mood of the boat was palpable. Excitement and eagerness. Gone now was the gloom, distrust and other problems they'd so recently experienced. Once again, Turner's ship was the efficient and happy set of men that it had been before coming into the Pacific. As his friend and mentor Dudley "Mush" Morton had told him when Turner had attended prospective commanding officer school:

"Art, a happy ship is an effective ship."

"Forward torpedo reports ready," Jarvis stated. After a few seconds, as he listened to the receiver of his sound-powered telephone, he then said: "After room reports ready, sir."

"Excellent. What've you got on your end, Chet?"

Chet Rivers, the boat's number one soundman and whose hearing was perhaps only matched by that of Lt. Joe Dutch, turned from his gear and pulled back one of his headset cups.

"I'm getting multiple sets of screws, sir," Rivers reported. "I believe three single slow screws... one set of fast double screws... and another set of fast... uhm... three screws. Assess three merchants, a tin can and a light cruiser, sir."

"Christ," Jarvis muttered.

Solomon Islands, New Georgia Sound - 9°8' S, 159 °38' E

"Lotta heavy metal to escort a handful of freighters," Turner opined. "Range, sonar?"

"Nearest is ten thousand yards, bearing three-one-five, sir."

"Up attack scope," Turner ordered.

Ted Balkley, the number one radarman, was acting as periscope assistant. He waited until Turner crouched low to the deck before hitting the appropriate control on the remote box.

The slim attack scope began to rise. Turner quickly flipped the control handles down and allowed the scope to haul him upright. He made a gesture, and Balkley stopped the scope's progress.

"Okay... damned good moon tonight..." Turner mused. "That storm is not far off now... Yup, I can see three freighters and their DD watchdog clearly. No sign of the CL, though. Hmm... still partially concealed by the horizon from this low. It looks as if two of the freighters are in line ahead and the third is off their port sides. The DD is slightly out ahead and to starboard. CL might be concealed in the rear. We're gonna use the same trick. We'll come up astern of the DD, send two fish his way, then shift targets to the lead freighter and give him four."

"And then?" Jarvis asked with a smile tugging at his lips.

"Then we pray," Turner said. "Down scope."

The minutes dragged by as *Bull Shark* worked her way out in front of the convoy. In time, Williams and Post both announced that the boat had reached Turner's waypoint. Turner ordered the helm to come to the same course as the five ships and reduce speed to one-third. This would allow the targets to close more quickly and conserve battery power.

Even from four-thousand yards off, the sound of the destroyer's screws could be heard resonating through the submarine's hull. It was thus far faint, yet the eighty silent men could tell that the distant ship was closing on them at an overtake speed of seven knots.

"Make your depth one-five-zero feet, Enj.," Turner said down the hatch to Nichols.

11

– July 2, 1942 – 2341 ship's time

"One-five-zero feet, aye," Nichols replied. "Planesmen, dive angle on the bow, fifteen-degree rise on the stern."

The ship took on a distinct forward tilt as the bow planes forced more water pressure over the ship's nose and the stern planes pushed the after end of the ship upward, thus allowing her screws to drive her deeper into the darkened sea.

"Chet, any idea of the separations?" Turner asked quietly.

The ship wasn't rigged for silent running, as the screw noises of the five vessels would mask most normal sounds. However, the habit of making as little noise as possible when making an approach was so ingrained in seasoned submariners it became an unconscious habit.

"I think about five hundred yards," Rivers said. "The DD is five hundred yards to starboard of the two-ship column, which is five hundred to starboard of the third merchant and the CL another five hundred. The DD is out front, maybe two hundred yards forward of the bow of the first freighter. The third freighter is a little astern of the second and to her left, then the CL a bit astern and further away. You could almost draw a line from the CL to the DD and intersect the two aftermost merchants, sir."

"You got all that, Elmer?" Turner said down the three-foot-wide deck hatch.

"Got it, Skipper," Williams stated. "You're gonna come up between the DD and the first freighter, a bit behind the DD, and shoot them both?"

Turner grinned. Williams knew him well. He reveled in the smooth way this attack was running and was thankful, "Roger that, XO."

"Recommend coming left two-five degrees for now," Andy Post stated. "Give it forty-seconds and then return to base course."

"Concur," Williams's disembodied voice said.

"You heard the man, Mug," Turner ordered.

"Sir my rudder is left standid'...," Vigliano said in his heavy Brooklyn. "...my helm is now one-tree-zero."

The ships were close by then. Well within a mile. Even without

Solomon Islands, New Georgia Sound - 9°8' S, 159°38' E

the benefit of the sonar headset, Turner could hear the ships' positions through the hull. The rapid swishing of the destroyer's twin fast screws churned over his right shoulder, and the slower, deeper chugging of the leading freighter's seemed to be coming from over his left, though further aft. Everyone listened as the swishing and chugging grew louder, closer and moved forward. With a seven-knot overtake speed, the convoy was closing the gap by two hundred yards every minute.

"Sir, my helm is now one-five-five," Mug reported.

"Tin can is abeam..." Rivers almost whispered.

"Very well..." Turner softly replied.

After another minute, the sonarman announced that the freighter was now abeam.

"Helm, all ahead two-thirds," Turner ordered, having to work to keep the excitement from his voice. "Frank, periscope depth."

Orders were acknowledged, and the boat angled upward. By the time the submarine was once again at sixty-five feet, the destroyer was five hundred yards ahead and the first freighter one hundred. Turner ordered the attack scope raised.

He did a quick three-hundred-and-sixty-degree sweep. There was nothing out there but his targets, which seemed shockingly close even in the darkness.

"Damn... the second ship in line isn't a freighter but a transport," Turner noted. "And they're headed for Guadalcanal... what goes on here? Pat, I want to give tubes one and two to the DD... a Fubuki... boy, these guys aren't screwin' around here... and then the rest to the freighter. Looks like a *Maratzu Maru*... use mast height of seventy-five feet. Depth still four feet. Here's your first bearing on the DD... mark."

"Bearing is zero-one-eight," Balkley read off the bearing ring.

Turner settled his targeting reticule on the big destroyer leader's mast. "Angle on the bow is one-niner-eight port... range... mark!"

"Six-five-zero yards," Balkley reported as he read the stadimeter scale.

– July 2, 1942 – 2341 ship's time

A few very tense moments, and then Jarvis looked to Turner, "Set. Shoot anytime, sir."

"Fire one," Turner said and then counted down from six. "Fire two! Okay, shifting targets to the freighter, Pat... got 'em... angle on the bow is one-five-six starboard... bearing mark!"

"Three-three-four," Balkley said excitedly.

"Range... mark!"

"Five-eight-five yards," Balkley reported.

"Run time on first two fish is thirty-five seconds," Pat stated as he cranked in the values. "About the same for the second batch... set!"

Turner ordered the last four fish in the forward room sent away. With each launch, the deck shuddered as three-thousand pounds of weapon was shoved into the sea by a blast of high-pressure air. In the next instant, that same volume of air, held in the tube by the seawater outside, was sucked back into the submarine by the poppet valve. Each time, the crew could feel the pressure in their ears as the boat's ambient pressure gulped thousands of pounds of compressed air back into the submarine.

"All fish running hot, straight and normal," Rivers announced.

"Ten-seconds on the Fubuki," Jarvis reported.

"Andy, get over here with your camera," Turner ordered.

In order for a submarine to be credited with a kill, some form of evidence must be obtained. That evidence could come in the form of a recovered life ring from a sunken ship, decoded intelligence reports from the enemy and best of all, photographic proof. It was Turner's habit, when possible, to have a photo taken after a ship had been hit as well as to allow the men in the conning tower to take turns looking at their handiwork.

Post appeared at his side with his small Kodak in his hands. Turner peered through the scope at the destroyer off his starboard bow, completely and strangely oblivious to the death racing toward her at forty-six knots.

Thwack! Ka-booom!

In his scope, the destroyer's stern erupted into a red-orange

Solomon Islands, New Georgia Sound - 9°8'S, 159°38'E

fireball. The torpex in the torpedoes blasting away the fantail and igniting the depth charges stored in racks above. Turner waved Post forward.

Andy first peered through the lens before placing the lens of his camera up to the eyepiece and snapping off three quick shots, "God all mighty..."

"Twenty-seconds on the freighter!" Pat remarked.

"Take a peek, men," Turner implored. "You just bagged your third tin can."

Rivers, Balkley, Jarvis and even Vigliano dashed to Turner's side and took a look at the death of the destroyer, already going down by the stern with her knife-like bow pointed toward the stars.

Turner took the scope back and rotated it toward the port bow. The freighter was turning, having seen the fate of her protector and knowing what must be coming for her as well. Unfortunately for her crew, the ship was neither swift nor maneuverable enough to avoid what was coming.

Once again, the peculiar crack and boom of the torpex explosion resounded through the ship. A huge geyser of red-lit water soared up the freighter's starboard bow. Six-seconds later, another bulge of seawater and raging fireball erupted amidships, followed quickly by a thundering roar that filled even the submarine. One or more of the ship's boilers must have exploded, the pressurized vessel dealing the doomed ship as much destruction as several fish combined.

Once again, Post shot a few pictures, and everyone took a look as the big black shape of the ship disintegrated into two halves, each of which hungrily devoured thousands of tons of seawater and plunging the ship and her sailors into a watery grave.

"Down scope!" Turner ordered. By now, the jig was most certainly up, and the light cruiser would be coming for them. "Helm, all ahead standard. Frank, get us down to three bills and make it snappy! Mug, come left to course two-niner-zero degrees!"

"We goin' after the rest of them, Skipper?" Jarvis asked wryly.

– July 2, 1942 – 2341 ship's time

Turner grinned, "Probably not, Pat. Don't want to press our luck too hard."

"Really?" Elmer Williams' head suddenly appeared in the hatchway like a jack in the box. "You mean we're not gonna surface and fire on all three ships at once? Seems conservative for Anvil Art Turner."

Turner chuckled, "Well... let's try caution this *one* time... if you don't like it, we won't have to do it again, Elmer."

That elicited a hearty laugh from the conning tower and the control room below. Turner was glad of that because they might just need it over the next few hours.

Oooooeeee... ooooeeee...

The eerie and ghostly sound of low-frequency sound beams probing the depths joined the frantic chugging of the civilian vessel's screws. The cruiser was actively pinging.

"Merchants are running for it, sir," Rivers reported.

"Exfiltrating at fourteen knots north and south. The CL is headed right for the sinkings... range fifteen hundred yards... not straight on, but she'll be close."

"Frank, take us down to five hundred," Turner amended his last. "Let's hope there's a layer down there someplace."

"Sir... chart indicates that we're in the hundred fathom curve off Savo," Williams cautioned.

"Good, then we'll have plenty of water under the keel," Turner replied. "Mug, back her down to two-thirds on both screws."

Ooee... ooee...

The cruiser's sonar probing was definitely getting closer.

"Rig for depth charge, rig for silent running," Turner announced.

Below, the sound of compartment hatches and ventilation flappers clanging shut reverberated through the boat. The air conditioning and refrigeration units were shut down, as was hydraulic power. Every bit of machinery that could make enough noise to give the boat away was quieted, as were the men.

Ping, ping, ping, ping...

"They've shifted to attack freq," Rivers whispered. "Christ, sir, they're close... five hundred yards..."

"Mug, all ahead one-third," Turner ordered.

"Depth now three-five-zero feet," Frank Nichols reported from the control room.

The rapid pinging suddenly grew louder, as did the chugging of the cruiser's three propellor blades. The boat's hull then echoed audibly as the Japanese vessel's sound beams found her, ponging loudly off *Bull Shark*'s steel and giving her position away.

"For what we are about to receive..." Jarvis muttered the age-old seaman's blasphemy.

Even without Rivers' report, it was obvious that the cruiser had located the submarine. The sound of her screws intensified as she accelerated and headed right for them. One saving grace for submariners in such a circumstance was that it was nearly impossible for a single ship to exactly determine the submarine's depth. Setting depth charge detonation ranges was a great deal of guesswork. It wasn't much of a comfort, but even a small comfort was something to cling to.

Another comfort was that the Japanese nearly always set their detonation depths too shallow. With the newer fleet submarines like the *Tambor* and *Gato* classes having a mean test depth of three-hundred feet, they could dive below the often-shallower depth charge explosions. In *Bull Shark*'s case, her test depth was half again deeper than even the *Gatos,* and she'd been down as far as eight-hundred.

"Splashes!" Rivers hissed. "Four of them."

"Depth now four hundred," Nichols said. "No layer yet, sir." Tensely the men of *Bull Shark* waited. The ashcans heading for them would take nearly forty-seconds to plunge to their current depth, if they made it so far. The cruiser had dropped them ahead, leading them so that the weapons and the target would meet.

Click, boom! Click, boom!

Two explosions followed rapidly by two more. The depth had been shallow, no more than three hundred feet. Although not too

– July 2, 1942 – 2341 ship's time

close, the pressure waves were still more than powerful enough to rattle the boat like a dog shaking a toy in its jaws.

Bull Shark bucked and plunged and rolled and heaved. Tiny bits of the cork insulation that lined the inner hull flittered about like a gray hailstorm. Light bulbs in every compartment shattered and men were tumbled about, banging painfully against equipment, valve handles and furniture. Not terrible, as depth charging went, yet no one was volunteering to receive another.

"Depth now... layer sir!" Nichols exalted from below. "Salt layer at four-two-zero!"

"Thank Christ..." Turner muttered. "Mug, left rudder. Make your course southwest."

There again came to the submarine's collective ears the sound of sonar pinging. Yet, now it sounded distant and attenuated into a very low frequency. As if the sender was miles off instead of only a few hundred yards. The heavier and cooler salt layer into which the boat was passing was stretching and bending the sound beams and robbing them of enough power to return a positive signal.

Minutes went by in silence. An eerie and heavy silence whose tension might have been weaved from heavy wool. From far off, not as far as it sounded but far enough, another set of thumping concussions filled the sea. Yet the tooth-shakers had been dropped half a mile off and had gone off too shallow. Hardly a ripple of their energy touched the submarine.

"Well, gentlemen," Turner said as he lit the second of Buck's borrowed Camels. "I believe we're not dead."

"It's a nice change," Jarvis quipped.

"Let's stay on course for another thirty minutes or so and then we'll go topside and scope the sitch," Turner said.

"A curious development, this. Wonder what the hell's going on out here...? Well, now that this bit of pleasantry is over... Elmer, pass the word to the galley. Let them know that we require a cake and that Doc needs to break out the depth charge medicine. We'll splice the mainbrace!"

Solomon Islands, New Georgia Sound - 9°8' S, 159°38' E

A quiet cheer went up through the tower and the control room. Williams's face split into a broad grin.

"A cake? That's terrific; it's my birthday after all."

"It's your birthday, Elm tree?" Jarvis asked cordially. "Well, I'll be a greasy someonabitch."

"That's true, Pat," Williams said, which earned another cheer and bout of muffled laughter.

Jarvis grinned, balled up a sheet of notepaper and chucked it at Williams' head. The XO caught it in his teeth, gave Jarvis a thumbs-up and vanished down the hatchway.

Turner smiled, enjoying the high spirits of his men. It felt damned good. It felt like home.

Chapter 2

Naval Air Station Midway – Midway Atoll 28 °12' N, 177 °12' W

July 6, 1942 – 0730 local time

Webster Clayton, Office of Strategic Services, was amazed at how much had changed on the small atoll in a little over a month. The last time he'd visited, during the epic battle of Midway, the base had been undergoing fortification for the impending Japanese invasion. He'd been there just after the battle, when the submarine he'd been aboard, USS *Bull Shark,* had put in before her return to Pearl Harbor.

On that day, the day after the battle, Midway resembled exactly what it was... the scene of a massive aerial attack. Many of the buildings, including barracks, airplane hangars, storage warehouses, fuel dumps and administration offices, had been smashed by Japanese bombers. He'd seen advanced showings of director John Ford's soon-to-be epic documentary *The Battle of Midway* and had been stunned by the destruction and the unbreakable will of the United States Marines and Navy.

Now though, as the Navy R4D transport and cargo plane, the naval version of the DC3, touched down on East Island's airstrip, the view from Clayton's window was almost unrecognizable. What buildings hadn't been badly damaged had been repaired, and new ones were being constructed in the place of those too far gone. Larger hangars, reinforced warehouses and other facilities had been, and were still being, constructed on East Island.

"I'll take that for you sir," a young Marine in olive drab said cheerfully as Clayton stepped down from the airplane. "PFC Joe Treadway at your service, sir. I'm to escort you to Captain Simard, sir."

Clayton handed the young man his small duffel, and the Marine smiled and began fast-walking across the apron to a nearby motor launch. Another impossibly young man, a seaman first-class, stood at the small boat's wheel and smiled.

"Another VIP, Joey?" the sailor inquired.

"You know it, Frank," Treadway said. "Watch your step, sir."

"I appreciate the treatment, Treadway... but you don't have to call me sir," Clayton said. "Mr. Clayton is fine, or even just Web if you like."

"Yes sir," Treadway replied.

The trip from East to Sand Island was a short one. Clayton noticed a bridge between the two and wondered why they hadn't just gone by Jeep, as he had the last time he visited.

"Why a launch instead of a car, Treadway?" he inquired as the sailor maneuvered the launch up to the main dock.

"Lot of construction and whatnot going on, sir," Treadway replied. "And Captain Simard thought you'd appreciate the special treatment, sir."

"Thoughtful," Clayton stated. "And stop calling me sir, Treadway."

"Yes sir."

Another thing that struck Clayton as the boat tied up to the small vessel section of the harbor was the number of large ships in the harbor. There was a heavy cruiser, several destroyers and a large freighter-like vessel with three submarines tied one against the other along the freighter's side. As Treadway led Clayton up onto the main pier, the OSS man was also surprised to see the China Clipper tied to

The Cactus Navy

her dedicated slip. The big Martin M-130 floatplane, a relic of the 1930s, had once flown a week-long route from San Francisco to the Philippines. Midway had been one of the overnight stops for Pan Am's wealthy passengers.

Even more interesting was the fact that Treadway wasn't leading Clayton toward the new admin building. Rather, he was leading the government agent to the Goonieville Lodge, Pan Am's hotel, which although damaged during the attack, had been repaired and was fully operational and had even been expanded upon.

"With sub crews coming in for resupply and R and R," Treadway explained, "the Navy has been trying to add some new facilities, sir. Midway is still pretty sparse, as far as fun goes, sir. Other than fishing, swimming and bird watching, it's not much in terms of relaxation, but that's gonna change in time, sir."

"We're not going to Captain Simard's office?" Clayton asked.

"No sir," Treadway replied as they approached the hotel. "The captain thought this meeting would be better in a more comfortable setting, sir."

"Treadway... I'll give you ten bucks if you stop calling me sir," Clayton said wryly.

"You got yourself a deal, sir!"

Clayton could only laugh. The young Marine led Clayton through the small lobby where sailors and naval officers were chatting and going about their business. Down a short hallway and into a plush conference room done up in teak, leather and brass. What struck Clayton most of all wasn't the décor but the human brass all seated around a large, polished conference table.

"Mr. Clayton reporting, sir!" Treadway announced as they stepped in.

"Thank you, Treadway," Captain Cyril Simard, the base commander, said. "Dismissed."

"Aye-aye, sir," Treadway replied and vanished.

"Come on in and grab a seat, Web," Simard stated, waving Clayton to an empty chair near the center of the table

"Coffee? Some breakfast, maybe?"

"Both, if possible, sir," Clayton said as he took his seat.

Simard grinned, "Treadway rubbing off on you, Web?"

"Yes sir," Clayton replied, and the two men chuckled.

A steward ambled over and poured Clayton a cup and took his order before heading out of the room. Clayton took the time to note the notables around him. Some of the men he knew and others he didn't, but to a man they were all highly important officers.

"Allow me to make the introductions, sirs," Simard said, rising. "This is Webster Clayton, Office of Strategic Services. Web was here during that little dust-up we had with the Japs last month and even did a short tour aboard one of our boats. Web, you know Admiral Nimitz, of course. This is Major General Alexander Vandegrift, First Marines. Admiral Robert Gormley, ComSoPac, Admiral Richmond Turner and Admiral Frank Jack Fletcher."

Introductions and handshakes were exchanged. There were two other officers, Marine Lieutenant Colonels both, seated near the end of the table. Unlike the Navy officers and General Vandegrift, who wore class-A's, the two colonels wore the new Marine frog skin battle fatigues. They were both rugged-looking men in top condition and exuded the confidence of seasoned combat veterans.

"These two gents are Lieutenant Colonels Merritt 'Red Mike' Edson and Evans Carlson," Simard said. "Commanders of the First and Second Marine Raiders battalions, respectively."

"Raiders?" Clayton asked as he shook the two men's hard hands.

"New special units," Edson explained. "Specializing in amphib, scouting and mobile tactical strikes."

"We're the guys who go ashore before the guys who go ashore," Carlson said wryly.

"All right gentlemen," Nimitz began the meeting abruptly.

"Now that the niceties are out of the way, let's get down to brass tacks... no pun intended."

A polite laugh floated over the table.

"As you all know, and I presume you too, Web, Admiral King has been pushing for an offensive in the Pacific almost since the Nips bombed Pearl," Nimitz stated. "The boys in Washington and our friends in the Army have been pushing back on this heavily. General MacArthur would prefer to have any offensive ground operations fall entirely under his purview. He's obsessed with his promise to return... yet his objectives don't gel with Cominch... or mine, for that matter."

Some shifting and uncomfortable mutterings rounded the table. The two Raider colonels simply sat as rigid as fenceposts, their faces set in hard lines that revealed nothing.

"For seven goddamned months now," Nimitz continued sternly, punctuating his statement by dropping a heavy fist onto the table, "the Japs have been kicking us in the ass and I, for one, have had enough of simply sitting around and taking it. Admiral King is of the same mind... and now, the decision has *finally* been made by the President and the joint chiefs to do something about it."

He directed his steely gaze in Clayton's direction. Although Clayton had always been a proponent of naval operations since day one, he was still technically a "Washington Weenie." However, Nimitz let him off the hook with a brief smile.

"What're we to do, sir?" Fletcher asked.

"What we've all been talking about for over a month now, Jak. The Army and Navy have agreed to shift the lines of demarcation between our areas of operation coverage by sixty miles," Nimitz replied. "It doesn't sound like much, but it does free up the southern Solomons."

"Tulagi," Admiral Turner, who was a surface-warfare officer, said.

"Tulagi," Nimitz stated. "I've recently received two pieces of intelligence that have given me what I need to put together an operation, which we'll code name Watchtower. As we know, the Japs have established... bullshit... they've taken *our* base on Tulagi. They've got seaplanes there, at nearby Gavutu, Tanambogo and even Florida Island."

Fletcher squirmed a little. The Japanese had taken Tulagi in May during the Battle of the Coral Sea. Although the operation was technically under the command of Admiral Bill Halsey, Fletcher had been there. The battle was considered a success because while Japan seized Tulagi, they were unable to take Port Moresby, their primary target.

"Yes, but the Jap isn't happy with what he's got," Nimitz continued. "On the first, one of our PBY recon flights spotted activity on nearby Guadalcanal. The Japs are building a large airfield on the northern coast, on the flatlands there, near Lunga Point."

"Christ..." Vandegrift groaned.

"And the next day, one of our submarines assigned to patrol the New Georgia Sound ran into a well-protected convoy," Nimitz said, casting a glance at Clayton. "A transport and two freighters protected by a tin can and a light cruiser out of Rabaul, most likely. Just off Savo Island."

"Reinforcements for Tulagi?" Edson asked.

"No... the course of the convoy indicates they were headed for Guadalcanal," Nimitz stated. "And so, then, are we."

"Did the boat attack the convoy, sir?" Carlson asked.

Nimitz chuckled, "Oh, indeed it did, Colonel. The skipper of this particular boat is... aggressive, to say the least. Sank a Fubuki destroyer leader and one of the freighters before the CL chased him off."

"Art Turner," Clayton stated and grinned. He then looked at Admiral Richmond Turner.

"No relation," Turner said and smiled thinly. "Too bad. Glad to hear we've got a bulldog submariner out there, though."

Nimitz chuckled, "*Bull Shark* has already racked up nine kills, four Nazis and five IJNs, and she's only been in commission four months. Anvil Art Turner loves to set his teeth into an enemy's hide... however, the point is that his after-action report clearly indicates that the convoy was headed to reinforce the Jap efforts on Guadalcanal.

Men, supplies and equipment for the airbase. We've got a couple of coastwatchers in the area that substantiate this."

"So, our mission is to land on Tulagi and Guadalcanal, Admiral?" Gormley asked.

"And the adjacent islands," Nimitz said. "You'll be in overall command, Bob. Under you will be Frank and his carriers, Rich and his surface ships and amphibious transports and Alex and his Marines, which will include the two Colonels and their special units here. Around twenty-thousand Marines. We move in, split up in the Sealark Channel and send about a third to the islands of Tulagi, Gavutu, Tanambogo and Florida. The other two-thirds land near the Jap airfield on the big island, Guadalcanal. My hope is that we can organize Watchtower in time to do all this *before* the Japs finish the airstrip. Because once they do, they can move fighters and bombers down from Rabaul and Bougainville and control one of our most important sea lanes between America and Australia."

"And we're not going to let that happen, sir," Vandegrift stated unequivocally.

"Damned right, we aren't," Nimitz reiterated.

"When do we go, sir?" Vandegrift asked with enthusiasm.

"I'd like to move by the end of the month, first week of August at the *absolute* latest," Nimitz stated.

Gormley looked pensive, "Sir... that's an awfully big order. We're going to need a lot of assets and men, not to mention a huge amount of supplies to pull this off... and so soon..."

"It is a tall order, Bob," Nimitz said. "But dammit... we've been on the defensive since December seventh. Admiral King and I feel it's time to take the fight to the Japs, Europe first be damned."

"What about Midway?" Fletcher put in. "We whipped the Jap but good, sir."

Nimitz drew in a breath and let it out slowly, choosing his words carefully so as not to offend the man who'd been in charge of that operation, "June four was a great day, Jack, no question. But we didn't so much *beat* Yamamoto as Nagumo *lost*, if you see what I mean."

Fletcher frowned. Nimitz using his less formal moniker didn't soften the blow much, "Sir?"

"We lost a lot of good men that day, and we got lucky, Jack," Nimitz said. "Please understand me; I'm not criticizing. Four Nip carriers sent to the bottom in one day was outstanding... yet we have to admit that the victory was partly due to the Japanese's mistakes as much as from our Ultra codebreakers and our own decisions. No matter what, though, we were on the defensive then. I want to *attack* now. I want to put these goddamned yellow bastards on the defensive, and that's just what you men are going to do. After Pearl... after the Bataan death march... these sons of bitches got it coming!"

Fletcher seemed discomfited but didn't protest any further. Nimitz's words, although they stung a little, were the truth.

"Jack, you'll have *Saratoga, Enterprise* and *Wasp*," Nimitz stated. "Bob, you'll have whatever surface assets Rich here can put together... I know we don't have the best landing gear right now, but we've got transports and Higgins boats and plenty of cruisers and DDs to play with. You men figure it out. Alex, you gather your Marines from wherever you need them and pick a spot you think will work for training. I know I'm asking a lot here, gents... but there's a war on, as I'm told daily, and war is a bitch."

A round of laughter, light but genuine, filled the conference room. Clayton looked to Nimitz, who nodded slightly.

"Gentlemen," Clayton began, "you're probably wondering why I'm here. Well, to begin, I'm plugged in to several key assets within the enemy camp, you might say. One of these, code name Shadow, is very highly placed on Admiral Yamamoto's staff. Through a rather... complicated communications network, my asset has been able to send in reports of Japanese ship movements and operations plans. That's how we happen to know about the more than one-hundred planes being slated for Guadalcanal. My source informs me that the airstrip is scheduled to be completed by the second or third week of August... thus Admiral Nimitz's timeline. Through the assistance of Ultra and Commander Rochefort's team at Pearl, I've been able to decipher and cipher communications between myself and Shadow, as well as with some other assets in the Solomons. I'm here because I need some help in supporting my assets, who in turn will support you gentlemen."

Everyone looked on curiously. Nimitz lit a cigarette and leaned back in his chair, "Go on, Mr. Clayton."

"As some of you know, we have what are known as coastwatchers in the islands," Clayton went on. "Some American and some British. They covertly and assiduously observe Japanese ship and plane activities all over the Solomons, often at or behind enemy lines. Well... one of these men, a man named Martin Clemens, is in a bit of trouble. He's been on Guadalcanal for some time now, and since the Japanese occupation and the withdrawal of European businesses, he and his team are hanging on by a thread. They're holed up in the mountains and are short on everything from smokes to food to batteries. Hell, Clemens's last report stated that he and his men's shoes are just about dissolving from jungle rot. They need replenishing, aid and assistance and they need it stat. And we need Clemens. He and his scouts could literally be the key to this whole operation... and I shudder to think what'll happen if we don't reach out to them."

"So, what do you want from us?" Fletcher asked. "An airdrop maybe? That might alert the Japs to their presence as much as anything."

"Normally I'd be in favor of that, Admiral," Clayton said, glancing at the two Raiders with interest. "But as you say... that might draw unwanted attention. No... I think what's needed is something a bit more subtle."

"A Raider team to go ashore and deliver supplies and assistance," Edson stated.

Clayton grinned, "Something like that, yes Colonel. I don't suppose you gents have a few of those special Raider types you could spare?"

"I'm sure we do," Carlson put in. "But the problem remains... how do we insert them without drawing the Japs' notice? Parachuters are out for the same reason already mentioned. A landing would leave the landing craft vulnerable and might tip the Empire off to our larger plans."

Nimitz met Clayton's eyes, and the admiral grinned, "I think Mr. Clayton has already worked *that* part out, eh, Web?"

Clayton returned the smile, "As a matter of fact... I have. I've had some very positive dealings with the submarine corps, gentlemen. One boat in particular... which has done some good work for me from the get-go."

"Anvil Art Turner," Admiral Turner said.

Nimitz nodded, "Just so. I can get him here in a week or so... he was vectored up toward Wake after his attack. Another eight or ten days back to the southern Solomons. However much time we need to keep them here... but certainly we can land what needs landing on Guadalcanal by the end of the month, I imagine. Any idea of a landing spot, Web?"

"I'd recommend the southern shore," Edson observed. "Much less trafficked than the Sealark Channel and the slot."

"Harder terrain, though," Carlson remarked. "Lot of coral reefs and the weather coast is rougher."

"That's what our boys are for," Edson added. "Mr. Clayton, I think I've got just the man for you."

"I'm much obliged, Colonel," Clayton said. "And to you, Admiral."

"This keeps up, Web, and Art Turner is gonna start thinking he works for *you* rather than me and Bob English," Nimitz said with a crooked grin.

"We're all on the same team, sir," Clayton said amiably. "Course... what I have in mind is a bit outside the normal wheelhouse for a sub driver. I'm sure Art will be okay with it, though."

Chapter 3

USS Bull Shark

– 975 miles south, southwest of Wake Island

It was at times like this when the boat's double-secret probation snorkel device certainly came in handy. The telescoping breathing tube allowed the ship to run her diesels at periscope depth which allowed her to maintain a cruising speed during the day that was much higher than any of her sister ships. For when operating in or near enemy waters, American submarines would run submerged during daylight hours to avoid enemy aircraft.

The uniqueness of the snorkel was something of a double-edged sword. It was by no means a new invention, having been devised by a Scottish engineer during World War One. However, no nation had put it into practical use as yet. According to intelligence reports, Norway was currently outfitting some of their new subs with the device... the American intelligence community knew of this because they'd been able to appropriate plans for the snorkel in 1941, and *Bull Shark* had been chosen as the testbed for the project. The double-edged sword aspect came into play in a variety of ways. First, while useful in moderate weather, the snorkel became inoperative in rough seas. The complex ball valve system that kept seawater out and allowed air to flow in and out of the tube clogged when it became rough. Secondarily, the snorkel was several feet across and left a large feather line on the surface that was much easier for an aircraft to spot. Further, the two periscopes and the radar masts had been reinforced to operate at higher speeds, thus giving them larger diameters and a larger wake profile as well.

Finally, because *Bull Shark* was of a class that would not be officially put into service for several months yet... being built of stronger and thicker steel and having the snorkel... she had become something of a special tool for use by United States intelligence agencies, specifically the Office of Strategic Services.

In short, Art Turner's ship, rather than being sent out on a standard war patrol and being allowed to dine heavily on Japanese merchant shipping, seemed always earmarked for one crazy mission after another. More than once, she'd been the personal spearhead for Webster Clayton. Not entirely unexpected, considering that Clayton had been involved with the boat's construction and with Turner's appointment from day one.

When Porter Hazard appeared in the conning tower hatch with several sheets of paper in his hand, Turner got the distinct impression, for no reason he could identify, that this was about to be the case once more.

Hazard was in his late thirties. A man of medium height and broad in the beam. His auburn hair was cut short, almost severely, and his face was open, pleasant and leaned toward handsome. His brown eyes were merry most of the time, and a smile was never far from his lips.

"Mornin' Skipper," Hazard said cheerfully in his heavy Georgia accent. Turner had to suppress a smile. The man really *did* sound like Foghorn Leghorn. "Mornin' fox, sir... and a directive from the bosses."

"Thanks, Porter," Turner replied, taking the sheets. "How are our four little darlings doing this morning?"

Hazard lit a Marlboro and leaned against the bridge ladder,

"Purring like kittens, sir. Kinda crazy, though, ain't it? Runnin' at radio depth with them rock crushers goin'? Never heard the like."

Turner chuckled, "Yeah... a mixed blessing, that. We don't get a break from the racket as often. You decode this?"

"Yessir," Hazard replied. "Me and Chief Weiss. That old boy knows his stuff."

"That he does," Turner said. "Excuse me a minute, Porter..."

Porter waited while Turner read the fleet broadcast and the specific orders for his boat. He groaned aloud and then chuckled softly.

"Skipper?" Hazard inquired.

"You read this, I'm sure," Turner stated.

"Yes sir."

"Well, you're new, Porter, so I'll read between the lines for you," Turner said. "We're being ordered to Midway with all possible dispatch. Essentially, having our patrol cut short by well over six weeks because we're about to be sent on some harebrained mission for an intelligence man I know."

Hazard grinned wryly, "You got all that from the order to proceed to Midway, sir?"

There were chuckles from the men on watch, and their captain joined in, "Porter, every damned thing we've done since this boat left dry-dock has been at the whim of an OSS agent named Clayton. We send in a dispatch about Jap activity in the slot, and suddenly we're to haul ass back to Midway. Bet you a bottle of fine Scotch that Webster Clayton is waiting there for us."

Hazard laughed, "Make it Jack Daniel's and you got a deal, sir."

"Mind you, it's not necessarily bad news," Turner said. "Just always something unusual. Nazi Q-ship or submarine aircraft carrier... anyway, on the flip side, I see we've received confirmation of my promotion list. Are those guys available at the moment?"

Hazard nodded, "In the crew's mess as we speak, sir."

"Good," Turner said. "'Preciate you taking care of this, Porter. I know you're not on watch."

"My pleasure, Captain," Hazard replied. "This is only my second patrol in the boats, and I'm anxious to get me some of them dolphins you fellas wear. Glad to pitch in wherever I can. Learnt that lesson early in the Corps."

"You'll have to tell me that story someday... unless it's something you'd rather not talk about," Turner stated.

"Oh, no, sir... not a big thing, really."

"Well, let's go down and give the boys some good news," Turner said, and the two men went down the ladder into the control room. "Mr. Post, do a sweep on both radars and then take us down to periscope depth. Got a little chore to take care of."

"Aye-aye," Post said. He was the assistant officer of the deck and watch diving officer. It was Nichols' idea to give him more practice to both help the ensign practice his trim and diving skills and to qualify for his own set of gold dolphins.

The crew's mess, just aft of the control room in the after battery compartment, was full of men at breakfast or just lounging at the tables. There were a few additional faces, including Eddie Carlson, the officer's steward, the COB, Chief's Duncan and Brannigan, as well as Walter Murphy and Walter Sparks.

"Attention on deck!" Rogers barked as the two officers entered.

"Good morning, gentlemen," Turner said formally, enjoying playing the part of the great man for once. "I've got a couple of announcements, so listen up."

The men, most of whom were off watch but a few who'd been specifically ordered to report, fell quiet and fidgeted nervously. The captain's tone wasn't angry, but it certainly meant something serious was up. None of them noticed the smiles threatening to break out on the chief's and LPO's faces.

"First off, and I'll post this on the POD later," Turner said. "We're headed for Midway. Got orders to stoke the furnaces. By now, you veteran *Bull Sharks* know what that means."

"Su'm crazy," a voice from the rear of the pack said, and a hearty chuckle filled the compartment.

The Cactus Navy

Turner smiled slightly, "More likely than not. However, that's not my primary reason for interrupting you men's meal. I've got a list of names here... a damned *long* list, men. Put together by your supervisors *and* the chief of the boat, for Chrissakes! And I have to say, I'm in *total agreement* with this list. This is no laughing matter, gents."

A heavy silence fell as Turner slowly looked over the men. Growing uncomfortable under the skipper's scrutiny, the men took to muttering and fidgeting to an even greater degree. The skipper was definitely serious. Turner glared them into stillness.

"Rivers, Hernandez, Broderick, Swooping Hawk, Jones and Parker. On *your feet!*" Turner growled.

The men in question rose, looking uncomfortable and unsettled to a man.

"I'm sorry, men, but by your actions and the way you attend to your duties... you've *earned* this. And may God have mercy on your souls," Turner said sternly and glowered. After a few seconds, he let the glower disperse, and it was replaced by a shit-eating grin that broke the chiefs and leading petty's into uproarious laughter. "It's a promotions list, boys! Ha-ha-ha-HA!"

The compartment broke into laughter. The standing men were pounded on the back, and catcalls and cheers rose up. The standing men flushed with relief and pleasure.

"That's dirty pool, Skipper," Tank Broderick said.

"Hey, what's the point of being the captain you can't bust your crew's nuts from time to time?" Turner said. "Almost makes the goddamned paperwork tolerable."

More laughter and cheers.

"Okay, listen up," Turner said, holding out the list. "Eugene Parker, you are hereby promoted to torpedoman one. Robert Jones, you are elevated to the lofty position of torpedoman's mate, third class. Fred Swooping Hawk to fireman one. Sherman Broderick is now a high and mighty electrician's mate third class. Chester Rivers is now sonarman's mate third class for his remarkably good ears."

"What's that, sir?" Rivers japed.

"You watch that smart mouth, Chet, or I'll bust you down to chief, and then you'll find out what workin' Navy *really* means," Turner replied with a chuckle. "Finally, our smartass from Long beach... Ralph Hernandez is now a first-class petty officer. Just one screw up from becoming *chief* quartermaster's mate, Hotrod."

"I am pleased to serve in any way I can," Hernandez stated. "For I am but a humble peasant, *señor*."

"See what I mean?" Turner asked. "Congratulations, gents. I'm very proud of you... of all of you. This is the finest damned crew in the boats, and before long you'll all be promoted and be wearing silver dolphins of your own. At the noon meal, we're gonna celebrate and splice the mainbrace!" A chorus of whoops and cheers rose.

"All right, as you were," Turner said. He went around and shook the hands of the promoted men before he and Hazard went forward again.

It was near the end of the second dog watch, and the sun had just slipped below the horizon. The last thin rays of sunlight lit up the foaming disturbance on the remarkably smooth surface of the sea and brushed against the glistening hull of the submarine as she broke out into the air. Water streamed from her decks and from the limber holes along her topsides.

Her periscope extended, turned a complete circle and then settled back down even as her two radar systems, one probing the sky and one across the surface, emitted their invisible beams before quieting. The bridge hatch opened, and men began to appear. Three climbed into the periscope sheers and a larger number than usual popped up through the hatchway and then went down on deck and gathered ahead of her forward five-inch deck gun.

"Steady on course zero-two-zero," Elmer Williams, who still had the watch, reported to his captain. "Running on all four at twenty knots, sir. I've posted Hotrod as quartermaster." "Very well, XO," Turner stated. "All right, men, I figured this would be a good time to go over what I know before I take the deck."

All of *Bull Shark*'s officers were at the impromptu meeting, even Williams and Nichols, who were still on watch for another thirty minutes.

"What's all the cloak and dagger stuff about, Skipper?" Jarvis asked as he lit a cigarette.

"As you all know, we received an order to report to Midway this morning," Turner said. "Well, I just got a for-my-eyes only from Midway along with the evening fox. Not much detail, as the source is pretty skittish about the Japs overhearing and decoding our missives. Since we've done it, then why can't they."

"This has got Web Clayton written all over it," Joe Dutch opined.

Turner chuffed, "Right you are, Joe. It's like this: we're to take on a special team when we get to Midway. A Marine detachment with whom we'll be training for a day. We're to put them ashore at an as-yet-unknown location... well, un *named* in the communiques, but I have a feeling I know where."

"The Solomons someplace," Jarvis offered. "I mean, we meet those Japs in the New Georgia Sound headed for Guadalcanal and then suddenly all this?"

"Makes sense to me," Nichols said. "Not a lot of coincidences when it comes to Clayton."

Turner nodded, "That's my feeling. Specifically, Guadalcanal. Japs are building a substantial airfield there. Anyway... there's more to this. In addition to the Marines, which means only one thing... an amphib operation... we're to provide specialists in the areas of mechanics, electrical and anybody who might have backwoods experience. And we're also to provide a command element for the purpose of evaluation. Yours truly, it would seem."

"You gotta be shittin' me," Jarvis said.

"So we're gonna send some of our men ashore too?" Post asked.

"Not just men... officers," Turner said. "I'm going, at least for a short time."

"I'll go," Hazard said. "Not only am I qualified in the mechanical department... I've got experience in ground warfare, sir."

"I'll go," Dutch offered. "Electrical and communications, for that matter."

At that, every man there volunteered. Turner grinned at them all, "I appreciate that guys... but somebody has to stay aboard and run the damned boat. Elmer, Pat, Frank and Andy will be staying aboard. Porter, Joe and I will go with the Marines. I'd also like to take an electrician and motor mac as well. I'll let you guys decide that. Ask for volunteers, though. Senior guys only, nobody below E3."

The officers weren't happy about the decisions. None of them liked the idea of staying snug and safe aboard the boat while their skipper went ashore into God knew what. Pat Jarvis was particularly non-plussed. While Turner would certainly like to take the big, strong and courageous gunner, he also felt better with him backstopping Williams.

"Don't fret too hard," Turner said. "Indications are that you boys aboard will be busy too. Again, the details are sketchy, and we'll learn them in time."

"I'd feel better about this if we knew more," Williams grumbled.

"So would we all," Turner agreed. "But orders are orders... and knowing Web as we do, this'll be something noteworthy. Maybe another medal in it for us."

Nichols scoffed, "Shit... we're due for one from that last mission, aren't we?"

That was received with a muted chuckle from everyone. Turner smiled and shrugged, "I hope so. Now that we're all gathered here in this makeshift hen party, Porter... how about giving us the cliff notes on how you come to our little group?"

Hazard grinned and lit a smoke of his own, "Well, sir... it's nothin' too exciting. I joined up with the Corps out of high school back in twenty-four after fartin' around on the family farm for a year. Little did I know I'd be packed off to Nicaragua to fight the damned Sandinistas for the next few years. Actually served under Chesty Puller, if you can imagine... anyways, spent a couple of tours there until twenty-eight when all the shoutin' was over. Stayed in another few years and made gunnery sergeant and then mustered out. Decided I'd like to maybe see what makin' a living with my head would be like 'stead of my hands and back. Took my pay and went to school for mechanical engineering... dumbass that I am, I thought gettin' a college degree would make me a glorified mechanic... which I guess it does."

Everyone laughed.

"Well... now when I get grease all over my good shirt, I can at least be proud I'm a college gradjiate," Hazard said with a grin. "Anyways, I got my bachelor's in forty and went to work for Fairbanks Morse as a junior engineer. Since I'd been with the fleet as a Marine, they put me in the Naval propulsion unit. Worked on submarine engines for 'bout a year and a half. Learned a hell of a lot there."

"Yeah, me too," Nichols said. "After getting out of MIT I went to work for GM for a bit and signed up with the reserves."

Hazard nodded, "Yeah, what I thought about doin', too. Once the grumblin' about war began in forty-one. Kept puttin' it off, though, until December... God damn... I heard about what happened on the radio that Sunday. I can still remember President Roosevelt's speech that night..."

"A day that will live in infamy," Turner said softly. "Me, Joe and Buck Rogers were there that day... it's like a dream still... well, a nightmare."

The men each added a little something about where they'd been that day. Hazard actually had to blink away tears before going on.

"I don't know... I felt like... I felt like I'd let the country down. Let the Navy down on account of I was safe and snug in Wisconsin while you boys were right in the thick of it," Hazard said, obviously struggling with his feelings even seven months later. "So I went to my nearest Navy recruiting office and asked to join up."

"How come not the Corps specifically?" Post asked.

"Well, way things were lookin'," Hazard replied. "This was gonna be, at least for a while, a Navy war out here in the Pacific. I wanted to get into the action as fast as I could. Figured becoming a squid were the fastest way to get to the front lines. Well, I was kinda surprised when I found that I'd be rushed in and as a J.G. instead of an ensign. My degree making me officer qualified and my prior experience in the Corps givin' me a leg up. So they sent me to indoctrination and then sub-school in Connecticut. Then I do a tour aboard an old R-boat under Mush Morton... any you guys know him?"

Turner chuckled, "Was one of my instructors when I was at PXO school. Damned fine sub driver, Mush."

"Yessir," Hazard said. "Course I was comm and commissary officer. Didn't see much action, though. Heard of some stuff... before coming out to Pearl, heard about some new boat went out and smacked around them fuckin'... 'scuse me sir... Krauts what was sinkin' our ships off the east coast. Wasn't I surprised when I got assigned to my new boat and found out it was you all I'd heard of?"

A round of grins flashed in the dwindling twilight.

"Well, I think I speak for everybody here when I say we're damned glad to have ya', Port," Jarvis said, clapping the man on the shoulder. "Course... now you gotta go back to some stinkin' jungle... never thought *that'd* happen, huh?"

Chapter 4

USS Bull Shark
– 3 miles west of Wake Island

"It's out there, Mug," Jarvis said quietly as he leaned on the bridge railing and looked off the boat's starboard beam. 'I can *smell* it."

Dick "Mug" Vigliano, quartermaster of the watch, puffed languidly on a cigar that Jarvis had given him. One of the gunner's last few stogies, Vigliano knew, and a very thoughtful gesture. Jarvis' own cigar burned aromatically not far away, and the truth was that the only thing Vigliano could smell was smoldering Cuban leaf... not that he minded."Damn shame," Jarvis went on softly. "Goddamned ridiculous, you ask me... there's still over a hundred Americans there, you know that, Mug? Most of 'em civilians.""Yes sir," Vigliano said, lowering his cigar and catching a whiff of the land. Or perhaps more accurately, the shallows that would be in view in daylight. "The real kick in the ass is what the hell did the Japs put so much effort into? Way I hear it, you can't even get a ship inside the reef."

"They got an airfield, though," Jarvis said. "The Marshals are only about seven hundred miles south, southeast. Makes Wake a good refueling stop between there and Guam."

"Just seems almost like... an insult," Vigliano said after a long puff. "So close to Midway and all. The Japs is in our backyard and givin' us the ole *brajole*."

Jarvis harrumphed, "Yeah, and they've enslaved our neighbors and are making them maintain the dump. Got a buddy from high school was a civilian contractor out here and got caught up when the fuckin' slants invaded. Might be dead, might be alive, I dunno. Frankly, I'm not sure which is the worse fate."

"Sorry sir," Vigliano said softly.

Jarvis drew in a breath and sighed, "Thanks, Mug. Anyways... it's pushin' one, better call down for a sweep... radar, bridge. Give me an SD scan and then a double SJ sweep."

The bridge speaker crackled, "*Bridge, radar... combat sweeps, aye.*"

Above the lookouts, the radar heads took their turn. The spherical SD air search broadcasting in a three-hundred-and-sixty-degree arc and then shutting down. Then the SJ surface search radar began to spin, sending out a directional beam across the sea to the visible horizon in two complete turns. "*Bridge, radar!*" It was the excited voice of Doug Ingram, electrician first-class. He was on watch and taking his trick at the radar gear. Since the incident in early June, Ingram had stayed away from any kind of dope and had proven himself to be an excellent electrician. His photographic memory making him invaluable at just about any duty station and allowing him to learn all of the additional systems to qualify for his dolphins rather quickly. "*Distant contacts! Bearing two-four-zero, range twenty-four thousand.*"

"What are they, Doug?" Jarvis asked. "Train the head on that bearing and take another reading."

A pause, "*Bridge, radar... assess multiple aircraft. Three birds on a constant bearing. Speed is one-two-zero. Altitude unknown as their coming up over the hill, sir.*"

"What the hell would be flying out here in the middle of the night?" Vigliano pondered.

The Cactus Navy

"Probably seaplanes out of Guam," Jarvis said. "Radar, bridge... alert the captain. And get me a couple of guys up here to man the ack-acks. Mug, take the way off her."

"Helm, bridge," Mug said into the transmitter. "All stop... what're you thinking, sir?"

Jarvis grinned ghoulishly in the moonlight, "I'm thinking those are supply birds and that we should smack them out of the sky. Up to the skipper, but I want to be ready."

Up through the bridge hatch came six men. Henrie Martin, the ship's cook who would act as ammo server on the 20mm Oerlikon. His assistant, Bill Borshowski, along with Leroy Potts, the baker, came after them to act as ammo servers and gunnery assistant for the big Bofors four-barrel Pom-pom. Behind them came Mike Duncan, chief of the watch and boatswain's mate Martin Janslotter who'd come aboard at Pearl a few weeks before to replace Steve Plank as boatswain. Duncan went to the Oerlikon and slid the butt strap over his backside while Martin opened the ammo locker and loaded two belts of 20mm rounds into the feed trays. Janslotter, Borshowski and Potts readied the big cannon forward.

In truth, the Bofors 40mm quad-barreled gun wasn't the original "Pom-pom" but had replaced the QF two-pounder just before the war. This original gun was shorter and had a slower muzzle velocity. It got its nickname from the pom-pom sound the shells made when fired. The much larger, faster and longer-range Bofors had replaced most of the older models and was still referred to affectionately as the Pom-pom... or the Chicago or even Devil's Piano.

Almost immediately, which was quite a surprise to the two men on the bridge, Arthur Turner popped up through the hatch wearing only a pair of shorts, "What's on, Gunner?"

Jarvis briefed him quickly, "They're about four minutes out now, sir. Three relatively slow birds... I thought maybe since we were here..."

"That we'd knock them down instead of just diving?" Turner asked wryly.

Jarvis shrugged, "Well, sir... it wouldn't be the first time. And I think we can handle three birds before they know what's really happening."

Turner grinned as well, "And you stopped the screws so we wouldn't make a visible wake. Okay, gunner, I'm with ya'. We are at war with these bastards, after all. The more we can deprive them at Wake, the sooner we can get them outta that hole. Officer of the deck, permission to prosecute the targets granted."

Vigliano grinned as Jarvis thumbed the transmit button, "Radar, bridge... status on contacts?"

"*Bridge, radar... sugar dog indicates altitude two thousand, speed decreasing to niner-zero knots... range now six thousand yards,*" Ingram reported.

"Okay men," Jarvis addressed the anti-aircraft gun crews. Pick your targets and walk your tracers. Don't give them a chance to react or go on the offensive. Your targets are just abaft the beam. Do not fire until I give the word."

A series of aye-ayes resounded from the forward Pom-pom and the Oerlikon mounted on the cigarette deck aft of the masts and periscopes sheers.

Jarvis held up his 7x50s and scanned the sky. The Japanese planes were descending and slowing for their approach to the landing strip on Wilkes Island. More accurately, they were slowing for their landing in the lagoon near the seaplane dock there. This would seem to indicate that none of the planes had yet to sight the long, low and slim shape of the menacing submarine directly in their path.

"They don't even see us," Jarvis opined. "Otherwise, they'd put on speed and arc away or come down for a strafing run. I've got 'em now... big boys, too. Flying boats... you see them, gunners?"

"Yes sir," Duncan said excitedly, his eyes glowing with a predatory fire.

"Barely," Janslotter admitted. "They ain't got no lights on or nothin'."

The Cactus Navy

"Course not," Vigliano said. "Wouldn't want any uppity round-eyes plinking at them from the surface, would they?"

"Looks like they're gonna pass astern," Jarvis said. "Mug, ring me up a back one-third bell on the port screw, huh?"

Behind him, Turner nodded his head in approval. The captain was always ready to let his junior officers take the lead in an operation, especially when it was their watch. It was good practice and added to the men's competency and confidence. Not that Jarvis lacked either, but Turner still enjoyed watching his men work.

"That's got it," Jarvis said as the boat slowly went astern, her aft end being pulled to the right. This put the targets more abeam and gave the two AA cannons better angles of fire.

"Got 'em clear now, sir!" Janslotter reported. He was a third-class petty officer of twenty-five from Wisconsin. He was a tall and lanky young man with a baby face and a shock of unruly brown hair over eyes the same color. He was an amiable sort, yet he knew how to buckle down and get men assigned to any detail he led to work and do so cheerfully.

The floatplanes were now close enough to be made out easily with the naked eye. Even in the darkness, their large bulky shapes were clearly visible, now less than a mile away. The breeze was light, and the throbbing of their big engines could also be clearly made out... especially when one of them began to rev up.

"Shit! I think they seen us!" Duncan shouted.

He was right. One of the planes, the closest in the angled formation, seemed to be throttling up and winging over toward them.

"Open fire!" Jarvis shouted. "Mike, you take out that ballsy fucker! Marty, you got longer range, go after the further birds! Borshowski, keep those mags coming... Potts, you help Marty train that big bastard and help Borshowski plug in those magazines, ya' hear me there!"

The peaceful night air was ripped open by the clatter of the Oerlikon, and the throatier crackle of the big Chicago Piano mounted on its blister forward and slightly below the bridge. Bright red tracer rounds soared into the sky and were joined by blue and even yellow from the seaplane.

Both Duncan's tracers and those of the onrushing aircraft were homing in quickly. It looked to be a neck-and-neck race, with the Japanese rounds sizzling into the ocean in a line toward the submarine while red fireflies angled straight for the aircraft.

Turner was just about to shout for everyone to hit the deck when Duncan's Oerlikon connected. The chatter of his cannon was joined by his scream of triumph as his 20mm, equivalent to .80 caliber rounds slammed first into the plane's starboard engine, turning it into a blazing fireball and then stitching their way to the right, smashing through the cockpit and then into the port wing, where they penetrated and ignited the fuel tank. The big flying boat, now only five hundred yards off, blossomed into a raging white-orange nova and plunged with almost majestic grace into the sea.

"Splash one slope!" Borshowski whooped in his heavy Chicago twang.

Janslotter was having more trouble hitting the other two aircraft. They were accelerating now and winging toward the south in order to escape. It looked as if they might do so until the angry red bees struck the further aircraft, more than a mile away, and it too exploded spectacularly.

Almost simultaneously, Duncan's Oerlikon found the final aircraft, the 20mm shells shredding the rudder and horizontal stabilizers but causing no explosion. The end result was just as deadly, however. Without the stabilizing effect of either the rudder or the elevators, the big plane immediately began to roll and pitch. Slowly at first, but more and more quickly as it began to tumble end over end and wing over wing until it cartwheeled into the dark sea and shattered into its constituent components and killing the crew instantly.

"Cease fire!" Jarvis called out. "Good Christ... nice shootin' lads!"

The six men at the guns cheered even as they began to secure their weapons for sea.

"A job well done," Turner said. "Mr. Jarvis, get us underway. Let's get outta here while the gettin' is good. Proceed on course at flank speed until the end of the watch and then take us down to ahead standard on three engines."

"Aye-aye sir," Jarvis replied. "Have a good night, Captain."

"Already have," Turner said and went below.

Once the guns were secured and the men dismissed, Jarvis and Vigliano once more stood quietly on the bridge as the ship headed east of north at over twenty knots.

"Still got half a cigar left," Vigliano said with a crooked grin. "Notfornuthin'... now we've got something to celebrate, huh Mug?" Jarvis asked and laughed, feeling pleased with himself and like maybe he'd gotten a little bit back for his lost friend."Just what in the *hell* did you think you were doing out there at Wake, Commander?" Captain Cyril Simard asked sternly three days later after *Bull Shark* had tied up at the pier at Midway. "You had no business gunning for those airplanes, dammit! Suppose they'd strafed you? Or bombed you?" Turner and Williams stood at attention in front of Captain Simard's desk. The only other man in the room, a Marine major dressed in the new reversible camouflage BDU sat in one of the interview chairs trying to keep a grin off his ruggedly handsome face.

"Sir, they were targets of opportunity, sir," Turner said stiffly. "You were ordered to proceed to this station with all possible dispatch, Commander," Simard snapped. "Not to dilly-dally and plink at passing aircraft, for Christ's sake! Your boat is far too valuable, under current circumstances, to risk on such a low-priority target as a couple of damned flying boats."

"It was three, sir," Williams unwisely corrected.

"Did I ask you for your assessment, *Lieutenant?*" Simard growled.

"No sir..."

"Sir..." Turner began to protest.

"Lock it up," Simard stated coolly.

The two submariners stood stiffly, rigidly at attention. To their right, the major had to cough to cover his amusement. Simard glared at them both, then in turn and then seemed to relax and sat behind his desk.

"At ease," he said more conversationally. "Take a seat. Officially, Lt. Commander Turner, I am hereby putting you on notice that in the future, you will *refrain* from attacking low-priority targets when under orders for transit. Barring a valuable surface target, naturally. Am I clear?"

"Yessir," Turner said as he took a seat.

"Unofficially," Simard stated firmly and then let a ghost of a smile appear on his lips, "and personally... I'm damned glad you gave those yellow bastards a kick up the ass. What I'd expect from Anvil Art."

Turner scoffed, "Sir, any credit goes to my torpedo officer, Lt. Jarvis. However, I accept full responsibility and any punishment you see fit, sir."

"I know," Simard said and then chuckled. "No punishment, Art. For Christ's sake... you and your officers are up for medals for that *Leviathan* thing. Not to mention sinking a goddamned Jap destroyer and freighter and three flying boats on your way back. Christ man... you're lucky you don't get a promotion to flag rank and get booted upstairs and into an office. Now *that's* punishment!"

The Marine finally broke into laughter. Simard grinned broadly, "Art, Mr. Williams, allow me to introduce Major Albert Decker. Al's with the First Marine Raiders, a new special operations unit and your new best pal."

Turner stood and shook hands with Decker, as did Williams. Decker was in his early thirties and two inches or so below Turner's height, making him five-foot-eleven or so. He looked like a typical Marine recruiting poster. Athletic build with a lean waist and broad shoulders. His hair was cut into a crew and his face was square, strong and hard looking yet amiable. His green eyes were sharp and looked past an aquiline nose that rested over full lips and a clefted chin.

"A pleasure to meet you, Commander," Decker said casually,

"and you as well, XO. I've heard a lot of good things about you fellas and your boat. Sound just like the kind of guys I need for this mission."

"And what is this mystery mission, sir?" Turner asked Simard.

The captain cleared his throat, "Based on recon data as well as your own information from last week, Art, it's pretty clear that the Japs are fortifying the southern Solomons. He's already got Tulagi, Gavutu, Tanambogo and Florida Island. Now he's building an airfield on Guadalcanal. The powers that be have decided that the time for waiting to respond to what the enemy does is over. We're going on the offensive and an operation is already being put together to invade the aforementioned locations. Carriers, warships and transports to support twenty-thousand Marines going ashore the first week of August."

"Jesus..." Williams muttered, "that's only a couple of weeks away."

"That's true," Decker put in, "which is why you've been asked to high-tail it back here. And why I'm here. We're the spearhead of the operation. There are a few small but critical things that need to be done before the main force arrives. There are assets on Guadalcanal that are in trouble and need our intervention and yesterday. Without them, the entire outcome of the operation could be threatened."

Just then the door opened, and Simard's yeoman poked his head in, "The gentleman is here, sir."

"Send him in, Baker," Simard said.

The door swung open and Webster Clayton, dressed in unadorned naval khakis, strode in, a wry grin playing on his features.

"I knew it," Turner said to Williams. "Glad I didn't bet you against this, Elmer... I'da done my dough cold."

"Art, Elmer, good to see you again," Clayton said, shaking hands and taking the remaining chair.

"What is it this time, Web?" Turner asked jovially. "Sea monsters, invading Martians helping the Japs... what?"

"Major Decker will explain the nitty-gritty details over the next few days while your crew gets a little R and R and you train," Clayton stated. "But the highlights are these: We've got coast watchers on Guadalcanal led by a British officer named Martin Clemens. Ever since the Japanese began to occupy the island, Clemens and his team, most of whom are Melanesians who live on the island, have had to take to the mountains and hide out. They're doing what they can but running low on everything. Food, medicines, ammo, clothing, the works. Their gear is crapping out, and they need help so that they can continue their absolutely *vital* observations. We think we can get your boat out there before the end of the month and put this stuff ashore."

"That's why they need mechanics, electricians and so forth," Williams said.

"Exactly," Clayton replied.

"But why me?" Turner asked. "I'm no ground soldier."

"I need a command-level evaluation," Clayton stated. "A man who can take stock of the situation and advise the Navy, so our invasion fleet has the best possible chance. Help us pinpoint a landing zone on Guadalcanal, for example."

Turner looked to Decker, "Can't the Major fulfill that role?" "He will," Clayton said. "But I want to be doubly sure. To have both a land and a sea officer's evaluation."

"It's going to be a small detail," Decker said. "You and I, Art, plus my five Marines, your chosen officers and a couple of ratings. No more than a dozen men, all told. We'll be bringing as much in the way of supplies as we can cram into the boat, too."

Simard cleared his throat, "This is the part you won't like, Art..."

Turner cocked an eyebrow, "Sir?"

"We're unloading all your fish," Simard stated. "Except what's in the ten tubes. No reloads. We need the space for men, gear and cargo."

Williams groaned and Turner leaned in, "Sir... that doesn't leave us with much of a defense."

"You shouldn't need much of one, Captain," Decker said. "One reason we chose a submarine, and yours, in particular, is that we can get in close and without being scoped. Get in close to shore by night, offload the gear and then *Bull Shark* can slip out to sea. All under cover of darkness. Either she can then wait offshore for us or proceed to the nearest naval base for replenishment. Once the delivery is made, the boat will have room again."

"What about picking us up?" Williams asked.

Clayton exchanged glances with Decker and Simard. Turner groaned aloud, "Apparently there's more than one thing I won't like about this."

"My men and I won't be leaving," Decker said. "We'll join up with General Vandegrift's force once it lands. In all likelihood, Commander, you and your men will be ashore at least until then. I'm told we can get to Guadalcanal from here in about ten days or so? A few days to train here before we leave, that puts us at the island on the second or third. The invasion is set to go that week, no later than the seventh. Hell, we'll need the better part of a week to get Clemens squared away and make final observations and recommendations."

"There's more," Clayton stated.

"Oh for Christ..." Turner sighed.

"In the last twenty-four hours," Clayton stated sternly. "I've received a coded message through my grapevine from Shadow."

Turner blinked in surprise, "Isn't that the Japanese first officer of the *Leviathan*... what was his name..."

"Ryu Osaka," Clayton said, Yes. He survived the sinking, Art. He informs me that a new Japanese strike carrier, *Sakai*, is currently loading up at Truk and will be headed for the southern Solomons. She could be a problem."

Turner scoffed, "Another of Yamamoto's secret weapons?"

"In a manner of speaking," Clayton stated. "Nothing as fanciful as a submarine carrier... but she *is* something special. Here."

Clayton opened his valise and handed Turner a typed sheet. The submarine captain looked it over and frowned before reading it aloud.

"Converted cruiser," Turner began. "Fifteen thousand tons and carries twenty airplanes... Vals and Zekes. Also equipped with side-mounted AA batteries and half a dozen one-hundred- and fifty-millimeter naval guns controlled by a gun director... equipped with radar as well as a full sonar suite for ASW operations... Christ, she carries forty ashcans, too? Top speed of thirty-two knots, range of over eight thousand nautical... escorted by a pair of Fubukis... Jesus Christ, Web!" "That's not all," Clayton said. "Because she's got a small air wing, she can recover, reload and launch very rapidly. Against a fleet she'd be no match, but cruising alone in the waters around Guadalcanal... she's a menace to our plans. Osaka indicates that she's there in response to your attacks, Art. No indication that the Japs suspect a full large-scale invasion... but they are sniffing around and want to hedge their bets." "And my boat is gonna be out there alone with ten fish against this predator?" Turner asked.

"Hopefully to *avoid* her," Decker said sardonically.

"Yes... but if the opportunity presents itself..." Clayton said. "Never rains, but it pours," Williams commented resignedly. "Especially on you, Elmer, since you'll be the man in the hot seat," Turner said. "We need to assume that ship is hunting a submarine after our little show earlier."

"Well, gents," Simard said, leaning back in his chair. "I suggest you get down to brass tacks. Commander Turner, you and Major Decker assemble a list of what you'll need. My supreq officer already has a partial. Let your boys come ashore for a few days, Art, but I think a departure for the twentieth is the goal."

"Aye-aye, sir," Turner said as he and the other men rose. He looked at Clayton. "Will you be joining us this time, Web?" Clayton looked chagrinned, "I can't this trip, Art... I've got other business to attend to in Hawaii for the moment."

"Ah, well..." Turner said wistfully.

"Don't worry, Mr. Clayton," Decker said ebulliently. "We'll bring you back something nice. Here them Japs use gold in their fillings... maybe a nice necklace."

The Cactus Navy

"Yeah, or maybe a shrunken head," Turner poked. "Would you like that, Web? Would you like a nice shrunken head for the mantelpiece?"

"Now I *know* I'm not going with you nuts," Clayton deadpanned and then laughed.

Chapter Five

"You gonna get that boat rigged out sometime this watch, or what, sailor?"

This question was asked in a sarcastic tone that was clearly evident, in spite of having been whispered. And although it drew snickers from several of the other men in the darkness, the contempt behind it was also clearly evident.

"You wanna give it a fuckin' try, leatherneck?" was the equally unfriendly response.

Two distinct groups of men stood on *Bull Shark*'s foredeck. They were arranged to either side of a large rubbery lump that was compressed into a cylinder roughly a dozen feet long and three feet high. The cylinder was held tightly together by a complex series of lines and knots and nylon webbing that was proving to be particularly frustrating to unravel in the darkness.

"Thought you squids was supposed to be good with knots and shit," derided Sergeant Philip Oaks, which again elicited laughter, albeit a bit nervous, from the other three Marines beside him.

Sherman "Tank" Broderick stood up straight from where he and Doug Ingram were struggling with the package on deck and glared at the silhouette before him. Both men were large, with Oaks having an inch of height on Broderick's five-foot-ten, but with Broderick having the advantage in weight with perhaps fifteen pounds on Oaks.

The two NCOs had clashed from the very beginning. Oaks had swaggered aboard the boat as if he owned the joint and had immediately taken to sneering at everything and everyone who didn't wear Marine green. Unfortunately, his three underlings, Corporal Dave Taggart, Corporal Chuck Lider and private first-class Ted Entwater, followed in their squad leader's footsteps both figuratively and literally. Whatever Oaks thought, the other three men thought, too.

Although it did seem to Tank that while the two corporals were whole-hearted in their support, Entwater was only going along because it was his duty. Broderick also received the impression that Entwater, a younger man who was relatively new to the unit, was something of an outsider.

Davie Taggart was the unit's explosive ordinance expert. He couldn't wait to tell anyone who would listen about how much he knew about everything from grenades to satchel charges to improvised explosives to bombs of all types. Lider was the unit's gunnery expert. He knew about every American, Japanese, German, Russian or British weapon made today or since the Revolutionary War and loved to brag about it. Both men, like their leading noncom, enjoyed strutting about and making sure that everybody aboard the submarine knew what badasses they were.

Teddy Entwater was something of a departure from the other three Marines. Where they were in their mid to late twenties, good-looking, fit and confident, he was quieter. Entwater was twenty-one and still a bit on the stringy side. Although six-foot-two, he only weighed perhaps one-sixty-five, and the impression of bookishness that his quiet and intelligent personality engendered was further enhanced by his heavy horn-rimmed glasses, known unflatteringly in all services as "birth controls."

Entwater, when not oppressed by his comrades, seemed more of a reserved and respectful kid. Born and raised in Missouri, he had mid-western manners and had already secretly apologized to Tank and Doug for his fellow Marines' behavior. The young man knew just about all there was to know about electronics, was a student of military history and always seemed to have a book in his hands when he wasn't on duty. He'd only just avoided having the label of Poindexter hung on him because with a well-found rifle in his hands, Entwater could knock the nads off a gnat at two-hundred yards

"Probably wrapped up by a jarhead," Ingram said from beside Broderick. "This thing's a mess, for Christ's sake."

It was two hours past dark, and the men had been loading and stowing gear, crates of supplies and other equipment since lunchtime. They were tired, hungry and irritable, and the tangled mess of the raft they were trying to deploy wasn't doing their moods any good. Broderick knew that if something didn't change soon, a brawl might ensue. For his part, he'd be more than happy to feed a knuckle sandwich to that arrogant sergeant... but that would only get them all in hock and it just wouldn't do.

"Maybe we should take five, Sarg," Entwater suggested calmly. "I could go for a smoke, and we can tackle it in ten minutes or something."

"We got a deadline to meet, Teddy," Oaks all but snapped, "and these squids here are holdin' us up."

"I hear a lot of bitchin' but no suggestions," Broderick shot back. "You sure do make a lotta chin music for a guy just standin' around with his thumb crammed up his ass, Oaks." "How 'bout if I cram my boot up your ass, *Tank?*" Oaks menaced.

"If you're lookin' for a free ticket to ride the bedpan express, then take your best shot, asshole," Tank jeered in return.

"I see you boys are still fuckin' around with this thing?" came a hard voice from aft. Chief Mike Duncan strode forward past the forward deck gun, his tall, long-armed frame intimidating in the moonlight. "Maybe you ain't heard, but we got a schedule to keep.

We're shoving off in the morning and you men haven't even loaded crate one yet. What gives?"

Even the Marines fell silent in the presence of a chief. Duncan was a good-natured man and ran his engine rooms with a firm but fair hand. However, everyone who knew him knew that that firm hand would go upside their head if they fucked around once too often. The Marines had picked up on that immediately when they found out that Duncan was to be the senior enlisted man in their little commando unit. His bearing was familiar to the Marines, just as it was to the sailors. A hard-edged working man's leader was the same in any branch.

"Your boys here can't seem to get this present unwrapped, Chief," Oaks said with mock cheerfulness.

"So you and Tank figure throwin' hands is gonna solve the fuckin' problem?" Duncan asked sternly. "For Christ's sake... we're all in the same Navy, boys. I don't know if any of you have heard, but there's a goddamned war on. We got Japs and Krauts out there tryin' to kill us. Ain't that enough? Maybe instead of squabbling like goddamned kindergarteners, you fellas might try working *together* on somethin'. For example, were you to yank your noggins outta your keisters, you might realize that you can just *cut* the goddamned frappings and the webbing and then we can re-stow it in proper Navy fashion later. We got five hundred pounds of supplies to row ashore, unpack and then row back here as *practice* for when we gotta unload the entire *ton* and a half at Guadalcanal."

The six men shuffled and muttered with appropriate sheepishness.

"And one more thing," Duncan said, leaning forward and glaring, his eyes oddly gleaming in the lights from the Sand Island shore a quarter of a mile away, "if there's gonna be any ass-whoopins around here, they're gonna come from *me*. And be thankful it's only me, cuz' if the COB catches you shitheads dickin' around like you're doin' now, he'd send your asses to the Solomons express airmail with a swift kick in the ass. Now let's play nice and get this goat fuck underway before sunrise, huh?"

"Damn," said Chuck Lider in his Alabama drawl. "I thought my DI at camp Lejeune was a hard-ass..."

"A first sarge is a first sarge," Davie Taggart added in his New Jersey accent and chuckled. "They just call them CPOs in the Navy."

"Okay, let's do as Mike suggests," Tank said, pulling his clasp knife from his jeans pocket. "I'll cut these lashings, and we'll see what we got."

Tank quickly sliced through the seizing's and found that once done and the spider's web of quarter-inch line was removed, the webbing was fairly easy to undo. It was secured with straps and buckles that, when loosened and released, freed the large raft.

"You boys about ready to load her up?" Marty Janslotter asked as he made his way forward with Smitty in tow. The men held boat hooks and a coil of half-inch line in their hands. "Like to do some boatswaining for a change."

"Boatswaining?" Tank asked as he and Oaks unrolled the big raft. Ingram and Entwater removed the four oars and loose planks that were to act as flooring.

"Industry term," Janslotter said.

"Okay, stand back..." Tank announced and pulled the inflation lanyard.

There was a whoosh that seemed to the eight men on deck to be enormously loud. They all looked about in surprise as the small canister of compressed CO_2 expelled its contents and turned the flattened rubber mass into a rigid lozenge-shaped boat.

The raft was twelve feet long and eight feet wide. The air chambers that made up its rounded-rectangle hull were twenty inches in diameter. In the center were straps where two thwarts would be placed, and outboard of these were oarlocks. Four men, sitting rather close together, two to a bench, would row the ungainly craft to and from the ship.

"Uhm..." Ingram said unhappily. "I think we were s'posed to put these floorboards in before we blew her up."

"Shit..." Lider grumped.

"Well, let's get as many in as we can now," Oaks suggested. "We'll remember when we do this for real next time."

Grumbles of assent were followed by the men shoving as many floorboards as they could into the bottom of the raft. Janslotter and Smitty then attached the bow and stern lines.

"Okay, let's load her up," Janslotter stated.

"Ain't we gonna put it over the side first?" Lider asked in confusion. "Ain't no way we can move it with five hundred pound of crate in'er..."

Ingram scoffed but said nothing. Janslotter chuckled and spoke before Broderick, who had something rather snide dancing on the end of his tongue, could respond.

"You're forgetting that this here is a submarine, Chuck," Janslotter said amiably. "We don't bring shit to the water... we bring the water to the shit."

"Huh?" Taggart asked.

"Let's get them boxes aboard and I'll show ya'," Janslotter said, pointing to the stack of hundred-pound wooden crates stacked near the five-inch.

Five boxes were loaded, three behind the rowers and two forward. Then Tank and Ingram took the rear bench while Lider and Taggart took the forward. Entwater sat atop the forward crates, and Oaks sat on the stern portion of the sponson, shoving his legs into the small, curved space behind the crates.

"Okay, now what?" Oaks asked sardonically.

"Now watch," Janslotter said, leading Smitty aft to the deck gun. He looked up to the bridge where Pat Jarvis stood as officer of the deck. Behind him and arranged along the cigarette deck were the rest of the ship's officers, including the captain and Major Decker. The only exception was Frank Nichols, who was manning the dive station. Paul "Buck" Rogers stood by as well.

"Sir, ready to flood down forward," Janslotter called up to Jarvis.

"Bout damned time..." Rogers muttered.

Jarvis grinned and thumbed the bridge transmitter to life, "Control, bridge, flood down forward."

From the bow to about the location of the deck gun, ballast tank vents were opened. A whoosh of pressurized air and small fountains of seawater shot upward as from the bow buoyancy tank aft, water was allowed to enter the ballast tanks and make the submarine heavy by the bow. The bullnose sunk below the surface and the foredeck disappeared almost to the mounting of the forward five-inch. Janslotter stepped up to where the stern line of the raft was tied to the gun mount. He undid the bowline and kept one wrap around a support strut to keep the raft from drifting off.

"Holy shit!" Taggart said.

"Welcome to the boats, boys," Tank stated and laughed.

"She's afloat, Marty."

"Permission to cast off, sir?" Janslotter asked.

"Granted," Jarvis said.

The boatswain undid his single turn, and Oaks gathered in the stern line. He turned forward again, now in command of the party.

"Rowers, give way," he said, surprising the navy men with this bit of sea knowledge. "Easy all."

"Damn," Ingram muttered as he and Tank took up their oars.

It quickly became clear, however, that while the sergeant might know some nautical terms, his two corporals didn't quite know how to manage a double-banked set of oars. Immediately they took to fumbling and splashing and clashing the blades of their oars against the two navy men in front of them.

"Jesus Christ..." Rogers muttered darkly from beside Jarvis. "Looks like a boatload of good time Charlies comin' back from liberty."

"Why we train, COB," Jarvis said without much conviction.

"For Christ's sake!" Tank grumbled. "Take it easy back there. *We're* the stroke oars. That means we set the pace. You guys just do exactly what we do and at our pace. Nice and smooth, we're not racing."

"Yeah, blow me..." Taggart cranked.

In spite of this, though, the two Marines soon got into something of a rhythm with the sailors. The boat had no rudder, so Oaks had to call out directions in order to alter course... which didn't go well at first. The Marines knew port and starboard, but they were facing aft, so there was some confusion as to which of them was which.

"Give way port... that's you, Chuck... no, you stop rowing now, Davie... Jesus Christ..." Oaks was griping, his frustration made even sharper by the tittering from the two sailors at the oars before him. "When I say give way one side or the other, that side rows while the other stops, got it? Okay... give way all... there you go... no, you're a bit slow, starboard... give way starboard... yes, that means you, Davie... okay... good..."

It went on like that for several minutes until the boat finally nosed up onto the beach. Entwater leapt out with the painter in his hands and hauled the boat another two feet or so onto the sand. Once done, the four rowers brought in their oars and jumped over the side and into shin-deep water. With the boat lightened, the four men clapped onto the handles attached to the sponsons and hauled the raft even further, with Entwater heaving as well. They got the forward end of the boat onto the hard-packed sand at the water's edge. Oaks then jumped out and sloshed ashore.

"Okay, let's set up a defensive perimeter while we unload," he ordered. "Ted, you, me, and Chuck. Fifty yards in either direction near the top of the dune. Pretend that's the jungle's edge. I'll take center. You other guys, get these crates ashore once we're in position. I'll time you when we're ready."

The three Marines quickly jogged off, Oaks moving only ten yards away.

"Pfft, yeah..." Ingram griped as he took hold of one end of a crate and Taggart the other. "Leave the guys what've been rowing to do the lifting..."

"It's just five boxes at fifty pounds a man," Taggart retorted. "Quit your belly achin'."

Ingram glared but limited his response to heaving his end of the crate up. As the two men moved off, nearly going to Oaks' position, Tank got hold of one of the crates and hefted it himself. It was a bear. Not so much the hundred pounds, which he could easily manage. It was the size of the thing. He had to stretch his arms out as far as he could go just to get a purchase on the big box.

"That ain't gonna fly, Tank," Oaks said when the big sailor set the crate down. "It took you almost twice as long by yourself."

"It ain't the weight," Tank cranked.

For once Oaks didn't ride him, "I know, it's bulky. I think two men to a box no matter what is faster and won't wear you all out. Remember, we gotta do this *six* times when we get there."

"Then we oughta have more guys or switch jobs," Tank said.

Oaks sighed, "Yeah, we should have dedicated rowers and all of us ashore to unload and guard. It'd be faster. But the skipper... both skippers, if you will... want to limit the number of guys goin' ashore."

"I'll have Mike talk to them about that," Tank said. "Maybe if we get all us enlistees ashore in the first load... maybe a light load, with two dedicated rowers from the ship... we can get ashore and send them back. More of us on the beach, and we can set up a better perimeter while we wait."

Oaks shrugged, "Yeah, maybe... we'll have what, eight or nine days to figure this shit out?"

"Hey, you guys gonna pitch in or what?" Taggart griped as he and Ingram trundled another crate up.

"You guys are doin' such a fine job, though," Tank teased.

"If it ain't broke, don't fix it," Oaks added wryly.

"You don't get your asses down to the water and help us," Taggart grumbled. "Somethin' will get fuckin' broke..."

"Geez... what a wet blanket," Tank said wryly.

Oaks grinned, "Yeah... nobody likes him much."

There was plenty of moonlight for them to see the one-fingered salute from both Ingram and Taggart.

The sun had barely cleared the horizon when *Bull Shark* lined up for her passage through the reef. The narrow channel could be treacherous at times, as the big swells or cresting waves that rolled across the vast open Pacific met the reef and created steep breakers and strong eddies through the passage.

The conditions were mild on that morning, though. Heading out was always easier anyway, and after lining up in the center of the passage directly astern of the escorting PT boat, Turner had Hotrod Hernandez order up a two-thirds bell on both engines and the big submarine pushed her way out into the open sea at ten knots.

Al Decker popped his head up through the hatch, "Permission to come to the bridge, Captain?"

"Granted, Major, come on up," Turner said.

Decker mounted and stood near the two men, inhaling deeply, "It's good to be at sea again."

"That it is," Turner said. "I trust you found your accommodations luxurious?"

Decker grinned. Turner had been kind enough to share his stateroom, allowing Decker to make use of the Pullman bunk in the captain's cabin, "Just dandy, Art. Hell, I've slept in worse places... way worse. I appreciate you letting me bunk with you."

"My pleasure," Turner said. "How about your boys? They doing all right in their new digs?"

"I think they're just thrilled they aren't hot bunking," Decker replied with a smile. "You should hear some of the horror stories we've been told about submarines."

"Probably true for the most part," Turner said. "Especially on the older S and R boats."

"Permission to come topside, sir?" Hazard asked. He was given permission, and he joined the clutch. "Morning, Major." "Morning Mr. Hazard," Decker said. Turner thought he detected just the slightest reserve in the Major's voice. "How would you rate our training exercises, Lieutenant?"

Hazard withdrew a Marlboro from his khaki shirt pocket and lit it, "A bit of a shambles, sir, to be honest."

"Uh-huh," Decker mused.

Turner, inspired by Hazard, reached into his duty shirt pocket and found that he'd neglected to place his own pack of Lucky Strikes there. He groaned and shook his head.

Hernandez grinned broadly and held out his own nearly full pack of the same brand, "I beg, *señor Capitan*, that you will accept this small token from an unworthy and simple peasant."

"How many times do I have to warn you about being a smartass, Hotrod," Turner pretended to chastise. "However, I'll overlook it *this* time on account of your kindness... but I shall commandeer no less than *two* smokes by way of learnin' ya' a lesson."

Decker and Hazard laughed as Turner withdrew two cigarettes, placing one between his lips and lighting it and the other in his empty pocket. That broke the slight tension of a moment before.

"What do you suggest, Mr. Hazard?" Decker asked, returning to their earlier subject. "As a naval officer and former Marine." "Well sir..." Hazard said, "seems to me that Oaks and Broderick are right. We should get the team ashore, then use *Bull Shark's* crew to do the shuttling. More men ashore and less wearing on the guys to both row and unload over three-thousand pounds of supplies."

Turner nodded slightly, "Makes sense. Only one problem." "We end up with four *Sharks* ashore on the last trip," Decker finished.

"No sir..." Hazard said. "The last ferry will be to get us lofty officers to the beach. Surely we can row ourselves."

"You mean... do manual labor?" Decker asked with wide eyes.

Turner chuckled, "Scandalous! Imagine, high and mighty officers... one a ship's *captain* for Chrissakes... working! After all, that's what your common sailor or Marine is for... right, Hotrod?"

"*Si*... it is the pleasure of we who are but simple folk to bend to the plow in order that the gentry may live a life of ease and comfort," Hernandez said. "It is the custom in my own village."

Decker could see that the quartermaster was joking. He grinned and asked, "And where is this village from whence you came, Hernandez?"

"Long Beach, California, *señor*."

Turner and the other men laughed. The captain puffed on his confiscated pill and sighed, "It's gonna be a *long* transit..."

"*Si*," said Hotrod.

Chapter 6

Strike Carrier Sakai – July 25, 1942
The Slot – Between Guadalcanal and Tulagi

"There she is, Ryu," Hideki Omata said, pointing through the windscreen at the group of toy-sized ships on the horizon. "And a good thing too... we are nearly on fumes."

"Can we land this floatplane on that carrier's deck?" Osaka asked dubiously.

Omata smiled, "No... we'll put down nearby. I'm told they have a crane that can lift us on deck or into the hangar. Quite an interesting ship, wouldn't you say? Small for a carrier... yet fast, maneuverable and versatile. Another one of our great Admiral's... experiments, do you think?"

Osaka grinned. He knew that his friend was referring to the experimental submarine carrier *Leviathan* on which they'd both so recently served. The ship had been defeated by an American submarine that was, as Osaka understood it, at least partially under the aegis of the Office of Strategic Services.

"I'm not entirely certain of that," Osaka admitted. "I believe she was already under construction when I came to Admiral Yamamoto's staff. However, I'd suppose that this was likely, considering the nature of the vessel."

Omata frowned, "Another outlandish scheme...? I don't mean to sound disrespectful of our venerable Yamamoto... but that monstrosity on which we served was a failure."

Osaka shrugged, "I would not say that, Hideki. It was our idiot captain who failed the ship, not the other way about. Kajimora is a foolish and arrogant bastard, and he's now enjoying the fruits of his own harvest, no matter who his relatives are."

Omata cast a questioning glance at his friend, "How so?" Osaka chuckled, "I believe he's now the IJN attaché to the occupying force on Attu, in the Aleutians. Quite cold there, I understand, even in the summer."

Both men laughed. Omata reduced his airspeed and began to descend toward the small strike force below.

Sakai looked odd between her two Fubuki destroyer escorts. Odd because the carrier was less than two hundred feet longer than the big destroyers, giving the odd impression that either the warships were oversized or that the carrier had been shrunken down.

Yet as the floatplane drew near, another impression was received. The carrier appeared somehow sleeker than her larger counterparts of the Kido Butai. Her bow seemed to be steeved at a greater angle. Her island was constructed in such a way that it appeared nearly vertical along its after end, while forward each deck was slightly shorter than the one below, giving it something of a right triangle appearance.

The aircraft spotted on deck amidships, only six at the moment, gave the ship her true perspective. The vessel's flight deck was just wide enough to allow two aircraft to be catapulted at once, wing to wing. A single large elevator just aft of the catapult allowed for two airplanes to be brought up from the hangar as well, with room aft of this for half a dozen aircraft to be readied to taxi up to the catapult. Abaft of the staging area was the arresting gear. Several more planes could be placed to either side, tails outboard, allowing nearly the entire complement of twenty birds to be readied on deck at once.

"As I understand it," Osaka was saying, "she carries ten zeroes

The Cactus Navy

and ten dive bombers. There are ordnance hatches on the flight deck to allow aircraft on deck to be re-armed and refueled without having to use the hangar. A very rapid launch and recovery rate, I'm told."

Omata nodded. As both a pilot and experienced air wing commander, he knew all too well the logistics of handling aircraft on the limited space offered by even one of the big carriers. It was interesting that in spite of this one's diminutive size, at least as compared to early monsters such as the *Kaga*, she was more efficient in spite of it.

Omata brought the aircraft down onto the gentle swell and taxied along the side of the strike carrier. Despite being only a hundred and sixty-five meters, or five-hundred and fifty feet in length, the ship seemed quite large once the small floatplane was beside her.

"I wonder..." Hideki pondered as riggers attached hoisting cables to the plane's upper surfaces. "Could this be the wave of the future? A larger number of smaller carriers rather than fewer giants?"

"It is something to ponder," Omata said. "It would take nearly twenty such ships to have delivered the same number of aircraft to Pearl Harbor as did the six fleet carriers of the Kido Butai... yet I wonder how *Sakai* might have fared against the American dive bombers at Midway. This ship is reputed to be as maneuverable as a cruiser. She might be able to dodge such an attack more effectively than her larger counterparts."

"Perhaps time will tell?" Omata asked.

Their plane was lifted from the sea. Yet rather than being hauled the forty feet up to the flight deck, or even twenty feet up to the level of the hangar deck, the aircraft was hauled only half a dozen feet above the surface of the sea. A sliding door in the hull had been opened, and the booms that supported the plane had been extended from within. They began to retract, drawing the floatplane inside a small garage just large enough to contain her.

The aircraft was settled, and the garage door sealed. One of the riggers, wearing an orange coverall, smiled and waved, indicating the two officers were free to exit the aircraft.

The young man bowed when Osaka and Omata climbed out and onto the deck, "Welcome, sirs. Captain Igawa is waiting for you in his at-sea cabin. If you will follow me, please?"

The young man slipped out of his coveralls, revealing the uniform of a freshly minted ensign in summer white. The coveralls were deposited on a shelf and the young man led them out into a narrow passageway. They went up a steep companion ladder and emerged onto the cavernous hangar deck. The single elevator was just being lowered from the level of the flight deck, and the innumerable hangar deck gang was readying two aircraft, Zeroes both, to be hoisted to the flight deck above. Several more birds were crammed together forward, and several more aft of the large elevation platform. Beyond this, several blast-proof doors were open into the ordnance magazines.

"As you can see, sirs," the young officer was saying, "some improvements have been incorporated. Heavily reinforced weapons' storage lockers, fuel tanks and transfer lines. This much protection has limited the number of aircraft we can put into action... yet it vastly increases the survivability of the ship."

"Quite interesting," Hideki noted, observing the layout of the hangar and the working of the men with a practiced eye.

For Osaka's part, he saw things from the perspective of a pilot as well. Yet his experienced eye also saw trouble. In his view, Japan was wrong for doing what she had done. Hirohito's and Tojo's lust for power and glory had blinded them to the larger viewpoint.

Like his mentor, Yamamoto, Osaka believed in his heart of hearts that a war against the United States was unwinnable. That despite an auspicious beginning, Japan was already sliding into a death spiral. While they did have an advantage over the Americans... hell, over everyone in the world... at the beginning of the war, things were changing. The confrontation in the Coral Sea and at Midway only served to underscore this.

America had roused herself from her neutrality and was putting her enormous industrial might to work. In spite of being behind in

The Cactus Navy

aircraft and ship-building technology, the United States was catching up quickly and had the manufacturing power to simply overwhelm anyone else on Earth. Unlike Germany and England, who could bomb one another incessantly from land bases between the two countries... one had to cross thousands of miles of sea to reach the American coast. And once you did? You'd find an enormous nation with dozens of seaports, hundreds of airports and a virtually limitless supply of resources.

No carrier force, no matter how massive, could deliver enough destruction to even slow them down. Conversely, Japan was an island nation. Her large islands required resources to be shipped in from Asia and the Pacific Islands. Like Britain, Japan was vulnerable to attacks on her seaborne trade. Like Britain, enemy submarines could be put to use to slowly but surely starve Japan out, in spite of Japan's much larger size.

And if the U.S. was still working with obsolete airplanes, they certainly had the long end of the stick when it came to submarines. American submarines, the new ones at least, were for the most part larger, more comfortable, faster and more heavily armed than any other nation's. They had distinct advantages in electronic warfare as well. High-quality sonar gear as well as radar and, in some cases, more than one type. It still galled and amazed Osaka that most of the Imperial Japanese Navy's surface fleet, to say nothing of her submarines, did not even mount a radar set!

How might the battle of Midway have turned out if the Kido Butai mounted radar systems aboard the carriers? They would've foreseen the American dive bombers and would have had time to vector their Zeroes in to defend them. Of course, Nagumo's indecisiveness had certainly not helped the situation.

And the old fool was *still* in command of the remaining carriers!

Osaka cringed inwardly. Japan would lose this war, whether it took a year or five years. The twisted concept of honor perpetuated by the emperor would force more and more Japanese into the fight. Slowly but surely, all of the experienced men would need to be replaced by younger, fresher and unseasoned men. The complex and rigid Japanese system of honor would force them to fight to the death... not simply their own, but their country's as well. When Japan finally capitulated to the Americans, and Osaka had no doubt this day would come, she'd be so crippled by war that she might become a third-world power for decades. Perhaps even having to depend on her former enemy for both protection and support.

To Osaka's way of thinking, the *faster* Japan's defeat came, the less horrible it would be. That's why he had decided to assist the United States. To pass vital information to Webster Clayton. It wasn't out of love for the Yankees... he neither loved nor hated them. It was to preserve as much of his beloved Japan as he could. To save as many young men's lives as possible.

Did that make him a traitor?

Osaka didn't think so. He tried to help America in order to help Japan. Because unlike some of his own people, Osaka knew enough about America to know that the country would be there to support his own once they were victorious. On the other hand, his ideals flew directly in the face of Hirohito's and Tojo's. They would doubtless consider him the worst possible traitor. *That* was something that Osaka could live with. If those twisted and evil fools would think of him as their enemy, then Osaka could live with that easily. He'd even take some measure of pride in it.

The ensign led the two senior officers out of the hangar and into the island, where they climbed two more sets of stairs to the level of the navigation bridge. The strike carrier had no flag bridge, as she was the sole command of her captain. The navigation bridge was quite spacious, considering the size of the vessel. The entire deck was walled in heavy-duty glass and surrounded by an exterior walkway. Behind the control stations and chart table were the radio, sonar and radar shacks. Aft of these areas a small corridor led to a head, three tiny offices and a cabin that took up the entire after third of the deck. Osaka's and Omata's guide rapped his knuckles on the door, and a smooth deep voice bade them enter.

The Cactus Navy

The cabin was, like the internal bridge, strangely large on such a compact ship. A comfortable-looking cot and wardrobe stood behind a screen that separated the sleeping place from the rest of the cabin. A desk occupied one corner, and the rest consisted of a sofa and several matching chairs around a coffee table with large bay windows that gave a panoramic view of the carrier's afterdeck, the sea to starboard and the flight deck below.

Captain Kenji Igawa stood from one of the comfortable chairs and smiled. He was a big man, nearly six feet tall, which was quite tall for a Japanese man. His shoulders were broad and the rest of his body stocky. His moon-shaped face was slightly on the puffy side but friendly and open. His jet-black hair was here and there sprinkled with strands of iron gray. Osaka guessed him to be in his mid-forties.

"Thank you, Ikane," the *Kaigun Daisa*, a full captain, said to the ensign. The boy bowed deeply and went out. "Welcome aboard, *Sakai* Commanders Osaka, Omata. Please be seated. You both come very highly recommended from Admiral Yamamoto."

"*Arigatou, Igawa san*," Osaka replied with a bow. Omata followed suit, and they sat.

"Would you care for some tea?" the captain asked, indicating the fresh pot on the table. "I have been reading your reports on the mission of *Rabaiasan*. Most interesting vessel... and most unfortunate that she was destroyed. Most unfortunate timing as well. A dark day for the Empire."

"*Hai...*" Omata said sadly. "We were at least fortunate to save two-thirds of the crew."

"Indeed... indeed... And the submarine that attacked you," Igawa went on, "the... *Bull Shark*, was it? Very aggressive. I was especially interested to learn of their underwater breathing tube."

"Yes," Osaka said. He would have preferred to leave that little item out of his report, yet he knew that was impossible. Hideki's own report made mention of Osaka's speculation. It wouldn't do to have something so important glaringly absent from Osak'a'sown account.

73

"However, I believe it was the aggressiveness of her captain that was the deciding factor."

"I have heard a rumor," Igawa stated, filling their mugs for them, "through our spy network and our communications network with our German allies. Evidently, they lost an important asset in the Atlantic coast off the shores of America several months ago. Reports from the ship's captain indicated that a new fleet boat was sent after them... and obviously succeeded in sinking the ship and her escort. According to Kriegsmarine records, the submarine was also called *Bull Shark*."

"*Kuso...*" Omata cursed softly.

Igawa chuckled with good humor, "Exactly, Commander Omata. Shit indeed. I believe we may have had our own encounter with this submarine and her captain, a man named Turner."

Osaka's brows rose, "Sir?"

"Oh, not directly," Igawa stated. "We've only been on station for a week now... no, I meant our fleet in this area. Several weeks ago, a small convoy consisting of two freighters and a transport and escorted by a light cruiser and destroyer were headed for Guadalcanal from Rabaul. They were bringing supplies and more men to reinforce the construction efforts at our Lunga Point airfield. An American submarine had the temerity to attack this heavily guarded convoy! They sank one of the freighters... unfortunate as it contained most of the additional heavy equipment and construction materials... and also sank the destroyer leader. Our light cruiser hounded them, but the submarine managed to slip away. We have heard, nor seen, nothing subsequently. Since *Sakai* has arrived, I've had regular patrols flown and have been circling the area doing echo location sweeps as well. No submarines, no surface ships... nothing. Only the occasional reconnaissance flight."

"And you believe that this submarine was the *Bull Shark?*" Omata asked.

Igawa leaned back in his chair and retrieved a pack of Golden Bats from a cocktail table. He used a golden Zippo to light it, evidently enjoying the entire process. "Ahh... we have no proof... yet after learning all of what we have so far discussed... I am inclined to think so. It has been suggested to me by my intelligence officer that this submarine may be under the auspices of the American Office of Strategic Services. It isn't far-fetched to think that they may have been here to keep an eye on our doings in the southeastern Solomons."

Osaka was compelled to agree, "Understandable."

"It is also understandable to assume that the Ame-cohs will make an attempt on one of these islands in the near future," Igawa stated matter-of-factly. "They've seen what we're doing on Guadalcanal. And we have known for certain that they have coastwatchers there. The strategic importance of the Lunga Point airbase is plainly obvious. And I have no doubt that between the *Bull Shark* and the coastwatchers ashore... the Americans are planning something."

Omata scoffed, "Coastwatchers... can we not... eliminate them, sir?"

Igawa chuckled, "It's more difficult than it sounds, Commander. We have well over two-thousand men on Guadalcanal. Aside from the garrison and workforce at the airfield, we have Army and Marine troops stationed at various points along the northern coast. Yet the island's interior, save the flatter areas of the northern coast, is dense jungle broken by steep mountains and valleys. You could walk right past a man hiding ten feet from you in that mess and never realize it... however, we have made some headway. Through investigations, patrols and the interrogation of captured locals, we've learned that there is a small group of coastwatchers led by an Englishman named Martin Clemens." "Excellent," Omata said eagerly.

Igawa smiled wryly, "Yes... but we have also learned that he and his followers have fled into the mountains. Our only hope so far is that they'll begin to run out of supplies and be hampered by the very environment which aids them."

"Have you flown sorties over the island to try and spot them, sir?" Osaka asked.

"We have," Igawa said. "Yet, as you know, our assets are limited. We have but ten fighters and ten dive bombers. I send every Zero we have up to act as our CAP, naturally. Flights from Tulagi using their seaplanes are generally used to scout the island. However, for the time being, our focus is on the sea and coasts, as you might imagine."

"We can aid in this, sir," Omata volunteered. "With the addition of our floatplane, we can fly a low and slow recon flight over Guadalcanal. Who knows? Perhaps we might detect something. Smoke from a cook fire..."

"Most generous," Igawa said. "I accept... in spite of the fact that you are here for a larger purpose. Did the Admiral brief you?"

"He said only that we were to advise you and observe," Osaka said. "Does this... discommode you, *Kaigun Daisa?*"

Igawa chuckled with good humor, "No, Osaka san. I am not Kajimora. I am a great admirer of Yamamoto's and appreciate his sending me two well-seasoned officers. You've dealt with the Americans and this special submarine, and you're both pilots in the bargain. On that note, let us begin. If our information is correct, we should expect an American assault sometime in the next few weeks. I should also think that we should expect this shark of theirs to arrive even sooner. What can you tell me of this Arthur Turner?"

Chapter 7

USS Bull Shark – August 1, 1942 – 1830 ship's time

12° 18', 161° 47'

– 112 miles south, southeast of Guadalcanal

"I hope you brought an appetite, Major," Art Turner said as Al Decker stepped through the green baize curtain into the wardroom. "Cookie fixed us up something special for our last meal."

"Christ, Art, do you have to put it like *that?*" Decker asked wryly.

The two of them, along with the other men in the wardroom, chuckled. The group included Joe Dutch and Porter Hazard, who were going ashore with the landing party. Pat Jarvis and Andy Post were also there. Williams and Nichols had the watch.

"Better enjoy the good chow, then," Hazard said. "Once we hit the beach, it's gonna be corned beef hash, B and C rations and whatever we might find ashore that's good eatin'. What've we got, Skipper?"

Eddie Carlson entered with a large soup taurine that he set on the pantry countertop next to a smaller pot of rice, "Our Cajun mess attendant made his special seafood gumbo for you all, sirs."

"Damn!" Hazard emoted. "That smells terrific, Eddie!"

Decker inhaled deeply and smiled, "Damned if it doesn't""That's not all," Turner said as Carlson began to scoop rice into large bowls.

– 112 miles south, southeast of Guadalcanal

He then ladled the thick and savory brown gumbo on top. "I've got a little something special I've been saving for an occasion to go with it."

Carlson began to set the bowls down in front of the six men. He then set a small basket in the center of the table that was covered in a cloth. When opened, it revealed freshly baked and slightly toasted French bread. He grinned and went out through the curtain.

"Well, dig in," Turner said, taking up his spoon.

Exaltations and appreciation of the quality were eagerly expressed as the officers began to devour the gumbo. Large pieces of chicken, shrimp, chunks of mahi-mahi and andouille sausage floated in the viscous tan liquid. The men dipped in lightly buttered French bread and were so intent on the food that no one spoke for several moments. Not until Carlson returned with a bottle in his hand.

"Whatcha got there, Eddie?" Jarvis asked.

"Remember Ned Tully out at Bermuda?" Turner asked. "He gave me a couple of bottles of twelve-year-old Glenlivet. Well, this one's been hiding in my stateroom for a couple of months."

A cheer went round as Eddie uncapped the bottle. He poured three fingers into half a dozen coffee mugs and added a couple of ice cubes.

"Figured we'd have a celebratory tot and a toast to good fortune on our last night aboard for a bit," Turner offered. "Pour one for yourself there, Eddie."

"Yes sir! Don't have to ask me twice!"

"Gentlemen," Turner said, hoisting his mug. "A toast for good luck. To those of us who go ashore, and to the men of *Bull Shark* who prowl the sea. May we prevail and sow confusion among our enemies!"

"Hey, hey!" Hazard and Decker exclaimed together.

"Here here!" Dutch and Post added.

"Hear him, hear him!" Jarvis intoned and grinned broadly.

"To wives and sweethearts," Decker put forward, holding out his glass. Everyone clinked and repeated the toast.

USS Bull Shark – August 1, 1942 – 1830 ship's time

"May they never meet," Jarvis finished and drew a laugh from everyone.

"You boys ready for this," Decker asked.

"Yes sir," Dutch said.

"Absolutely, Major," Hazard stated.

Turner smiled thinly, "It's a bit strange for me... leaving my ship... but if what we're about to do makes it even a little easier for our Marines when they come... then I'm all in."

"Yeah, well, I'm not happy about stayin' back here," Jarvis said. "Just feels like... I dunno... like we're being left out and not doin' our part, y'know?"

"I think you'll be busy enough, Pat," Turner said. "Remember, aside from the invasion force, we've got that Jap strike carrier out here someplace. It's a wildcard, and I don't like it. I know I'll feel better knowing you're here backstopping Elmer. And with two qualified engineers too, plus Buck. I think we'll be able to focus on our parts better knowing you guys are in good hands. You do your part, and we'll do ours. Should have this war wrapped up in two, three weeks max."

That drew another round of laughter and clinking of glasses. "Believe me, Lieutenant," Decker said to Jarvis. "You're not missing much. Guadalcanal isn't some tropical island paradise. It rains over a hundred inches a year... place is loaded with spiders, leeches, giant wasps, tarantulas, crocs, fire ants... and if that's not exciting enough, jungle rot, dysentery, ringworm and malaria. Oh yeah... and two thousand Japs who don't much like round-eyes."

"Other than that... it sounds nice, though," Dutch added sardonically.

"You're not much of a salesman, are you, Major?" Hazard teased.

Decker chuckled, "Just laying the cards on the table, fellas. Rough as it might be for us for a short time... Martin Clemens and his group are in a living hell and have been since the war broke out. I'm glad to suffer whatever hardships we face in order to bring them just a little comfort and provide them with the gear they need. These

– 112 miles south, southeast of Guadalcanal

coastwatchers, here and all over the Pacific, have proven to be a Godsend. This little op is the least we can do."

That received expressions of agreement and another toast. Things in the after battery compartment weren't quite so cordial. Unlike the officers, the men of *Bull Shark,* at least for the most part, hadn't taken very well to the four enlisted Marines. Between the seemingly innumerable crates of supplies that were stuffed into every available space and the four men who bunked in the after torpedo room, the crew's already limited space had vanished to almost nothing.

Added to that was the fact that the boat was short by fourteen torpedoes. All she had were what had been loaded into the ten tubes and nothing more. To the crew, it felt as if their ship's teeth had been drawn. These stresses had combined to throw up an invisible wall between the sailors and Marines that had made the ten days of the passage uncomfortable.

Even Tank, Ingram and Duncan had not yet been able to get past the barely veiled animosity between themselves and the four Marines with whom they'd be going ashore. With one exception, however. Ted Entwater had managed to break through the wall of inter-service rivalry and irritability that pervaded. His quiet and friendly demeanor had slowly but surely gained him acceptance with his Navy shore party members and even the rest of the crew.

Part of this was the young man's eagerness to learn. He expressed an open fascination and admiration for the submarine service and spent every waking moment in the maneuvering room and engine rooms. He asked pertinent questions, pitched in with daily chores and seemed to pick up on the technical side of things quickly. It was clear that after only a day or two, he and Doug Ingram had become fast friends. Both men were of an age, and both had the kind of powerful memory that allowed them to absorb new information quickly. Ingram, although new to the boat, had made friends aboard and was somewhat more outgoing than Entwater. So when the other

USS Bull Shark – August 1, 1942 – 1830 ship's time

men saw the two getting along, Entwater received their approval by osmosis as well.

This had somewhat worked the other way about. For although Entwater was something of a dork in the eyes of his fellow more manly men Marines, he was a Marine. He was valuable to the Raider team, and he *could* shoot like a son of a bitch. That pushed his stock up in the eyes of the other enlisted Marines. And since they had at least a moderate regard for Entwater, they'd also accepted Ingram.

So it was not particularly unusual, therefore, when Ted and Doug took their garbage catchers... slotted dining trays... loaded with gumbo, French bread and bug juice over to the table where the other three Marines were already eating. The table could seat six men in a pinch, and the Marines made room for the two new men.

"Damn good chow," Oaks commented between slurps of gumbo. "One advantage of riding with the Navy, huh Davie? Chuck?"

"Hell yeah!" Lider rejoined. "Nice of the squids to give us a lift to the real war, ain't it, Davie?"

"You got it," Taggart said, tapping his spoon on his bowl.

"You guys are a riot, y'know that?" Ingram asked. "Oughta join the Bob Hope show when we get back to pearl."

Entwater grinned briefly.

"Aw, we're just ridin' ya' a little bit, Dougie," Lider said."Yeah, well..." Ingram observed, "maybe it's talk like that keeps the rest of the guys aboard from taking to you all. Ever think of that?"

Oaks only shrugged, "Hey, it don't matter much. After tomorrow, we'll be gone anyways. Then these sewer rats can get back to cruising around in their comfy air-conditioned pipe and their good chow. We'll be ashore sloggin' it out with the Japs and the creepy crawlies and shit. Sorry if we don't work so hard to make friends, Dougie, but we ain't here for that."

A silence fell over the table for a moment. It was broken a moment later by the angry voice of Mug Vigliano. He, Smitty, Fred Swooping Hawk and two other men, members of the so-called "black

– 112 miles south, southeast of Guadalcanal

gang," the engine room crew, stood in a clump holding trays and glaring at the Marines.

"You boys are at our favorite table," Vigliano said tersely.

Oaks glanced up and shrugged, "Hey, what can I tell ya, pal. Table's a table. Just take another one."

"There ain't no other one," Smitty growled.

"First come, first served, buddy," Taggart added.

"Yeah, you guys can't find a seat... why don't ya' go up on deck and eat," Lider said, and the Marines, except Entwater, laughed raucously.

The submarine was currently cruising at a depth of two hundred feet until dusk.

"You shitheads are *guests* here," Vigliano said dangerously. "Yinz oughta friggin' act like it, *capisce?*"

"Look, *Mug*," Oaks retorted sternly. "WE got here first. We're eatin' our last good meal aboard before we go off into the jungle. You can have the fuckin' table when we're *done*. Cuh-pish?"

"Oh-A! How'd you like to wear that fuckin' gumbo, *stronzo?*" Vigliano asked, receiving supportive chuckles from his shipmates.

"Come on guys..." Ingram held up a hand. "It ain't worth—"

"What're you doin' sittin' with these assholes anyway, Doug?" Smitty asked. "What're you gonna trade-in your dungarees for camos now?"

"Hey, Lider!" came a boisterous voice from the vicinity of the forward hatch. Walter "Sparky" Sparks entered, followed by Buck Rogers.

Sparks was one of the few *Bull Sharks* that the Marines did respect. Particularly Lider, who was a fellow Alabaman. He and Sparky had spent many an hour trading fishing stories and discovering who among their friends and family were common acquaintances.

Sparks had immediately sized up the situation the second he'd put his head through the hatchway. He could smell a fight brewing a mile away, and the one that he and Rogers saw was only seconds from breaking out.

USS Bull Shark – August 1, 1942 – 1830 ship's time

The appearance of the two senior men, not to mention their imposing statures, seemed to throw a small amount of water on the fire. Lider looked up and grinned at his new friend.

"Hey Sparky! What's goin' on?"

"You tell me, Chuck," Sparks said, sauntering up. "Me and the COB here was just coming aft to grab some of Henrie's damned fine gumbo. Looks like you fellas are having a disagreement or somethin'?"

"Yeah!" Lider said. "These boys is got their panties all bunched up on account they claim this is *their* table. We didn't see no name on it, though."

"They fuckin' know we sit there every meal," Vigliano growled.

"Lookie-here, boys," Sparks said, smiling. "Nobody owns any goddamned tables in this mess. You get one when you get one; that's the way it's always been. Mug, why don't you and you other boys go sit at the fuckin' chief's table. Ain't nobody there now."

That received uncertain mutterings and grumblings from the sailors. Rogers held up a hand.

"It's fine, boys. I got some more work to do before I sit down. It ain't worth fightin' over. In fact, who sits at what goddamned table *ain't* gonna be somethin' to fight over. And anybody who thinks it is will find themselves at the wrong end of an ass-whippin' from me and Sparky here. Then after you stop cryin', I'm gonna put you to work scrubbing the heads with a toothbrush... Marine or sailor. We clear?"

As he said this, Buck met each of the men's eyes in turn, sailors and Marines alike. All the men backed off and nodded, even the Marines. Even Oaks wasn't eager to scrap with the two big sailors. They both had a well-deserved reputation as men not to fool with.

"Come on guys," Sparky entreated. "We's all in the same fuckin' Navy. We're all on the same side. It's the Jap that's the enemy, not each other, ya' hear?"

"Besides," the COB said with a smile, "you want a fight, then we got a couple of doozies coming in over the squawk tonight. Willy Pep and Joe Louis, Jake LaMotta and Joe Walcott... oh, and Sugar Ray

– 112 miles south, southeast of Guadalcanal

Robinson is up against Rocky Graziano. Let's all relax and listen to a bunch of other guys beatin' hell outta each other, huh?"

An hour later, just as the last vestiges of twilight were glowing dully in the western sky, the dark and deadly shape of the *Balao*-class submarine broke the surface and raised her radio mast. The search periscope also went up, slowly rotating through a complete circle. Satisfied with what was... or was not... seen through its lenses, the bridge hatch opened, and lookouts scrambled out and up into their perch. "Ship rigged for surface," Frank Nichols reported.

"Very well," Elmer Williams said as he climbed into the conning tower. "Notify the captain. Arnie, standby to receive a coded transmission... oh, and let the mess know the boys can tune into the fights, huh?"

Williams ascended the ladder and saw the men in the tower attentive to their gear. Ted Balkley was performing his radar sweeps, Chet Rivers listening intently to the JK sound gear, Wendel Freeman was taking a trick at the wheel and Ralph "Hotrod" Hernandez was on periscope watch, in addition to his duties as quartermaster.

"How's it look up top?" Williams asked.

"Radar negative on SD and SJ," Balkley reported.

"All quiet below," Rivers announced. "Except for a family of whales maybe ten miles off."

"Visual scan reveals *nada*," Hernandez reported. "Lookouts posted."

"Great," Williams said. "Ready to get a breath of fresh air, Hotrod?"

"I am, sir," Hernandez said. "Although the smell of that gumbo is making me *hungry*. Enough to drive a man *loco*."

Williams grinned, "I know. But our watch is over in a bell. Just enough time to go topside and have a smoke or two."

The ship vibrated to the rumble of her four powerful diesels. Williams ordered Freeman to ring up an all-ahead standard, and he and Hotrod went up through the bridge hatch into a pleasantly warm

USS Bull Shark – August 1, 1942 – 1830 ship's time

evening. Far off in the distance, however, a low rumble of thunder rolled across the calm sea.

"Sounds like weather," Hotrod observed as he lit a cigarette and lit William's as well.

"Yeah… and from the north, too," Williams said. "Right where we're headed. Maybe that'll be a blessing once we hit the island, though. Cover of a storm for the landing operation might be a good thing."

"And a big pain in the ass, sir," Hernandez said with a small smile.

"*Bridge, radio,*" Arnie Brasher's voice filtered through the speaker. "*Incoming coded message.*"

"Very well, radio," Williams replied. "Alert Chief Weiss and the skipper."

A few minutes later, Turner himself came up through the bridge hatch with a message flimsy in his hands, "Evening gents. How's the watch?"

"Welcome topside, Art," Williams said. "We're on a three-four-zero running at ten knots, currently. We've just reached the 100-fathom curve and I estimate that once we top off the charge and accelerate, we should make landfall by zero-four-hundred. Diesels one and two on battery charge, three and four on propulsion. Batteries are currently at twenty-five percent. Fuel tanks two able and baker currently online. Ship rigged for surface, air accumulators topping up and no sign of enemy vessels on sound, radar or visual."

"Excellent," Turner said and then noticed the illusory flash of lightning far off over the horizon almost dead ahead. "Looks like we're sailing into weather."

"Yes sir," Williams noted. "Hotrod and I were just speculating that maybe that'll be helpful for cover later on."

Turner sighed, "Yeah, but it might make things ugly. Well, XO, aside from the evening fox, here's a little something you should look over."

Williams accepted the message and read it. He nodded,

– 112 miles south, southeast of Guadalcanal

"Authorization for our landing as scheduled. Hmm... this is cryptic... beware the shadow?"

Turner chuffed, "Shadow is one of Clayton's contacts. I didn't actually meet him... but it turns out his name is Ryu Osaka. He was the XO of that sub carrier we sunk. Also, an aid to Yamamoto. Occasionally funnels information to the OSS. I think this is Web's way of telling me that Osaka is out here. Maybe aboard that strike carrier you'll be dodging."

Williams frowned, "So what's this mean for us?"

Turner shrugged, "I'm damned if I know. You know how all this spook shit goes, Elmer. Layers inside of layers... maybe Osaka can help us, maybe not. However, regardless of the situation, *Sakai* is a legitimate target."

"You think I should go after her?" Williams asked dubiously. "Once I'm gone, Elmer, you're the captain," Turner said. "You're gonna have to make the hard decisions. However, my advice would be to keep a weather eye open for her. She's got two Fubukis escorting her, and as you know from the material we received, that small carrier has her own ASW teeth. So, I'd say if the opportunity arises, try for her. But only if you have to. Don't go *seeking* trouble, Elmer. Remember, you've only got ten pickles aboard."

Williams drew in a breath and let it out slowly, "Christ... it can't ever be easy on this boat, can it, sir?"

Turner chuckled and patted Williams on the shoulder, "I've got faith in you, Elmer. You've earned your stripes now. You've got the training, the experience and the headpiece for this. You'll be a great skipper. Besides... ya' got Hotrod here, so what else could you ask for?"

"This is true, *señor*. I am *muy temido* by the Japs," Hotrod affirmed. "This means that the Japanese fear me much, sir." "Is that true, Art?" Williams asked with a twinkle in his eye. "S*i*!" Turner replied.

Chapter 8

Honolulu, Hawaii
– 1755 local time

"Hi Mommy!" Dotty Turner exclaimed as soon as Joan Turner stepped through her front door.

"Hi Mom," Arty enthused almost immediately.

"Hey gang," Joan said, smiling and kneeling on the living room floor to give and receive hugs and kisses from her two children. "What're you two up to?"

It was plainly obvious what they were up to. The small living room, almost a parlor, really, featured only a sofa and love seat. The Turners had elected not to include a coffee table so as to open up the floor space.

Said floor space was now dominated by a two-story dollhouse and a variety of dolls and their clothing strewn about. The rest of the floor was currently being used as a combination construction site and shipyard.

Arty had both his Lincoln Logs and his Tinkertoy sets out, several sets of each now accumulated. His complex fort was being joined by what looked like the skeleton of a naval vessel.

"Just waiting for you to come home," Dotty said as she plopped herself down in front of the house.

"Mrs. Finnegan says we can listen to Jack Benny while we eat," Arty said with pleasure.

As if to underscore this, the large radio set along one wall broke into an announcement:

"This is an NBC re-broadcast from our home studios... We now present to you the Grape-Nuts radio program starring Jack Benny!" Applause and music began to play as the show began. Joan smiled and walked into the kitchen where Gladys Finnegan was just straining a pot of potatoes. The pretty brunette turned and smiled at her friend.

"Welcome home, Joanie, dear! How was work?"

Joan laughed as she slipped out of her Navy WAVES uniform coat and hung it on a hook in the small hall closet. "Lots of numbers and letters, as usual. Joe Rochefort was in rare form today, though, Gladys. Bedroom slippers, A pair of corduroys, an Aloha shirt and his hair looking like he just got out of bed!"

"What time was *that?*" Gladys giggled.

"About an hour ago!" Joan joined in. "The Old Man's up to something, dammit! He says... the Old Man is Yamamoto... and we've got to decode this pronto. That's when I grabbed my purse and got the heck outta there."

Gladys chuckled, "And my Joe?"

Joan drew in a breath and looked sad, "He... he didn't make it, honey."

Both women broke up, and Joan helped to set up the plates. Gladys had laid out six of them, and Joan looked at her questioningly.

"Oh, Joe got out," Gladys said. "He called about ten minutes ago from the office. He says he should be here any time and is bringing an old friend of yours. Asked if we had enough for six and I said sure, plenty to go around. Between your and my Sunday meat ration, I was able to get a nice pair of roasting hens."

"Terrific," Joan said. "By the way, it smells *divine*, Gladys. I'm famished."

"Hey, hey! Anybody home!" Joe Finnegan's voice called out from the front room. It was met by enthusiastic greetings from the kids. Joan and Gladys heard Finnegan talking to the two Turner kids, inquiring about how they were and telling them how nice it was that they were around since his two were visiting their grandparents in Massachusetts.

There was another man's voice too that Joan didn't immediately recognize. Not until Finnegan strode into the kitchen/dining room with a civilian in a dark blue suit trailing in his wake.

"Web?" Joan asked in confusion. "What brings you to our humble home?"

Webster Clayton gave Joan a quick hug and kissed Gladys' hand, "I actually went down to the dungeon to find you, Joanie. Joe here said you'd gone home and that I should come back with him. I hope you don't mind me popping in uninvited for supper... but I did want to talk to you about something."

Joan felt a brief flutter in her belly, "Is... is anything wrong, Web?"

Clayton smiled reassuringly, "Oh, no. Art's fine. No, it's actually work-related, and I think you might be just the one to help with this. We can talk more after supper, though. It smells great! Roasted chicken and mashed taters?"

After a very pleasant meal and the laughter from the Jack Benny Show and then a live broadcast of a concert from the Park Sheraton Hotel in New York, Gladys and Dotty began to clean up the dinner dishes while Joe and Arty went for a walk down the street to a small park where they could play catch on the empty ball field. Joan told Gladys she'd be happy to wash dishes since Gladys cooked, but her friend waved her off, stating that she knew Web wanted to talk with her.

Clayton and Joan then went out to the covered back porch and sat. Clayton lit up a cigarette while Joan enjoyed a glass of wine.

"Okay, Web, what is it this time?" Joan teased. "Want me to ask Hitler out to the movies or maybe work as Mussolini's secretary or something?"

Clayton laughed, "No, nothing so spectacular this time, Joanie. But I do have a special project I think would work out well for you and allow you to be home with the kids more."

Joan waited expectantly.

"Okay..." Clayton began. "As you know, we're about to launch a major offensive in the Solomons."

Joan nodded, "Marine division and a fleet assault. We've been pouring over Japanese transmissions for weeks now trying to discover if they have any idea of what we're up to."

"And do they?" Clayton asked.

Joan frowned, "No... although there has been some speculation. Losing a couple of ships near Guadalcanal at the beginning of July put them on edge. I think the consensus among the upper echelons is that we're going to strike some time. They just don't know when... although one transmission I read gives us a clue."

"The airfield on Guadal," Clayton said.

Joan nodded, "Yeah. It seems to be Matome Ugaki's opinion that we're going to invade *before* it's completed. And the estimates for that were the first week of August, but with the loss of that freighter, it's been pushed back to the end of the month."

Clayton drew heavily on his cigarette and sighed out the smoke, "Yeah, I was afraid of that. Makes sense, of course... but at least it's not a definitive date so that they can build up forces."

"What's this got to do with me, though?"

"Well, Joanie... you've heard of the coastwatcher program, right?"

She nodded.

"We've got some on Guadalcanal, which we're code-naming Cactus," Clayton explained. "Anyway, our Cactus group is in trouble. Your husband, in fact, should be just about to the island now, or before morning at any rate. He's delivering supplies and a small team of Marines to assist Captain Martin Clemens, a British Solomon Islands Protectorate officer who was stationed there and is now acting as our chief coastwatcher and advisor."

Joan bit her lower lip, "Is Art going ashore too?"

The Cactus Navy

Clayton drew in a breath, hesitated and then nodded, "Yes. As I understand it, he, Joe Dutch and his new second engineer, Porter Hazard are going with a couple of sailors. Hazard is a former Marine, and Art's going to act as command-level observer for us. The plan is to re-supply Clemens and his people with enough to keep them going until the First and Fifth Marines arrive. Then Art and his crew will extract back to *Bull Shark*."

"Jesus..." Joan breathed.

"I know, Joanie," Clayton empathized. "But this is a war... and your husband has proven to be... very effective."

"I know that... dammit... but that doesn't make it any easier, Web," Joan stated. "Hell, sometimes this new career of mine makes it worse, you know? Now that I'm on the inside of the loop and really know what's going on? Only after the fact, of course, and it's not like I can even talk with him..."

Clayton nodded and managed a small smile, "Which brings me to my point. One of the things that Clemens is running low on... hell, it's everything in truth, including shoes... are batteries for his radio station. In the gear *Bull Shark* is delivering are batteries along with additional radio equipment. The problem is that radio transmissions are easy to intercept. However, there are some bands that can still be useful and aren't as carefully monitored by the enemy. So long as the operators are cautious, they can be a big help. Ever hear of ham radio?"

Joan nodded, "Yeah, people who sit in their basements and talk to folks in China and whatever... is that what Clemens does?"

"It's what he *will* do," Clayton clarified. "At least until the Marines arrive. For the next week or so, Joan, he's going to be sending in quite a lot of information, both officially and unofficially... and that's where you come in. I'd like to set up a ham station here at the house. I'd like you to monitor it and report whatever you hear. I've already gotten permission from Rochefort. You'll be at your station several times a day, at stated intervals. You talk to them, take notes, provide coded info and so forth. We've already worked up an entire cover story, fake names and the like so that you can speak plainly, but still in code, if you see what I mean."

"Do you think I could speak with Art?"

"Absolutely," Clayton reassured. "Interested? It's only for a couple of weeks, mind you. You'll be back to the dungeon in no time."

"Swell," she intoned dryly and then grinned. "Okay, Web, I'm your man. What do we need, and when do we begin?"

Southern coast of Guadalcanal – 0347 local time

"I'd call it a mixed blessing," Major Al Decker said from *Bull Shark*'s cigarette deck.

"I call it a giant pain in the ass, with all due respect, sir," Paul Rogers said as he supervised the hauling up of cargo through the forward torpedo room loading hatch and engine room hatch aft. "Seas running six feet at least... gonna be a ball buster once they hit them breakers."

The submarine was hove-to a quarter-mile from a wide stretch of deserted beach on the windward side of Guadalcanal. The sand stretched about fifty yards from the mid-tide line and ended at a dense jungle that was nothing more than a black line in the black night.

The storm had passed at least, leaving behind a partly cloudy sky that occasionally blotted out the moon and plunged the sea and land into impenetrable darkness.

"Least it ain't rainin'," Chief Mike Duncan said as he passed by on his way down to the main deck.

"I think our boys' idea of using dedicated rowers is a good one, Captain," Decker said. "We're going into this totally blind."

"According to the dispatch, Clemens or some of his people should be meeting us," Turner said without much conviction. "But I hear you, Major... all right, let's load up the raft with you and the Marines on the first run. We'll need four rowers, though. It'll be a battle for them to get out past the surf line."

The Cactus Navy

"Can we take Tank, Ingram and Duncan as well?" Decker asked. "That'd give us eight men ashore, including me. If something does pop off, that's two squads' worth of men."

Turner frowned, "If you all cram in, you could do it... but the boat'll be a lot more unstable with you all sitting on the chambers..."

Decker frowned, "Yeah... damn... how close can you get in, Art? If we could position the submarine parallel to the beach, she'd act as a breakwater."

Turner blew out his breath, "We're already in fifty feet. I could probably get a hundred yards, maybe two hundred, closer. I wouldn't want to go in less than twenty-five feet, though. We'd have less than a fathom under our keel in a trough. Maybe... maybe we can do it. Get you off and then move the ship closer just long enough to ease the swell behind you a bit. We'd have to move off again right away, though."

"The raft will be more stable with cargo in it, though, right?" Decker asked.

Turner nodded, "Yeah, lower center of gravity. Okay, let's do it. Get your men and what gear you need to establish a beachhead. We'll tell off parties to load and row. Once all the cargo is ashore, I'll come off with Joe and Porter. Just us. We'll find a place to hide the raft. You never know."

Decker nodded and cleared his throat, "There's one thing we haven't really discussed, Captain... and I hope this doesn't cause a problem. We've worked well together so far. Our boys have had their share of head-butting, but I think that'll go away once we're in the thick of it."

Turner waited, sensing what was coming.

"You and I are the same substantive rank," Decker said. "And aboard ship, you're also the captain and are clearly the senior officer. However, once we go ashore..."

"It's your show, Major," Turner said. "I understand that. Land warfare is your bailiwick. I've got no problem with that. Hell, I'm not so arrogant that I think I know more about it than you do. I hope I'll learn something and hope I'm more of a help than a hindrance."

Decker grinned, "Somehow, I doubt that you'll be a hindrance, Art. You've gone through basic training, same as any of us. You're physically fit, brave and smart. And I appreciate your acceptance of this. I think we'll do just fine."

At first, the run in to the beach was easy. *Bull Shark* flooded down, and the raft and its twelve men got clear of the ship before the rolling swell began to make itself known. Out in deeper water, the swell actually aided the rowers, gently pushing the raft toward the dark shore. However, as the raft neared the surf line, the swells began to steepen as they met the rising bottom. By the time they began to break, they were easily eight-foot-high cresters that made everyone aboard the raft cringe.

"We can do this two ways, sir," Mike Duncan, the senior sailor in the group, stated as the raft held herself just outside the line of breakers. "We can row like mad, surfing in as best we can... or we go in backwards."

Duncan and Decker sat on the curving stern of the raft, Taggart and Lider to either side and forward of them. Next were the two thwarts with the four *Bull Shark* rowers. Next to either side were Tank and Ingram with Oaks and Entwater sitting in just about the same spot as Decker but facing aft.

"The thing's the same back or front," Decker noted, wiping spray from his eyes. The storm had passed, and the rain was gone, but the fifteen-knot wind still blew spindrift off the tops of the swells. Between that and the working of the sea, every man in the boat was nearly soaked and several inches of water sloshed about at their feet.

"Yes sir," Duncan explained, "but if the guys row backwards, that is to say, pushing us forward, they can then stretch out and row hard when one of them big breakers comes up on us."

Decker nodded, "Pushing back so we don't go ass over tit... I see what you mean, Chief. What about the regular way?"

Duncan frowned, "It might be the same... but them breakers look nasty, plus it's dark..."

"Okay, let's do option two," Decker decided.

"Give way port! Back water starboard! Smartly now, dammit!" Duncan, who was acting as coxswain, bellowed.

The clumsy overloaded rubber boat began to turn, rolling hideously in the trough of two big swells. Every man aboard except the oarsmen leaned to seaward to counteract the butt-clenching roll.

"That's it! Back water all!" Duncan ordered. "Sir, *Bull Shark's* moving in closer!"

A cheer went up from everyone who could see the dark silhouette of the submarine to seaward. She was working herself in closer and turning, putting her three-hundred- and eleven-foot beam to the swell and acting as a temporary breakwater. To the men in the small boat, she looked enormous. Almost dangerously close.

It was working. The swell, although not completely blocked, seemed to shrink down to a modest two-or three-foot height. Even as the raft entered the line of white water, it was clear that the submarine's bulk was both reducing the wave size and pushing the surf line closer to the beach.

It couldn't last, though. Even in the darkness, the men could clearly see *Bull Shark* swaying to the swells, and they all knew that she was slowly but inexorably being pushed toward shore. She'd have to move off again and reset or risk bottoming out. And who knew what rocks or corals lay below the surface. The charts weren't that specific.

"Hundred yards to go!" Oaks called out from his spot, now the stern.

The waves were increasing in size and power rapidly as the raft moved out of the submarine's blockage zone. That was also being magnified by the fact that the boat was already turning and headed further offshore.

The raft's pitch began to grow alarmingly steeper. First her stern rising so that Oaks' and Entwater's feet were as high as Decker's head. Then the foaming, churning hill of water would roll beneath the boat, flexing her twelve-foot length until the men in the bow had to look down to see the tops of the foremost men's heads.

"It's about to get dicey, boys!" Duncan called, gripping the straps with white-knuckled intensity. "Back water... little more starboard... okay... here comes a doozy... give way all! Pull! *Pull* goddamit!"

A huge breaker blotted out the horizon and the retreating form of the submarine. Clouds were in the process of obscuring the moon, and the barely visible breaker became a mountainous dark shape with just a hint of ghostly coloring at its crest.

The wave slammed into the boat, and she seemed to stand up nearly vertical as every man aboard leaned into the rise. The men at the oars threw themselves bodily on the looms, digging their blades in and fighting to propel the raft backward against the tremendous force of the wave. Foaming seawater poured over the men, filling the boat and then swirling out again.

Suddenly the wave was past, and the boat slid down the backside. Thankfully, the backs of the breakers weren't nearly as steep.

"Back water!" Duncan shouted. "Come on, guys! For all you're worth now!"

"Almost there!" Entwater shouted. "It must shelf up because the breakers are pretty light just ahead of us."

"Get ready!" Oaks shouted. "Here comes another one... almost... here she comes!"

"Give way all!" Duncan roared.

The towering wave struck the floundering boat and heaved her bow toward the cloudy night sky. Once again, Decker felt as if he were being thrown onto his back and that every man in the boat was hanging directly over his head.

Unfortunately, the angle of this wave had been slightly different from the last. It caught the boat on its quarter, and even as the raft began to level off over the foaming crest, the raft suddenly slewed sideways and began to surf, being dragged along with the wave and heeling precariously over. As the men shouted and screamed, they felt the big wave break, hitting the shallows and blasting apart as its energy was dissipated in a swirling, roiling maelstrom. All that saved the raft from capsizing was the fact that it was nearly full to the gunwales with seawater.

"We're in!" Duncan announced and laughed maniacally.

The raft spun slowly in a sea of foam with only the meagerest of ripples. They were only ten yards from the shore and a quick test with the oars showed that it was only three feet deep below them. The raft was quickly rowed to the beach and the men tumbled out, hauling her up onto the shore and patting one another on the back and laughing.

"Holy Christ, Chief!" Decker said with a smile. "Think I shit my skivvies."

"Well then you're doin' better'n me, sir," Duncan said wryly. "My asshole was clamped down so hard I coulda cracked a walnut."

"Okay, form up," Decker said, suddenly turning all business. "Taggart, Entwater, you move off left, Oaks, you and Lider move right. Recon the tree line and set up a perimeter. Tank and Ingram, you station yourselves directly ahead at the jungle line. Take a peek inside but don't lose sight of the beach. I'll stay here with the chief. Each team send a runner back to report once you've made a thorough inspection. If it's clear, Doug and Tank can start hacking us a path inland."

A chorus of aye-ayes were made in reply before the men paired up and moved off. Decker and Duncan helped the four sailors turn the raft over and empty the water out.

"Sir..." Duncan began. "I don't like sending these guys out alone without a coxswain. Not under these conditions. Permission to accompany them back to the ship, sir."

Decker looked at the four sailors. They were walking back and forth in the sand, shaking the stiffness from their legs and arms. Each one was among the fittest aboard the submarine. Swooping Hawk, the Navaho, Janslotter, the new boatswain and two burly diesel motor machinists hand-picked by Duncan.

"Granted, Chief," Decker said. "One more man shouldn't make that much difference. And I hear you... that was a rough landing. Think you'll be okay headed out? How about the next trip in?"

Duncan sighed, "Going out should be easier, sir. We'll be able to meet the surf head-on. Coming back... I hope that with some of that cargo lashed in, it'll make the boat more stable. I'll also talk to the skipper about keeping *Bull Shark* in closer again, but for a little longer."

"Okay, good," Decker said. "Wait until we get the report. Couple of minutes to let these boys rest and then head back out, Chief."

Five minutes later, Entwater, Ingram and Lider trotted out onto the moonlit beach and up to Decker. Quick salutes, a sip from their canteens and then a negative report.

"No sign of anybody, sir," Entwater said.

"Our side either, sir," Lider reported. "We went a good hundred yards to the east."

"Nobody ahead," Ingram reported. "Both Tank and I split up a bit and made our way into the brush. It's dense as hell sir, but there appears to be a rough path not far to the left there. Not sure where it goes, but you can see it's been used, even as dark as it is."

"So, where the hell's Clemens?" Decker asked no one in particular. "Okay, Chief, you'd best get moving. Gonna take half a dozen trips to get that shit ashore... we'll be lucky if we're done by daybreak."

Chapter Nine

Remarkably and thankfully, the landing of the three-thousand or so pounds of supplies went relatively smoothly. With *Bull Shark* able to work to within two-hundred yards of the beach, it gave the raft a reduced sea in which to operate.

The task was tedious, however. The ship would have to work in close, flood down, launch the raft and then turn sideways to the sea. Then, as the raft entered the break zone, the boat would then have to be worked out again to twice the distance to avoid being shoved up onto the beach. This made the row out less placid, but as the raft was empty of all but five men, it was less wearing as well.

Seven times this process was repeated. Load up the raft with five hundred pounds of crates... it could hold more but became too top-heavy... then row it ashore, unload and then back to the boat for more. Finally, as the sky was lightening in the east, Art Turner, Porter Hazard and Joe Dutch got into the raft and took the oars. Turner sat alone on the after thwart to act as stroke oar, and the other two officers doubled up behind him. Chief Mike Duncan, who'd been acting coxswain throughout, sat in the stern on the floor, not even caring about any water that came aboard. He'd long since been soaked through to the bone and looked to his captain as tired and bedraggled as a drowned rat.

"You guys take care of yourselves, huh?" Elmer Williams said as he stood on deck near the raft. "This is the most harebrained thing..."

"We'll be fine, mom," Dutch joked.

"You better be," Pat Jarvis put in. "Cuz if anything happens to any of yous, I got a nice butt-whippin' for ya."

"Here you go, sir," Buck Rogers said, placing a large rubber bag in the bow of the raft. "Couple changes of clothes and some other goodies in this watertight sack. Skipper... you sure I shouldn't come along? Kinda feel bad, lettin' you guys go without me."

"Trying to horn in on our shore leave, Buck?" Turner teased. He smiled what he hoped was a reassuring smile at the three men. "I feel better knowing you're here to watch over these boys, COB. They are but officers, after all. We're leaving you guys short-handed, and I personally feel better knowing you're here for Elmer and Pat to rely on. We'll be fine. A few short days and we'll all be back together again. You guys mind the Japs, now."

With that, the boat was flooded down for the final time and the raft rode the swells toward shore. There was only one brief moment of terror when the raft got caught in an eddy and was spun completely around, but it happened just inside the break line where the waves, although still four feet or more even with the attenuation provided by *Bull Shark*, had been robbed of most of their power and were little more than foam. The raft arrived on the beach just as the sun was peering over the horizon with four wet, but otherwise unharmed, men.

"Captain Turner," Al Decker said, extending a hand to help the captain out of the raft. "Welcome to Guadalcanal."

"I hereby claim this land for Spain!" Turner joked in an over-the-top Spanish accent. He drew in a lungful of humid tropical air heavily laced with the pungent aroma of life. "How are we set up so far, Al?"

The Cactus Navy

"We've moved the stores into the jungle there out of direct sight," Decker said, leading the men up the beach as Tank, Ingram, Lider and Entwater emptied the raft and began carrying it into the jungle as well. "So far this morning we've seen no sign of anybody. Not Clemens or his people, or the Japs."

"Have you done much scouting?" Turner asked.

"Not much," Decker admitted. "There's a partially worn-down path right here... but once you enter this jungle, it's blacker than a coal miner's asshole. Even in daylight it might be tough. Awfully dense canopy. However, your sailors did go a little way in and discovered that the path eventually breaks out into a sort of open area that might be a road. Now that it's light, I'm gonna send out a couple of scouting parties."

"How are we supposed to get in touch with Clemens?" Dutch asked.

Decker sighed, "That's not clear. According to Clayton, he's supposed to let Clemens know where we're to land and when. But part of the problem is that *we* haven't heard anything from Clayton."

"Which could mean Clemens couldn't respond," Hazard opined. "With his radio gear in such a bad way."

"Or it means he didn't get the message at all," Decker said unhappily. "Which means we're on our own. We'll have to find him ourselves."

"Christ..." Dutch cranked. "And hump a ton and a half of supplies ten or twenty miles into those mountains?"

"Welcome to amphibious warfare, gents," Decker said, pulling a pack of PalMals from his combat utility blouse pocket. He shook out several and held them out for the officers to take. "By the way, we need to get you boys changed out of those khakis and into Marine BDUs. Believe it or not, there's still rainwater dripping in the trees there. One spot is so heavy you should be able to rinse completely off before putting on your utilities. I recommend it. All this salt, once dry, will fuck up your skin something awful in this heat. Just watch for creepy-crawlies."

"And killer parrots?" Dutch asked wryly as the ubiquitous birds began to chirp and squawk from within the dense jungle.

Once Turner and his men had "showered" and put on their frogskins with the jungle pattern outboard, they'd assembled back on the beach to gear up. Each man received a Colt 1911 .45 semi-automatic with two extra magazines. They also were issued a Thompson sub-machine gun with two extra magazines and a bandolier with four grenades. Aside from this was a rucksack with several days' worth of C-rations, bug repellant, hand-held radios with admittedly limited range, two-quart canteen and a few other items, including a new prototype Marine Corps combat knife called a KA-BAR that they all strapped to their thighs.

"Look at you boys," Decker said cheerfully as the entire team paraded themselves on the beach. "Look like real Marine Raiders. Okay, here's the deal. We got four officers and seven working men here. Six sailors and five Marines."

"Sir," Hazard held up a hand. "Six Marines, sir."

"Ah, yes," Decker said with a grin. "Our Mr. Hazard who walks both in light and shadow. Okay, that's good. Now, as the two most important guys, Captain Turner and I will stay safely in the rear."

That drew laughs from the Marines and even the sailors.

"Okay, okay, all kidding aside," Decker got serious again. "We're here, but have no idea the location of our objective, nor if he is even aware we've landed or that we exist. We've got pretty good maps drawn from recon overflights. Problem is the maps aren't too detailed. We know there's a small river about two klicks west of us, that the foothills to the mountains start about five or six klicks inland and—"

"Uhm..." Dutch raised a hand and flushed with embarrassment. "What's a klick, sir?"

There was some muffled tittering from the enlisted Marines. This drew a hard look from their major and it stopped immediately.

"Back in the Great War," Decker explained patiently, "we had to start using the metric system to adapt to the French and their maps. Been using it ashore ever since. A klick is shorthand for a kilometer,

Joe. About six parts of a mile. Two klicks is about one point two miles. Actually, a kilometer is pretty close to half a nautical mile, if that helps any."

"I knew that," Turner said and grinned at Dutch, who elbowed him lightly.

"I'm glad everybody's in good spirits," Decker went on. "We'll need them, I think. Now then... we know most of the big landmarks but not the details. No idea what roads or trails there might be. Not sure what settlements there are. There must be some because more than fifteen thousand people live on this island and not all at the coconut plantations on the north side where the Japs are building. Point is that unless and until Captain Clemens shows up or sends a guide, we're on our own. Which means we're gonna have to scout, and it means we're gonna have to find him on our own, I suspect."

"What about all the stuff we brought ashore at risk to life and limb, sir?" Duncan asked.

"It's safe for now," Decker said. "If we do decide to trek anywhere far, we'll take a few essentials. Like the radio gear. That's critical, and should we run into Clemens, he needs that just about more than anything, aside from shoes."

"Request permission to recon forward, sir!" Oaks put in.

"Granted," Decker said. "But here's how we're gonna do things. I want two fire teams with three men each. Two Marines and a sailor. Captain Turner and I will stay here at... basecamp... for lack of a better term, until one of you scouts finds us someplace a little better. Lieutenant Dutch and Ted here are our electronics experts, so they stay back. We'll set up the radio and try and contact Clemens that way. Red team is Oaks, Taggart and Broderick. Blue team is Hazard, Lider and Ingram. Lt Hazard mustered out as a Gunny if I recall, so he's team leader. Both teams have an electrician and over the past week or so, I've learned that both Tank and Doug here are crack gunners."

"What about me, sir?" Duncan asked.

"Chief, there's an open patch in the jungle about a hundred yards in," Decker said. "We think it's a coast road. Not much more than a mud track, but something to follow. I'd like to station you at the head of the path that leads to it. Normally I wouldn't send a man out alone, Chief, but you're only a couple of minutes away. Red and blue teams, you'll move down the road east and west for about an hour. That ought to put you at about extreme walkie range, especially in this dense jungle. Chief, you'll conceal yourself and act as relay man. This is a scouting mission, men. If you see a Jap patrol, you are to conceal and report. Do not engage unless forced to. Everybody clear? Good, then move out. Oh, and one more thing, men."

The men had already begun to assemble. They all turned back to the major.

Decker placed his hands behind his back and examined each man in turn, "I know that there's been some inter-service rivalry going on between you sailors and you Marines. Well, I'm telling you that this shit stops *right now*. For all intents and purposes, we're all Marines as of this moment. We're all in the Navy, too. We're brothers in arms and we treat each other accordingly. Anybody who can't get with that program can swim his ass back to the ship... wherever she might be. *Understood?*"

A chorus of "Sir, yes sir!" from all the men, even the sailors. Decker nodded approvingly and waved them off.

Turner looked at the break in the jungle where his men were swallowed up the second they entered it.

Decker placed a hand on his shoulder, "They'll be all right, Art."

"My guys are good guys," Turner said. "But they aren't infantry trained... not much, anyway."

"They'll be with my Raiders," Decker said. "They'll watch out for them. Hazard knows his stuff; I've spent some time talking with him. It'll be all right."

Turner drew in a breath, "Best we get to work ourselves, then."

Bull shark – prowling the 50-fathom curve off Guadalcanal

Elmer Williams couldn't shake a cold sense of worry. He couldn't divorce himself from the idea that he'd seen his captain, his friends and his men for the last time. He couldn't shake the feeling that he'd abandoned them to their fates as well.

With only four officers left aboard, Williams had worked out a new watch bill. Every officer would stand a watch and have a chief or LPO as his junior officer of the deck. He'd have Hotrod Hernandez, who would also double as diving officer, as would the other JOODs. Jarvis would have Harry Brannigan, Frank Nichols would have Sparky Sparks and Andy Post, as the most junior officer, would have Buck Rogers backstopping him.

There was another chief aboard. Clancy Weiss, the chief yeoman, was an experienced man, but his duties would be even more strenuous now. Williams knew Weiss could handle a watch and would likely do so, yet he also knew that being the only yeoman aboard, Weiss had enough to do. That was true for Brannigan as well, but at least he and Sparky had men to take up their slack.

"How's your depth, Hotrod?" Williams asked from his position at the master gyrocompass table.

"Holding at one-five zero feet, sir," Hotrod said. "Good trim."

"You okay with this duty, Ralph?"

Hernandez smiled reassuringly at the XO, "No sweat, Skipper. Had plenty of practice. We all have. This is why we work so fast and so hard for these."

Hernandez tapped the silver dolphins pinned to his shirt. "We won't let you down, sir."

Williams grinned, "Thanks, Hotrod. No wisecracks about how you're a humble Mexican peasant or something?"

Hernandez smiled crookedly, "Being a smarty-pants is frowned upon in my village, señor."

Williams laughed, "No wonder they kicked you out then."

"*Si.*"

The captain pro-tem went up the ladder and into the conning tower and moved to sit at the vacant TDC. He placed a Winston between his lips and lit it. He didn't really want the smoke, in truth, but it gave him something to do.

"What'd'ya hear, Chet?" Williams asked softly.

Rivers was lounging in his seat, leaning back as far as he could with his hairy legs splayed out before him. Like most of the men aboard, Rivers wore the standard working submarine rig in warm climates. Sandals with no socks, white skivvy T-shirt and khaki shorts. Williams himself wore the same, except that like his captain, he threw on his khaki uniform blouse over the T-shirt and left it unbuttoned.

"All quiet, sir," Rivers said. "Other than biologics, of course. Crackling shrimp, an occasional whale song... distant, though. No Japs this morning as yet."

Williams sighed, "I'm not sure if that's good or bad news, Chet. Some action would be a good thing, I think... but with only ten pickles aboard, I'd hate to run out of ammo on our first day. We got six or seven days of this before the Marines arrive... although who really knows on that score...?"

Rivers frowned, nodded and seemed to focus his attention on his headphones.

"Well, keep your ears open," Williams said. "I'm gonna take a turn through the boat."

The Exec. turned skipper went below and forward to the torpedo room. There he found Sparky's torpedo gang lounging in their racks or playing cards around a collapsible table. When some of the men saw him duck in through the hatch, they began to come to attention.

"At ease," Williams said. "Don't let me disturb you, boys. Just taking a turn through the boat. Where's Sparky?"

"Crashed out in Chief Duncan's rack," Perry Wilkes said. "Was up all night helping with the freight."

"Not much to do up here now, I guess," Williams said, leaning casually against an empty torpedo rack.

"Nah.... But we figured we'd routine these six fish today," Tommy Perkins said in his smooth southern California surfer drawl. "Might as well, since it's been a while, and these are all we got."

"Think we'll get to use them, sir?" Eugene Parker, a relatively new member of the crew, asked.

"I hope so, Parker," Williams said. "Although I'd prefer if it was later rather than sooner. Like maybe we could do some good sinking a few ships before the task force arrives... well, I'll leave you guys to it."

Various expressions of goodwill followed Williams as he went aft and into the forward battery compartment. He ducked into the wardroom and found it empty. Just about everyone had been up all night and was riding their racks. With the absence of three officers, the area felt deserted to Williams.

"Get you a cup of coffee, sir?" Eddie Carlson asked quietly, appearing as if by magic from his small pantry.

"Yeah, that'd be great, Eddie," Williams said. "Just touring the boat, checking on things, you know..."

Carlson prepped Williams' coffee the way he liked it and handed him the mug, "Mind if I give you a little advice, sir?"

"Advice, Eddie?"

"Well, more advice from my grandma," Carlson added.

"Shoot."

"My grandma always told me that whatever was for me wouldn't pass me by, sir," Carlson said, his dark face beaming. "So, I shouldn't worry about what might be. It'll be comin' along directly, so I was just to be patient."

"Your grandma sounds like she was a wise lady," Williams said. Carlson was around thirty and the XO figured Eddie's grandmother had passed on, like his own.

Carlson chuckled, "Still is, sir. Seventy-five and you'd think she was forty. Everybody started pretty young in my family."

"That's nice, Ed," Williams said. "Nice having your granny around... well, I'm off. Thanks for the joe and the good words."

Williams proceeded back through the control room and then into after battery. He chit-chatted a bit with the men as they sat at the mess tables reading, studying or playing Acey-deucey or backgammon. He snitched a sweet roll from Martin's countertop as he went by and into the forward engine room. The compartment, like the next one aft, was quiet now. With the boat being submerged for the day, the four big sixteen-cylinder diesels and even the auxiliary generator were quiet. Men on duty were performing a variety of maintenance tasks. The two water evaporators were offline and were undergoing routining as well.

Eventually, Williams entered the maneuvering room. This room was never totally quiet nor certainly empty. It was from this compartment that the submarine's motor systems were controlled, as well as all major electrical functions routed through. Men manned circuit breakers, and at least two men sat on the padded bench before the large control console. Sometimes, but not always, men would go down through the hatch grating and into the motor room where *Bull Shark's* four massive General Electric motors drove her propellors.

"Come to join the pahty ahyah, sir?" Electrician's mate second class Danny Pentakkus asked wryly.

Pentakkus had come aboard at Pearl just before they'd set out for their patrol of the Solomons. He was a good-natured young man in his mid-twenties whose freckles and shock of unruly fiery red hair made him seem like a teenager. Pentakkus was from Kittery, Maine and had worked as an electrician at the Portsmouth Naval yard. He spoke with the odd twang of northern New England, which sounded a bit like that of Boston, only slower... almost the countrified version.

"So how is it actually going to sea in one of these cans, Pentakkus?" Williams asked. "You enjoying playing that organ?"

"Oh shuwah..." Pentakkus drawled. "Been around boats all my life, y'know sir. Been workin' down to the shipyahd since I was fourteen. A bit of a change goin' to sea, but figyid it was about my time."

Williams enjoyed listening to Pentakkus. His mode of speech was so different than what Elmer grew up with in Indiana. There, folks just spoke English without any inflections, dropped Rs, drawls or anything. Yet aboard this small ship, Williams had men who spoke with almost every regional dialect in the country around him. Surfer, Northern mid-westerners don'tcha know, southerners of several varieties, a Cajun, a few guys from the Chicago area, New Yorkers, New Englanders like Jarvis who spoke in an accent that was close to the typical New York but not quite so harsh, and then Pentakkus whose Maine drawl was something different again.

"Harry leave you in charge for the watch?" Williams inquired, mostly just to hear Pentakkus talk again.

"Ayuh..." the electrician stated. "Went up to the goat locah, he did."

That got snickers and titters from the half dozen other men in the room, including Pentakkus' mate sitting next to him. The Mainer only grinned and shrugged.

"They's all think it's funny, way I talk," Pentakkus explained. "Been like that ever since I got to Pearl Hahbah. A wicked shahk fuh me, sir... back home, anybody who ain't from Maine is eithah a flat landah or just from away, y'know. Guess the boot's on t'othah foot now, ain't it."

"Join the Navy, see the world, Danny," Williams said and patted the man on the shoulder as he headed aft, trying very hard not to burst into tears of laughter.

The XO had just poked his head into the after room when the 1MC hissed and Hotrod Hernandez's voice echoed through the ship, *"Captain to control! Captain to control! We have sonar contacts!"*

Chapter 10

Southern Coast of Guadalcanal

"Place is like a fuckin' oven..." Sherman Tank Broderick whispered as he and his two teammates crouched in a stand of birds of paradise at the edge of what their maps said was the Nombor River. He was right, too. It was just after nine a.m. and the temperature was already almost ninety.

Even being on the windward side of the island, the constant trade winds that blew ashore couldn't penetrate the rainforests all around them. The jungle acted like a sponge, retaining water and absorbing heat and radiating it back out again in waves of nearly total humidity. All three men were already soaked with sweat after only an hour's walk along what had indeed proved to be a road.

The road was also what Decker had stated it to be. A muddy track about thirty feet across that cut through the jungle, giving the only glimpse of sky one could see when not in the foliage. There were ruts in the muddy road, which indicated that there must be a few vehicles on the island. That was promising and alarming. Were they vehicles belonging to the Melanesian residents or the Nips?

"They look comfy," Taggart opined, nodding toward the small village on the right bank of the river.

The men were perhaps a half-mile inland from the ocean. The Nombor, which had its origins in the craggy mountains ten miles away, wound down to the sea where it became a Mangrove estuary. It was probably still fresh at this location, based on the small habitation the men observed.

Across the two-hundred-foot-wide river, a collection of huts had been constructed in several acres of cleared rainforest. There were perhaps a dozen small houses and a larger communal structure at the center, all of which had large cisterns built onto their roofs. Behind the homes were small fields with a variety of crops growing in them. Most likely rice, beans and perhaps some root vegetables. Several canoes were lined up along the riverbank, and tied to a dock was what looked to be some kind of homemade boat. The boat had a small pilothouse and open deck aft for transporting cargo. Two dozen people in light clothing milled about, doing chores and going about their daily business.

"I wonder if any of those people knows Clemens?" Oaks pondered.

"Let's ask one," Tank said wryly.

"Yeah, well, when you figure out how to get over there, you let us know," Taggart quipped.

"Must be a crossing someplace," Tank opined, pointing at the coast road.

The road turned abruptly to the north and followed the river for some distance before cutting away and back into the jungle. For perhaps a quarter of a mile, fronting the village on the other side of the river, the road ran along the left bank and was wide open without a stick of cover.

"I sure as shit ain't swimmin'," Taggart noted and pointed to their right.

Sunning itself on the bank of the river no more than fifty yards from their position was an enormous saltwater crocodile. The beast must have been at least twelve feet long and didn't present the air of gentleness that invited a close approach.

The Cactus Navy

"Them fuckers is all over this hell hole," Oaks stated. "Wonder if we can train 'em to get a taste for slopes."

That received muffled titters from the other two men. The laughter stopped abruptly when a trio of men appeared from the largest of the village structures. The men wore khaki trousers and cotton shirts so light they appeared almost beige. Every man wore a red sash belt around his middle and a cap with cloth flaps that fell to their collars as sun protection. They also carried rifles and ammo packs.

"Shit..." Tank grumbled. "He ain't tasted them yet. Fuck *me*..."

"Since you're the electrician," Oaks said. "That makes you our radioman, Tank. Better call this in. Don't like Japs being so close to our beachhead."

"Think you can handle that, Navy?" Taggart jeered.

"We use radios in the boats too, wiseass," Tank grumbled and pulled the bulky walkie from his backpack, extended the antenna and switched it on. "Macaw, Macaw, Red team..."

A crackle of static over the speaker and Tank lowered the volume slightly before Duncan's voice said: *"Red, Macaw, I read, over."*

"Bob Hope is at the show, and he's got waterfront seats, over," Tank reported. This was some of the pre-established code they'd chosen. It meant that the Japanese were in a village at the river's edge.

"Roger... will relay to Houdini... what do... ow! Fuckin' cock!" Duncan swore vehemently over the open channel.

"Macaw?" Tank inquired.

"Fuckin' centipede just bit me... stung me, whatever... Christ, there's a bunch of 'em in here... goddammit... I'll have to shift," Duncan cranked. *"Place is like a fuckin' horror movie. Goddamned centipedes and ants and fuckin' giant spiders could carry a man off... fuckin' Bob Hope can shove this fuckin' place straight up his ass! Oh yeah... fuckin' over and out!"*

Oaks and Taggart quaked with mirth as they held their hands over their mouths and tried not to guffaw. Tank was smiling as well, but he did feel bad for the chief. Suddenly Oaks flinched and swore under his breath.

"Jesus..." Oaks said, shifting slowly away from his spot. "What're these things everywhere?"

The radio crackled again, "Red team, Macaw... Houdini asks how many performers and how many guests at the show?"

Tank shifted to try and get a better look through the dense, broad leaves of the banana tree like bird of paradise.

"I see three Japs," Taggart whispered. "Maybe two dozen civvies."

"Macaw, looks like three players and two dozen or more attendees, over," Tank reported. "Wait... wait one, Macaw... some shit's goin' down over there..."

At least half a dozen more Japanese soldiers appeared, some from inside the central hut, one or two more from a couple of the smaller huts and another handful from the fields. One of the newcomers from the big hut was clearly an officer. His uniform was slightly more decorated and leaned more toward the medium green range of the khaki spectrum. He also wore a sword at his side. The officer began to speak in a harsh voice, giving quick orders to the men. Six of them formed up and began to move along the riverbank to the north.

"Wonder what that officer has up his ass?" Tank asked rhetorically.

"He's ordering a squad to go upriver and cross over and do a sweep on this side," Oaks said. "He also used some ungentlemanly expressions about the natives and the men."

"You speak Jap?" Tank asked in shock.

Oaks grinned, "A bit. Enough to get the gist of most conversations. Know all the bad words, though."

Taggart snorted.

"I'll be damned..." Tank said.

"We ain't just ignorant gomers, y'know," Taggart quipped.

"One thing I did hear was *marui me wo fac*," Oaks said with less humor in his tone now. "Better update the chief, Tank."

"What's that mean?" Tank asked as he hefted the radio again.

"It pretty much means fuckin' round-eyes," Oaks replied. "And I don't think they were talkin' about the villagers."

"Well, you said this was boring," Taggart teased.

"Phooey..." Tank grumbled. "Macaw, Macaw, Red team... The USO tour has just expanded. Repeat, Bob Hope has more entertainers and a director, and they're moving into the crowd, over."

"We'd better shift positions," Oaks said. "I think this is about to get interesting."

Tank reported the numbers to Duncan and then said they were moving to a better position and would report back soon. As the three men backed out of the flora in which they hid, picking cockroaches, centipedes and leeches off their clothing, a distinct man-made sound began to grow over the sound of the birds and insects of Guadalcanal's jungle.

It was the sound of a vehicle engine.

It seemed like they'd been walking forever, yet it had been less than an hour. Lider was on point with Hazard taking up the rear. The three camouflaged men hugged the edge of the road along the foliage line as best they could with eyes and ears peeled.

It was no mean feat, as the cacophony of the jungle was overwhelming. Parrots cawed, birds cheeped, and monkeys chittered. Insects in all of their dizzying varieties sang from the jungle by the millions. As for sight, the sun was just now beginning to rise over the trees and turn the narrow canyon between the dense patches of rainforest from deep gloom into bright daylight.

Of course, this brought a more intense heat as well. The sweltering August temperature and humidity had been oppressive at dawn, but now that the sun was truly exerting itself, the heat was becoming thick and palpable... and heavy. In spite of the new camo's wicking effect, the men were soaked in sweat and had to take large swallows from their canteens to stay hydrated.

"Jesus..." Ingram grumbled. "Hotter'n the devil's balls out here..."

"Just be thankful we're in the southern hemisphere," Lider quipped. "It's winter now."

It became clear to everyone very quickly, from the officers to the Raiders, that however fit they thought they were was insufficient against Guadalcanal's climate. Months aboard ship or submarine hadn't done much to enhance or maintain their stamina for the sort of slogging they were in for now. Everyone was physically fit and strong, yet the endurance required to operate in such a steamy tropical climate was lacking.

Lider moved to the southern side of the road, where some shade from the trees still existed. This would slightly reduce the wear on the men and conceal them better should they run into any surprises. The road seemed to be headed south of east and began to rise as the trio rounded a gentle curve.

"Ten minutes," Hazard managed to announce without panting. "Then we post up, observe and make a report."

"Aye-aye," Lider said. "I'd like to see what's on top of this hill, though, sir."

"I got five bucks says it's more jungle," Ingram grumped. "Christ, who'd ever want to live out here in banana land anyway?"

"Coconutville, Doug," Hazard corrected with a chuckle. "Got a lot of coconut plantations on the island. Up north, where the task force is headed."

"You'd have to be coco-*nuts* to set up house in this oven," Ingram declaimed. "And oh look... the hill's gettin' steep. That's *aces*...."

"Now don't complain, Navy," Lider tossed off, huffing a bit. "Just think how many broads you'll impress when this is over."

"That's right, Doug," Hazard puffed out. "A little while from now, this'll all be just a *happy* memory. Fifteen... twenty years... you'll look back and laugh."

"Swell..." Ingram cranked, but did manage a grin.

Lider was about twenty feet ahead. The hill was indeed rising rather steeply. So much so that even from six paces behind, Ingram's head was only at about the level of Lider's ass. Even the jungle appeared disinterested in the climb. At least on their right, the heavy rainforest was thinning a bit.

Lider suddenly stopped just before he'd reach the crest of the ridge. He held out a hand behind him, palm out, indicating that the other two men should stop. Lider crouched lower, gazed back and forth for a minute or two and then waved the others forward as he began to inch his way up to the crest of the hill.

Ingram and Hazard flanked him, and they reached the top. It was an unremarkable hill, perhaps fifty or sixty feet above the jungle floor to either side of it. To the left, the foliage was still dense enough that even from their elevation, the men could see nothing beyond. They did have a commanding view of the road leading down either side of the hill for about a hundred yards before the rainforest swallowed it up again.

To the right, however, the thinning continued to the point where the rainforest was more of a collection of low-level flora and a few palms and other tropical trees. Some hardwoods, rattan, and giant ferns, and viny things that seemed to grow in every direction at once. A narrow path led to the right, toward the ocean. There were footprints in the sand... perhaps because of the elevation, the storm the night before hadn't turned the crest of the hill into a mud patch.

Lider pointed at the prints. Hazard bent over and gazed at them. They'd been made by boots, but they were odd. There appeared to be an indentation at the toe end of each print, as if the person who'd walked here had cloven hooves for feet.

"Those are Jap boots," Lider hissed. "They got these weird separations between the big toe and the others. Made of softer material. Supposed to make hiking easier or somethin'."

"What the hell are the Japs doing here?" Ingram hissed. "Thought they was all on the other side of the island at that airfield."

"Guess not," Lider said with a shrug.

"Let's see what's down this path," Hazard said. "I got a hunch."

"Sir, these tracks are fresh," Lider advised.

"Good, then maybe we'll get to stick a few yellow bastards,"

Hazard said, drawing his combat knife. "I'll go alone. Ingram, you report back to base. Lider, you keep an eye out here. I'll sneak in, have a peek and come back to report."

Lider frowned. He didn't like the idea of splitting up, "Sir..."

"We was sent out to scout, Corporal, and scout is what we'll do," Hazard said definitively. "If there are Japs down this path, maybe watchin' the coast, we need to know that."

With that, Hazard slipped into the foliage along the path. Lider had to admit that the beefy man moved quietly.

Ingram activated his walkie, "Macaw, Macaw, Blue team... do you read, over?"

"Roger, Blue, go ahead," Came Duncan's voice.

"Reached observation point," Ingram stated. "Found signs of the USO tour... Bob Hope may be in town, over."

There was a short string of oaths before Duncan said: *"Red team also reports similar... can you confirm, over?"*

"Blue one went to the box office," Ingram said.

A pause, *"Will relay. Standby."*

Ingram and Lider stood stock still, heads swiveling yet not saying a word. Over the lowered volume on the bulky walkie-talkie, the two men listened to a one-sided conversation. The unit had an effective range of two miles or so. Even walking slowly both teams had gone at least that far in an hour, putting Red and Blue four miles apart... or about seven klicks in Marine parlance.

All they could hear was Chief Duncan's side of his conversation with Red team. However, it sounded to the two men as if Oaks' group had found something near a river. Possibly Japanese, as Duncan had asked for numbers and clarification. After a few minutes of this, the chief directed his attention back to Blue team.

"Blue, Blue, Macaw," he said. *"Have advised Houdini. Request clarification, over."*

"Roger. Will advise when Blue one reports," Ingram replied.

A hundred feet to the south, and it might as well be the far side of the moon considering how isolated it felt, Porter Hazard was nearing the far end of his path. He'd grown up in the backwoods of Georgia and knew how to move through brush. Growing up hunting with his dad and uncles had honed his woodsman's instincts. Then spending years in the Marine Corps, some of which had been trudging through Central American jungles not dissimilar to the one in which he found himself, had put a razor's edge on his instincts.

He moved slowly, placing each foot carefully and being mindful of everything around him. Each fern leaf, each overhanging branch of rattan or rosewood was carefully moved aside. The raucous rainforest sounds helped, of course, yet on this elevated hillock and nearer to the sea, whose salt scent could now be distinguished even through the greenness of the forest, the foliage was far less dense.

Finally, after ten minutes, the path opened, and Hazard could see that the forest ended rather abruptly onto a semi-rocky outcropping. Small chest high grasses grew along with stubby palmetto-like trees. Even from his hiding spot, the sailor could see that the promontory looked out over the Pacific from a height that would give an observer a fair observation position to examine the curving beaches in either direction or the sea out to perhaps a dozen miles or more.

Which was exactly what the lone Japanese soldier seemed to be doing. The man, dressed in the beige uniform of the Imperial Army, or *Kaigun Rikusentai*, the Japanese Marines, stood behind a telescope and that was currently trained along the beach to the man's right. In a west, northwest direction... right at the spot where Hazard and his team had landed.

Hazard couldn't tell from his vantage point, yet from the intensity of the man's concentration and the fact that he wasn't swinging the scope to make a wider sweep told the naval officer all he needed to know. The bastard was zeroed in on the landing spot and probably had a bead on Captain Turner and the others still working on the radio.

With deliberate slowness and stealth, Hazard brought the blackened and razor-sharp blade of his KA-BAR up. His right hand briefly brushed the butt of his .45, but he rejected that idea immediately. This must be a fast and silent kill.

The American stepped out from behind his concealment and took two deliberate steps forward. The man at the telescope was only five yards from the path. Now that Hazard was in the open, he could rush forward and slit the man's throat before the Japanese soldier could react.

Yet even as he gathered himself to spring, his well-honed instincts told Hazard that he'd made a mistake. He'd reacted too quickly. He hadn't spent the critical moments to remain concealed and examine the scene more closely. If he had, he would've noticed the abundance of boot prints in the dusty soil that covered the volcanic ridge.

The realization came too late, however. From behind him, the unmistakable sound of steps and a metallic click told Hazard he'd failed. In the next instant, the harsh and almost guttural Japanese order froze him in place.

Hazard didn't speak the language, but one didn't need to understand the dialect when one heard an order to freeze. He risked turning his head to see two more soldiers standing just behind and to his left. Then there was a swish, something solid striking the side of his head, and Porter Hazard's world erupted into fireworks that swam before his eyes. He hardly even felt his knees striking the ground.

Chapter 11

Between Guadalcanal and San Cristobal Islands

"Should we sound general quarters, sir?" Buck Rogers asked as Williams entered the control room.

"Not sure yet, Buck," Williams replied. "Let's see what we've got first."

The XO went up the ladder and moved to stand by Chet Rivers, who was listening to his headphones intently and watching the Magic Eye display on his sonar set. Not wishing to distract him at a critical moment, Williams only touched the young man on his shoulder.

"Contacts are really faint, sir," Chet acknowledged without looking away from his gear. "I *think* there's three of them... kinda hard to tell now. They're at extreme range... about forty-thousand yards bearing zero-three-zero."

Williams glanced at the chart laid over the dead reckoning indicator, "Hmm... off the northwest shore of San Cristobal. Any idea of their heading, Chet?"

Rivers frowned and made some minor adjustments, "No sir... they probably aren't all headed the same direction. Although... sir, I think I've got two sets of light, fast screws and one set of three heavier screws. The big boy *might* be headed somewhat in our direction... the other two seem to come and go."

Williams tapped his chin thoughtfully, "Like escorts circling or picketing around their charge... I wonder if we've found our strike carrier group...?"

"Only one way to find out, sir," Rivers said wryly.

"Run over to them on the surface and ask?" Williams inquired with a crooked smile. "Helm, come right and steady up on course zero-six-five. Make turns for four knots."

"Zero-six-five," Wendel Freeman said. "Maneuvering answering four knots at all ahead one-third, sir."

A rather dull but expectant hour passed. Williams sat at the TDC and would occasionally put on the spare set of headphones to listen in. Both he and Rivers agreed that the three ships were staying together and that the two smaller ships were patrolling back and forth along the larger's course. Rivers established that the lead ship was on a rough heading of three-two-five and traveling at four knots.

"That's odd," Williams stated. "If it is our friend the *Sakai,* then she's capable of speeds almost as fast as her Fubuki friends. Wonder why they're moving so slowly?"

"Maybe they're trying to conserve fuel oil," Came Pat Jarvis's voice from the open hatch. The big torpedo officer climbed the rest of the way up and leaned on the bridge ladder. "Just taking their sweet time."

Williams sighed, "Or they're looking for us? Or any subs in the area? We're not even sure it's them, really. How far are we now, Chet?"

"Thirty-thousand yards, sir," Rivers stated. "Almost dead ahead of us now."

Williams drummed his fingers on the TDC, "I'd sure like to get a closer look at 'em, Pat."

"Thinkin' about taking a shot?" Jarvis asked hopefully.

"Not sure yet," Williams said. "With just the ten fish, I'd hate to waste them so early."

"Getting rid of a Jap carrier, even a small one, wouldn't be a bad thing, Elmer," Pat opined.

"Yeah... but we're still a week out from our task force arriving," Williams said. "I wonder if it wouldn't be better to wait until they're closer. Then sink this bastard. Sort of... clear the path, so to speak."

Jarvis pondered that for a long moment, "I see what you mean, Skipper... on the other hand, Noah didn't build his ark in the rain. We don't know *exactly* when the invasion is set, so..."

"Maybe not, Pat, but Noah didn't have to evade two tin cans and an ASW-equipped strike carrier with twenty planes," Williams half-chided.

"Pssh..." Jarvis replied with a lopsided grin.

"Freeman, left standard rudder," Williams said. "Steady up on... three-three-five. Let's shadow these fellas for a bit and see what jumps off. It's nearly noon now. Maybe by dusk we can work in close enough to scope them. What's for lunch anyway?"

"Pork chops and gravy over rice with peas," Jarvis said. "And since I'm on watch soon... and since we're not sinking any Japs at the moment... I'll go down below and see how the meal is. Test it out for ya', Elm."

"You're a real peach, Pat," Williams quipped.

Guadalcanal – left bank of the Nombor River

Oaks led his team across the muddy road and into the trees on the other side. Although the jungle there was dense, it did feature quite a few hardwoods. Mahogany, rosewood, lignum vitae and teak among them. Mixed among these were hibiscus, thorny bougainvillea, orchids, ferns and viny growths. The hardwoods were large and aggressive enough species to hold back some of the smaller flora enough so that the humans could work among them and take up fairly decent firing positions from behind the harder trees.

The sound of the engine was growing louder, but only slowly. Tank found himself behind a lignum vitae, or ironwood tree, between

Taggart and Oaks, who were crouching behind trees of their own five yards to his right and left.

"Are we gonna take these slants out?" Tank asked.

"Maybe," Oaks said. "Let the chief know what's coming and request command advise. I'd like to avoid giving our presence away so soon... but then again..."

"We can use that vehicle," Taggart finished.

Tank made his report quickly. They couldn't see the vehicle yet, but it was drawing close. Duncan instructed Tank to standby, which he did. However, the wait time began to draw out. After more than two minutes, Tank got impatient.

"Macaw... Macaw... do you read? Macaw... where the hell are you, dammit..."

"Bag it," Oaks said. "He might not be able to answer right now. Let's not give the Japs any more notice than we have to. I think I see the vehicle now... looks like a flatbed truck... perfect."

"Think they're listening in?" Tank asked as he cleared his weapon.

"No idea," Oaks said. "But possible. Okay... I see four men riding on the bed and a driver. Hold fire until I give the word. And whatever you boys do... don't hit the damned truck!"

Guadalcanal – Windward overlook

The butt stroke from the Japanese soldier's Arisaka rifle hadn't hurried Porter Hazard into unconsciousness. Either the man hadn't swung hard enough or didn't want the American to be knocked out.

Rather, Hazard found himself floating in a haze, where his vision tunneled down to a narrow gray tube that wavered and occasionally flashed with shooting stars. The soldiers stood around him for a long moment, chattering away in clipped Japanese but not directly addressing him.

Two pairs of hands roughly dragged Hazard to his feet, and his ruck was yanked off and his body patted down. His vision was just beginning to clear when the man at the telescope squared off in front of him. The soldier's uniform markings indicating a higher rank than the other two men.

"Who are you?" the soldier, perhaps a sergeant, asked in heavily accented English.

Hazard took some perverse pride in the size difference between himself and his captors. Although a well-set man, Hazard was of average height, and yet not one of the Japs stood taller than half a head shorter than himself. A vicious backhand struck the side of the Georgian's face when he didn't answer quickly enough.

The coppery taste of blood filled Hazard's mouth. The pain of the blow was nothing as compared with the wave of hatred that suddenly swelled up inside him. He didn't grunt or wince, only met the soldier's eyes defiantly.

"Who are you!?" the sergeant asked again, this time shouting the question directly into Hazard's face.

"Elmer Fudd," Hazard said.

The sergeant's odd cloven-hoofed boot buried itself into the American's guts, forcing the air from Hazard's lungs and driving him to his knees once more. He clenched his jaws and forced his gorge not to rise.

The strange thought occurred to him, even as he struggled to draw breath, that he'd like to spew all over this yellow fucker's uniform. However, a disconnected part of his mind told him that in this climate, he couldn't afford to lose the fluids or the precious calories.

"You Marine!?" the sergeant bellowed. "How you get here!? Where is ship!?"

Hazard was still quite disoriented. When he heard the rustling from behind him and the shouts that didn't quite sound Japanese, he grew confused.

Had Ingram and Lider come for him?

If so... then why did they sound foreign?

Hazard was just gathering himself for a clumsy and probably

fatal lunge for the sergeant. If nothing else, maybe he could push the bastard back and over the edge of the cliff. He looked up, drew in as much air as he could and... and the sergeant's head exploded into a cloud of red mist even as his body flew backward and knocked over his telescope.

"The *fuck*...?" Hazard muttered, struggling to his feet.

"American?" a man asked in a good accent slightly tinged with an odd accent that sounded part Spanish and part African.

Hazard turned to see the other two Japs laid out on the outcropping, clearly dead. Three men in ragged clothing who looked part negro and part Hawaiian stared back at him. Two had pistols and one a heavy club.

"Uhm..." Hazard said, "yeah... American. Who are you?"

The man who seemed to be in charge grinned and saluted, "I'm Jacob Vousa. Sergeant major in the British Solomon Islands Protectorate. Assistant to Captain Marty Clemens. At your service, sir. Marine?"

Hazard laughed even as the man with the club reached out and offered him a steadying arm, "Well, I'll be... Not exactly. I'm Navy. But I'm a Marine now. My skipper is at our landing point with a shitload of supplies for you boys. Got a team of eleven here. Some Marines, some Navy. Lt. Porter Hazard at *your* service, Sarge."

Vousa chuckled, "God bless you, sir."

Guadalcanal – Chief Duncan

"*Got five Japs in a flatbed, Macaw,*" Tank was saying. "*Red one requests Houdini authorize we take them out, over.*"

"Standby Red team," Duncan said.

He had shifted position more than once. First, he'd hidden in the middle of a small group of banana trees but found that quite a few centipedes and tarantulas had the same idea. He'd then shifted over close to a large hardwood tree of some type only to discover, much too late, that he'd chosen to stand just a little too close to a fire ant nest. Finally, he'd moved twenty yards west up the road and nestled himself between a stand of ferns and an ebony tree that provided shade, cover and had fewer bitey and stingy neighbors.

He'd just completed his request to Turner and Decker when something caught his ear. Something had moved deeper in the jungle behind him. He'd only been half-listening, but there was something unnatural about the sound... something sly and predatory about it.

Duncan dropped his radio and spun, hauling his .45 out to confront whoever or whatever it was when something hard and heavy struck him from behind.

Duncan wasn't a woodsman by any means. He'd grown up mostly a city boy, although he'd done his share of camping and hiking as a kid. What he had spent many hours doing, however, was learning to box. With his height and unusually long arms, Mike Duncan had done well in the middle-heavyweight division. He'd even fought golden gloves after entering the service.

Duncan quickly tucked and rolled away from whatever had hit him, using his momentum to get away and back onto his feet. His opponent... to his surprise, neither a Jap nor a wild ape or something... had done the same and was facing off with the chief holding a wicked-looking short sword in his brown hand.

Both men's expressions comically matched one another. First rage and savagery, then surprise and finally cautious puzzlement. Duncan figured the man must be an islander, and the islander thought that Duncan must be an American based on his camouflage.

"Yankee?" the man asked in a deep, heavily accented voice.

"Who's askin'?" Duncan asked, easing into a fighter's stance but not quite all the way.

The man chuckled and lowered his sword, "Batu. I savvy Clemens 'e kopo sendalong yankees meetum. 'E say you save."

"Huh?" Duncan asked in confusion, the man's garbled English nearly unintelligible at first. "Uhm... I'm American and have brought help... you're with Clemens, I take it... seen any Japs?"

Batu spat, "Bloody butterheads... You people savvy belonga east find, altogether. Naponapo 'e watch savvy cliff top."

"Christ..." Duncan snapped. "We gotta warn 'em!"

Batu held up a hand, "Is okay, Yankee. We got scouts near close. You people at river, but... some Nips 'e come. Not many much."

"Shit..." Duncan said, retrieving his dropped pistol and walkie. "Come on, Batu, I want to introduce you to my CO... maybe he can understand what the hell you're jawin' about..."

Guadalcanal – landing zone

"No response as yet, sir," Dutch said as he and Entwater finally connected the components of the radiotelegraph. "But then again, I'm not sure if Clemens's unit is even powered."

Turner frowned and glanced up and down the wide sandy beach for what seemed like the hundredth time, "I don't like this, Al. We're exposed out here, and we've already made contact with a group of Japs only two miles away. Hell... what the hell are they doing on this side of the island, anyway?"

Decker shrugged, "Damned if I know. Probably being thorough, I'd guess. That's why we need to make contact with Clemens. We're operating in the dark here. He's supposed to fill in all the intelligence gaps for us."

Turner harrumphed, "I don't like coincidences, Al. There isn't shit going on down on this side of the island, and yet we're not ashore a couple of hours and we're surrounded by Japs?"

It was then that Chief Duncan exited the jungle leading a man dressed in mildewed trousers and shirt that had seen better days. The man's skin was dusky, and he was clearly an islander.

"Chief, what the..." Turner began.

"This is Batu, sir," Duncan stated. "He's got some things to tell us... kinda..."

Decker and Turner stepped forward and shook the man's hand. Although thin, the wiry Melanesian still had a strong grip.

The Cactus Navy

"You come meetum Marty?" the man, Batu, asked.

"Yes," Decker said. "We've brought supplies. We'll need transportation to move them, however. About three thousand pounds worth. How is Captain Clemens?"

"Is altogether okay, sir," Batu said. "We savvy safe go to in mountains. No savvy transportation... I altogether savvy you men 'e find now."

He pointed to the west.

"Sergeant Oaks says there's a truck comin' up the road by the river," Duncan added, intrigued that he was beginning to understand the pigeon language a bit. "They're going to attempt to take it. Sir... there may also be trouble over yonder. Lt. Hazard was following a path that way but has not yet reported in. Batu says the Japs may be watching up there."

Turner looked at Batu with a question in his eyes.

"No savvy altogether," Batu said. "Vousa, 'e come two men belonga find-out scout. Is mound 'e Naponapo scoutum."

"Good vantage point," Decker guessed.

Duncan's and Decker's radios crackled and spluttered. Both men turned up the volume, and both called for a repeat of the transmission. However, nothing could be heard but static.

"All right, time to move out," Decker said definitively. "Chief, you're with me. Mr. Batu, since we haven't properly outfitted you yet, please stay here with my team. Art, you stay here with Entwater and Dutch. You can take up the chief's position at the path head if you like."

"Where are you going?" Turner asked.

"We're going to the west to the river," Decker said. "At last report, that's where the action is gonna be. Art, please provide Mr. Batu with a rifle and... and some shoes, would ya'?"

"All right, Chief," Decker said, swallowing half his canteen, "Drink up and let's move. It's the shoe leather express. Double time!"

The two men vanished into the rainforest, leaving the other four men to look after them. Turner drew in a breath and moved to the trees where the crates had been stored. He located the appropriate one and opened it, revealing clothing. He gave Batu two pairs of socks and found a pair of boots that fit him. They then opened the small arms crate and found that it was not filled with Tommy guns. The ones the landing party had were drawn from *Bull Shark*'s own small arms locker. Instead, the crate was loaded with Springfield M1903 bolt-action rifles.

"No rat-tat-tat?" Batu asked in surprise.

"I guess not," Turner said, withdrawing one of the rifles and an ammo pouch. "I'm familiar with this weapon.... It's a good gun... but seems a little slow for what we need. Still..."

Batu took the rifle and examined it. He shrugged, seated the five-round feeder magazine in and fixed the bayonet, "Is number one gun. We takum rat-tat-tat belonga *Naponapo*. This we savvy word Japanese."

Turner sighed. He'd been left behind at what passed for camp. He had nothing to do except stand around and wait for other men to do something. He was ill-suited for it.

"Forget it, you guys," Turner said to Dutch and Entwater. "I think we've made as much contact with Clemens as we're gonna get until we move to his location. Save the batteries. Pack it up and get ready to travel. Come on Batu..."

Turner entered the jungle path with the Melanesian right behind him. Upon exiting onto the road, Turner activated his radio.

"Blue team, Blue team, Houdini..."

A crackle and then a weak voice, "*Houdini, this is Blue. Go ahead.*"

"What's your sitch?" Turner asked.

A pause before Ingram's voice said"

"*We've met some entertainers, but they were dealt with by theatergoers. One wishes to speak with you.*"

"Tell them to do it in person," Turner reported. "We've met a local as well. Several of us here have gone to the big Bob Hope show with Red team. You guys hightail it back here pronto."

"Vousa altogether savvy you men," Batu said with a smile.

Turner sighed once again and began to pace, "Dammit all..."

"You want fight?" Batu asked. "You are soldier?"

Turner chuckled, "No, I'm a sailor... but yes, I want to fight. I'm the captain of a Navy submarine."

"Big water boat?" Batu asked in amazement. "Then why 'e come here?"

Turner chuckled, "Good question, my friend. Good question..."

Chapter 12

Bank of the Nombor River

"What the fuck...?" Tank grumbled under his breath.

The flatbed truck came to a halt a hundred yards away. It sat there, idling and resting on its semi-deflated tires. For long moments, nothing seemed to move. Not the Americans and not the Japanese in the truck.

"Do they know we're out here?" Taggart asked just loud enough for the other two men to hear.

"There's no damned way," Oaks said.

"Uh-oh..." Tank muttered.

"What?" Taggart asked worriedly.

"Can you guys see the village?" Tank asked.

"Nah..." Taggart said.

"My view is blocked," Oaks said. "Why?"

"Cuz there are two Nips over there settin' up a goddamned machine gun on a tripod," Tank stated. "And it's pointed more or less in our direction. *Somebody* musta spotted us."

Taggart swore, and Oaks joined him, "That's why the truck stopped... okay, I'm gonna try and work my way closer to that truck.

You boys try and take that machine gun out. It's less than a hundred yards; you should be able to hit them."

"Sarge, soon as we open up, they'll home in!" Taggart stated.

Tank took another peek around his tree, "They've got partial cover... behind a pile of logs, firewood I guess—"

The sounds of the living jungle around them suddenly rose in pitch and discord as the machine gun across the river began to fire. From a distance of seventy-five yards or so, the throaty grumble of a fifty-caliber automatic weapon was little more than a mild crackle. What was far more distressing was the sudden swarm of lead bees that seemed to travel into the trees all around the Americans.

Leaves fluttered with the passage of heavy rounds. Tree trunks thumped and shook and splintered as a fusillade of bullets swept over the men from right to left and then back again.

"Jesus Christ!" Tank exclaimed. "How the fuck do they *know!?*"

"They don't!" Oaks said even as he began to crab walk toward the north. "We're just in an area with good cover. They're *assuming* we're here! Fire back when they reload and open up again!"

"He's outta his goddamned mind!" Tank cranked as he poked the barrel of his Thompson SMG through a crotch in the tree behind which he hid.

"Why, for moving off toward the Japs, or for thinking we can hit those fuckers across the river with these trench brooms?" Taggart asked bemusedly as he angled for a shot as well.

Although the Thompson sub-machine gun was a solid weapon and fired a heavy .45 caliber round, it wasn't known for its long range because of that. Made famous by the gangsters during prohibition, the Tommy gun had tremendous knockdown power from close range but was only really effective at less than a hundred and sixty yards, and pinpoint accurate at less than half of that.

In spite of the fact that the two Japanese manning their machine gun were perhaps no more than two or three-hundred feet away, they had partial cover from their woodpile. Their weapon was also far more effective at longer ranges.

The Cactus Navy

Once again, the rainforest was splattered with finger-sized rounds as the Japs worked their death machine back and forth, scything the air and the foliage around the two Americans. Tank gritted his teeth and waited for the watery sound of rounds passing overhead to move off to his right, quickly aimed his SMG and squeezed the trigger.

The gun clattered, emptying the thirty-round magazine in less than three-seconds. In some disconnected corner of his mind, Tank realized that the Thompson did indeed sound like a fast typewriter, earning it one of its notorious monikers, "Chicago typewriter."

"Down!" Taggart all but screeched as the horde of bees returned, nearly zeroing in on the two men. The barrage only stopped when the fifty cal across the river ate through its belt of ammo.

"Guess I didn't get 'em," Tank said.

"No, but you did piss 'em off!" Taggart snapped. "Come on, we gotta move!"

"We got cover!" Tank argued.

"Rule number nine-hundred and sixty-eight point five of ground warfare, Navy... you don't fire from the same place twice!" Taggart said. "Deeper in and north! Follow me."

Taggart began to crawl deeper into the jungle, using his knees and elbows to push himself forward with surprising speed. Tank swore under his breath and followed suit, trying not to think about the million crawling things that were all around him greedily seeking his blood.

"And don't forget to reload," Taggart quipped even as the Japanese opened up again, peppering their hiding spot and turning the area into a cloud of splinters. "See? The *Japs* know how to reload..."

"*Fu*-ckin'..." Tank grumbled as he fumbled the empty magazine from his SMG and slapped in a fresh one. He'd had to stop to do so and had almost lost track of his teammate.

Over the screams of birds and melodious songs of uncounted insects, the two men distinctly heard the roar of the truck's engine as it started up once more. Tank and Taggart had no idea how far Oaks had gotten, but they hoped it was far enough to be able to open fire on the soldiers coming for them.

"Hear that, sir?" Duncan puffed from beside Decker.

The two men were jogging down the muddy road and after only a mile, both felt as if they might collapse... both from exhaustion and from the oppressive weight of the sweat in their clothing.

"Sounds like a machine gun..." Decker stated. "Christ... hold up, Chief."

Both men stopped their jog and panted heavily in the mid-day sun. The jungle all around them seemed to be steaming and radiating the heat outward and over them. There wasn't even a hint of the steady trade winds that had made the beachhead almost pleasant even in the heat.

"Sir... we gotta keep goin'..." Duncan heaved.

Decker grinned, "Nobody's gonna accuse you of bein' a softy, Chief... but I'm about to pass the hell out if I don't rehydrate. Won't do our guys any good we die before we get to 'em. Take a drink and we'll walk for five. Matter of fact... you got your D-rations on ya'?"

Duncan pulled what looked like a chocolate bar from one of the pouches in his BDU, "Not really hungry, sir."

Decker chuffed, "Me either, but we need the calories. This type of environment, Chief, it saps a man's strength like you wouldn't believe. You get dehydrated fast, and you need to replace not just water but salt and energy, too. Lot goes into this type of jungle warfare. It's kinda like being at sea. The environment does everything it can to erode you and your gear. Gotta keep the guns oiled, and you'll be amazed how fast any unsealed food molds, how quickly our clothes will start to disintegrate... hell, by the time the invasion force arrives, them boots you're wearing will look a year old, if they're not coming apart."

"Jesus..." Duncan muttered. "I'm just a gearhead on a submarine, sir. What the hell am I doin' here? What are any of us?"

"Necessity," Decker explained. "Even our invasion plan is half-assed and thrown together. Our guys are already calling Operation

Watchtower Operation Shoestring... and with good reason. Twenty-thousand Marines are gonna attack Guadalcanal, Tulagi, Gavutu, Tanambogo and Florida Island with only enough food for a week or two. They won't have nice new M1 Garands or Thompsons, but those old Springfields we brought. It's gonna be a shit show, and this little slapdash op we're on might be the lynchpin it all hangs on. They're waiting on confirmation from Turner and me on the landing zone and the date."

"Yeah... no pressure though," Duncan said. "A handful of Raiders and squids who don't know shit about this jungle crap."

"Don't try to bite that... use your knife, trust me... like this," Decker showed Duncan how to shave slivers off the rock-hard D-ration bar with his combat knife. "And I hear what you're sayin', Chief... but submariners are a tough bunch of dudes. And what I hear, you and your boat have been through the wringer. You know how many guys in this war can say that, even after seven months? Maybe one in ten. The Marines at Midway, a few troops who've made it to Europe and Africa... a few Navy ships, the ones that ain't been sunk... hell, we can hardly put together enough gear for this operation because the powers that be want to focus on Europe. There's a big deal called Torch that's supposed to put a shitload of Army pukes and Marines ashore in Africa."

Duncan chewed thoughtfully on the rather bland chocolate-like food slivers, "That'll change, sir."

"Yeah, in a big way," Decker said. "But still, the war is young, I'm afraid. We got years of this shit, Chief. Admiral King and Dugout Doug's idea is to hop from island to island across the Pacific right up to Hirohito's front porch. So right now, we gotta do what we gotta do. And the men of *Bull Shark* are some of the most seasoned of the war right now. You guys have seen and done some shit. And your skipper has already shown himself to be worthy of his ship's name."

Duncan grinned, "He's a bulldog for damned sure. It's just that we ain't trained for this, sir."

Decker laughed, "Know how many of the Marines slotted to hit this beachhead have seen combat, Chief? None. Just the older dudes, officers and non-coms. Ninety percent of the kids that'll be landing here next week have just come from basic. They know how to march and shoot and dig a trench... but it's all theory, you see? You Navy guys get the same basic training, and on top of that, you've been *tested* in battle. I'm not sayin' we should take guys off ships and send them ashore... but in a pinch, I believe that you boys will do us proud. You'll learn from us the finer points of this jungle business and your technical expertise will come in handy. You got the guts and the grit, and that's more'n half the battle."

"Hoo-rah, sir," Duncan said and grinned.

"Damned straight," Decker said. "Now polish that jawbreaker off, and let's get this show on the road, Pilgrim."

This last was said in a pretty damned good John Wayne. Duncan laughed and made a concerted if not speedy attempt to finish the iron-hard ration.

Both Lider and Ingram had been more than mildly surprised when Hazard led a group of three dark-skinned Melanesian men out of the trail. They'd heard the shots, of course, but were still debating on what their next moves might be when they heard rustling from the jungle. The kind of hurried rustling that wasn't concerned about concealment.

After running down what had happened, Hazard led the men back down the road toward the trail that would lead to the beach. He introduced Vousa and his men, and then Vousa himself explained how they'd been making their way toward the Jap position when Hazard had appeared. They'd killed the Japanese and stripped the bodies of everything they could, including boots.

When the report came in over the radio that something was happening at the village, Hazard and his now six-man team began a slow jog toward Turner's position. Even at that, it would take at least sixteen or seventeen minutes to cover the distance. Hazard knew all too well what could happen in sixteen minutes.

From behind the team, a low rumbling growl began to make itself heard over the jungle noises. Hazard held up a hand and the men stopped, listening intently.

"Oh, what new hell is *this*..." Ingram grumbled.

"Into the forest, either side of the road, now!" Hazard snapped.

He noticed that Vousa and his men didn't have to be told. They had already begun to move even as Hazard began to speak.

"Don't aim straight, aim upward," he told his men on the south side. "Don't want to hit one another."

The sound of the diesel engine grew louder as it must have crested the hill. Due to the curve in the road, none of the men could see whatever it was yet, but the growling of what might be an uncowled engine sounded close.

"Thought this was a backwater island with a buncha natives on it," Lider hissed. "What's with all the rides?"

"Lotta folks lived and worked here before the Japs came," Hazard said. "Plantations and shit on the other coast... what the... is that a tractor?"

Sure enough, a rather new-looking front-end loader was plowing its way down the coast road on muddy tracks. Heavy black smoke billowed out from the exhaust stack and two men were seated in the control cage. A driver and another man with a rifle. Neither was Japanese, in spite of the hieroglyphic type characters on the bright yellow side of the machine.

Hazard was surprised when Vousa and his two companions stepped out of the jungle waving' their hands and smiling at the approaching vehicle. Hazard exchanged glances with Lider and Ingram, shrugged and stepped out into the road as well.

"This is Vonni and Fento," Vousa explained. "They don't speak English."

"Where'd they get the tractor?" Lider asked.

"Stole it from the Naponapo," Vousa explained as if this were obvious... which it was.

"Bet they ain't happy about *that*," Lider quipped.

"No... but so far they haven't followed," Vousa explained. He exchanged a few short sentences in whatever language they spoke and then turned to Hazard. "Fento says that the fuel is nearly gone. They stole this machine from Lunga Point, which is sixty kilometers from here. It only goes twenty kilometers per hour and has perhaps less than an hour's fuel remaining."

"It'll get us to the river though," Hazard said with a grin. "Faster'n we can walk. Think we can all pile on?"

"You gotta be puttin' me on..." Ingram said, shaking his head.

Vousa grinned, "Many of us can ride in the front."

Fento angled the scooping blade so that it could accommodate passengers. All but Vousa and Hazard piled in, and then the two leaders climbed up onto the rumbling machine and found spots for themselves on the protective fenders that covered the tracks near the control cage.

"Damndest horse I ever seen but... charge!" Hazard shouted ebulliently.

Now that he was closer and wasn't looking mostly head-on, Oaks thought that the flatbed truck the Japanese soldiers were riding in was just about the oddest thing he'd seen in a while. It had the cab of a truck and a flatbed... but where a grill should be, there was what looked like the prow of a boat. He also saw the English letters D.U.K.W. written in large blocky white letters on the odd flat side of the thing. It was painted green and, to the Marine's further surprise, also sported a large white star on the driver's door.

"It's an American truck!" Oaks whispered and then cursed as the damned crazy thing stopped again.

He cursed because while the truck/boat whatsits was almost side on to him now, it most certainly was not blocking the fifty cal across the river that was pumping bucketfuls of hot lead into the trees where his other two men were huddled.

Oaks wasn't sure when he started thinking of the sailors as *his* men. Up until the previous night, he and his fellow Marines, with the exception of Entwater, had done nothing but trade snipes and engage in a long-running pissing contest with Tank, Ingram and Duncan. It

The Cactus Navy

wasn't that he *liked* the squids... but he had to admit they were tough and brave. He figured it probably happened during the rafting evolution. That'd been pretty hairy, and the squids turned leathernecks had been there all the way.

The thirty-foot-long amphibious truck shut its engine down once more, and the five Japs squatting on the long-raised flatbed jumped down to the muddy road. The driver remained behind the wheel. Three of the soldiers landed on the far side, and two landed right in Oak's sights, no more than twenty yards away.

"Bad move, Tojo..." the Raider muttered as he lined up the first man in his iron sights.

He drew in a breath and let it out slowly, and eased the trigger back. The powerful SMG jerked backward, and the first soldier flew off his feet as if someone had jerked a giant string. Oaks carefully lined up his next shot and fired once more, the second soldier toppling over in a vermillion mist that flowered from his beige uniform shirt. Oaks actually cringed when the resounding gong of the man's head striking the steel of the truck echoed across the intervening space.

Instantly he began to move. The three on the far side of the truck had homed in on where they thought the shots were coming from and three Arisaka rifles began to chatter as a hail of 7.7mm rounds sizzled through the foliage all around the Marine.

He didn't have good cover. Although the foliage was dense between himself and the truck... there was no way the Nips could see him... it was mostly ferns and hibiscus and other insubstantial vegetables. Oaks rapidly belly crawled north again, trying to work around to the rear of the truck. If he could get out of the three soldier's field of fire, he might be able to move to the edge of the road for a charge.

There were long moments where all that could be heard were harsh Japanese curses and orders, only half of which Oaks was able to understand. This cacophony was joined by the rapid chatter of the Arisaka rifles and the distant but throatier roar of the tripod-mounted machine gun. And yet... and yet... was that another engine he heard getting closer?

"Oh, for Christ..." Oaks cranked. "What now!?"

There was enough of a break in the foliage so that Oaks could see a few dozen yards down the road. Almost to the turn where he, Taggart and Tank first hid. Suddenly, something happened beyond his sight, because the shouts of the Japanese grew more alarmed and the diesel engine roared louder.

Oaks inched his way forward so that he could get a better look and was startled to see something large and yellow appear around the corner. The Japanese saw it too, because all three men near the truck and the men at the machine gun across the river turned their attention entirely on the new threat.

"It's a fuckin' tractor!" Oaks heard Taggart yell from fairly close.

The sergeant tried not to laugh as he watched in amazement. Taggart had been right. A large, tracked front-end loader was rumbling around the corner, its big wide horizontal shovel raised slightly and acting as a shield for the driver. Rounds by the hundreds pinged and gonged off the heavy steel as the growling monster came to a stop. Oaks knew an opportunity when he saw one. He quickly slapped in a new magazine and got to his feet.

"*Charge!*" he bellowed as he leapt forward, crashing headlong through the brush and straight for the rear left corner of the amphib truck.

Astonishingly, none of the Japanese soldiers next to the truck noticed. Their attention was drawn to the new vehicle and the eight men crouching behind its track and firing.

Oaks burst from the trees only ten feet from the truck just as Tank erupted out of the greenery fifty feet to his left. Taggart, swearing a blue streak, came right after him. Oaks, letting out a fierce battle cry, shouldered his weapon and opened up on the Japanese soldiers.

All three went down quickly, two from his own Tommy gun and one from Taggart's. Tank, who let his weapon fall and hang from its

The Cactus Navy

strap, lunged for the driver's side door of the truck just as the driver was aiming a pistol out of the open window.

Oaks gaped as the big sailor dove and rolled to the mud as the driver squeezed off several rounds. Tank rolled up next to the truck, popped to his feet and yanked the door open. He reached in and grabbed the screaming Jap inside and hauled him out of the truck, swung him bodily in the air and then slammed the terrified man's head into the sidewall of the truck with a gut-twisting clunk. The soldier went limp, and Tank let his body crumple to the mud.

"Looks like we got us a new ship, Sarge!" Tank whooped.

Oaks laughed with elation and was just about to shout a much-deserved compliment when he heard a distinct *thwump!* In the corner of his eye, across the river, a bright flash and thunderous bang drew his attention.

A pillar of smoke and dust rose from the ground only a few feet in front of the woodpile where the Japanese machine gun was mounted.

"The fuck was that?" Tank asked as Taggart ran up to join the other two men.

"Grenade launcher!" Oaks said. "One of our buddies on the tractor must have an M1 mounted to their 1903!"

"Anybody know how to drive this thing?" Taggart asked, waving a hand at the truck.

"No sweat," Tank said, climbing into the driver's seat. "Get on the bed and we'll head over."

"Seriously? You can drive this beast?" Oaks asked incredulously.

"Go Navy!" Tank said with a big smile.

The Japanese in the machine gun nest were pouring all they had at the tractor. Although not even fifty caliber rounds could damage the heavy steel that made up the construction machine, a few rounds must have penetrated the air vents on the engine because the machine belched black smoke, chugged and vibrated horribly and then conked out.

It did them little good, however. The man with the Springfield mounted grenade launcher fired again, and this time his aim was true.

The hand grenade soared through the air and struck the woodpile just in front of the machine gun, and a heavy boom sent logs and splinters and fragments of jagged steel flying in all directions. Mostly they flew into the vulnerable flesh of the soldiers and turned the two men into a horrific bloody pile of gore.

Tank got the engine started and struggled with the gear shift, grinding the transmission and swearing until he got the truck into first. He then stepped on the gas and turned the wheel, driving the big amphibious truck straight into the river, where it promptly began to float and spin its wheels uselessly.

"Hey, Captain Nemo!" Taggart said, rapping his knuckles on the rear window of the cab. "I think ya' gotta engage the prop."

"Hang on!" shouted someone from the tractor as a group of men in BDUs and ragged clothing approached. Oaks was surprised to see that one of them was Decker and another was Turner.

"What the hell do you three think you're doing?" Decker asked bemusedly.

"Floating in three feet of water on account Magellan up there can't drive this damned... whatever it is," Oaks jeered.

"Hey, you wanna give it a shot, smartass?" Tank asked, smiling crookedly.

"You said you could drive this thing!" Taggart accused and laughed.

Tank shrugged as he finally located the separate transmission lever that controlled the front axle and prop shaft, "What can I say... I'm an optimist."

"We was gonna clear out that village before more slopes start firing on us," Taggart stated.

"To hell with it," Decker said and looked at Turner for confirmation. "We got us a ride... that floats... and we got a shitload of cargo to transport."

"Shouldn't we clear the area sir?" Oaks asked.

"Probably," Decker said with a sigh. "But humpin' that cargo and finding Clemens is priority number one."

The Cactus Navy

"Sir," a burly man in his late forties that Hazard introduced as Jacob Vousa put forward. "If you can put me and four of my men across with a three-day pack each, we'll clear the village, speak with the locals and make our way back to the camp."

Turner looked at the man curiously, "Just five men?"

Vousa nodded, "Batu knows the way back, so he can guide you in the truck. Besides, five less men is less weight. Now that we've gone and broken our new toy, this amphib is our only ride."

"That tractor's got Jap writin' on it," Oaks teased Vousa.

"Yes... we stole it from the airfield, of course," Vousa said.

"I thought you was a cop?" Ingram joked.

Vousa lit a cigarette from a pack Lider had given him, "I resigned."

Chapter 13

Off the northeastern coast of Guadalcanal
– 1945 local time

"Sun's down... finally," Elmer Williams noted from his position behind the attack periscope. "Still got the task force in sight, but either they're picking up speed, or our angle is just opening too far."

"I think they *are* increasing speed, sir," Rivers announced from his sonar set. "Turn rates increasing... estimate ten knots... wait... I think there's a fourth contact..."

"You think?" Pat Jarvis asked. "We need to be sure. Petty officers don't guess, Chet."

"Yes sir..." the sonarman's mate fiddled with the knobs on his gear. "Yes... yes, sir! Fourth contact, light, slow screws. Weird that I didn't hear him before. His screw noise is different from the other ships. Smaller vessel, I'd imagine."

"Hmmm..." Williams pondered. "They creep around at four knots all day, and then as dusk comes on, they throttle up. Seem odd to you, XO?"

Jarvis puffed on his Camel thoughtfully, "Yeah, that does seem strange. As strange as the fact that we didn't detect the fourth ship, whatever it is, until just now."

"I'm about to lose them over the hill," Williams said. "Frank, take us up to radar depth. And get the rock crushers online. Let's put this snorkel thingamabob to good use for once. Phone talker, maneuvering to stand by to answer bells on diesels."

Frank Nichols, who was at his customary place at the diving station in the control room, acknowledged. Jarvis made a note on the chart desk and took his maneuvering board and slid down the ladder to the control room. There he'd update his plot with the new information on the new contact.

The ship angled upward by twenty-five feet and leveled off. This not only allowed the SD and SJ radar masts to operate above the water but gave Williams a periscope height of nearly thirty feet, more than doubling his visible horizon. The submarine began to vibrate as her four big sixteen-cylinder diesels growled to life.

"Helm, all ahead two-thirds," Williams ordered. "Make turns for ten knots. Frank, better put one and two on battery charge... hmm... battery charge..."

"I'll be damned..." Jarvis' disembodied voice floated up through the hatch. He and Williams must have had the same idea at the same time.

Although the conning tower was a separate watertight chamber from the control room below, connected only by a thirty-six-inch hatch, the acoustics of both compartments were so good that even conversational voices floated between and were easily overheard.

"You thinkin' what I'm thinkin', Pat?" Williams asked.

"That we don't have nearly enough dancing girls aboard?" Jarvis asked.

Williams waited for the laughter to die down and grinned, "Well, sure... but also that the reason the carrier group was plodding along all day was that they were escorting... or being escorted... by a submarine."

"Concur," Jarvis said in a much more serious tone. His head appeared in the hatchway. "Now they can speed up and run at a decent speed while the Jap boat charges her batteries... just like us. Recommend radar sweeps, Captain."

Williams shivered slightly at the label. While Turner was away, he was technically the acting captain and Jarvis the acting XO, yet he felt uncomfortable in the role. As if he were usurping Turner's position... or trying to slip into a pair of shoes several sizes too large for him.

"Concur," Williams replied. "Teddy, give me a full sweep on the sugar jig and then home in on our friends out there. Then do a sugar dog scan for good measure."

Ted Balkley began to quickly operate his bulky radar equipment. The *Bull Shark* was equipped with two separate radar systems, the SD air search and the SJ surface-search radars, both manufactured by RCA Victor. The SJ rotated through an entire three-hundred-and-sixty-degree arc and could also be directed on a particular bearing. Designed to sweep the visible horizontal surface of the Earth, the SJ unit returned its data on a small CRT screen in the form of a bright green line. When a contact was detected, the line would spike, and the height of each spike would indicate the range of each target. Additional gauges would return this data in numeric form as well. However, a good radar operator could determine the relative size and even guess the type of contact from the intensity of the spike.

Furthermore, the SJ unit came with a top-down display known as the PPI or planned position indicator. Another cathode-ray tube screen, this one could display a chart and then overlay the data from a radar sweep as blips. In this way, the operator had very good range, speed and bearing data to work with.

The SD system was somewhat less advanced and simpler. Rather than sweeping, the SD simply sent out an omnidirectional pulse. An early form of radar, the SD gave only a range return without indicating bearing. Should it detect an aircraft flying at greater than one-thousand feet, it could only return a range, and the operator could determine speed over time should the unit be left operating. It was, for all intents and purposes, a proximity alarm only. And although it had yet to be proved, the prevailing theory in the fleet was that the Japanese could detect the SD in operation and use the signal to home in on the originating submarine.

"Definite three contacts on SJ. Bearing three-five-zero, range twelve-thousand yards," Balkley reported after a moment. "One large and two a bit smaller... possible fourth, but I can't be sure. The signal is weak and being light-shaded by what must be the carrier, sir."

"The boat is out front," Jarvis opined.

"Switching to SD..." Balkley said and then jerked in his chair. "Sir! Multiple airborne contacts, range eight thousand... possibly multiples!" Balkley all but shouted.

"Easy, Ted, easy..." Williams stated. "Probably the CAP and probably about to trap, what with the sun going down. Kill the sugar dog and switch back to sugar jig. One-minute full rotation sweeps. Let's see if we can snag them coming in low."

"It still might be light enough for them to see our wake from the snork, Elm," Jarvis pointed out. "Thing's three feet across, for Chrissakes. If you want to stay a secret..."

Williams sighed, "Yeah, I know... but I want that damned flattop, Pat. I want at least *one* of those bastards."

There was a grumble of ascent from the men in the conning tower and below. Jarvis grinned as well, but he still felt inclined to advise caution.

"I'm hearin' ya, Elm... but our orders aren't to engage unless necessary," Jarvis said. "We make ourselves known, and things could get real dicey out here."

Williams bit his lip. It seemed uncharacteristic for the big outgoing torpedo officer to take the conservative view. Yet the acting captain knew Jarvis was right, at least for the time being.

"Helm, all stop," Williams ordered.

"Maneuvering answerin' all stop sir," Mug Vigliano said.

The boat glided on for a minute or two more while she shed her velocity. The light level was low enough that without the feather line wake of her exposed masts and structures, the pilots of any nearby aircraft shouldn't be able to spot them.

"Contacts on sugar jig!" Balkley reported. "Four contacts, bearing zero-three-zero, descending through one-thousand... all in a line. Looks like they're headed for the carrier group, sir."

Williams nodded, "Very well. Standby."

Another minute went by, and Balkley reported again. Now there were only three contacts, and they appeared closer to the carrier. Several minutes later, there were two, then another few sweeps and there were none.

Williams watched through his periscope and could actually see the carrier, even from six miles off and in almost total darkness now. There were bright lights burning on her after deck, which suddenly winked out after Balkley reported the final aircraft had vanished from his scopes.

"They've recovered their CAP," Williams said. "Good. Helm, all ahead full, come left to course three-four-zero."

"You're goin' after them?" Jarvis asked.

Williams swung his scope around in a complete arc, stopping at nearly dead on the starboard beam. "And there's the moon... perfect... yeah, Pat, I want to shadow them and see what happens. They're headed north, northwest and the moon's rising from about zero-seven-five... we should be out of her gleam from their perspective."

"Maneuverin' answerin' all ahead full, sir," Vigliano said. "Can only give yiz twelve knots on two engine speed."

"Very well," Williams replied. "XO, standby to surface the ship. Radar, keep your SJ trained on the Japs. Five-minute scan interval."

A buzz of excitement sizzled through the conning tower and the control room below. The captain hadn't ordered the general quarters alarm as yet, but his increasing speed to overtake the targets and the preparation to surface certainly implied an impending night surface attack.

"Once we get on top, Pat," Williams said, slipping a Winston from the pack in his duty blouse and lighting it. "Let's dismiss the watch below. We're not gonna attack, at least not for some time, and this stalking game we've been playing has already delayed the evening meal. We've got all night to decide what to do, if anything. I suppose I should radio in for advice on this."

Jarvis nodded, "Probably. This being one of old Clayton's operations. Our job, as I understand it, is to stay quiet and be here should the shore party need us. Not to mention we only got ten fish in the tubes."

"Well," Williams said and smiled around the cigarette in his lips. "That's one each for the two Fubukis, one for the Jap sub and maybe two or three for the carrier. Hell, Pat, we'd still have enough to sink a couple of freighters for good measure."

"Well, Elm tree, I admire your... let's call it moxie," Jarvis replied with a chuckle.

The moon was now a third of the way across its path and shone its face down on a placid sea. In the wide silvery streak of her reflected face, three angular blobs of shadow cruised, barely hull up on the dark horizon. They plowed along at a steady ten knots, seemingly unaware that six miles off their port beams, five pairs of eyes watched them unceasingly. Five pairs of eyes that held within them curiosity and the shared glint that hinted at the predatory thoughts behind them.

Frank Nichols had the watch. He stood on *Bull Shark*'s tiny bridge and studied the small group of ships off his starboard side with a steady intensity that belied his inner thoughts. After a moment, he allowed his Bausch and Lomb 7x50 binoculars to hang loosely around his neck and proceeded to light a cigar.

Nichols was a quiet man. In spite of his compact frame and sharp good looks, he was a thoughtful and intelligent sort. He was often called a brainiac, although rarely ever in a disobliging manner. His gold-framed specs seemed an odd addition to a face that was strong and square and looked like it might be at home on a big screen.

As he pondered the carrier group that may or may not be *Bull Shark*'s next meal, he found himself of two minds. First, as a young

Naval officer, a reservist called up when war was declared and proud to serve his country. Proud also to be able to utilize his master's degree in mechanical engineering aboard such a complex machine as a fleet boat. The military was almost always first at developing and testing new technology, and Nichols was pleased that he could expand his knowledge and experience while doing his part to pay back the Japanese for attacking his homeland.

Another part of his mind contemplated his homeland. He thought of growing up in Connecticut and going to school in Boston. He thought most of all about his young wife, June. The vision of her on the day they'd met that late spring day at Boston Common. How they'd chatted as they watched the swan boats and then how they'd impulsively decided to ride on their own together, laughing and chatting and holding hands...

He thought of her in Hawaii, waiting for him to return, and anxious all the while should he not. He thought of how shy she could be around new people and new situations... and yet how her shyness concealed a very intelligent, exuberant and passionate spirit. The vision of the fire in her eyes when they made love... how uninhibited she was when it came to sex. So unlike her usual demure temperament in public.

He contemplated her friends as well. Of May Dutch's somewhat matronly attitude toward June and the rest of the "spring girls." How April, the newest member and soon to be wife of young Andy Post, brought a larger-than-life ebullience to the group and how Frank knew that June secretly envied April's ability to be so unabashed... and how June wasn't even aware that she herself was beginning to bloom as a result of being around the other women so often.

He ruminated on Joan Turner as well. The pretty blonde who possessed such poise, intellect and good nature. A natural leader who, without even having to try, had slid so easily into the role of heart and soul of all the women of the *Bull Shark*. She was so much like Art, Frank thought fondly. So easy-going but with an intensity of personality that oozed from her pores. The Turners could so easily guide and lead without having to force themselves or their points of view.

His mind wandered over all of this and was mostly glad. Yet he was a little sad, too, as might be expected. After all, he was out here, and June was back there. No way to communicate, to share or to comfort one another. Even letters were hard to exchange. Submarine duty was called the silent service... yet when a man stood mostly alone on watch on a dark night, it could be a deeply lonely service, too.

"Think we'll pull ahead soon, sir," Wendel Freeman said quietly, breaking into Nichols' musings. "Think we should slow down to pace them?"

"No... skipper wants to get out ahead," Nichols said. "If they do follow the Guadalcanal coast, they might head more west soon and better we stay ahead in case we need to go to seaward."

"So how come we don't slide in behind them, sir?" Freeman asked.

Nichols smiled at the young man, "You're striking for quartermaster, aren't you, Wendel...? Why don't you tell me? You've got our position recorded, and you know the chart. Why would we get out ahead and cross over if we need to?"

Freeman flushed. He was being tested and no longer quite felt he was as ready for a promotion as he'd thought himself just a month or two earlier. Back then, he'd generally been paired with Lieutenant Tom Begley. Although Begley had been kind toward Freeman... one of the few... he'd also been far more focused on his own schemes to teach the young man anything helpful.

Now that the former XO and second engineer were gone and the original XO had returned, Freeman found himself feeling somewhat inadequate. Yet, he was also grateful for the fact that anytime he was stationed as acting quartermaster, the officer of the deck was friendly and eager to help him along.

"Well... I guess, first of all, there's the moon," Freeman started. "If we cross behind them, especially if they come more to port, we'd be silhouetted."

Nichols grinned, "That's one reason. What else?"

Freeman swallowed and frowned for a moment, gazing out over the water at the distant silhouettes of the enemy, "Uhm... oh! Nuts! Well, the prevailing trade winds would waft our engine exhaust in their direction. Maybe somebody could smell it on one of their fantails or something?"

"Very true," Nichols said and then chuckled, "I actually hadn't thought of that, Wendel. Probably not a big concern, as we'd be far enough astern for the smoke to dissipate... but maybe not. There is one more reason, though."

"We're already in the Sealark Strait and over the 50-fathom curve," Wendel stated with more confidence than he felt. "It'll continue to shoal, especially if they decide to hug the coast. So we want to be too seaward so we've got plenty of water under our keel if we gotta dive."

"That's two points and a bonus," Nichols said.

Wendel grinned, "I'd like to go down and check the plot one more time, sir... because I think we may have to make a course correction soon. Permission to leave the bridge?"

Nichols granted it, and the young man dropped through the blood-red circle of the open hatchway. Nichols puffed on his cigar and enjoyed the warm night air for a moment. In rather less time than he'd have thought, Freeman re-appeared on deck with a frown on his face.

"Well?" Nichols inquired.

"I think we'd better put on some speed, sir," Freeman said. "Unless they are headed for Tulagi, they may be about to turn soon."

Nichols nodded, "About what I figured. Very well, quartermaster. Ring me up a full-speed bell. We should be about topped off, so order number two put back on propulsion."

Freeman depressed the bridge speaker's transmit button, "Helm, bridge. Alert maneuvering to put number two on propulsion. Then all ahead full."

"*Bridge, helm... maneuvering answers number two on prop, all ahead full,*" the duty helmsman reported.

The ship began to increase her speed, her creaming wake growing larger and the apparent wind increasing as her speed climbed up. In the moonbeam that painted the sea, the menacing silhouettes of the strike carrier and her escorts began to slide slowly astern.

"*Bridge, helm... Bendix log indicates one-five knots,*" the helmsman reported.

"Sir!" one of the lookouts called down excitedly. "I think the group is altering course, sir... yes, they're coming left and fast!"

Nichols brought his binoculars up to his face and found the enlarged images of the ships. In particular, he saw the blocky shape of the small carrier begin to foreshorten as she turned toward the submarine.

Nichols depressed the transmit button, "Radar, bridge, give me an SJ sweep from zero-six-zero to one-two-zero and then home in on our targets."

There was an acknowledgment, a pause and then electrician's mate Paul Baxter, taking his turn on the radar gear, responded, "*Bridge, radar... aspect change on targets. They're coming to course two-eight-zero, range decreasing... new contact! Fourth contact now visible, sir. Definitely part of the group, but low profile.*"

"That'll be the submarine, I'd bet," Nichols said. "Very well, radar. Have the messenger of the watch—"

"Sir!" the starboard and aft lookouts both shouted in unison and in alarm.

Their report was unnecessary. The three ships were arranged in a half-phalanx formation with the carrier at the center. Astern and to port, one *Fubuki*-class destroyer held station three-hundred yards away. The other destroyer held herself at the same distance off the carrier's starboard bow. Evidently, the submarine had been positioned off the outer destroyer's starboard beam and was now visible to radar as the ship's turned toward *Bull Shark*.

What had alarmed the lookouts was the sudden bright magnesium-white flare of brilliant light over the task force. A star shell had been fired from the outer *Fubuki* and now hung in the night air, casting a brilliant glow over the water as the flare slowly descended toward the sea.

"I don't like this..." Nichols said, biting his lower lip. Until this mission, he'd hardly ever stood a watch as OOD. Now, he was in command and had to make a decision that might affect the safety of the ship. He cursed and grabbed at the diving alarm, pulling it twice. "Clear the bridge! Hard dive! Hard dive!"

Even as the lookouts scrambled down from their posts and Freeman proceeded them down the hatch, the bridge speaker crackled with an alarmed report from Baxter, "*Bridge, radar! Detecting broad scale contact pattern... looks like a squall, but...*"

Nichols knew what Baxter was seeing. One method for detecting enemy radar was for its broadcast to show up on your screen. Another was that your signal would intercept the other set's signal and bounce back in a dispersed return pattern that resembled a low-density mass like a cloud bank. However, the night sky was clear, so it could only be one thing.

"*assess enemy radar sweep!*" Baxter blurted.

"Christ..." Nichols said as he watched the three lookouts dropping through the hatch.

He followed, yanking the lanyard and freeing the big hatch from its holding mechanism. Freeman was hanging on the edge of the ladder and reached up to dog the bridge hatch even as Nichols slid down to the conning tower's deck.

"Secure radar!" he called out with more excitement than he felt was proper. "Sound general quarters! Battle stations torpedo!"

Chapter 14

Hours earlier... 10 miles northeast of Aola Bay, Guadalcanal
– 1930 local time

Lt. Commander Ryu Osaka had the stick. He and Omata Hideki were completing a six-hour recon overflight of Guadalcanal and were looking forward to getting back aboard *Sakai* for a warm meal and warmer sake.

"I honestly do not know what we're supposed to find down there," Hideki was saying as he stowed his clipboard and notes. "The damned island is so overgrown it's difficult to even see the roads... what roads there are."

Osaka shrugged, "Certainly we will likely not fly over a coastwatcher's camp and see a large sign or a great Union Jack fluttering in the breeze... yet one can never quite tell, can one?"

"Guadalcanal is one-hundred and fifty kilometers long and forty-five kilometers wide at its widest," Hideki stated. "At eighty knots, we were able to fly over the length of the island four times, covering every square kilometer visually. And what did we see? Our airbase being constructed near the Lunga River, a smattering of villages... and nothing else."

"You seem annoyed, my friend," Osaka commented. "Did you expect anything else? If Clemens and his team are still alive, then they're set up in the foothills or even the mountains. Even a third of the way up the island's highest elevation and they can easily see Savo, Tulagi, Gavatu, Tanambogo and Florida Island. Yet we'd be hard-pressed to see them from more than a few hundred meters away. And should we actually do so... how do we know it's Clemens and not just some islanders?"

"Precisely," Hideki grumped. "We're out here wasting our time. This is simply masturbation."

Osaka cocked an eyebrow at his friend and chuckled, "We need to get you a geisha, Omata sama... look, there is our task force. In less than ten minutes you'll be swimming in warm rice wine. I'll circle around and come in from their bows... I dislike landing into the sun."

Osaka slowed his airspeed to just above a stall and turned slightly to starboard and the northeast. He began to descend from one thousand meters down to two hundred. In this way, he could do a lazy visual scan of the ocean surrounding the carrier as well as stay well below and behind the flight paths of the four Zeroes that would be preparing to land for the evening. The sun was already nearly down and would vanish below the horizon in just a few minutes. Osaka could simply continue his arc and land from astern of *Sakai* if he wished, yet he felt it was good practice to do a complete orbit.

"What's that?" Hideki asked, pointing ahead of the float plane's nose. "Do you see that, Ryu?"

Ryu hesitated as he looked. There did seem to be something out there. A shadow below the surface? And was that a dissipating line of foam off to the right...?

Both men were pilots and had pilots' sharp eyes for detail. However, Osaka was also a submariner. He could see things from a different perspective and knew all too well the signs that a submarine could leave on the surface. If traveling at periscope depth in the clear Pacific waters in daylight, a boat could easily be spotted. As if that weren't enough, any periscope or mast that poked up through the surface of the sea left a wake. A foamy line of disturbance that slashed across the blue surface like a scar. If one

The Cactus Navy

truly knew, and had a truly sharp and trained eye, there were other subtler signs as well.

For example, a two-thousand and more ton object moving beneath the water displaced an equal mass of water. Even hundreds of feet below, unless the boat was moving very slowly, it created a hump above it on the surface. A slight disturbance that moved as it moved.

And Ryu Osaka did indeed have sharp and well-trained eyes. And he kept those eyes trained forward now, lest they betray him.

What was his duty? What was the best course of action now?

Hideki had almost certainly seen the tell-tale signs of a submerged submarine. And Osaka knew it was *not* the I-123 that was even then waiting patiently below the carrier for daylight to diminish so she could surface. No... it could only be an allied submarine stalking his current home.

In his unique position as Yamamoto's aid and as a pipeline from the IJN to the American Office of Strategic Services, Osaka was often faced with such conflicts. He did what he could in order that the United States and her allies could more efficiently subdue Japan... yet he truly believed that this was in the best interests of his country. His goal was not to help the allies kill Japanese... no... it was to help them win more quickly and *spare* Japanese lives!

Yet if he failed to report the presence of this submarine and she fired on one of the ships in the task force and sunk her... then was he not culpable? Conversely, should he report the presence of this boat, and that boat was then sunk by the destroyers and the carrier... then was he, Osaka, only prolonging the conflict?

He *could* get away with saying nothing. He could inform Omata that he'd been mistaken, and it was simply a trick of the sunset light, or a whale, or any of a half-dozen reasonable explanations. He could even circle around and try and locate the object. By then, the light would be too low to see the black silhouette of a submarine even just below the surface. The foam would have dissipated and there would be no proof. The small group of ships was already on alert for

American submarines... so nothing would truly change whether Osaka spoke up or not.

One final thing troubled him as well. Nearly two months earlier, he'd actually met the man with whom he'd been secretly communicating. He'd met some of the men from the submarine that had vanquished *Leviathan*. He'd found Clayton and Jarvis, and even their COB to be open and even friendly men.

What if that *were Bull Shark* down there?

The odds were low, of course. Already the Americans were building new submarines at an astonishing rate. They must by then have nearly a hundred in service. And why should it matter what boat it was anyway? He had no particular love for any of them... not even *Bull Shark* and her captain, for whom Osaka *should* harbor feelings of resentment... yet he did not. He admired the man and his crew, to be sure...

"I don't know, Omata," Osaka finally said. He decided that he wouldn't go out of his way to cover up the presence of an American submarine, but neither would he go out of his way to ensure her destruction. "It was probably nothing... but I'll circle around and take another look."

He banked the Aichi floatplane into a wide clockwise arc. As suspected, the light was too dim to see below the surface. Also, as he'd expected, the minute traces of an old wake had been all but obliterated by the slight but consistent action of the waves.

"Perhaps I'm simply paranoid," Hideki said wryly. "Seeing ghost ships everywhere."

"Seeing what you want to see, eh?" Osaka teased. "There's nothing to fear, though, I think. I wouldn't be surprised to learn that there was indeed an American submarine out here. After all, the presence of one in the early part of the previous month is what prompted *our* being here. Yet it would be a foolish sub commander indeed who would attack two *Fubuki*-class destroyers and a nimble strike carrier that herself had anti-submarine capabilities."

"Foolish or dogged, my friend," Hideki pointed out as Osaka

The Cactus Navy

turned the plane back toward the landing lights of the carrier. "Like that man who hounded us when we were aboard *Ribaiasan*. What was his name... Turner?"

Osaka chuckled, "Most submarine captains are bold, Omata."

Soon they were being hoisted up and into their little hangar, and the task force had increased its speed. The sun had set, and I-123 had surfaced and the entire group was running northwesterly at ten knots. The two pilots made their way up into *Sakai's* Island, where they were seated in the captain's sea cabin to dine.

A table had been set up to accommodate four. In addition to Osaka and Omata, the carrier's captain and her first officer, Takashi Sato, were in attendance. Sato was in his mid-thirties, a full *Kaigun Chusa*, Commander, and was somewhat short. Although what he lacked in stature, he made up for in burliness.

"Good evening, gentlemen," Captain Igawa stated and bowed from the shoulders. "Thank you for joining me. Please be seated."

Osaka and Omata both bowed to the senior men and sat themselves at the two empty settings. A large *tokkuri* filled with sake sat in the center of the table over a three-candle warmer. There was also a pot of green tea and a basket of warm, freshly baked bread and soft butter.

"Wine?" Igawa asked.

Both pilots nodded. The two stewards proceeded to fill their teacups and their *choko* with sake for them. The stewards then buttered several slices of bread and served them to the officers and went out.

"To a successful flight!" Igawa proposed, lifting his small sake vessel high.

The other men acknowledged and sipped. The rice wine was of a fairly good vintage, although being heated did help in disguising the fact that it was hardly of the top-shelf variety. It did go down well, however.

"Successful in that we returned unscathed," Hideki jested. "Though otherwise..."

Sato nodded grimly, "You found nothing."

"We found nothing that we recognized as something," Osaka corrected slightly. "The difficulty is obvious. A small number of men can easily hide in such dense jungle."

"Yet must they not be in the mountains?" Sato asked. There was a subtle but detectible tone of impatience in his voice. "High enough to be able to observe activity as far as Savo and Tulagi?"

"Probably so, sir," Hideki said. "Yet even several hundred or even a thousand meters above sea level, the rainforests are dense. There are also frequent mists and so on."

"Is it impossible to find them, do you think?" Igawa asked.

"Not impossible," Osaka reassured. "Simply a matter of time. Yet, in truth... does it really matter? We have regular flights, men on the ground and our own coastwatchers. *We're* here and the Americans continually fly patrols and even bomb our captured territory. What we're doing here is hardly a secret."

"But this Clemens is *spying* on us," Sato declared angrily, slapping the table and causing the *tokkuri* to rattle on its warmer's wire frame. "He reports back to his American puppeteers on *everything* we do. And sooner rather than later, the Yankees will come in force... all because of *him*."

"Be easy, Takashi," Igawa soothed. Osaka and Hideki exchanged furtive dubious glances. "What will be, will be. Let us not get worked up over things we cannot immediately control. Did your scouting flight reveal anything else, Osaka san?"

Here it was. He'd been asked directly, and if he chose to stay silent about what Hideki saw, it might appear strange to his friend. Once again, he reconciled himself to the fact that the sighting was now more than an hour in the past and that the task force was on alert in any event.

"Omata thought he saw something on the surface," Osaka stated. "However, when we circled back to verify, there was no sign."

"Something?" Sato asked. "Such as?"

"A submarine's wake," Hideki said. "I thought I saw a shadow and a line of foam... however, it was more likely just a trick of the light. As Ryu says, we saw nothing definitive when we re-examined the location."

"And you did not report this *immediately?*" Sato asked tersely.

"We determined there was nothing to report," Osaka stated.

"Perhaps that's for your *superiors* to decide," Sato griped. "As a scout, your job is to report everything you see."

"Notes were taken, sir," Hideki said, shifting uncomfortably in his chair.

"Takashi, these two gentlemen come directly to us from Admiral Yamamoto," Igawa soothed. "I think we can trust their judgement. Let us not get this pleasant meal off on the wrong foot, eh?"

Sato appeared as if he wanted to say more. Instead, though, he drew in a breath and let it out by way of calming himself. He smiled thinly, 'Of course, sir. Forgive my outburst. As the Brits say, gentlemen... a glass of wine with you."

The four men drank again as the soup came. It was a simple broth with bits of onion and dried mushroom. Simple but tasty. Next came a seaweed salad and handmade sushi rolls. After this, a stir-fried mixture of frozen vegetables and meat was served. The vegetables consisted of carrots, zucchini and onion. The zucchini was a bit soft due to the freezing but otherwise a satisfying meal.

The men talked companionably for an hour or so. They shared their family histories, tales of their experiences in this war and the previous wars and even managed to laugh a few times. Despite Sato's earlier pique, he seemed to warm to the newcomers.

Long after the sake was gone and the dishes cleared, the captain passed out Cuban cigars and invited the men to join him on the observation bridge. The night was comfortable, and the moon was bright.

"We're about to alter course to the west," Igawa was explaining as the men puffed on their quality cigars. "We'll skirt the coast up to about Cape Esperance and then turn south and circumnavigate the coast once more."

The officer of the deck stepped out from the navigation bridge and up to the captain. "Sir, we are preparing to come about. Permission to fire the star shells."

"Granted," Igawa said. "After you do, please activate the radar and keep it active throughout the maneuver."

The young officer, a Lieutenant, looked surprised. "Keep it on, sir? The turn will take several minutes. And the likelihood of any aircraft being in the area this late..."

"Understood," Igawa said patiently. "While our radar is mainly used for aircraft detection, it may detect something else, as well. There is certainly no need for stealth on our part."

"*Hai*," The officer bowed and vanished.

From forward and to starboard of *Sakai*, a boom resounded from the vicinity of the leading *Fubuki*. A second later, a small star erupted in the night sky, casting the destroyer in a ghostly eldritch glow as the shell gently parachuted toward the ocean. Another was fired from port and aft from the trailing destroyer. Finally, from the bow of the carrier, a third shell was sent aloft ahead. For nearly three minutes, the miniature suns cast several square kilometers of ocean in an eerie brightness. Not as if night had become day, but more than enough that any object within their sphere of light would have been seen.

None was, of course, and the lookouts perched on the observation deck and in the perch above the bridge itself reported no sightings.

The four ships, *Sakai* and her two destroyer escorts along with I-123 to starboard of the leading *Fubuki*, began to turn to port as one. Their turn was leisurely, not being completed until the last star shell had fizzled into the Pacific.

A messenger suddenly appeared and, in an excited tone, said, "Sir! Sir! Radar reports that they've detected... something."

"Something, seaman?" Sato snapped irritably. Osaka and Hideki began to wonder if this were his true nature and that the amiability he'd displayed since supper was but a veneer. "What do you mean, *something?*"

The Cactus Navy

"Unknown, sir," The lad answered nervously. "I've been asked to inform you and with Lieutenant Arawi's respects to join him."

The four officers followed the young man into the navigation bridge and then aft to the small radar shack. Lieutenant Arawi, the same officer of the deck who'd spoken to them earlier, stood behind the technician and studied the fuzzy blob on his screen. Igawa entered the small room and Sato leaned against the doorframe. Osaka and Hideki stood just outside, pressing against one another and the opposite side of the hatch in order that they might see as well.

"What have we got, Arawi?" Igawa asked.

"Unknown contact, sir," the OOD answered, visibly stiffening at having so many senior officers literally breathing down his neck. "Very faint contact at ten thousand meters. Yet it appears to be growing fainter by the second."

"I've lost it, sir," The technician stated, fiddling with his gear. "Contact has disappeared... the screen is clear."

"Blast this damned equipment!" Sato cranked. "We need more than a simple air search system. We need a directional system for surface search... what do you suspect it was, Arawi?"

The OOD sighed, "I can't say, sir. It could be nothing. With this simple radar, we may have even picked up an echo from the mountains on Guadalcanal itself. Although very distant, our equipment might have registered it as closer than it actually is."

"What else could account for this?" Igawa asked.

Once more, Osaka felt a twinge in his belly. He had a very good idea of what their radar had detected. Should he speak up now or...

"Something on the surface that sank below it," the technician said. "This is similar to other returns I've seen from submarines we picked up on the destroyer on which I last served."

Sato spat out a curse and glared at Osaka, "A submarine, Commander. Perhaps what you saw earlier was *not* a trick of the light!"

He pushed past them and across the small passage to the sonar shack, "Sonar! Active ping now! Signalmen! Signalmen! Send to both escorts to begin active ping.

Possible enemy submarine in the area."

"It might be nothing," Hideki said uncertainly.

"Or it might not," Osaka replied, looking at Igawa.

The captain only shrugged, "Pay no mind, Commander. Takashi is a bit... high-strung, but he's a competent officer. Better safe than sorry, eh?"

Osaka turned and moved out into the navigation bridge and past the men working there at the chart table and helm stations. He moved out onto the dark observation platform in time to see all the running lights on the carrier and the destroyers only three hundred meters away wink out.

"Do not blame yourself, Ryu," Hideki said soothingly at his side. "We couldn't have known."

Osaka sighed, "No... it is just unfortunate, Omata *sama*... it casts us... or at least myself... into doubt."

Hideki chuffed, "Only in Sato's eyes, perhaps. I think Captain Igawa still has faith in us."

"Let us see how the night progresses, Omata," Osaka said. "Then we'll know."

And what will we know? Osaka mused inwardly. *That I am either an incompetent fool... or perhaps something worse?*

Chapter 15

Several hours earlier
– the Guadalcanal interior

Between the supplies and the men, the Chevy amphibious truck was making hard work of what passed for roads on the big island. Most of them, once they'd left the vicinity of the windward shore, were little more than game trails. The average speed of the truck was hardly more than ten miles per hour and not as much in some places.

All during the hot afternoon of loading supplies onto the flatbed and winding their way north and west, there were no less than four scares caused by low-flying Japanese aircraft. They flew regular sorties over the island using Kawanishi seaplanes and often came in quite low. At one point, an Aichi floatplane buzzed overhead, although at more than a thousand feet. Each time, the truck was driven into the brush in hopes of concealment. It was, thankfully, painted olive drab, which did blend in well with the surrounding jungle. It became painfully clear as evening approached, however, that the truck would have to go.

"Where'd this thing come from anyway?" Turner asked.

He, Decker and Batu were crammed into the cab with Tank. In spite of his rough start, Tank did know how to drive a truck.

"Naponapo bring over Tulagi," Batu answered. "Was belong Americans then when Japs come they savvy use it here."

"Makes sense," Decker said.

"This far as we go with road no more," Batu explained, pointing ahead where the jungle trail they were all but crashing through opened up. The road... more of a goat path in truth... stopped abruptly at a somewhat more open area dominated by a fast-rushing river cutting its way through a rocky ravine that was at least thirty feet deep.

"Christ..." Tank grumbled as he stopped the truck and set the emergency brake.

"Where are we?" Turner asked.

"Altogether we savvy near Vushicoru," Batu said. "Is small village high in mountains."

"Is that where Clemens is hiding?" Decker asked.

Batu frowned, "Sometime yes, most time no. He main spot were Palapao, but then Japanese 'e come, Clemens savvy altogether move to Vungana. In hills and savvy whole north side."

"So... how do we get all this gear to him?" Turner asked, jerking a thumb toward the rear window. "There's only a dozen of us."

Batu frowned, "Is... half sun up walk to Vushicoru. Savvy... five miles?"

"Aw hell..." Tank grumbled. "Takes an hour a mile or so? Five or six round trips? We'll never do it, Skipper."

Batu brightened, "Altogether 'e carriers come. Many much men belonga! One trip savvy."

"Oh, if I understand you right," Decker said, "you've got men employed to hump gear around the island on foot."

"Yes, savvy," Batu replied.

"Looks like it's time to unload," Turner said. "Then we can hide the truck somehow."

"We still need to find Clemens and let him know we're here," Decker said.

The Cactus Navy

"I go," Batu stated. "Savvy the way, even 'e night come. Return morning time, much men 'e quicky-quicky."

"Leaving us alone out here in the middle of who knows where..." Turner grumbled.

Decker frowned and opened his door, "Do we have a choice? We can set up the radio gear again and try and contact him that way. Let's you and me scout the area, Art."

The rest of the Marines and sailors had climbed down off the truck, stretching their legs and sipping from their canteens. Even approaching sundown, the heat from the jungle was sweltering. Although Turner did notice that it wasn't quite as humid or hot as it had been on the coast road. Their elevation must have changed, and they might be several hundred feet above sea level now.

"All right, gang," Turner told the men. "Have yourselves a smoke and then we gotta unload the gear. This is the end of the road."

"Road," Chief Duncan scoffed. "I seen deer paths better marked than this, Skipper."

"Hey, least the Japs can't hardly see us from the air, Chief," Oaks said with a grin.

"Well, it's all worth it then," Duncan said, brushing at a heretofore unnoticed spider that had been crouching on his shoulder. He did a little dance, swiped himself all over and yanked a pack of cigarettes from his blouse and managed to string together a formidable number of curses even as he lit the pill.

"Our man Batu is gonna head back to Clemens's camp and bring back a party of men to help us hump this stuff up the hill," Turner explained. He grinned at Duncan as he reached into his own blouse pocket and then frowned. "We'll probably have to bivouac here for the... oh, what the..."

Joe Dutch laughed uproariously, "Forget somethin', Art?"

"God *dammit*..." Turner grumbled. "I gave my pack to Batu..."

"Here you go, sir," Entwater said, holding out an open pack of Lucky Strikes. "Take a couple if you like."

"Thanks, Ted," Turner said, removing two cigarettes from the pack. "You're a prince among men. Nice to have *friends*."

Dutch widened his eyes, "What... I'm your friend?!"

"Says the guy who didn't offer me a butt," Turner said, walking away and chuckling. "Lt. Dutch is in charge of unloading detail. Make sure he pitches in, boys."

The jungle opened rather abruptly onto a promontory of gravelly land overlooking the stream-cut ravine. The thirty-foot-deep canyon was perhaps fifty feet across, and the mountain stream that flowed through it roiled and churned as far as the eye could see in either direction. To the right, however, the cliff edge appeared clear, if a bit narrow, as it wound its way into the mountains, now towering high above them in the near distance.

Turner watched as Batu quickly and expertly moved along the ravine. It was clear by the islander's confident stride that he knew the terrain. He disappeared around a bend a few hundred yards off, leaving only a wisp of cigarette smoke behind.

"Should be enough space here to camp for the night," Decker stated.

Turner nodded, "Yeah... and a bucket on a line will provide us with what looks like good, fresh water to refill the canteens."

The open patch was a good fifty paces wide and half as many from the jungle to the edge of the precipice, "Think we're protected enough, though, Major? I mean, should the Japs come scouting?"

Decker unfolded a map of the island and oriented it to the north. On it, he'd made a few pencil marks over the several hours of their trip, "We came ashore west of Merao Sound and Talisi... right about here."

Turner nodded, "Yeah, matches with our charts."

"So here's the coast road and here's the Nombor River," Decker stated, tapping the map. "I wonder if this stream here is the Nombor... could be. I tried to keep track of our drive, but it was tough with all the curves and switchbacks and whatnot... But I think we're about here."

"Looks like maybe ten, twelve miles from Lunga Point as the crow flies, north, northeast," Turner said.

"Yeah, with seven-thousand-foot mountain peaks in between," Decker grumbled. "I don't know where this Vushacoru is, or Vungana or even Palapao... but they have to be in the central or northeastern sector. That's where the Japs are building. They got troops at Lunga Point, Coli Point and Aola and a few other places, I think."

"Clemens will know," Turner stated.

"Yeah, or we're gonna find out," Decker said. "Operation Watchtower is set to begin within a week or so... Christ, I wish they'd told me the *actual* date... We've got to make contact with Clemens and do a thorough recon of the potential landing beach and surrounding Jap emplacements. Our guys need to know what they're in for when they hit the beach."

"Think we can hold out that long?" Turner asked, glancing over his shoulder where the nine men were hefting crates and boxes off the DUKW.

"I don't know, Art..." Decker said, sounding a bit worried. "There's enough food here for twenty guys for about a week. In this environment, you gotta eat a lot. But now if we need these carriers to help us... they're gonna want to be paid. More likely than not in food. Then there's Clemens and his regulars. How many of them?"

Turner sighed, "So we're way understocked is what you're saying."

Decker chuffed, "Probably would be if it were only our guys. You know what we brought. Aside from food, there are boots, socks, skivvies, a few toiletries, some BDUs and a bit of survival gear. We got guns and ammo, a bit anyway. But a lot of our weight is in radio parts and fuel. New batteries for Clemens's teleradio, a new charging motor, spare parts, fifty gallons of fuel and the ham radio set with the big aerial and booster. All that shit adds up fast. Suddenly three-thousand pounds doesn't sound like much."

Turner shook his head as he watched the men sweating under their burdens, "No, it sure... ham radio set?"

Decker eyed him sidelong, "Clayton didn't say?"

"Does a spook ever say much?"

Decker laughed, "Touché. Clayton has this idea that with a ham radio set, Clemens will be able to converse with anybody on Earth. But especially station K and station H... in Pearl."

"I assume in some kind of code."

"Right... and from what I understand, he's got a ham operator in Hawaii set up to relay information both that Clemens has to report as well as intel from ultra and other sources."

"And all it takes is for a handful of Marines and sailors to make their way into occupied territory, through a dense jungle full of deadly beasts and find a guy who's now become pretty good at hiding himself," Turner said sardonically. "And hope that the enemy, both on the ground and in the sky, doesn't sniff us all out... and once we do all that, we're responsible for directing the landing of twenty-thousand men."

"Pretty much."

"Well, what'll we do after lunch tomorrow?" Turner asked.

Although the camp was only a few hundred feet above sea level, it cooled down to something like tolerable after the sun had gone down. The alcohol stove was broken out, and the men ate a hearty supper of corned beef hash, some sort of weird, canned bread, canned green beans and canned fruit. Some papayas also grew near the camp, and several were picked and eaten as well.

The truck was driven a half-mile down the track and, through sheer force of six-wheel drive horsepower, backed into the jungle and covered with creepers. There were seven or eight gallons of diesel left in the tank, so the position was noted for future reference.

About an hour before midnight, the sky darkened and opened up in a torrent of heavy rain. The cargo had been piled up near the edge of the jungle and covered with several green tarps. These served as both camouflage and rain covers, which were now proving their worth.

The landing force hadn't brought any tents, but their gear did feature a number of tarpaulins and plenty of rope. The Marines showed the sailors how to rig a reasonably dry shelter using tarps and cut bamboo poles, and the men slept three to each on bedrolls, staying mostly dry if a bit damp under the canvas. The two sentries were not as fortunate and had to stand exposed out in the tropical deluge or under what shelter the jungle overhang could offer.

To Tank Broderick's waterlogged mind, standing watch was a contradiction in terms, at least during this goddamned monsoon. He couldn't see shit, let alone a pack of blood-thirsty Japs creeping up on them. Every now and then, lightning would cast the entire area in a flashbulb of actinic blue light. In that brief moment, he could see the tents, the pile of freight, the dark gash across the land that was the trench and Dave Taggart, huddled in the dubious shelter of a big-ass banana tree.

Tank briefly thought that it was sort of ironic that here he was, a submarine sailor, and that he was getting more sopping wet on so-called dry land than he ever had in the boats.

"Including that time we almost bought it at eight hundred feet," Tank said aloud, with hardly enough volume to even hear his own words. "The fuck are we *doin'* here..."

Like Taggart, Sherman Broderick had grown up in New Jersey. Where Taggart had lived in the rural northwestern part of the state in a farming community not far from Grover's Mill, Tank had grown up on the Jersey shore. Maybe that was why Taggart had chosen the land warrior route and Tank the sea.

On their long ride Tank had learned that Taggart remembered the Orson Well's *War of the Worlds* radio play. He'd just graduated from high school that year and was working on his family's farm before joining the Corps. He said that while some locals flipped their lids, on account of Grover's Mill, the supposed landing site of the Martians, was only six miles away... not many had really panicked. Unless you came into the story a bit late, it was pretty clear that it was a Halloween radio show.

On the other hand, Tank had been living in the town of Keyport.

When he was only three, there was a big national sensation when five bathers were attacked by sharks along new Jersey's coast. The final three in Matawan Creek, not far from his home. Taggart had whistled in genuine awe that after that horror, which he remembered reading about as a kid, Tank would go into the Navy.

And here was Broderick, not facing down the gaping maws of hungry sharks... but hanging around in a dank rainforest waiting for spiders, insects, rats and Japs to come out of the dark and scrag him. What a goofball thing war was.

The promontory on which the landing party camped was situated in such a way that the narrow track that led from the jungle opened up to the northwest. The river flowed sort of northeast to southwest. If Tank stood looking directly at the canyon... if he could actually *see* anything... he'd see the nearby shoulders of craggy volcanic mountains ahead of him and a dense tropical rainforest behind. He, therefore, didn't stand facing forward, as nothing on foot could really come from that way, except possibly to the north, northeast where Batu had gone. Instead, he faced in the direction that the river flowed, and Taggart, his opposite number, faced the direction that Batu had gone.

In this way, they could keep an eye on each other, on the surroundings and cast regular glances into the blackness of the jungle and the tempting pile of cargo nestled halfway into its fringes.

It was because of this position, therefore, that Tank caught some kind of movement out of the corner of his eye upon the occasion of the next brilliant flash of lightning. The area lit up for no more than a second or two, but in that brief flash, the electrician thought he caught something large disturbing the foliage not far behind the tarp-covered gear.

Instinctively, Tank dropped to his knees and brought his Thompson up to his shoulder. With his left hand, he fumbled a small waterproof flash from his left hip pocket and clicked it on and off in three rapid bursts in the general direction of Taggart. He then stuffed the penlight back into his pants and began to inch forward toward the stockpile, hoping for another flash and hoping that he'd seen whoever it was first.

It was bad enough to have to stand guard duty, but to do so in this deluge was not only a virtual impossibility, it was deeply frightening. Though Tank would hardly admit it to himself, the goose flesh that suddenly popped out on his skin, the prickling sensation along his hairline and the now rapid thumping of his heart were sure giveaways that he was scared shitless.

Sherman "Tank" Broderick was no softy. He was a big, strong and tough man who'd come up rough and who'd been hardened further by ten years of service. Yet he was, after all, only human. And what he didn't realize was that his fight or flight response had been awakened to its full potential the moment he'd set foot on the alien landscape of Guadalcanal.

His ancient lizard brain had reacted exactly as it was supposed to. His primordial survival instincts had been activated by the unfamiliar environment, so filled to the brim with strange and pungent odors, odd sounds and the trepidation generated by his higher brain. Without even realizing it, Tank, like his fellows, was far more aware of his surroundings than he usually was. And in the current circumstance, where his oh-so-depended upon eyes were all but useless and his hearing was simply overwhelmed by the roar of the rain and the jungle life, he was beginning to rely on more ancient and not very well understood survival mechanisms. Mechanisms far older than the pyramids... far more ancient than even his primate ancestors who first fell from trees on the African savannas millions of years before. These were raw, primal instincts as old as the oldest dinosaur. Instincts that had vanished from the consciousness of the homo sapiens who left the wilds and moved into the safety and comfort of manufactured dwellings thousands of years earlier... yet these reptilian instincts still existed and were on full alert.

Tank *knew* someone was out there. He could *smell* them... or so it seemed. He crept forward until he brushed gently up against the hard edge of a tarp-covered crate. There, he paused and listened with his entire being. Almost without cognizant thought, Tank slowly drew the large and deeply reassuring heft of his combat knife from its scabbard on his thigh. He adjusted the sling of his rifle so that it hung across his back and waited. He knew that the gun wasn't his best friend now. He knew that only the cold steel of a seven-inch blade would serve him.

A gust of wind, a sudden pelt of rain and then just as suddenly, a lull... and was that something snapping...?

Electric-blue light sizzled across his vision for just an instant. In that instant, peering over the upper-left edge of the roughly shaped pyramid of the boxes, Tank's eyes met those of another's. In the brief instant of the flash, the two men held each other's gaze in both fear and shock before the world was plunged into inky wet blackness once more.

The submariner turned soldier threw himself to his left, flattening his body and then tucking, rolling and coming to his knees just as something wet and heavy lunged for where he'd just been. Tank lurched forward and threw his arms around the thing, feeling the lean but hard body of a man. He bellowed in rage as the two combatants crashed down to the muddy gravel and began to tear at each other and beat at one another.

"Tank!?" Taggart's voice shouted from what might have been a mile off to Tank's ears, now roaring with the pounding of his heart.

"Intruder!" was all Tank managed before a hard fist slammed into his guts.

Another blow, from the man's other fist, slammed into Tank's thick neck, doing no harm and being hardly noticed. Somewhere in his addled mind, Tank realized that his opponent held no weapon... and that he still held his combat knife in his left hand.

Using the leverage of his legs and his great upper body strength, Tank heaved the other man onto his back and fell on top of him, one hand pressing the smaller man's left shoulder down and the razor-sharp edge of his blade pressing against the unseen assailant's throat.

As quickly as that, the fight was over. The smaller man went rod stiff, making no move and doing nothing to earn him a cut windpipe. Voices began to stir, and lights began to click on as men clambered from their tents to see what all the fuss was about.

Tank hauled his captive to his feet, and in the bright glow of Taggart's flash, he saw that the man he'd grappled with was a young Melanesian man with wide, frightened eyes.

"Who are you?" Taggart barked.

"I..." the man squeaked. "Panota... Michael Panota. I am policeman! I work altogether with Marty Clemens."

This man's English was much better than Batu's. Still some pidgin in it, but much more refined.

"Then what the hell are you doin' sneaking up on us in the middle of the night and in a storm, Goddammit!" Tank growled.

"What's on here?" Turner's voice snapped from out of the darkness. He and Decker appeared in the small circle of glowing flashlights.

"Caught this guy snoopin' around our stash, sir," Tank said, shaking the man. "Says he works for Clemens."

"It's true!" Panota protested. "I sneak up account you no savvy me in the dark. Didn't want scare you and get altogether head blown up."

"Jesus Christ..." Decker grumbled. "You sure chose a bad way to make friends, kid. All right, false alarm. Everybody go back to bed."

Grumbles, curses and a few chuckles as the now wet men went back to their damp bedrolls with the idea that sleep might actually come.

"At ease, Tank," Decker said. "Put the pig sticker away. How'd you find us, kid?"

Tank slid his knife back into its scabbard but kept his hand on the grip.

"I was altogether visit father Estacio at Talisi," Panota explained. "Vousa told me to come report if anything savvy strange. I hear gun shots this morning and..."

"Tracked us here," Turner said. "Terrific."

"Want me to search him, sir?" Taggart asked.

"Yeah, I do," Tank said.

"Go ahead, Dave... Panota, this is just a precaution," Decker stated.

Taggart patted the young man down. He found a knife, still sheathed and was surprised to find a bulky walkie-talkie clipped to the man's worn leather belt near the small of his back. He pulled it out and examined it in his light.

"A radio?" Turner asked dubiously.

"I take from my posting when the Jap 'e come," Panota explained a bit shakily.

"I didn't know you guys had two-ways like this," Decker said thoughtfully.

"Sir... look at this," Taggart said, thrusting the radio toward Decker's face and shining his light on it. "This thing's on, sir... the talk button mashed down. And... and ain't that Jap letterin'?"

All four men probably had the same thought at the same time. However, as much to his surprise as to anyone's, it was Art Turner's mind that first formulated the thought and acted upon it.

"Birddog!" he shouted, grabbing at both Tank and Decker and heaving them all to the side. "Infiltrators!"

As if to prove him correct, the already voluble night was further disrupted by the rapid-fire of half a dozen automatic weapons.

Chapter 16

10 miles off Aola, Guadalcanal
– 2225 local time

"Forty-five feet," Chief Brannigan said from the diving station.

"Close main vents," Nichols called down from the conning tower. "Helm, all ahead standard. Chief, give me full dive on all planes until we reach two-hundred feet."

"Should I blow negative?" Brannigan asked nervously.

He was trained for this, yet this was the first time he'd ever been both JOOD and diving officer and on a real dive. He'd done a few trim dives for practice, but now this was the real deal.

"Not yet," Frank said. "We may have to go deep, so there's no sense in dilly-dallying."

Elmer Williams and Pat Jarvis shot up through the hatchway. Jarvis went immediately to his TDC, and Williams came to stand beside Nichols at the scopes.

"What's the story, Frank?" The XO turned skipper asked.

"The task force turned east and started firing stars," Nichols reported. "Then our SJ sweep caught a broad-spectrum return."

"Assessed air search radar, sir," Torpedoman Peter Griggs replied from the radar gear.

"So I ordered a hard dive," Nichols continued. "And battle stations torpedo... just in case we needed or wanted to take somebody out up there."

"Active pinging!" Chet Rivers, who'd come up after the officers and slid into his customary place, reported. Torpedoman's mate Paul Baxter, who'd been taking his trick at the gear, made as if to move away, but Rivers held him back. He pointed to a second set of headphones. "Low freq as of now... and I'm getting the task force's returns, too. Still nine thousand yards off and coming abaft the beam."

"So they probably haven't spotted us," Jarvis opined.

"How long have they been pinging?" Williams asked. "And how many ships?"

"All four, sir," Rivers stated. "But far as I can tell, they seem to be staying in their formation... ain't that right, Paul?"

Baxter frowned and then nodded, "I'd say so, Chet."

"As for how long, they just started right as we dove," Rivers announced.

"One-five-zero feet!" Brannigan called up from below.

"Yeah, but sir," Baxter interjected, "They been goin' active every half hour or so... so this could just be a precaution as they make their turn."

"Well, either way, let's not give them much to hang their hats on," Williams said. "Helm, slow to all ahead one-third. Chief, blow negative to the mark. Level us off here and let's see what our friends upstairs do for now."

"Sorry sir, I was..." Nichols fumbled uncertainly.

Williams put a hand on his shoulder. He found it strangely odd how much easier it was to quell another man's uncertainties than to deal with his own. Odder still, he realized that by reassuring Frank, he was also reassuring himself. He smiled at his engineer, partly out of comradeship and partly because he understood that Art Turner knew this was exactly what would happen.

"Don't fret, Frank," Williams said. "You're doing fine. Nothing wrong with being conservative in a submarine."

"We gonna attack, sir?" Wendel Freeman, now standing at the DRT and chart desk, asked.

Williams pondered, "I'd sure like to. The trouble is that we *can't* sink all four ships up there. The minute we attack, we lose our advantage. They'll know we're here and might hunt us relentlessly. Even should we sink one of them, they can do active sweeps around the island, send up aircraft... make our lives miserable... maybe impossible for us to stay on station."

"They could do that anyway," Jarvis pointed out.

"Yeah, but if they're *certain* there's a Yankee sub prowling around, they'll do all they can to protect themselves and either chase us off or blow us outta the water," Williams bemoaned.

"Nearest target is seven thousand yards, bearing one-two-five," Rivers reported after a few minutes of silence. A silence in which the very faint and distant *oooo-eeee...* of low-frequency search echolocation could be heard through the hull. "Light slow screws, assess the submarine, sir... wait... something's happening... I think the fleet is breaking formation."

"Speed increases on two of the light, fast screw ships!" Baxter exclaimed. "Bearings are changing, too!"

"Uh-oh..." Jarvis muttered.

"Either they can hear us, or they're getting more aggressive," Williams said. "Hey down there... Chief, twenty-degree down angle on the stern planes. Find me a layer if you can."

Above and several miles to the east, Ryu Osaka was having to wrestle with his demons. Unlike everyone else aboard the carrier, with the exception of Sato, he was certain that the brief radar contact they'd made was *not* the distant mountains but a low-profile surface ship... a submarine.

Sato was sure, but his surety was more that of a man who *wanted* to be sure without the actual data or the experience. Not a bad thing in such circumstances, Osaka had to admit. After all, it was better to be paranoid and *assume* an enemy boat was lurking out there in the darkness... biding her time to strike at the perfect moment... than to arrogantly assume they were safe.

Yet Sato wasn't a submarine sailor. And for all the new *Sakai's* anti-submarine equipment, neither was he seasoned at this sort of work. He might blunder about blindly and never find the American submarine that was surely near them.

Osaka, however, had such skills and experience. And the men around him, those that mattered, knew it. He *could* simply stand back and say nothing... yet that might cast him in a paltry if not suspicious light.

Once more he had to pit his skills against the people who he was secretly trying to aid. He must use his knowledge to aid his people, the people he loved. Help them to defeat the Americans, whom he neither loved nor hated... but on whom he hung his hopes for Japan's future.

"I believe that we have indeed detected a submarine," Osaka finally spoke up. He noticed that Hideki smiled when he did so.

Igawa turned away from the big chart table and grinned, "It is fortunate then that we have... what do our American friends call it? A... ringer... yes, a ringer on board."

Sato glared at Osaka. In his eyes there was a war going on. He was not pleased that Osaka had failed to report the sighting. In his mind, it lowered the commander's worth. On the other hand, Osaka was a submarine sailor, and his expertise was undeniable.

"You have a suggestion?" Sato asked tersely.

"Only if it is desired," Osaka said with equal tension.

"Perhaps if you'd reported this earlier," Sato began coldly.

"It would have made no difference, *yakuin*," Igawa said soothingly. "And there is no proof that Commander Osaka was wrong. It may have been a shadow. We deal with where we are now, not the past. Yes, Osaka san, please advise us."

"They will likely not attack," Hideki interjected. "Not with so much firepower up here."

"Not the point," Sato said. "If there's an American boat out there, I, for one, would like to sink them. One less problem for us."

"Then we need to expand our capabilities," Osaka said. "Order the *Inetu* and *Ragatsu* to begin an orbital course, using *Sakai* as the pivot point. Opening each circuit out until they achieve a five-kilometer radius, with each destroyer diametrically opposed to one another and traveling in the same direction. Then cycle back in toward us. Active sonar going the entire time. Order the I-123 to form up with us as close as they can. Beam to beam and maintain our speed. Perhaps fifty meters or less. If the Venturi effect from our hull's passage is too great at such close proximity, then we can slow down or increase the range... but the closer they are, the better."

"Why so close?" Igawa asked with honest curiosity.

"To mask their machinery signature," Hideki said proudly. "And so that even should our enemy use directed active echolocation, she couldn't distinguish the submarine from us so close."

Osaka grinned, "Precisely... very good, Omata... it will confuse them. They won't know where *our* submarine has gone."

Igawa nodded, "Make it so, *Yakuin*."

Sato moved to the observation bridge to speak with the signalmen there. He wouldn't try to explain the complex maneuver Osaka had suggested using the signal lamps, but he would have their signalmen alert the two destroyers and the submarine to prepare to receive a short-range radio transmission.

Sato then strode back into the control chamber and aft again to the radio shack, casting a flinty-eyed glare at Osaka. A moment later, he returned.

"Message sent," he reported. "I-123 will get close and then speak to us over a megaphone."

Several minutes went by. A signalman from the starboard signal bridge rushed into the compartment, "Sirs! I-123 reports unable to get any closer. They are perhaps seventy meters off."

Sato frowned, "Helm, reduce speed to one-third. All engines. Make turns for five knots."

The order was acknowledged, and the ship slowed. A moment after, the same lookout reported that I-123 was now less than fifty meters to starboard and holding station.

"Excellent," Igawa said, rubbing his hands together. "Now we see if we can find a needle in a watery haystack."

"With our speed reduced," Sato warned. "We make an easier target, sir."

"Sour bastard..." Hideki muttered only loud enough for his friend to hear.

Osaka schooled his face and said: "Perhaps... we're also more tempting. Our foe may be lulled into foolhardiness. Our ability to detect sound *is* increased as well."

"They're slowing down, sir," Rivers reported tensely. "No... not exactly..."

"Well, which is it, man?" Williams just managed not to snap.

"It sounds like the carrier has slowed down," Rivers said in momentary confusion. "And the destroyers have sped up and are moving off in opposite directions..."

"What about the sub?" Jarvis asked.

"Uhm..." Baxter muttered. "We had him... but I can't hear him anymore, can you, Chet? Maybe they stopped?"

Rivers frowned and then shook his head, "It sounded to me like they were moving toward the carrier. Now their screw noise is gone... assess they're right up against the carrier to hide, sir."

"Now passing three-hundred feet," Brannigan reported from the base of the conning tower ladder. "No halocline yet, sir."

"Very well," Williams intoned. "Let's keep them in sight... hearing... helm, right standard rudder. Rig ship for silent running."

Bull Shark began a lazy turn to starboard, moving in a wide arc that would eventually put her astern of the *Sakai* at both ships' current speed. With the ship now at silent running, a sort of mechanical quiet prevailed. There was the sound of equipment being worked, albeit very subtle. Yet the background noises of the air conditioning and ventilation systems went silent. Hydraulic power was shut down, and all planes, the rudder and acoustic sound heads had to be worked manually.

And outside, eerie in the ominous silence, the ghostly wail of sound beams echoed. Probing, seeking... ceaselessly plumbing the depths for even the smallest signal.

Then a new sound reached through the dark waters and began to slowly but steadily permeate the boat's hull. It was the sound of fast screws churning the sea and getting closer.

"One of the *Fubukis,* sir..." Rivers whispered. "From what I can tell, they're circling the central ship, banging away with active."

"Where's the carrier?" Williams asked.

"Bearing zero-nine-five... range four-five-five-zero yards..." Rivers said.

Baxter's face went ashen, "Hey Chet... doesn't it sound like..."

"Now passing four-hundred feet... salt layer, sir!" Brannigan softly called from below, triumph in his voice.

"Sir!" Rivers suddenly hissed. "We're driving right into that destroyer's path! Range one-one-zero-zero! Speed... twenty-five knots, sir!"

"Christ... this is gonna be close..." Williams muttered, crossing his fingers.

Oooo-eeee... ooo-eee... oo-ee...
Shoo,shoo,shoo,shoo,shoo...

"Fuck... fuck me..." somebody muttered.

Even as the sound of the screws grew enormously loud, nearly on top of them, the sound of the sonar beam began to attenuate. It seemed to stretch and bend and warble as it met the saltier colder layer and was dispersed and reflected. Everyone in the control room held up a fist and grinned in triumph. They were below the halocline.

"Four-five-zero feet," Brannigan announced.

Although the sonar beam was deflected, the crew could still hear the churning of the destroyer's screws as it raced overhead. Strangely, however, they suddenly grew faint and then stopped altogether.

"What the...?" Nichols asked.

Williams frowned, "Not sure... helm, all stop. Chief, hold our depth here."

The down angle began to shallow as the stern planes were set level and the bow planes angled slightly up. What small sound from the electric motors that could be heard through the ship's hull eased, and *Bull Shark* began to drift into a thick and heavy silence.

"*Inetu* reports that they may have detected... something," the radio technician said as he stepped from the shack.

"*May* have?" Sato asked with a frown.

"They cannot be certain, sir," the radioman stated. "A very faint signal and then... nothing."

"Another false alarm?" Igawa asked.

Osaka frowned and then looked at the tech, "Order *Inetu* to go silent. Cease echolocation, kill their engines. Quickly!"

The young man darted aft, and the other senior officers stared at Osaka.

"If the submarine is out there," Osaka said. "They may have found a salt layer."

"Then we've lost them," Sato groused. "We can't locate them with sonar."

"Perhaps not, although this isn't always the case," Osaka instructed. "Some haloclines are stronger or weaker than others. However, low-frequency sounds *may* be detected even through one. The longer the waveform of a sound, the easier it is for it to penetrate matter. Therefore, if the destroyer comes to a complete stop, and if the submarine commander is wise, he will also... then it becomes a waiting game. If but a few hundred feet separate the two vessels, then *Inetu's* sonarman may hear when the submarine attempts to move off. No submarine is entirely quiet, after all."

"And if you're wrong?" Sato asked.

"Then no harm is done," Osaka said. "Even if we lose them, the task force, but for *Inetu* moves off. We have many more opportunities to relocate this ghost submarine in the future. We will continue on while *Inetu* waits. Patience is what allows a surface vessel to win a submarine contest, Commander, not aggression, necessarily."

The three officers in *Bull Shark*'s conning tower exchanged bewildered glances. For nearly an hour, the boat hung motionless in the inky darkness at four-hundred and fifty feet. The mood throughout the boat was tense. The uncertainty, coupled with the forced quiet, had a way of eroding men's nerves.

"Did they move off?" Nichols asked after glancing at his wristwatch for the tenth time.

Jarvis and Williams exchanged questioning glances. Jarvis frowned and shook his head. Williams nodded in agreement before saying: "I don't think so, Frank. The salt layer wouldn't have attenuated their screw noise so quickly. No... I think they went silent and are sitting up there waiting for us to make a move. The crafty sons of bitches must have gotten *something* on us."

"So we just sit here and park our thumbs then?" Jarvis asked with a wry smile.

"Be my guest, pat," Williams quipped. "We have to be patient now... of course..."

"They can afford more patience than we can," Nichols said glumly. "They can't run out of air."

"Not a lot of good options," Williams sighed.

Jarvis leaned back in his chair and met Williams' eye, "Elmer, there is one other."

Everyone in the control room looked to Jarvis. Williams thought he knew what his XO was about to say and felt a fluttering in his gut. Jarvis' confidence made him bold... and bold men preferred action. Williams admired the trait, so long as it didn't get them all killed.

Jarvis drew in a deep breath, "We don't sit and wait. We slowly rise above the layer and listen. Chet and Paul and our good gear will tell us *something*. At least then we can make a decision based on some information... sir."

Williams chuckled softly, "Spoken like a man with brass castanets, Pat... but I can't help but agree. I don't relish sitting down here in the dark until we can hardly breathe, then coming up only to find that Nip bastard waiting to pounce. No... the *Bull Shark* just ain't that kind of boat. When told by one of his officers that circumstances weren't right for an attack, Napoleon responded, 'Circumstances be damned! I *create* circumstances. We attack!'"

A hushed cheer went up through the room. All except Nichols, who grinned crookedly and asked: "Didn't he end up *losing*, Elmer?"

"Shut up, Frank," Williams said as he laughed quietly. "Nobody likes a dead battery."

"Want me to take the dive station?" Nichols asked.

Williams pondered that for a long moment and then shook his head, "It's still your watch, Frank. You're officer of the deck. Give the orders."

Nichols drew in a breath, "Brannigan, pump auxiliary tanks to sea. If that doesn't give us a positive buoyancy, then slowly... I mean *slowly*... begin using the two-twenty-five to push the water from safety and what's left in negative."

"That'll make some noise, sir," Brannigan reported.

"I know... but we've got no choice," Nichols said and was reassured by Williams' nod. "The layer should mask us long enough to get the job done."

Every piece of machinery aboard the boat made some kind of noise. The trim and drain pumps, even though muffled for maximum sound suppression, still thumped audibly. Blowing high-pressure air from the manifolds into the tanks made a detectible hiss. There was just no way around it.

The pumps, at least, could be regulated. They could run more slowly so that pushing water out into the open sea could be done quietly, if not quickly. It took nearly ten minutes then to pump the auxiliary tanks to sea. The boat did begin to rise, but so slowly that it would take days to reach the surface.

Two-hundred- and twenty-five-pound air was then forced into the partially empty negative tank and the full safety tank. At four-hundred-and-fifty feet, the exterior water pressure sat at just under one-hundred and ninety PSI. Just enough of a difference for the air to force the water out. The depth gauge needle above the helm began to twitch and move visibly.

"Looks like we're positive, sir," Brannigan reported, his head popping up through the hatch like a prairie dog. "I calculate a foot per second."

"Good," Nichols said. "Good, that's nice and slow. Let me know when the bathythermograph stylus stops jinking, Chief."

Once again, the men of *Bull Shark* had to sit and wait. Yet this waiting was of a different quality than before. It held an expectation. A tautness that would continue to mount until something happened.

And that something, and something spectacular, *would* happen wasn't even in the slightest doubt for any of the seventy men aboard.

Chapter 17

Deep in the jungle

"Kill them lights!" Decker roared.

The Marine Raider commander had been impressed by how quickly the submarine captain had reacted. As the three of them fell to the muddy gravel, Taggart ducked down low and scrabbled across the mouth of the trail and to his original position.

Decker was not pleased that their only cover was the pile of precious supplies they'd brought ashore. Brought ashore with a great deal of effort and no small amount of peril to every man on his team.

"The fuck's goin' on?" Chief Duncan's voice called out from the vicinity of the tents.

"We've been betrayed!" Decker shouted. "One of the islanders led a patrol of Japs to our location! Arm yourselves and stay down, for Christ's sake!"

Their only advantage was that it was pitch dark. The low heavy rain clouds completely obliterated the meager light from the moon and stars, and Decker couldn't see his hand in front of his face. He could *hear*, though, and in spite of the rain, he could clearly hear the discharge of six Arisaka rifles coming from the trail.

That was one more advantage. Unless the Nips hacked their way through the jungle, they'd have to come at the Raiders through this one narrow choke point. Their own element of surprise had already been neutralized by Turner, so it would now be a slog-fest. Who's blind shooting would kill the other team's men first.

Taggart and Tank were already firing. Both men had their weapons set to automatic fire, but both were using strict fire discipline and shooting in short bursts. Decker wasn't surprised by Oaks, of course... yet he was once more impressed by the sailor's discipline and cool-headedness under fire.

Suddenly from out of the watery darkness, another man scrambled up and slid onto his knees, "It's Hazard."

"Where are the others?" Decker snapped.

"I sent the chief, Lider and Oaks over to Taggart," Hazard said. "Dutch, Ingram and Entwater I told to stay low and move north along the ravine. What the hell's goin' on?"

Turner, who'd taken it upon himself to pinion Panota's arms behind his back and push him roughly to the ground, growled angrily: "This little bastard somehow found us. He had a two-way on him with the talk button pushed down so he'd transmit. The Japs must have used their own radio to home in on us. Sounds like six of them out there, trying to work up to us."

"Could be more," Decker added. "It *sounded* like six rifles, but it could be that some men haven't' fired yet in the rear. Could also be only three or four Japs out there."

"Good point," Turner said unhappily. "So we could be facing down three Japs or a whole goddamned platoon."

"Welcome to the jungle, Captain," Decker scoffed.

Turner snorted derisively, "It gets worse here every day... and it's only been one. So what do we do now, Davy Crockett?"

"Might have to send a fire team out there and work in closer," Decker said. "Use their muzzle flashes to home in."

Just then, a sustained automatic burst shattered the stormy night.

Dozens of rounds sizzled through the brush, and quite a few thunked into the crates that were the six men's only refuge.

"Dammit!" Turner grumped. "They keep shooting up the cargo and we might as well just go home."

"I'll go, sir," Hazard said, addressing both the other officers. "This is my kind of fighting... or used to be. I'll take Lider with me. Couple of southern boys like us are used to the backwoods."

Decker frowned, "Okay, Porter. Good man. *LIDER!*"

A moment passed by, and the Alabaman slid into their little circle, "Sir? We can't see nothin' over there. Maybe a couple of muzzle flashes... but I don't know..."

"You and Hazard are gonna work your way through the brush and get up to the Japs as close as you can," Decker ordered. "Stay low and try and be quiet, although I know that's practically impossible. Least the rain will help cover you."

Suddenly, a memory struck Turner and he reached out and gripped Decker's wrist briefly, "Al! Back in early May, when we were on our way out from New London, we met up with a couple of Jap destroyers. I noticed something odd about them. Whenever they'd fire off their five-inch guns... there were no muzzle flashes."

"Some kind of flashless propellant?" Decker asked.

"I think so," Turner said. "Now, I don't know if that's something they can use in a rifle, but..."

"Have to chance it," Hazard said as another burst flew mostly over their heads. "Sounds like they're less than a hundred yards down the trail, but maybe packed in."

"How many are there, asshole?" Turner growled, cranking Panota's arm up behind his back and eliciting a howl of pain. "Answer me, fucker!"

"I... I no savvy!" the young man pleaded. "Naponapo captain come and 'e say I find American soldiers. He savvy radio and say I no find, they kill altogether at Talisi mission!"

"Jesus Christ..." Hazard spat. "How the fuck you s'posed to fight a war and help the natives when the natives go all Benedict Arnold on ya'?"

"Very carefully," Decker cranked. "Like you two are gonna be. Now get movin' and stay low."

"Okay, but don't shoot us in the back, sir," Lider tossed off as he and Hazard crawled past Tank and into the thick underbrush.

"Hey, what about that grenade launcher you guys used this afternoon," Tank said as he aimed at where he thought the trail went and emptied his magazine.

"Almost forgot about *that* little toy," Decker chided himself. He turned to call over to the other group of men ten yards away. "Who's got the M1?"

"I got it, sir!" Oaks shouted.

"Well, then send our friends a care package, for Chrissakes!" Decker shouted back.

"Can't see for shit," Oaks retorted.

"Aim for the sound," Decker said. "Don't much matter, it'll make a point, I hope."

"I think the rain's slackening," Tank said as he slapped home a new mag. "Might get some light in a bit. Isn't that wonderful?"

"Oh, it's dandy, Tank," Turner replied. "Then all the slants in the bushes will be able to see us by moonlight."

"That's the spirit, sir," Tank chuckled. "Let them yellow pricks see just what they should be scared of."

There was a *crack, thump,* and a few seconds later, a bright flash appeared some way into the jungle. It was accompanied by shrieks of alarm. Oaks whooped in glee.

"I think I got 'em, sir!" he stated. "Leastways I scared the rice puddin' out of 'em."

"Great, Sarge, now give 'em another!" Decker hollered.

This was followed by another volley from the enemy. They were most certainly moving closer.

Oaks cried out in agony, and his major's heart leapt into his chest when the noncom exclaimed: "I'm hit! Oh fuck! I'm *hit*!"

"Here, watch this piece of shit," Turner stated and lunged away from the cover of the stockpile before Decker could even open his mouth to protest. Turner scrabbled on elbows and knees to where Oaks' voice had come from. Tank was right, the torrent of the thunderstorm had slowed to a steady soft rain, and now that Turner thought of it, there hadn't been a flash of lightning in several minutes.

Yet, it was still pitch dark with the overcast. After several minutes of praying, he'd gone the right way, the submarine commander bumped into something. He reached out and felt Oaks' body lying prone in the mud. He also felt the hard shape of the Springfield, which he quickly slung over his back.

"Oaks, it's Turner! Where are you hit?"

"Ungh... my leg, sir... and shoulder..." the Marine rasped, clearly in agony.

"Can you move?" Turner asked as another burst of rifle fire lit off from the jungle. He could have sworn that he felt the passage of the rounds directly over his head.

"Don't... don't think so, sir... send another pineapple downrange, sir... distract the fuckers..."

Turner would rather just get the man back to the relative safety of the stockpile, but the Raider sergeant was likely correct. Turner unslung the rifle and inspected the grenade attachment. He then fumbled around for a grenade on Oaks' bandoleer.

"Ever toss a grenade, sir?" Oaks gasped.

"Yeah," Turner said. "Been a while, though."

"You gotta hold the handle down and pull the pin," Oaks instructed shakily. "Then slide it into the barrel of the launcher. The tube holds the handle down. Then you just aim and fire... only thing is, though, sir... you gotta kind of put the butt of the rifle on the ground. Try and shoulder it and you'll be sorry when that launcher kicks."

"Okay..." Turner said, yanking out the pin and quickly seating the bumpy explosive into the launch tube. "How far would you say they are?"

"Uhm... fifty yards maybe?" Oaks replied. "Gonna have to use high elevation. Thing has a range of almost two hundred yards. My first shot... ungh... was about thirty degrees elevation."

"No problem," Turner said. "We sewer rats are good at that kinda shit... okay, here goes nothin'..."

The long gun bucked as Turner pulled the trigger and the shell propelled the grenade up and away. He tossed the weapon as hard as he could in the direction of Decker and Tank, almost laughing out loud when he heard Decker curse. Then Turner helped Oaks to sit up, threw his good arm across his shoulder and bent low.

"Hang on to me tight," Turner instructed. "Like a piggyback ride only horizontal."

The brief explosion acted as a small lightning flash. In the half-second or so that Turner could actually see anything, he caught a brief glimpse of the stockpile and started to crawl.

The distance was only about thirty feet, yet it felt like a mile. Oaks was having a hard time hanging on. Turner hadn't had time to inspect the man's injuries and wondered how much blood he was losing. Each time he crawled forward, the captain would have to reach back and help Oaks to adjust and stay on his back. Finally, he stopped and helped Oaks to his knees.

"What're ya' doin', sir?" Oaks asked dreamily.

Turner ignored the question, put his shoulder under the man's armpit and an arm under his crotch and heaved them both up, leaning half-forward to spread Oaks's weight across his back and then half-ran, half-stumbled to Decker's position.

Turner collapsed to his knees and laid Oaks out on the ground as gently as he could, "Light!"

A flash clicked on, and both Turner and Decker inspected the sergeant's wounds. Both the left side of Oaks' BDU blouse and his left trouser leg were dark and slick with blood.

"Where's what's his face?" Turner asked as he gently probed with his fingers.

Decker held up his .45 and met Turner's eye with a stern expression, "He's not a problem now."

Turner experienced a shudder of revulsion. Decker had killed the man almost in cold blood. Yet, almost immediately on the tail of that thought came the cold anger. This was war. Panota had betrayed them, no matter what his reasons, and now one of their own men was in danger of his life.

"Where's the first aid kit?" Turner asked.

Decker shrugged, "In one of the packs... probably in a tent."

"Swell..." Turner cranked, unbuckling and whipping off his belt. "The shoulder is bad, but I think this leg is worse. I'm gonna make a tourniquet with my belt. We need to find something to press into the shoulder, though. It's high up, above the clavicle, so I think it's relatively minor as compared to his leg."

The shooting from the jungle suddenly grew very fierce. A lot more than six weapons were firing now. To the Raider's ears, it sounded like twice as many, and several had the heavier, throatier sound of the .45 caliber Thompsons. There were a great many screams. Screams of fear, pain and anger. None were in English, however.

Then a sort of silence descended. It wasn't quiet, by any means. The soft patter of the passing storm, the now audible chatter of insects, birds and monkeys was hardly silence... but the lack of weapons' fire was stark by comparison to what had gone before.

Decker tore his blouse off and then his undershirt. It was soaking wet and sweaty, but it was also cotton, and he pressed it to Oaks' shoulder.

"Skipper!" Porter Hazard called out from somewhere in the jungle. "We're clear! And we got company!"

"Who's he talking to?" Decker asked bemusedly.

"You're in charge of this mission now," Turner said. "I'm just a useless sub driver."

Decker chuckled, "Says the guy who ran out into the line of fire, shot off a grenade and then carried a wounded man back."

"Gee whizz, it sounds kinda heroic when you say it," Turner quipped as he cinched the belt tight.

"Yeah, and crazy as a shithouse rat... Report!" Decker shouted.

"Can we get some light?" Lider's voice inquired.

All the men, including Taggart and Chief Duncan, activated their flashlights. After a minute or so, a group of dark figures emerged from the trail. The rain had now become a mere drizzle, and to the east and north, the clouds were breaking up, allowing a faint glow of moonlight to filter through.

It was enough for the men to see that Hazard and Lider were leading a group of six men into the camp. Six men dressed in a variety of ragged clothing and one man dressed in light-colored khakis. The man in the khakis had a red band around his middle.

"Vousa?" Turner asked.

Sergeant Major Jacob Vousa's smile gleamed brightly against his dark face, "That it be, sir."

"Who's your friend?" Turner asked.

"Captain Yoshi Hinto," Vousa said. "We captured him when we cleared the village."

"And you guys marched all the way up here since then?" Turner asked.

"I know a shortcut," Vousa joked.

Off Aola

"Anything?" Frank Nichols whispered to Chet Rivers and Paul Baxter at the sound gear.

Bull Shark had just risen above the halocline and was in isothermal water at three-hundred and ninety feet.

"Nothing sir..." Rivers replied softly.

"Like a graveyard out there..." Baxter added and then smiled ruefully at his ill-chosen simile.

"Pat," Nichols said softly. "Order both rooms to open their outer doors as quietly as they can."

The Cactus Navy

Jarvis had the sound-powered telephone set around his neck and spoke into it. After a moment he said, "Both rooms acknowledge, Frank."

"How about the task force; can you hear them?" Frank asked the sonarmen.

"Way off now," Rivers said. "Very faint at maybe... eighteen or twenty-thousand yards. I think two ships."

"That submarine could still be masking her screw noises in the carrier's," Williams opined.

"What we need is something that we can push out of a tube that makes some noise," Jarvis stated. "A decoy."

"Lot of stuff that would make sub warfare more effective," Nicolls said. "Wish Beau Ord would get their shit together."

"Christ, they can't even agree that our fish are no good," Jarvis cranked. "If we hadn't modified them, we'd never sink anything out here."

Williams sighed, "Yeah... funny ain't it? Tryin' to fight a war and the guys who are supposed to be helping us are making it twice as difficult... well, just think of how we pioneers will change things for the next war. Wonder what kinda toys our kids will have on their submarines?"

Jarvis grinned, "Hell, I don't want any kid of mine doing this shit. Rather them be something less dangerous like a cop or a firefighter or test pilot."

Everyone chuckled, but softly.

"What if we were our own decoy?" Frank asked.

"What do you mean, Frank?" Williams inquired.

"Well... we're almost four-hundred feet down," Nichols said, tapping his chin in thought. "Suppose that Jap is up there waiting and listening. What if we gave them something to aim at but then moved away so that by the time he gets over it and drops his ashcans, we're far enough out to fire a couple of fish."

"Sounds bat-shit crazy, Enj.," Jarvis said, wearing a crooked smile. "I like it."

Williams raised his eyebrows.

"We could burp some diesel oil or even a big air bubble," the engineer said.

"Done that before," Williams stated. "Off Cay Sal Bank. But in the daytime. They might not see the oil slick or the bubble bursting."

"Maybe not... but what if they *heard* it..." Chief Brannigan's head expounded from the hatchway. "We inflate a couple of Mae West's, right... and then load them into the escape trunk in the forward room..."

William's eyes lit up, "And then open the outer hatch while it's full of air. There's your bubble. But when it breaks the surface, it bursts and then the life jackets pop, on account of the pressurized air expanding."

"Yeah, but we're at normal air pressure in the hull," Jarvis pointed out. "The life jacket will simply compress and then expand back to normal if we just let it out."

"Unless we blow them up with compressed air," Nichols stated, doing some rapid calculations in his head. "We pressurize the forward room to about one-twenty-five. We have the guys inflate the Mae West's manually, with the compressed air in their lungs. Load 'em into the trunk, bring the pressure back down in the boat and then let them go. They ought to burst close to the surface anyway."

"Brilliant," Williams said. "Except there's no way to make sure the life jackets pop on the surface, right?"

Nichols shrugged, "Don't have to. Even if they go off fifteen feet down, the pops should alert the *Fubuki*."

"Okay, let's see it done," Williams said. "Chief, start flooding the negative tank and level us off. We're gonna need to control our depth, and once we start moving, we can plane up."

"We'll need to send somebody forward to manage all this," Nichols said. "Plus, figure a way to get the escape trunk open. It operates manually. I think that should be me, sir. You can handle the attack."

"Nope," Williams said. "I'm gonna do what Art's done for me. I'll handle the approach; you handle the attack. Pass the word for Chief Weiss."

A few seconds later, the chief yeoman popped up through the hatch, "Sir?"

Williams quickly explained their scheme, "You're a math whiz every bit as good as old Frank here, Yo. You can figure out the numbers. Go forward and see what you can do and let me know."

Weiss frowned, shrugged and smiled thinly, "Yes sir."

The yeoman, whose duties usually amounted to office work, was excited to find himself doing something more interesting. Yes, he had helped with plotting parties and such. His head for numbers worked well for that type of work. Of course, like any man who made chief aboard a boat, Weiss had his silver dolphins. He could stand at any station... but the opportunities were usually not there. Not until he'd come aboard this boat, of course.

He ducked into the forward room to find the men there mostly sitting idle on the deck, on empty torpedo skids or in their racks. Eugene Parker's tall, lean frame was standing below the JP sound head's manual wheel. Tommy Perkins and Perry Wilkes, the room's second and third petty officers, were down in the bilges operating the JK heads. Walter "Sparky" Sparks stood between his gleaming torpedo tubes, a half-burned Camel dangling between his lips and a hard look in his eyes.

"You look like you lost a fin and found two bits," Weiss joked as he walked over to Sparky.

The big torpedoman's mate scoffed, "Never been real good at this fuckin' waitin' game, Chief. What can I do ya' for?"

Weiss quickly explained the plan that the men in the conning tower came up with. Sparks all but inhaled the last of his butt, lit another and shook his head.

"In all my years in this man's Navy," Sparky muttered, "I ain't never been on a boat whackier'n this'n here. The day we actually run a textbook attack will be the day I know the world's gone ape shit... okay, only problem is that the way the trunk works is that the dudes inside gotta open the outer hatch once the chamber done fills up. So how'n hell we gonna do that from in here?"

"Well, that's dumb," Weiss stated. "Why don't they build in a backup mechanism so it can be operated from in the room?"

"Christ, Clance," Sparky grumbled. "I'm just a simple workin' Navy man. Why the Navy does anything is beyond my pay grade... but okay, let's see... Grigsy, close the hatch and the flappers. Jonesy, you operate the salvage air. Okay, here's my thought on this shit show, Chief..."

Weiss chuckled as he and Sparky began pulling inflatable Mae West life vests from a locker, "Once we're at pressure, we blow up four of these. Now, we're at three-seventy. Accordin' to the pressure gauge, the water pressure is about a hundred and fifty-five."

"Gotcha."

"Now, we gotta get that trunk hatch open and let the air inside and them vests float to the surface," Sparky pondered.

"Undog the hatch," Perkins said in his smooth surfer accent. "Undog it and leave it that way. The water pressure'll keep it shut. Bring the pressure in here up just under the outside and shut the lockout door. Then we tell control to start headin' up..."

Weiss's eyes grew wide, and Sparky hooted softly, "Then the high-pressure air'll pop that hatch when we go up a bit! Goddamn!"

Weiss pondered for a moment while he did the math in his head, "One-four-five is what we need, Sparky."

"Okay, Jonesy, put a hundred and forty-five pounds in here. Lemme go undog the hatch... shit, hope we ain't wrong in our calculations... Grigsy, tell conning what we're a'doin'."

In the conning tower, Jarvis' eyes widened, and he chuckled irreverently, "Forward torpedo reports the vests are in the trunk. Sparky has undogged the lockout hatch. When we rise fifteen or twenty feet, the pressure in the trunk will blow the hatch and send the air and vests topside. Probably make enough racket all by itself to alert the Japs."

The Cactus Navy

Williams cringed and looked to Nichols. The diving officer grimaced and lit a cigarette.

"Helm, all ahead one-third," Nichols ordered. "Diving officer, five degrees up angle on the stern planes. Everybody cross your fingers."

The submarine began to move, vibrating gently as her four big electric motors began to turn the twin propellor shafts.

"Maneuvering answering one-third," the helmsman reported. "Bendix log indicates three knots... depth now three-six-five... six-four... six-two..."

"Think that inner door on the forward escape trunk will hold once all that seawater rushes in?" Jarvis asked quietly.

"*Now* you bring that up?" Williams asked.

"Three-five-eight..." the helmsman read the depth gauge repeater at his station. "Three—"

From forward, a surprisingly gentle *pop* resonated through the ship. Nichols smiled with relief. The smile vanished in the next instant when a tremendous roar seemed to fill the entire boat as several hundred cubic feet of air blasted free of the ship, carrying the life vests with it. As the air vacated the trunk, seawater rushed in. It lasted only twenty-seconds or so, but compared to the quiet that had gone before, it was as if the world had exploded.

"Jesus Christ!" Williams exclaimed, a bit pale.

"Think the Japs heard that?" Jarvis jibed, wiping sweat from his brow.

"Pat, how's the forward room?" Nichols asked, visibly shaken.

A moment went by, "They're all right. The inner door held. Sparky requests a half dozen buckets and mops be sent forward, on account of everybody up there shit their pants, Skipper."

The quiet laughter was cut short when Rivers and Baxter both quiet-shouted, "Active sonar! Screw noises!"

"That got their attention," Nicolls said.

"Screw noises," Rivers reported more calmly. "Bearing two-one-five, range five-hundred yards."

"Okay, here we go," Williams said. "Helm, come left and steady up on one-eight-zero. Make turns for four knots."

"Pat, order after room to set depth on their weapons to four feet, speed fast," Nichols ordered. "Diving officer, fifteen degrees up bubble."

"This is gonna have to be a leading shot, Frank," Williams said. "We might not have good data. But assuming the DD runs right for the location of our sounds, we can fire a pair of fish to intersect them."

Nichols bit his lower lip and turned aft, "Can you do that, Pat?"

Jarvis was already working the torpedo data computer, "Pretty straight forward... or afterward... Frank. I'll give the fish a two-degree spread. If I can get some sonar data..."

There was a sudden rapid series of pops that echoed through the ship. Although faint, they sounded like small firecrackers going off. Rivers grinned.

"That was our vests," he said. "Directly astern... about a hundred yards. The DD is moving at twenty knots, and I think straight for it."

"Let's see..." Nichols calculated. "Ten yards per second... it'll take him fifty-seconds to reach that bearing... and we'll have gone only another hundred yards... not far enough for our fish to arm, dammit!"

"Helm, increase to full," Williams ordered.

"Pat, you'll have to fire the fish with a minus ten-degree gyro," Frank said. "Aim for where the DD will be ten or fifteen-seconds after it passes the bearing of our noise."

"Lotta guesswork to waste two fish on," Williams complained.

"Bendix log indicates eight knots," the helmsman reported.

"Let's just hope the *Fubuki* is too busy pinging to hear the noise we're making now," Nichols said. "Okay, Pat, you about ready... ten seconds to firing..."

Jarvis grimaced and worked his dials and quickly, "Okay, I've got a solution."

"Standby to fire nine and ten," Nicolls stated. "This is gonna be close..."

The churning of the DD's screws could be heard over the high-frequency echo ranging astern. Nichols was pumping his fist, and his face was a rigid mask of concentration.

"Fire nine!" he said, still counting and then after six-seconds. "Fire ten!"

As the two fish were ejected by huge fists of compressed air, the deck below Nichols' feet shuddered. All the men had to work their jaws to clear their Eustachian tubes as the boat's internal pressure rose with each shot.

"Both fish fired electrically," Jarvis reported.

"Both fish running hot, straight and normal!" Baxter enthused.

"Helm, hard left rudder," Williams ordered. "All ahead one-third. Diving officer, bring us to periscope depth."

"What's he doing, sonar?" Nichols asked tensely.

"Still running on course, sir!" Rivers announced, sounding almost giddy with excitement.

"Periscope depth!" Brannigan called from below.

"Up attack scope!" Nichols ordered.

The slim scope rose, and he slapped the handles down, spinning to look off the boat's port quarter, "Christ, it's raining... I can hardly see—"

"Number nine passing through projected bearing now," Rivers interrupted. After a few seconds, he sighed. "Think we missed, sir."

Nichols was about to curse when something brilliant lit up his lens. He turned a bit more to his right, and there, in the magnified view of the attack periscope's optics, a brilliant white-orange fireball lit up the sea. In the incandescent glow, he could easily make out the big destroyer... or what was left of it.

The second torpedo had struck the ship directly amidships, coinciding almost perfectly with the sub-surface explosions of four depth charges. It blasted open a rip in the steel below the waterline and ignited two of the destroyer's boilers. This even larger explosion had set off the depth charges on her fantail and wrought mortal devastation. The entire rear third of the ship had been blown off, disintegrating even as it lifted from the sea. The bow section lurched, burned and immediately began to settle, rolling to starboard as its knife-like bow rose high into the night. Before the sea extinguished the flames and the darkness took her entirely, Nichols swore he could see tiny figures. Some were no more than dark silhouettes, and others turned into living torches but all tumbling from the ruined ship and into the sea.

"God help the poor yellow bastards..." Nichols breathed in awe as he watched.

"Congratulations, Enj.," Williams said, slapping Nichols on the back. "You just bagged your first Jap. Now put us on the roof, get the diesels going and let's exit the area toot-sweet before the carrier comes back to look for survivors."

"My God..." Nichols said in awe. "We really got 'em... I really got 'em..."

"Welcome to the club," Williams said, and everyone in the conning tower and the control room laughed and cheered in excitement, victory and relief.

Chapter 18

Honolulu, Hawaii – August 3, 1942
– 1130 local time

"I still don't understand how this little radio set lets us talk to somebody over two-thousand miles away," Joan Turner marveled.

"Yeah, it's nutty, isn't it?" Clayton asked. "I'm no technical expert... but as it was explained to me, the AM band, or amplitude modulation, has such a long-range because the radio waves bounce off the ionosphere, then back down to Earth and so on like a pinball machine. Long as they start with enough power, you can transmit all the way around the world. Course it gets a bit scratchy... but that's why you can listen to Jack Benny out here live from New York."

"So that's what this amplifier does then?" Joan asked, pointing to the humming box beneath the simple ham radio set.

"And the big aerial attached to the house," Clayton replied. "Ready to give her a whirl? Art and his Raiders should have made contact with Clemens by now. They started going ashore on Guadalcanal late on the second... ought to be set up by now."

Joan drew in a breath and activated the power switch. The tuner knob was already set to the frequency pre-set by Clayton and his team. The unit hummed, and a burst of static broke from the speaker.

Clayton grinned and adjusted the volume and another knob, "Okay, let her rip, Joanie."

"2X2L calling QR1Z... QR1Z, you out there, Joe?" she asked, trying not to sound desperately hopeful.

While she certainly wanted their mission to go well, her hope was more to hear the sound of her husband's voice. If Martin Clemens could respond to her, that meant that Art and his team had been able to locate him and deliver the radio equipment to allow them to talk. It might even be Art himself who answered. It wouldn't be Clemens, of course. They couldn't take the chance of having a conversation on an open channel in the event that the Japs happened to tune in. They would likely recognize his voice by then.

Everything would be made up, of course. The names, the coded questions and responses. In all likelihood, Joan would be conversing with one of the Marines or one of Art's crew to maintain the illusion of two Americans yakking innocently over the airwaves.

There was a heavy sense of disappointment that bordered on despair when no answer came. Guadalcanal was three hours behind... or ahead? Joan had trouble keeping track of how the international date line worked. In any case, it should be just a bit after sunset there and one of the scheduled times to talk.

"What's the date out there?" Joan asked Clayton by way of conversation and to mask her unexpected black mood.

He chuckled, "Christ... I think it's tomorrow night... the fourth... you all right?"

Joan sighed, "I just... I guess I just had a lot riding on this conversation tonight, Web."

He saw her eyes growing moist. He reached out and took her hand and spoke gently, "Hey... it doesn't mean we won't make contact. They might be setting up still... or having a smoke or something. Remember, they're out in the middle of a jungle. Could be a monkey ran off with the mic or something."

She smiled and chuckled a little, "Thanks, Web... sorry."

The Cactus Navy

"Nothing to be sorry about," Clayton stated. "It's okay to be human Joan."

She heaved a heavy and stertorous sigh, "I should be stronger... I'm a Navy officer now. Can't act like a flouncy girl."

Clayton chuckled then, "I don't know many people, men or women, who can claim more strength, Joanie. Feeling scared or sad or disappointed isn't a weakness. Christ, we're in the middle of a war. Who wouldn't feel bad once in a while?"

"Do you ever?"

He scoffed, "Me? Of course not... I'm no sissy."

She punched him lightly in the arm, and they both laughed. It felt good and helped to drive away some of her gloom. When the radio crackled and spluttered and a man's voice filtered over the speaker, Joan found her emotions once again soaring up the roller coaster.

"*...you 2X2L?*" the garbled voice asked.

Clayton made a few adjustments. The static, while not disappearing altogether, sunk into the background.

"Sure it's me... that you QR1Z?" Joan asked hopefully.

"*Hiya Mary,*" the man's voice came in much more clearly now. Joan was surprised to recognize it. While the contact codenames were Joe and Mary, the man on the other end of the connection was indeed a Joe. Joe Dutch.

"Hey there, Joe... how's tricks?" Joan asked, her heart pounding in her chest. "You guys make it to the Yankees game okay?"

"*Oh sure... parking was a pain in the neck, but we managed to find our seats,*" Dutch reported. Joan saw Clayton frantically making notes on a pad.

Joan laughed, "How was the stadium?"

A pause, "*Crowded! A lot more Orioles fans than I woulda thought. Pretty much a packed house!*"

Joe was essentially stating that they'd gotten ashore, although it wasn't easy. He reported that they'd managed to find Clemens but that there were more Japanese on the island than they thought. He then stated that even some of the Yankees' fans were rooting for Baltimore... meaning that some of the islanders were beginning to turn on Clemens and the other coastwatchers.

Joan glanced down at her own sheet of notes. Coded questions to ask and cleared her throat, "Have you guys met up with Phil and Don yet?"

A calculated laugh, "*No, although Jack has touched base with them. We're supposed to get together for brewskis soon... certainly before the end of this series anyways.*"

Jack was Martin Clemens. Phil and Don... all these names were taken from the Jack Benny show... were F. Ashton "Snowy" Rhoades and a man called MacFarlane. Both of whom were coastwatchers on Guadalcanal as well. While Clemens had occasional contact with them, the other men weren't able to get to him.

"Glad you boys are having a good time," Joan said.

"*Oh, it's swell here...*" Dutch replied ironically. "*Oh, hey... Rochester wants to say hello, Mary.*"

Joan and Web exchanged a confused glance. There were no provisions for anybody named Rochester... although it did fit in with the theme.

"*Hi Mary.*"

Joan's heart leapt into her throat at the sound of her husband's voice. The tears that she'd been holding back now burst like a dam. Somehow, she managed to keep the quaver out of her voice when she replied: "Oh, Rochester! It's... it's so good to hear your voice."

"*You too, Mary... how's everything back on the farm?*" Turner's own voice wasn't entirely level.

"Good...good. We miss you," Joan half whispered, so overcome was she.

"*Me too, baby... me too.*"

Clayton tapped his watch and smiled apologetically. Joan cleared her throat, "Well, I know it's way after midnight in New York... so I should let you boys rest. Don't fill up on too many hot dogs and peanuts at the ballpark, okay?"

A soft chuckle, *"Oh, don't worry... the stadium says they're running low on red hots. Apparently there's some kind of war on or somethin'."*

Although this joke did bring a laugh to both Joan and Clayton, Art Turner was actually reporting that their supplies were not sufficient for the duration. Yet the fact that he could joke about it was reassuring.

"Yeah, I think I read something about it in the papers," Joan said wryly. "Well, give my love to everybody... and mine to you, darling."

Art Turner had to bite down on his tongue to keep from blubbering. It wouldn't do for a high and mighty ship's captain to start sobbing in front of his men, Clemens's people, and the Marines. He forced a grin and squeezed the microphone so hard he feared he might crack it.

"Thanks, Mary... we all miss and love you too... especially me. Goodnight."

Martin Clemens switched off the set and squeezed Turner's shoulder, "She sounds champion, mate. A right fine woman."

Turner drew in a breath and tried to swallow the huge lump lodged in his windpipe. He managed to croak, "She sure is."

Clemens's small black hybrid dog of uncertain breed, Suinao, ambled up and leapt into Turner's lap. The dog was perhaps twenty-five or thirty pounds and had long legs for her size. She was friendly enough, and her wagging tail and sensitive amber eyes brought a smile to Turner's face.

Martin Clemens was in his middle-to-late twenties. In spite of the shaggy beard he wore so as to disguise himself, he was a handsome man. Tall and ruggedly built, Clemens exuded a courage and steadfastness that Turner had come to admire in the short time he'd known the man.

After Vousa and his men had arrived the previous night... or more accurately early that morning, Decker and Turner had gathered their men back together again. With the rain stopped and the threat of a Japanese patrol neutralized, they'd turned to the wounded.

One of Vousa's men had also been wounded. Evidently, when they'd come upon Hinto, the captain had fought savagely and managed to slice a spectacular wound in one of the men's arms with his sword. The islanders had bound it for the time being and made their way back toward Clemens' position. Then there was Oaks, whose shoulder and left leg had been brutalized by 7.7mm rounds.

The islander, Mevao, was in better shape than he looked. The gash in his left bicep, while long and deep, hadn't severed any major blood vessels. Fortunately, the medical supplies brought from *Bull Shark* hadn't been damaged. There were plenty of bandages, rolls of gauze, boxes of sulfa powder and mercurochrome. In addition to this, there was a full suite of surgical instruments and a fair quantity of sutures, needles and so forth. Perhaps most important of all were several hundred tablets of Prontosil, a moderately effective antibiotic. Finally, they had brought with them some of the new penicillin, which was a natural antibiotic and purported to be very powerful at fighting infection. A must in the damp and malodorous environment of a tropical jungle.

Mevao's arm had been cleaned and stitched. Oaks' shoulder had been patched up, and his leg cleaned, although it would need more than a simple stitching. However, they were able to stabilize him, get an I.V. going and used some of the penicillin to help his body fight the infection.

Not long after sunrise, Batu had returned with a large number of men. Together, they'd separated the freight that the team had brought ashore into roughly fifty-pound loads that the sixty men could carry between them. A stretcher had been rigged from the empty crates, and Oaks was carried by an alternating party of two on the five-hour hike that took the party along the riverbank and then higher into the mountains to the village of Vushicoru. Upon reaching this location, the sailors, Marines, Vousa's men and the carriers gratefully set their burdens down and a hearty meal was prepared for everyone, including the villagers, of whom there weren't many, and Clemens himself. The stoic British officer was overcome with joy to see

The Cactus Navy

American soldiers and sailors. He greeted them all heartily, and something of his wry sense of humor, which had been sorely tested over the last few months, returned.

"Blimey..." Clemens had said as he shook the American's hands in turn. "When Townsville said we were to receive help... they didn't say we'd be getting seven sailors and five Marines."

"Oh, you think it's too much?" Decker asked.

"Yeah, should some of us leave... y'know... just to make things sporting?" Turner asked wryly.

"Well..." Clemens drawled, laughing heartily. "You've got one bloke wounded... I suppose that's at least a nod to fair, eh?"

One of Clemens' official followers was a medical practitioner who'd worked at the hospital on Tulagi. While not a doctor, the man's skills were far superior to any of the Marines or sailors. He went to work immediately on Oaks. The shoulder wound, which had been a through and through, was cleaned once again and stitched. Then he used a local anesthetic to widen the thigh wound and remove the bullet that had lodged against the femur. Fortunately, although several bone splinters were removed, the thigh bone itself hadn't been broken. A cat-gut suture in the iliac vein, a saline rinse, a handful of inner and outer stitches and a course of penicillin and the man stated that the Marine would be on his feet again in a few days, if not particularly agile. It was also fortunate that Tank Broderick and Ted Entwater had the same blood type. Both gave a pint which was then pumped into Oaks to help him get a jump on replacing the blood he'd lost.

After that, Dutch, Ingram, Duncan and Entwater went to work on replacing what parts they could on Clemens' telegraph radio set. Tank set about examining any other electrical equipment and seeing what he could do. Clemens, Decker, Hazard and Turner went off a way to have a private conference.

"Let me begin by stating that I'm heartily glad you lot showed up," Clemens began, visibly enjoying the cigarette from the pack he'd been given. "Ah... haven't had a fag in weeks... anyway, jolly good show, coming ashore on that rough weather coast and all... yet I could've wished you'd been able to bring more with you."

Turner sighed, "I know, Captain... three thousand pounds sounds like a lot, but when you're feeding damned near a hundred people..."

"Not to mention what we lost during the attack," Decker lamented. "Not too much, thank Christ... but only twenty of the fifty gallons of gas we brought... some other damage to a few cases of canned food. Some of the clothing took a few rounds, too..."

Clemens grinned, "That doesn't signify, really. Good togs with a few air holes poked in sure trumps wrappin' yourself in palm leaves, what? Lord... these boots alone are a Godsend. Been trampin' about the bush on my own bare pins this past fortnight and more. The medical bits you brought, they'll last a while... but the food... any notion when the invasion is meant to happen?"

Turner and Decker exchanged glances and then sighed almost in perfect unison. Turner let Decker field that question, as he was the Marine.

"We don't quite know," Decker stated. "Possibly within a week, possibly less. We weren't told exact dates and times for obvious reasons. It was *supposed* to happen on the first... but logistics being what they are, the hope is within a week of that... we'll just have to see, I suppose."

Clemens nodded, "Right. Mum's the word, need to know and all that rot. Yet your team seems an odd bunch."

"What we could scrape together for both mobility and usefulness," Decker replied. "My guys are obvious. Young Teddy there is a crack gadget man. But you can hardly beat submariners for both ingenuity and skills. Got three electricians who can also work on motors, know something about comm gear and can shoot damned well."

Clemens grinned, "I'd give my right arm to mount an offensive against the Japs. Little yellow bastards have been multiplying over this island like the damned white ants... yet we're just so outnumbered it'd be foolhardy at best, I'm sure. And what of you, commander. What's a sub driver doing creeping round this tropical resort, eh?"

Turner chuckled, "I'm here as a command observer. Part of our mission, Captain—"

"Cripes, call me Marty," Clemens said genially. "We're going to get mighty cozy over the next bit, gents, and we might as well drop the formalities, if it's all the same."

Decker grinned, "I'm all for that, Marty. Then we're Art, Al, Joe and Porter."

"I'm the good lookin' one," Hazard quipped.

Turner grinned, "So my job is to assist you in your observations and then make recommendations back to the powers that be. To that end, we've brought you some gear to help you keep your teleradio going... but we've brought something else, too."

That's when Turner explained the ham radio set and the coded ruse of some people in the U.S. jabbering back and forth to save on long-distance charges. After their little clandestine call, the officers gathered outside of Clemens' little hut and shared a few cigarettes while the coastwatcher told the newcomers about his travails since the beginning of the year.

"Jesus, Marty..." Joe Dutch said in awe. He squatted down and began to scratch Suinao behind her ears, much to the dog's delight. "You ought to get a medal just for what you've done so far."

"Amen to that," Hazard put in.

"It's been a challenge," Clemens said in his inimitable British manner. "The bloody Japs fly over twice a day for hours in those seaplanes... more and more of late. In spite of our chaps and yours coming in and bombing every day. Can't tell you how many close calls I've had myself... blimey... just yesterday, in fact. Was down in the stream, giving myself a bit of a how's your father, when a Kawanishi all but scraped the treetops overhead. Was all I could do to climb out and get under something green before the bastard swung back round for a second gander. Your bloody Nip is a blood-thirsty brute..."

"This spot here, though," Turner opined. "Seems fairly safe. Although your viewpoint isn't so good in spite of the elevation."

"Struth," Clemens admitted. "We had to bugger out of Vungana last week on account of so many overflights. Capital spot, though, Vungana... when the mists clear, you can see for fifty miles and more. Clear view of Savo, Tulagi, even Florida Island. Palipao was better, of course. Lower down, but more suited to living. Had a right fine garden planted and such... Vungana, which I'll show you when we return, is a bit like a natural fortress. It sits on a sort of promontory of rock amidst a great precipice. Only a narrow path leads to what amounts to a patch of ground fifty paces across. Bit of a bother to get in and out of... yet quite defensible, as one might expect."

"But not from the air," Decker put in.

"Correct," Clemens nodded and puffed heavily on his Lucky Strike. "And while there's plenty of fresh water, it's a few hundred feet down, and one must go down, collect it and bring it back up to the station... in bamboo rods, no less. Quite enough to drink and cook with... but having oneself a smashing scrub down is right out."

"Sounds like that's where we need to go soon," Turner stated. "For several reasons. Not the least of which... is that I'm sorry to have to tell you, Marty... some of your folks here are working for the Japs."

Clemens sighed heavily and shook his head with a world-weary sadness that was plainly evident, "Aye... I'm aware of it. Can't be helped, really... bloody shame, though."

"One of your men, a young kid named Michael Panota was the one that led the Japs to us this morning," Decker stated, his face hardening.

"God help us..." Clemens intoned. "Such a shame. A good lad was Michael... worked with me as a liaison to the missionaries on the island. I don't suppose..."

"He's dead," Decker said still in that toneless dry voice. "I executed him, Marty. I know that's cold, but between his action and trying to guard him..."

Clemens face hardened as well, and he glared, but not exactly at

Decker. It was more an anger born of the horrible necessities of war. Finally, he closed his eyes and nodded, "Couldn't be helped, I'm sure. A tragedy... and what's worse is it'll hardly be the last to touch this island. I don't blame you, mate. I'm sure you acted for the best."

Decker's features softened then, and he smiled, a thin and grateful smile, "Thanks, Marty. I'm sorry all the same."

"Less said, soonest mended, eh?" Clemens said a bit more cheerily. "Well, it's getting on and I suspect we've got a busy day ahead tomorrow. By the by... I don't imagine you lads brought any of those pin-ups you Yanks are so proud of? Wouldn't mind casting these weary eyes on Rita Hayworth or Margaret Lockwood, perhaps? Haven't seen a blonde in an age, eh? Nudge, nudge?"

The men shared a hearty laugh and went off to catch what would be one of the few unbroken nights rest they'd get for quite a while to come.

Chapter Nineteen

"Right, then," Martin Clemens was saying as he, Decker, Turner and Hazard stood around his small table in his guest hut. Decker's map of Guadalcanal was spread out before them. "Here's Cape Esperance on the northwest, and here's Merao Island and Merao Sound which lies on the southeastern side of the island. There's at least one schooner hidden in the mangrove swamps there, of which I'm aware. That might be of some use should we find ourselves in need."

"To sail off?" Hazard asked dubiously.

"Last I heard from Mac," Clemens stated, "he was to try for the Sound, or even Talisi, where another boat is supposed to be moored."

"That's where that Panota kid came from," Decker stated. "Says the Japs came in and held the missionaries there hostage... nuns and all."

"Bloody yellow bastards..." Clemens growled. "Although I can't say I'm surprised, unfortunately... they seem to be crawling all over this rock of late... well then... this here is Aola, our former district office operations area. Held by Japs. Here's Coli Point, Lunga Point and the Lunga Road... all held by Japs. This is the Lunga River and the Tenaru River... and this spot here in between, this is where the airfield is going in. Right in between. Last I saw, they were making right fine progress, the swine... red clay and gravel runway. Should they finish that strip..."

"The Jap will control the sea lanes from Truck to Rabaul to the New Hebrides," Turner said tersely. "That's why we're here, Marty. That's why the Marines are about to come down on this place like stink on a monkey."

That got a round of subdued chuckles.

"Several things are needed then," Clemens opined. "First, we need to move this first-rate operation back to Vungana. From there, we can see all the way across the Channel and lay eyes on the airfield into the bargain."

"Which means a recon mission to make sure your former location is clear," Decker stated. "And we also need to get close. To scope the airfield and get a more exact idea of the whats and wherefores."

"Precisely," Clemens enthused. "I've got my people working on it... but I'm somewhat dubious of that now, what with Michael's actions and such..."

"That notwithstanding," Decker said, "we're here for a reason. And it's not just to drop off some new boots. We're here to make an assessment and recommend a landing spot, among other things. I suggest I lead a small recon party to this Vungana. We'll hump in some supplies so that should the location be clear, there's some things there when you arrive, Marty. Then we can work on moving your gear back. I'll take one of your locals with me. Somebody you're absolutely sure you can trust. That Batu fellow seems a good choice. Vousa does as well."

"Jacob Vousa's loyalty is beyond reproach," Clemens stated with certainty. "I believe the same is true for Batu. Then there's me, of course."

Decker shook his head, "Out of the question, Marty. You're far too valuable to risk. As you say, the Jap is all over this island, and we've seen that for ourselves. Not to mention the fact that we've had

The Cactus Navy

two run-ins with them over the past few days. They may or may not have reported to their bosses that some round-eyed devils are here... but it's best to assume they know. Whatever scouting we do, it's with small mobile fire teams. Three or four men. I'll take one team to this village. I've got three marines, so we can split them up into at least two teams."

"I've got men too, Al," Turner said. "Including Porter here, who's a former Marine himself."

"No such thing as a *former* Marine, sir," Hazard put in with a lopsided smile playing at his lips.

"I think Tank and the chief are certainly battle-hardened, Decker agreed. "Ingram though... that kid's a whiz with the gear. I'd hate to risk him on a scouting mission. Tank's a damned fine electrician, and the chief a crack gearhead, of course... but they've got more experience..."

"Don't count Doug out," Turner said. "I've seen him in action. He can shoot, and personally bagged at least one Jap floatplane during Midway... on the other side of that coin is your boy Entwater. He kind of reminds me of Ingram. Capable, but his head is definitely inclined toward the tech. Maybe those two we keep with the core team, including Joe. Like them, Dutch is a technical whiz... but he's not really a soldier. Not the type, I think. Got a good head piece and cool under fire... but..."

"Then there's you and me, Skipper," Hazard stated.

"The most expendable of all," Turner said wryly.

"You're not, Art," Decker shook his head emphatically. "You're the *least* expendable. A ship's captain and a sub captain to boot."

Turner chuffed, "Yeah, about as useless as tits on a bull as Porter might say. But I'm also here to make observations and recommendations... which means I can't sit around on my duff."

"Struth," Clemens agreed. "And good on ya', mate."

Decker drew in a breath, "Okay then... we got three officers, two Raiders and two hard-nosed submariners. Sounds like two fire teams with Art bouncing between. Me, Taggart and Tank. Porter, Lider and the chief. Each team can take either Vousa or Batu, unless you've got anybody else in mind, Marty."

Clemens shook his head, "I believe you're in the right of it, Al. Now see here... this is Tyvu point, about twenty miles east of the airstrip. We know for certain sure that the Japs have established a camp here. They've also massed some troops or at least a perimeter at the Matanikau River, west of the Lunga River."

"Those are the bookends our landing forces would need to worry about once they take the airfield?" Decker asked.

Clemens nodded, "Indeed. We don't have exact counts, but we believe there are nearly three-thousand Japs on this island... although the vast majority are construction workers and probably civilians and Koreans forced into labor. We must assume that at least a thousand IJA soldiers are here, however. Them and the *Riikusentai*... their Marines."

"Then we know what we need to do," Turner said, tapping the map. "First, we secure Vungana for Marty... and then we get in close to this Matanikau River and the airfield site."

"I'd like to scope Tyvu Point as well," Decker sighed. "But that's a hike and a half in this jungle. No way it could be done in a single day."

"It's about thirty miles from here," Clemens agreed.

"Through dense rainforest. Unless you go out onto the northern plains... but then you've got to contend with the Japs and the kunai grass... grows as high as a man sometimes and sharp as dammit. No, I think for the time being, we best focus our efforts on the airfield and any nearby positions. If I had to guess, lads... and I were to land... how many Marines do you think?"

"Not entirely sure," Decker said. "The First Marines including the First and Second Raider Battalions... the Fifth Marines as well... I think something like close to twenty-thousand men."

Clemens whistled, "Bloody hell... glad to see somebody is finally taking this seriously!"

"Some go to the other islands, naturally," Decker said, "but I

The Cactus Navy

think close to fourteen thousand are coming here. That should be enough to secure the airfield and establish a perimeter that the Japs won't be able to breach with a couple of companies."

"Righto... then if I had my druthers," Clemens stated, tapping the map himself at a point just to the east of the airfield location, "I'd put ashore here, on this beach. Good sloping shore, wide-open space past the tide line and not many places for your Jap to hide himself."

"We'll scope it," Decker stated. "All right, gents, time to roll up our sleeves and get to work."

"One more thing," Turner said. "What about our Jap captain? Since we've got this prisoner who's going to eat up our supplies... shouldn't we interrogate him? He might know something useful."

"Indeed he might, sir," Clemens said with a wicked gleam in his eyes. "You leave that to us. By the by... don't suppose any of you chaps speak Japanese?"

Decker grinned, "Oaks does. At least to a passable degree."

"So does Joe Dutch," Turner said. "Although I think not as well. He's been boning up on it ever since we were assigned to come out to the Pacific."

"Good show!" Clemens enthused, rubbing his palms together. "Then you lads trundle off into the bush, and we'll stay back here and plumb the depths of what wellspring of knowledge our *guest* may hold, what?"

When Chief Duncan and Sherman "Tank" Broderick entered the small hut in which Philip Oaks had been assigned to recover, they found that Dave Taggart and Charlie Lider were already there. The two Marines looked up, Taggart with a small but welcoming smile and Lider with a neutral expression. Oaks, for his part, grinned broadly and waved them over to his makeshift cot

"Mornin' Sarge," Duncan said cheerfully. "How ya' feelin'?"

"Like I'm no fan of the Japs," Oaks tossed off.

"Well, you're in a big club then," Tank stated.

"You guys heard the news?" Taggart asked.

"Lemme guess... Lana Turner, Veronica Lake and Betty Grable

are here and takin' a nude bath down in the stream," Duncan replied with a chuckle.

"Hell, I'd get up for that!" Oaks said and laughed.

"Nah, we're doin' some scoutin', the four of us," Lider said but with less good humor than the other men. "More Navy and Marine teams are headin' out into the bush again after breakfast."

Tank snorted, "Good thing we motor macs and electricians came along, huh Chief?"

Duncan only shrugged, "It's a livin'."

"It ain't a joke," Lider said coldly. "This is serious and dangerous business out here. Christ, we ain't been here hardly more'n a day, and we already got a wounded man.

One of *our* men. Maybe you clowns should start takin' this seriously."

"Jesus, what's up your ass this morning?" Duncan asked with slitted eyes.

"Take it easy, Charlie," Oaks said. "These fellas have shared the same dangers we all have. Proven themselves to be good Marines, too, I'd say."

"Yeah, come on, Charlie," Taggart prodded good-naturedly. "No need to get sore. We been pretty hard on these fellas, and they done real good so far. Shit, it was Captain Turner that ran out and got the Sarge here... so why not just lay off, okay?"

"Maybe he wouldn't be lyin' there with a couple of holes in him if we'd had a team made up of *just* Marines," Lider said. He made a rude noise and stalked out, shouldering past Tank on his way.

"And here I thought we were startin' to get along," Duncan sighed.

"Don't let him get to you, Chief," Oaks said. "I think he's just feelin' a bit guilty on account he wasn't on guard when the Japs hit. Just blowin' off steam. A good long, hot patrol will set him up."

"But hey, that ain't all," Taggart said with a lopsided smile. He switched on a bulky portable radio and extended the antenna. "Listen to this..."

Taggart switched on the set, and the tubes warmed up, catching a scratchy version of *Blues in the Night* by Woody Herman near the end of the record. After about a minute, the song ended, and a woman's voice began to speak.

"*Good morning my Yankee brothers, this is your Japanese sister, Tokyo Rose coming to you live with the real truth,*" the woman spoke in flawless English without even a hint of an accent. Her voice was low and husky, and it was easy to see why she was so popular with American servicemen in the Pacific, in spite of the poison she spewed. "*I'm sorry to have to be the one to tell you this, you brave but misguided sailors and G.I. Joes out there... but the facts can't be denied... your leaders are putting you men into terrible danger. You boys in blue out there in the American Navy, you're headed for a world of pain and suffering simply because President Roosevelt thinks nothing of pitting you against the superior forces of Japan. He sits back in his comfortable palace while you true-blue guys go out on carriers and battleships and especially submarines and commit war crimes without even knowing it.*"

Duncan swore under his breath.

"*This show goes out especially to the brave men of the submarine service,*" Tokyo Rose went on. "*Men who* bravely *sneak up on unsuspecting Japanese civilians and send them and their ships to a watery grave. Just last night, in fact, an American submarine* courageously *torpedoed an innocent and unarmed Japanese passenger liner in the Solomon Islands. Over two hundred civilians, including women and children, now sleep forever at the bottom of the sea... thanks to the brave men of USS Bull Shark. Well, Bull Sharks, this murderous deed won't go unpunished. The Imperial Japanese Navy will come for you. They don't want to sink you... but they have no choice because your insidious president is forcing you into this illegal war. So long, Bull Shark, and here's a little something for you to enjoy from your good friend Tokyo Rose...*"

"What the fuck...?" Tank muttered. "Passenger liner?"

Oaks scoffed, "That's her propaganda bullshit. Illegal war my ass!

Who bombed who? Nah, *Bull Shark* probably sank a destroyer or a freighter or somethin', and that bitch is just twisting it around."

"Wish she was here now," Duncan said. "I'd show her a much better use for that mouth of hers…"

"Wonder how they know?" Taggart pondered.

"Probably broke some of our codes," Duncan opined. "Like we have. That or it's just a guess. Interesting though… if there's even a little truth in her words… the XO bagged himself a Jap ship last night."

Tank scoffed, "Wonder what she'll say about us? Nothin' but a lousy fake aloo artist and a turncoat. Tokyo *Rose* my ass… She can kiss this sailor's bright, red rosy on main street anytime!"

Taggart chuckled, "I guess we'll see. Well, Sarge, we gotta grab some chow and hit the bricks. We'll check in on you later, huh?"

"Good luck, boys," Oaks said, sounding regretful. He didn't like having to lie around doing nothing while others… his men… put themselves in danger.

"What're you fellas up to this fine morning?" Turner asked as he walked up to where Dutch, Ingram and Entwater were crowded into one of the thatched-roof cottages. The men had the components of Clemens' teleradio set partially disassembled. The small charging engine was chugging away just outside the door, and the two new and two old batteries were wired into it.

"Trying to figure out a way to get more life outta these components, Skipper," Ingram said enthusiastically. "The vibrator is okay, but the receiver and transmitter seem like they short out a lot, according to Mr. Clemens."

"It's this damp environment," Dutch said. "Up here it's a little better. Not as hot and the humidity is tolerable, but still… down where he needs it it's like a damned sauna."

"Plus, that charging engine is kinda wonky," Entwater stated. "The chief helped us out with it. Had to sort of cannibalize parts from the old one and the one we brought to make something that's sort of… new-ish."

The Cactus Navy

"How do you mean?" Turner asked.

"Marty says that he'll put the electronic components under a table and open up the cases," Dutch explained. "Put a lantern right up against it to burn off some of the humidity. Works pretty well. Long enough to send and receive his reports... as for the motor, his old one was wearing out. But our new one got shot up last night. Managed to save the dynamo, spark plugs, crankcase and muffler from ours... but the fuel system's shot, one of the pistons is blown... so what we've got is better but hardly off the shelf, if you see what I mean."

Turner sighed, "Par for the course, I guess.... Listen, boys, most of us are headed out on a scouting mission. Marty has to get back to Vungana, his second-string observation location, if you will. It gives him a good view of the north side of the island and the others across the channel... but he had to bug out last week on account of heavy Jap flights and such."

All three men raised their hands to volunteer. Turner smiled and shook his head.

"Thanks, but we've got our teams already," the captain said. "Joe, I'm leaving you in command. The three of you need to get Mr. Clemens gear tweaked and ready to travel."

"Who's all going?" Dutch asked.

"Decker is taking Taggart and Tank," Turner said. "Hazard takes Lider and the chief. Each team has a local guide, and I go with one or the other."

"Shouldn't Mike stay here?" Dutch asked. "He's really our only true mechanic. And you sure as shit shouldn't go out there, Art!"

Turner chuckled, "Chief's good in a fight, and as for me... the whole reason I'm here is to observe and make reports back to headquarters to try and give them enough info to decide when and where this invasion is to be. If I sit back and stay safe, I might as well have stayed aboard the boat... nope, your favorite submarine hero is now a Marine Raider, intelligence specialist and a swell dancer, too."

That drew the laugh he'd hoped for. Yet in Dutch's eyes, Turner saw the concern was still there. He smiled at his friend and nodded in thanks.

"Don't worry, lads," Turner said cheerily. "You'll get your chance to go bush and get bitten by centipedes, shot at by Japs and gnawed on by crocodiles."

Ingram grinned, "Sounds ducky, sir."

"I did have an idea, sir," Entwater put in, sounding more animated than Turner had heard from the man since day one. "What we need is a vapor barrier of some kind... and I think the island has what we need. Do you think when you all come back from patrol you could bring back some coconuts?"

"Coconuts?" Turner asked in confusion.

"Yeah! I mean... yes sir..." Entwater said. "There aren't any palms up here, really. But down where you guys are headed there should be some... anyways, the fibrous husks, or coir, is a really useful material, sir. It's extremely buoyant for one. My thought is to strip out a bunch of it and have the villagers here weave some small mats and then put that inside the gear to act as insulation."

Turner was duly impressed, "Damn, Ted, that's brilliant."

"Not to mention the nuts are good for food," Dutch said.

"Also, the remaining husks make good beds for fires," Ingram said. "Read a thing in popular science not long ago about how when you burn coir it creates a smoke that acts as a natural bug repellent."

"Okay, I'm convinced," Turner grinned. "We'll bring back as many nuts as we can."

Dutch smiled, "Well, *all* you nuts better come back, y'hear?"

Turner grinned, "It'll be fine, Joe. We're just sending a bunch of white men out into a hostile tropical jungle filled with giant spiders, stinging insects, voracious lizards and blood-thirsty Nips... what could be saner than that?"

Chapter 20

USS Bull Shark – Northwest of Florida Island

August 4, 1942 – 0830 local time

Elmer Williams sat alone in the wardroom and sipped his coffee. Laid out on the table before him was a roughly drawn map of Guadalcanal and the surrounding islands. Written on this map were what at first appeared to be a random set of numbers written in pencil. Yet upon closer inspection, some order could be gleaned from the scribblings.

After the boat had taken out the destroyer, Williams had ordered the ship northeast and out of the immediate area. No doubt the *Sakai* and her one remaining escort, as well as the submarine, would reverse course and come looking for them. There could be no doubt now that an American submarine was prowling the waters of the slot.

Williams knew that he was playing a dangerous game. The submarine's skipper and some of her key personnel, not to mention half of her officers, were absent. She now had only eight torpedoes remaining in her tubes. Worst of all, *Bull Shark* was alone deep inside enemy-held territory and had, rather spectacularly, advertised this fact.

The baize curtain slid aside, and Pat Jarvis entered, yawning and rubbing sleep out of his eyes, "Mornin', Elm tree. Doodlin' again?"

"You know me, Pat," Williams said, sounding a bit weary. "Can't keep my mind on the job."

Eddie Carlson stepped out of the tiny pantry and set a cup of coffee in front of Jarvis, "Here you go, sir. Either of you gent's care for breakfast? Henrie's got pancakes and sausage this morning."

Jarvis grinned, "Sounds good, Eddie, thanks... course knowin' that crazy Cajun, the sausage is probably Andouille, and the flapjacks are probably sprinkled with cayenne."

"Yeah, I'll take something, Ed, thanks," Williams said a bit distractedly as he studied his sheet of paper.

"What's eatin' you, Elm?" Pat asked, leaning forward to study the map as well.

"Our current situation is not... comforting," Williams stated. "In a word, Pat... we're surrounded."

For the past day and a half, the boat had prowled the shallows around Savo, Tulagi, Gavatu and Tanambogo and Florida Islands. Both during the day and at night, the submarine had made careful observations of the Japanese activity there. The numbers on the sheet of paper represented, as near as could be determined, the number of soldiers on the islands as well as aircraft and ships. In addition, there was an X marked almost equidistantly between Savo, Tulagi and Guadalcanal marking the location of the strike carrier. They'd snuck up on the task group twice since their initial meeting, and the two surface ships had not moved. What was further distressing was that *Sakai* had now been joined by three other lighter destroyers.

Since then, the carrier had been sending up air patrols twice per day. That was in addition to the Kawanishi seaplane patrols from Tulagi and the occasional overflights by Jap Betty bombers, probably out of Bougainville.

"The area is hotter than one of Henrie's gumbos," Jarvis commiserated.

"Yeah, and it was me that stirred up the hornet's nest," Williams lamented. "I just had to be cute... had to pull some kind of crazy maneuver and sink that *Fubuki*."

The Cactus Navy

"Oh, come on, Elm," Jarvis said gently. "That was a world-class job. Hell, what else could you have done? That DD was sitting on top just waiting for us."

Williams sighed, "We could've gone deep, Pat. Might have found another layer and snuck away. Might have done that anyway. Even at a knot or two. Put a mile or two between us and then come up and engage them. Or just leave the area. Not pull some stunt with life vests and waste two of our fish."

Jarvis drew in a breath and pondered. For all his skill with both machines and people, Elmer Williams still had some doubts about himself. It wasn't nearly as deep as when he'd first come aboard, but Jarvis felt that Williams still needed a little seasoning.

Elmer was still dedicated to the book. To submarine doctrine that had been established before the war. And while he'd seen what an aggressive and creative commander like Art Turner could do, he perhaps hadn't been in the fire quite long enough to fully season.

Williams had missed their last patrol. A patrol in which they'd had to hunt down a Japanese super-sub, all while dealing with some rather distressing internal problems. He hadn't been there when the boat had plunged to over eight hundred feet, leaking like a colander. He hadn't been through the internal struggle that Pat had, where he had to override the XO and save the ship.

Yet now here was the XO once again returned to the ship and immediately thrust into a tense and unusual situation. He was suddenly the captain and had to make the big decisions. Pat knew it could be overwhelming... but he also knew that Williams had the knowledge and the grit to handle it. He just needed to stay in the fire.

"It's a war, Elm," Pat said gently. "Nobody promised it'd be easy. Not especially for us. When the Japs first attacked, our Pacific fleet was crippled, at least for a time. The only thing we had that could *immediately* be put toward an offensive effort were these boats. And you know as well as I do that the old rules, the pre-war book, isn't worth much of a *damn* out here. We need aggressive guys like Art Turner and Mush Morton. We need to toss the old book out and write our own new one. The Japs sure as shit ain't playing it safe or conservatively, are they? And now, for the first time since December, we're about to really push back! Not just defend ourselves... but go on the *offensive*, Elmer. We're gonna take these fuckin' islands from the Jap, and we're gonna *keep* 'em. Then, in a couple of months, we're gonna move up. Island by bloody island. And for right now, this boat and our guys on Guadalcanal are the keys to the whole shootin' match."

"God..." Williams breathed. "Was that speech supposed to make me feel better, Pat?"

Jarvis grinned, "It's supposed to light a fire under your ass, Elm."

Williams frowned, "I *will* fight the war to the best of my ability... it's just sometimes I don't know if that ability is good enough. I'm not sure I'm like you and Art, Pat. Not sure I'm really tough enough."

Jarvis shook his head, "Sure you are, Elm. I've seen it, and so has the skipper. You think you'd be in command right now if he didn't have faith in you?"

Williams sighed, "I'm no Anvil Art... he'd know what to do right now. Instead of sitting here and looking at this map and feeling overwhelmed."

Jarvis sipped his coffee and thought for a moment before asking: "And what would he do, Elmer?"

Williams grinned, "Probably charge the carrier on the surface and in the daytime, guns blazing and fish sailing outta the tubes."

Jarvis laughed, "Yeah... but what else?"

Williams frowned, "He'd be aggressive. He'd go after every ship that tried to supply or support Tulagi and Guadalcanal until every torpedo and every five-inch round was expended."

"So?" Jarvis prodded. "What do you think you should do, then?"

"It's not our *job*, though, Pat," Williams protested. "We're supposed to be out here staying hidden. Ready to support the captain and the landing force. Making observations. Clayton wants—"

"Let me tell you something, pal," Jarvis said sternly but not unkindly. "Webster Clayton isn't out here. *We're* out here. We're the front-line soldiers in the Pacific, Elm. We're the thin blue line between Tojo and our nation. You want my unsolicited advice? Toss the rulebook aside, put Clayton's wants and needs in the background and do what Elmer Williams thinks is best."

Williams drained his mug and considered his friend for a long moment. He nodded slowly and then grinned, "You're pretty sharp for an ignorant New England fisherman."

"Hey, I'm not just another pretty face," Jarvis replied with a wink.

"That's true."

Eddie returned with plates of food for the officers. As he set them out and poured more coffee, Williams snatched the phone off the bulkhead near his head.

"Control room, this is the skipper," he said confidently. "Have the quartermaster of the watch plot us a course to put us in the fifty-fathom curve northeast of Savo. We're gonna go kick some slope ass."

Both Jarvis and Carlson whooped and shook their fists in the air. They could all hear the hearty cheer that echoed forward from the control room.

"My, my, sir," Carlson said. "You sounded just like John Wayne."

"That's right, pilgrim," the XO replied in a very admirable John Wayne. "And just as soon as I finish my pancakes, we're gonna go and teach the yellow man a lesson."

It was just after 1500 when *Bull Shark*, traveling submerged at five knots, reached the general position that Williams had ordered earlier. Andy Post had the watch with the COB standing as AOOD down in the control room. Post found himself feeling a bit unsettled by the current state of affairs, although he endeavored not to show it.

This wasn't his first time standing a watch. Since the captain and the others had gone ashore, he, the COB, Chief Brannigan, Chief Weiss and even Sparky had been obliged to take their trick as watch officers. Yet something was different about this watch.

Lieutenant Williams, the captain pro-tem, had declared that they were gonna go and kick some Jap ass. That meant that the submarine would be going on the offensive and would soon be attacking *something*. With eight torpedoes remaining and a shitload of Japanese ships and planes all around, it made Andy Post want to keep his butthole clenched.

It wasn't that he was afraid to fight. He'd gotten over that a long time ago. It wasn't that he was afraid of the retaliation from surface ships. He'd been through enough depth chargings and shipboard emergencies that he knew he could handle things.

No, what troubled young Post was that he'd screw up at the worst possible moment. Captain Turner, and now the XO, had developed a policy aboard *Bull Shark*. In most submarines, it was the captain who took over during an attack. He'd handle the approach and setup, relying on the XO or the officer of the deck.

Yet in *Bull Shark,* things were different. Certainly, there were times when the skipper took over and handled the attack himself, yet Art Turner was as much a teacher as a warrior. He felt that his officers should get the chance to learn by *doing* and not just by watching. It was customary, therefore, that when an enemy ship was sighted and earmarked for an attack, the officer of the deck would handle the setup. He might even manage the approach as well. Although Turner liked to split those jobs up, thus allowing more men to practice and to learn to rely on each other and work more smoothly.

Andy had never run an attack before. He'd seen it done, heard it done... but never did it himself. He was often tasked as diving assistant, part of the plotting party or sent aft during a depth charge attack to his station in maneuvering. Now, though, the XO had decided to go on the warpath, and Post was worried that before the final hour of his watch was over, he'd be taking *Bull Shark* and seventy men into peril.

Hot on the heels of that thought, almost as if to mock him, Chet Rivers's voice broke the tense silence in the conning tower.

"Contact!" he said excitedly. "Heavy, slow screws bearing zero-four-zero... range sixteen thousand yards... turn rate... ten knots, sir."

Post swallowed and was at least grateful that the A-team was on watch with him, "How many, Chet?"

"Indeterminant so far," Rivers stated. "Sound is a bit muddy at this range... but I suspect more than one. I'm hearing at least two screws, and if they're merchantmen, they probably only have one apiece."

"Very well," Post said, outwardly cool as a cucumber, but inside the two ham sandwiches he'd had for lunch felt like a brick of lead in his belly. "Hotrod, station the plotting party. Bring us up to periscope depth. Mug, slow us to all ahead one-third."

Mug Vigliano acknowledged. Ralph Hernandez slid down the ladder to the control room to take over the plotting party.

"Periscope depth, aye," Buck Rogers' steady voice filtered up from below. The sound of it comforted Andy some.

"What's their heading, Chet?" Post asked after Rogers reported they'd levelled off at sixty-five feet.

"One-two-five, sir," Rivers reported. "Definitely two of them."

"When do we cross their track?" Post asked.

There was a delay, and then Hotrod called up, "We're about a thousand yards from their baseline course, sir. But we don't have any data yet on their zig-zag pattern."

"Helm, hard right rudder," Post decided, feeling butterflies again. They were still eight miles from the targets, which put them well below the horizon from a periscope sighting at that depth. Yet, Post knew that the approach to an enemy convoy was as critical as the actual shooting. "Steady up on course three-zero-five."

"Hard right rudder, comin' to course tree-zero-fiver," Vigliano replied, turning his wheel all the way to the right.

"Fiver?" Ted Balkley, acting periscope assistant and radarman, asked.

"Hey, fuhgetaboutit?" Mug replied genially. "We got a niner... so why not a fiver?"

Post chuckled, "You're a silly bastard, you know that, Mug?"

"Same thing my Uncle Aldo told me day before he committed suicide, sir."

"*Ay dios mio*... he killed himself?" Hernandez called up from below. "What happened?"

"He was so distraught that he owed five hundred dollars to the Banano family he stabbed himself in the back wit an icepick nine times then trew himself off the Chrysler buildin'," Vigliano deadpanned.

"Wow... you're *really* fucked up, Mug," Balkley muttered with a head shake and a chuckle.

"Can yiz' blame me?"

"Jesus Christ... we're all gonna die..." Post muttered, grateful for the banter. "Chief, you'd better sound the general alarm."

The cathedral bells began to gong throughout the ship, their fourteen-tone chime alerting everyone aboard that their magnificent fighting machine was about to do what she did best.

By the time the alarm had ended, Pat Jarvis was stepping up into the conning tower and sliding into his place at the TDC. Elmer Williams' head popped up through the hatch and smiled at Post.

"What've we got, officer of the deck?" The XO asked.

"Two potential freighters, sir," Post said. "I've altered course to intercept on a parallel. We're still figuring their track. Estimate twenty-six minutes to visual range."

"Very well," Williams said. "I'll go assist the plotting party and let Hotrod come up here and work the approach at the chart desk."

"Uhm... don't you want to manage the attack, sir?" Post asked. "Or determine if we *should* attack at all?"

"Why, you don't think you're up to it, Andy?" Williams asked with an arched eyebrow.

"Well... now sir... I mean, yes sir... it's just..."

"You're OOD, Mr. Post. It's your turn to dance with the one-eyed lady," Williams said sternly but with a twinkle in his eye. "We're short-handed, and I need every man to do his best... more than his best. You're in charge of the boat for the moment, so I'm leaving it up to you. England expects every man to do his duty, Mr. Post."

Post caught Pat Jarvis grinning out of the corner of his eye. Interesting, the grin wasn't only directed at him but down at Williams as well.

"Aye-aye, Admiral Nelson," Post said confidently.

"Atta boy," Jarvis said softly.

Not for the first time, Elmer Williams was intrigued by the thought of how much easier it was to reassure his juniors than it was himself. As if giving them the encouragement they needed somehow bolstered his own confidence. By helping others to conquer their own fears and doubts, his own seemed to diminish with each application. He knew how this worked, of course. Yet it still amazed him... and amazed him further when he understood that his own captain had figured this out long ago and applied it regularly.

Every time Williams lifted up a man under his command, he strengthened himself in the process. As he slid down the ladder, he caught Pat Jarvis's eye and knew that the other Lieutenant understood this as well and was somehow aware of exactly what Williams was thinking.

"Aspect change on targets," Rivers announced. "Turn rates staying steady but... they're altering course to starboard... new heading appears to be zero-niner-five."

Hotrod Hernandez stood at the chart desk with a maneuvering board in his hand. He made a pencil mark on the chart and then a note on his board. He also checked the dead reckoning indicator repeater and nodded.

"I think I've got an idea of their pattern," he said to Post. "But we'll have to see over the next few minutes or so to be sure."

In order to help them avoid submarine attacks, surface ships would often zigzag off their course. By continually changing their heading, it made it difficult for an enemy submarine to calculate the correct torpedo angle so as to ensure a target and a weapon met. However, over time, a submarine could observe the target and, by carefully tracking their movements, establish both the base course upon which the ship was traveling as well as their pattern of evasion.

With enough data, the attacking submarine could predict where a ship would be several minutes in the future and therefore be able to place a torpedo in its path. This was tricky out in the open sea, yet among the many islands of the Solomons and having a clear understanding of a ship's destination, the problem was simplified somewhat.

The two freighters or tankers were doubtless heading toward Tulagi or even Guadalcanal. Their general direction made that clear. If Hotrod and the plotting party had enough time, they could observe enough zigs to establish a hard pattern and then Post could position his submarine for the final attack.

"Range now ten thousand yards," River stated. "And... yes... I'm getting a third contact, sir. Now that the convoy is more bows on to us, I can tell there are definitely two single-screwed merchant ships... and one set of fast, light screws. Assess enemy destroyer escort."

"So, the game is afoot, eh?" Williams muttered from his position at the master gyrocompass and chart table.

"Should we bag it, sir?" Post called down.

Williams briefly considered this. It would take a minimum of four torpedoes to sink the freighters. It was possible to do it with one, yet there was no guarantee. That would only leave the *Bull Shark* with two forward and two aft. Yet two fat merchantmen were tempting targets. No doubt filled with vital war and construction materiel that the Japs couldn't afford to lose.

"No, Andy," the XO finally decided. "We can make a final judgement when we sight them... but sinking two supply ships may be worth a great deal to our invasion force when they arrive. Forget the DD, though. Only the freighters."

Post nodded and saw Jarvis do the same. The convoy was headed right for the submarine and closing the distance quickly. It was time to set up for the attack.

"Mug, hard left rudder," Post ordered. "All ahead two-thirds.

Come to course one-two-five. We'll assume that's their base course until we know for sure. Ted, up search scope."

Balkley hit the appropriate button on the control box, and the forward search scope began to rise. Post flipped the handles down and pressed his face to the eyepiece when the scope was at eye level.

He swiveled to face off the submarine's starboard quarter, "Okay... I've got a couple of sticks. Foremasts only thus far, but they look like goal posts. Mug, what's our speed?"

"Bendix log indicates four knots, sir."

"Hmm... Chet, are they turning again?" Post asked. In the magnified view of his scope, Post saw the yards that made up the mast's cargo booms begin to foreshorten.

"Roger that, sir," Rivers reported. "Sounds like... give me a sec here... heading one-five-five. I've lost the DD."

"If I had to guess," Hotrod opined, "their base course *is* one-two-five. That puts them right for Tulagi harbor. Probably zigging thirty degrees off course for ten minutes and then doing a sixty back the other way for twenty, then going back to port again."

"Concur," Williams said from below.

"Then we need to get them where their starboard zig meets their baseline course," Post decided. "Hotrod, give me a course and speed for that."

A minute went by, and the quartermaster smiled. "Come to one-four-zero, speed three knots. That should put us within a thousand yards of the leftmost ship when they cross their own baseline."

"You heard the man, Mug," Post said. "Pat, have the forward room open their outer doors. Down scope."

For the next half hour, the submarine slowly moved through the sea. Although she was going less than a third the speed of the convoy, their constant jigging reduced their speed made good toward their destination and allowed the slower submarine to position herself ahead and to port of the convoy, ready to attack.

"Up attack scope," Post ordered.

Balkley raised the slimmer attack scope, and Post peered through the lens. With the targets just over half a nautical mile away, he could clearly see their black hulls. He whistled softly.

"Look like *Tokashi-Maru* class," he said. "Loaded too. All the way down to their Plimsoll marks."

Hotrod quickly consulted the ONI-208-J ship recognition manual, "Seven thousand tons, mast height of eighty-five feet."

Post drew in a deep breath, trying to quell his nervousness.

"One step at a time, Andy," Williams said, suddenly and magically by the younger man's side. "You've got this in the bag."

"Okay... okay..." Post said to himself, breathing deeply. "Here we go, Pat... we're gonna go for the further ship first. Constant bearing... mark."

Post lined up the reticule on the stack of the outer ship. Balkley read the bearing ring off the scope.

"Zero-three-five," he said excitedly.

"Angle on the bow is three-three-zero port," Post reported. He activated and adjusted the range finder. His view in the scope suddenly split, showing two ships, one inverted over the other. By adjusting the knob below the right periscope handle, Post brought the two images together until they were exactly matched up, like a reflection in a pond. "Range... mark!"

"One-one-eight-five," Balkley said.

"Depth on all fish to six feet, Pat," Post ordered. "Order of tubes will be one through four."

"Set," Jarvis said.

"Fire one!" Post ordered.

The deck shuddered as the twenty-foot-long weapon was hurtled from the ship. Everyone sensed the small increase in pressure as the poppet valve in the torpedo room drew back the column of compressed air that had initialized the torpedo's journey. Below, Paul Rogers was making minor adjustments to the trim of the ship to compensate for the loss of weight and increased buoyancy.

"Tube one fired electrically!" Jarvis reported.

"Fish running hot, straight and normal!" Rivers chimed in.

"Okay, constant bearing," Post said, settling his reticule on the ship's foremast and adjusting the range once more. The information was fed to Jarvis, and almost immediately he was ready to fire.

"Fire two!" Post said. "New target... constant bearing, mark!"

"Zero-four-two," Balkley said breathlessly.

"Angle on the bow is three-four-two port... range, mark!" Post announced, his heart pounding in his chest.

"Nine-eight-zero yards!" Balkley said.

Again, Jarvis announced ready.

"Fire three... fire four! Down scope!" Post all but shouted.

"Time for torpedo one is forty-three seconds," Hotrod announced. "*Muy bueno*, Andy."

"Let's hope so, Hotrod," Post declared.

"Don't let them track back to us from our torpedo wakes, Andy," Williams reminded Post gently from below.

Post cursed under his breath, "Mug, come left to course zero-five-zero."

The boat turned to head ninety degrees away from the path of her torpedoes. Even should they sink the two freighters, the destroyer would be able to trace the wake from the weapons' steam engines back to the original firing point. It was best to get away from that spot immediately.

"Ten-seconds," Hotrod announced.

"Up attack scope," Post said. "Teddy, get your camera."

The water had just cleared from the lens when Post saw a gout of frothing water shoot up from the further freighter's middle. The column of water was soon joined by a flash, a roiling pillar of red flame and thick black smoke. A moment later, the unmistakable *thwack, boom* of a torpex explosion resounded through the hull, eliciting cheers and whistles from all around Post.

Miraculously, though, the wounded ship was not sinking, or at least not obviously so. Not until the second fish struck, however. This one struck about a third of the way back from the four-hundred-and-forty-foot freighter's bow and cracked the hull open like an egg.

Immediately, the ship began to roll ponderously to port, listing further and further, her blasted open steel being invaded by hundreds of tons of seawater each second.

Finally, she went over beyond her center of balance and capsized. Post stepped aside to let Balkley snap a photo.

"Holy cow!" the radarman said as he took a quick peek after taking his picture.

Post jammed his face against the eyepiece once more and saw that his third torpedo had struck amidships of the second target. Further aft this time, the explosion set off the ship's boilers and she broke in two huge pieces in a devastating display of smoke and fire.

"Get a quick shot and then get the scope down," Post said. "How about fish number four, Chet?"

"Passing through the bearing now," Rivers said. "A miss, sir... but no loss. You got 'em both! Congrats... oh shit!"

"Naturally..." Vigliano was heard to mutter sardonically.

"I've got the DD," Rivers clarified. "And her *friend*, too! Apparently, there was a second escort masking herself behind the freighters, sir."

"And?" Post asked almost against his will, the elation of the kill now gone.

Rivers turned to him, "Both on a direct bearing for us, sir. Turn rates increasing and I'm getting active, attack-level pinging."

Williams poked his head up through the hatch and grinned, "Congrats, Andy. Of course... your actions have put us in grave danger. Whose idea was this anyway?"

Post, in spite of his nervousness, jabbed a thumb back toward Jarvis, "Pretty sure it was Pat's, sir."

Williams cocked an eye at Pat, "That's right! Nice goin', Pat."

"Hey... I got a big mouth, just ask anybody," Jarvis said with a chuckle.

"That's true," Mug tossed off.

"I'll buy that," came the COB's disembodied voice from below.

The Cactus Navy

"In the ancient and humble land of my birth," Hotrod drawled in his best Mexican peasant. "Such a man is known as *boca grande loco*."

"You guys can go pound sand," Jarvis pretended to grumble. "And hey, not to throw a monkey wrench into your good times, but maybe we should, I don't know... dive or somethin'?"

"Not a bad idea," Williams admitted. "IN spite of how you've nearly doomed us, Pat. What do you say, Hotrod?"

"*Si.*"

Chapter 21

The jungles of Guadalcanal – several hours earlier

The first few hours of the trek through the jungle and northward toward the coast were uneventful. Although the heat was sweltering in the rainforest and grew hotter as the two fire teams descended, it was at least peaceful.

They were on the northern side of the high mountains that made up Guadalcanal's volcanic spine. The terrain was rough, cycling from patches of dense jungle to deep ravines that slashed their way through high mountains and hills. At no time could any one of the nine men see more than a few hundred feet in front of them.

This was fortunate, as more than once during the six-hour hike, the unmistakable roar of aircraft engines could be heard in the sky above the canopy that shielded them. From the sounds, it seemed that things were indeed heating up in this part of the Solomons. Both Japanese and Allied aircraft roared overhead, and the distant rumble of air-dropped ordnance floated across Sealark Channel and penetrated the cacophonous music of Guadalcanal's riotous fauna.

"We are nearly to Vungana," Jacob Vousa stated when the team stopped by a fast-flowing stream that cut its way into an oxbow ravine. "From here, the path is narrow and winds its way up several hundred feet to the village."

"Thank Christ..." Chief Duncan said. "Feel like I've lost five pounds since breakfast."

Vousa grinned at the Americans, "This is why so much food is required here. I recommend draining your canteens and refilling them before we go up."

"No water altogether dry time up high," Batu added. "Long time 'e come much work belonga drinky savvy Vungana."

"Meaning there's no water up there, and it's a bitch to carry it up," Tank said.

"You understand this guy?" Taggart asked.

Tank shrugged, "You catch on. Growing up, I had a granny who lived with us from the old country. Italy. My mom's mom. Anyway, she didn't speak a whole lot of English, but she tried. Sort of talked in this Italian and English mash-up. Not unlike pidgin. I kind of got used to it and was always my job to translate for the folks who didn't know Italian."

"Well, then I guess Batu is on our team," Decker said. "Vousa, you can go with Hazard's. Might be a good idea if you can communicate better since you're headed toward Palapao."

Vousa nodded, "Sounds reasonable."

"So, how'd you learn to speak such good English?" Lider asked Vousa.

"Lived in Aus when I was a boy for a while," Vousa said. "Learned to speak English then. Came back to the islands when I was in my teens and lost my accent. Still understand pidgin... but it's a lot harder to speak it now."

"You sure you're up for this, Jacob?" Hazard asked the protectorate officer.

Vousa, a strongly built and hearty man of medium height, cocked an eyebrow at that, "Why? Cuz I'm forty-seven? Fifteen years older than any of you puppies? You just try me on, Yank."

Hazard smiled. Vousa's reproof hadn't been delivered angrily. He even smiled sardonically and winked.

"Maybe I should go with Porter's team as well," Turner put forward. "Get a closer view of things from Palapao."

Vousa frowned, "It's closer to the sea, it's true, Captain... but I suspect the village has been overrun."

"Danger and I are old companions by now, Mr. Vousa," Turner replied.

Vousa considered him for a long moment and then nodded. The sergeant major could tell a man of substance, courage and grit when he saw one. A man who'd seen some things and who was a natural warrior, "I'm sure, Captain... but you're too valuable to risk for now. We'll sneak in, see how the land lies, grab some coir for young Entwater and then beat feet back here. You lot go up and get the bird's eye view."

Turner drew in a breath and let it out in slow resignation, "You're the expert."

"Okay, let's get crackin' then," Decker said, gulping down the remaining water in his canteen and moving to the edge of the stream. "Do we need to purify this water, Jacob?"

"It's a very clean source," Jacob said. "You shouldn't need to even add iodine. This stream is too fast for the animals to use, not until it gets a little lower and the land levels some. It actually feeds the Matanikau."

"Okay, you heard the man, load up," Decker ordered. "And Baker team, give us any gear you don't need that we can hump up to the village. The lighter you can travel, the better."

This done, the men broke up into Able and Baker teams. Hands were shaken, shoulders patted and luck wished. Decker's team watched as Vousa led his team into the jungle, and within seconds the four men had vanished, melting into the dense greenery like ghosts.

Decker noticed Turner's frown and squeezed his shoulder, "They'll be all right, Art... or are you just sore cuz you're not going on the more exciting mission? Anvil Art Turner don't like hanging back, huh?"

"Both," Turner admitted with a crooked smile playing on his lips. "I'm not good at hanging back, that's true. I'm worried about Hazard and the chief. They're submariners, not soldiers."

Decker smiled reassuringly, "Hazard was a Marine, don't forget. Fought the Sandies in Nicaragua. Not that different than this. As for the chief... he's a tough nut. Men learn fast under fire, Art, as you well know. And a man with grit picks it up even faster. They'll be all right. Besides, they've got Vousa and Chuck with them."

Turner nodded, "I know... and I'm worried about those two boys, too, Al, not just my lads."

After resting for another half hour or so at Batu's insistence, Able team gathered itself and began the rather arduous climb up to the village. Clemens had told the teams about this trek, and Turner found that the man had certainly *not* exaggerated its difficulty.

The jungle trail that had seemed somewhat rough before was a stroll in the park compared to the steep and narrow rocky ridges the five men now trudged upon. Loose shale and mud made footing treacherous, and there was one point where the path became so steep that the men had to form a line. Up this line, passed from hand to hand, went the rucksacks, a five-gallon jerry can of gas, several satchels of canned food and weapons. Finally, after what seemed an eternity, they came to the upper lip of the ravine, and a row of ten houses could be seen. Unfortunately, they had to hike another mile around the rim of the oxbow before they could gain access to the castle-like column of land upon which Vungana sat.

"What're you *shittin'* me?" Taggart cranked as Able team faced its final trial.

Batu only grinned and shrugged, "Naponapo 'e come, 'e find much savvy gotem no easy. No easy we, no easy 'e."

"If it's tough for us, it's tough for the Nips," Tank said with a sigh. "It's like some kind of fort."

The ravine yawned before them, plunging three or four hundred feet to the river below that surged and roiled through the exaggerated oxbow that flowed around the outcropping that supported the village. The village itself sat on a mostly flat piece of land that was no more than fifty yards across at any one point. There was a row of small houses and a few bamboo trees and betelnut palms, although none were much higher than the thatched rooves of the cottages. Low mists of cloud seemed to cling to the land almost low enough to touch, giving the scene an other-worldly feel.

Between the men and the village was a narrow knife-edged bridge-like spit of rock no more than four feet in width. As if this weren't daunting enough, at the end of the fifty-or sixty-foot-long path was a vertical wall more than ten feet high into which hand and footholds had been cut.

"For all the trouble to get to this dump," Decker admitted. "It looks like a fine observation point. If I don't mistake, we should be able to see for thirty miles or more. Once these mists float away, of course."

"Well, as the Brits say," Turner said, being the first to step out onto the connecting path, "growl you may, but go you must. Let's get it done."

Although mildly nerve-wracking, the trip across the chasm wasn't very far, and even the climb up the rock face was fairly easy with the large holds that had been cut into it. The five weary men found themselves on a flat gravelly space partially covered in grass, a few sparse trees and some bushes. A small group of natives met them, smiling and chattering away in a language that only Batu could understand. After a moment, a lean and angular middle-aged man approached.

"This head man Okanu," Batu explained. "He savvy us, waitem altogether longa days, savvy we come."

"Sir," Decker said, extending a hand. "We come from Martin Clemens. He wishes to return, and we have been sent to ask your permission and ensure the village is safe."

The idea of asking permission hadn't been discussed. Decker had simply thought of it at the spur of the moment. Turner saw the pleased look cross the head man's face and knew the inspiration was the correct way to go.

"You welcome," the headman stated formally. "When Martin comes?"

"We must send a message back to Vushicoro," Decker stated. "He will come soon. We have brought some things... is there a place where we may rest and observe the naponapo?"

"Yes, you come my house," Okanu said, bowing slightly. He seemed honored that the soldiers were in his village. He also spoke better English than Batu, which was a Godsend to Decker. "Is dry. I show you savvy spot for looking."

Okanu showed Taggart, Batu and Tank where they could sit by a fire and relax. He then led them into the largest of the huts, although it was hardly much to brag about.

The headman's "mansion" was a one-room shack with a thatched roof and a betelnut palm floor raised two feet above the ground. He was particularly proud of the veranda. Inside was a table and two chairs, along with several rudely constructed cots made from lashed bamboo poles. The officers gratefully shucked their rucksacks and followed Okanu back outside and past a smallish open-sided structure that resembled some sort of kitchen. Beyond this, on the northern edge of the village's roughly circular top was a small pile of rocks that Okanu indicated proudly with an open-handed gesture.

"Good see, many distance," he explained. "Have telescope from Martin. I bring?"

"A telescope, by God!" Decker asked enthusiastically. "Yes! Yes sir, please bring it."

Okanu puffed up proudly and strode off. Decker and Turner exchanged grins and looked toward the north.

It was nearly four in the afternoon and the mists had already cleared. Although the village was remote and extremely difficult to access, the view it afforded was nothing short of spectacular.

As Turner looked out over the vast expanse of island and sea

The Cactus Navy

before him, he decided that this must have been what the Gods of Olympus experienced when they viewed the world from their lofty perch. He could see Cape Esperance far to the west and a little north. He was able to identify Savo Island, as well as Tulagi and the associated other Florida Islands. The northern plains were in view as well, although most of the grasslands were blocked by the hills below. However, he could see the ocean's edge and the green tops of the coconuts in their plantations.

He could also *hear* activity. He heard the distinct rumble of construction equipment working far below and miles away. After a moment's search, he found the Lunga airfield. He could clearly see the big bulldozers, shovels and loaders, shrunken to micro-size by the miles that separated them from his post. He saw Lunga Point to the east and saw a warship, possibly a light cruiser, anchored there.

"I feel like Zeus," Decker commented, eerily reflecting Turner's own feelings.

"Yeah... too bad we can't fling lightning bolts down on those yellow bastards over there," Turner pointed slightly to their right.

Decker chuckled irreverently, "That's hardly the only target. I can see right into Tulagi Harbor... and it's got to be thirty miles from us. And look there."

Decker indicated a point somewhat to the left, nearly equidistant between Guadalcanal, Savo Island and Tulagi. "There's a tempting target."

Turner saw what the Marine was indicating. There, floating in the azure blue of the Pacific waters, were five tiny ships. So shrunken by perspective that he could blot each one out with an extended thumb. Yet what drew his attention was that the ship in the center of the group was clearly an aircraft carrier. Its flat deck and small island easily made out from sixteen miles away. The other ships around the carrier appeared to be destroyers, although one was slightly larger than the other three.

"That carrier isn't a whole lot bigger than those others," Decker opined. "Think that's the *Sakai* Clayton warned us about?"

Turner nodded, "Yeah, I do... but she's got four escorts instead of two. Interesting... wonder why the extra security?"

Decker shrugged, "Dunno. Our bombing runs are getting more frequent, Marty says... maybe more AA cover? Hey... look out there, past Savo. See that?"

Turner looked to the northwest and saw two black specs on the horizon. They were so distant he couldn't make them out, other than knowing that they must be ships.

"Damn, you got good eyes, Al," Turner said, shielding his eyes from the sun. "Freighters or tankers, maybe."

Okanu returned with a battered metal tube and tripod, which he set up on the two-foot-high rock pile, "Is old but good glass. You see."

Turner stepped forward, patted Okanu on the shoulder and aimed the scope for the very distant horizon. He first pointed it at Tulagi and played with the focus knobs until the harbor came in clear. The magnification was only twenty times, but it provided amazing detail. From their height, Turner could make out planes, ships and even vehicles along Tulagi's waterfront. He thought he could make out figures moving, but couldn't be sure.

He then turned the telescope out to sea. Keeping one eye glued to the lens and the other he used to guide his movements, Turner found the ships in the far distance. He settled them in the eyepiece, adjusted the focus once more and studied them for a long moment.

"What've we got, Skipper?" Decker asked amusedly.

"Two freighters," Turner said. "And two tin cans off to their starboard. Probably a supply run."

"Two DDs?" Decker asked. "For two cargo ships? I'm no expert, but that seems like a lot of security."

Turner stood back from the scope and rubbed his eye, "Yes, it is... but they lost a freighter and destroyer to a submarine attack early last month."

Decker grinned, "You?"

Turner returned the grin, "Yessir. So they suspect an American boat is prowling around the islands... and they're right. Maybe that's why the extra security for the strike carrier, too."

"Hmm... remember that Tokyo Rose broadcast? Maybe *Bull Shark did* sink a Japanese ship... just not a passenger liner."

Turner nodded, "Yeah, maybe one of the—holy Christ!"

He pointed off to the northwest, where a flash of light appeared briefly over one of the small black specs. The two men exchanged glances, and Turner once again put his eye to the telescope's eyepiece.

"Oh my god..." he breathed. "The left ship is on fire... Jesus! Another explosion! Take a look, Al!"

Decker took Turner's place and gawked, "God, she's burning and rolling over... what the hell...? A torpedo attack? Could that be—wow! The other ship just got hit! Goddamn, Art! She's broken in two!"

Turner was laughing with almost giddy delight, "I'll bet you a bottle of eighteen-year-old Scotch that *Bull Shark* just made herself known! Ha-ha-HAA!"

Decker was laughing and hooting as well until his face slowly fell, "Uhm... Art... those two destroyers just changed course. I can see them beam-on... think they're headed to the east..."

"Toward the origin point of the torpedo wakes," Turner said with far less enthusiasm. He drew in a deep breath and sighed. "Part of the game. Elmer knows his business."

Although Turner believed in what he said, he was also trying to convince himself. His boat, without him aboard, was about to be depth charged by two destroyers. It wasn't the first time... yet he was suddenly seized in a vice-like grip of guilt. He should be there, not watching from thirty miles away.

But he wasn't there. Elmer Williams was. Turner squared his jaw and turned away from the scene, "We've got our own jobs to do."

Baker Team

It wasn't much longer that the clearly evident downward angle of the trail levelled off onto a wide plateau. Not long after reaching this level, the jungle path opened up and became an actual road. Although muddy and rutted, the road was wide enough for the men to walk side by side should they choose.

Of course, it also meant that the afternoon sun beat down with merciless directness and increased the power of their thirst.

After about an hour of steady walking, the team came upon a moderately sized clearing in the rainforest. A small collection of homes squatted haphazardly around a central gathering area, and behind them were several small but thriving garden fields of yam, papaya and coconut palms.

There were islanders about, some in the fields and some working at the communal area cooking, weaving and tending the fire. Half a dozen small children flittered about, running among the adults and in the fields and even as far as the stream behind the fields. It was a scene of tropical tranquility that nearly made one forget about what was really happening on Guadalcanal.

"This is Carambuta," Vousa explained as he led the team up to an elderly couple that sat near the fire. "We stopped here briefly on our way up to Vushicoro a few weeks ago."

Vousa spoke with the elderly couple, the headman and his wife. Neither of them spoke even pidgin English, and Vousa had to speak in their native tongue. Some Melanesian dialect or other that none of the Americans could possibly follow.

After a few minutes, Vousa turned to Hazard, "He says that no Naponapo have appeared in the village nor passed by. He has seen their flying machines, and when on a trading journey to Matanikau he has seen them and their works."

"So he knows nothing of what they're up to?" Hazard asked.

Vousa met his gaze and there was something in it that Hazard picked up on, although he couldn't quite say what it was, "He *says* he

The Cactus Navy

knows nothing of their doings. He *says* he can't communicate with them or with white men... he says we are welcome to stay the night if we wish."

Hazard caught the meaning then. The way Vousa kept emphasizing *says* was subtle, but to the English-speaking ear, it was clear. Vousa didn't believe the headman about his ignorance of the Japanese nor his inability to communicate.

"Tell him thanks," Hazard decided. "We may take him up on that kind offer someday... but we have to move on while there's light."

Vousa nodded ever so slightly and turned back to the headman. More words were exchanged, and the team waved goodbye and moved down the road.

"I told him we were headed to Aola," Vousa said.

"You don't trust him, sir?" Lider asked.

Vousa shook his head, "No, Corporal, I don't... can't quite say why... I've met him before... and he and his wife have always been honest and friendly... it's just something didn't seem right in their attitudes. I dunno..."

"Better safe than sorry," Duncan contributed. "Look what happened with that Panota kid."

Vousa nodded, "A lot has been happening on this island over the past few months. The Japanese have been making contact with just about everybody on the coast. They bribe headmen and local leaders with friendship badges and even money. Sometimes gifts of rice and beans. Rumor has it the Japs are taking a census to try and account for everyone... and between threats and bribes, Marty and the rest of us are no longer certain of our friends or foes."

"Jesus..." Hazard muttered mournfully.

"What are friendship badges?" Lider asked.

"A symbol that lets other Japs know you're on their side," Vousa spat angrily. "A mark of a traitor as far as I'm concerned."

"Why would these people turn against you and their other islander friends?" Duncan asked.

Vousa sighed, "Many don't feel they have a choice. Food is scarce.

The Japanese have technology and weapons that the islanders can't stand up to. Stories of murder, torture and rape have already circulated among these people... sometimes, they just feel there's no choice. Collaborate or die... or worse. Have your wife and daughters taken away, or gang-raped while you're forced to watch..."

"God all mighty..." Lider breathed. "What kind of people are we fightin'?"

"The worst kind, mostly," Vousa said. "Brutal, arrogant and absolutely convinced that they're both superior and right. That they have a divine *right* to what they do."

The men trudged down the road in silence for a time. Each one pondering Vousa's words and the variety of aches and pains that grew stronger with each passing hour.

Finally, in the late afternoon, they reached what Vousa called the village of Bumbagoro. Although, village was a generous term for it. Bumbagoro was little more than a handful of huts and a small garden plot in a relatively open area. The stream that roughly paralleled their course was now a river over a hundred feet wide and much slower. A crude bamboo picket fence had been erected along its edge to keep the crocodiles out, Vousa explained.

"There's the shelter house," he said, pointing to a dilapidated hut for which the term ramshackle would be generous. "It's not much, but it'll keep the rain out for a night or two."

Although the rainforest opened up to the north, the flat land stretched on for over a mile, and nothing could really be seen except the edge of the plateau where the land descended, and the jungle began again in earnest. Hazard frowned as he looked around.

"Hardly a good place for observation," he commented.

Vousa shook his head, "No... why we moved to Vungana."

"Are we staying here tonight?" Lider asked.

"We can," Vousa said. "Palapao is only about an hour's brisk walk, though. I think we should keep going and give it a look. We can always backtrack here after dark."

The Cactus Navy

"What's so important about this Palapao anyway?" Duncan asked.

"We've got a cache of supplies there," Vousa stated. "I'd like to see if it's been raided or not. Also, I'd like to find out if the Japs have occupied the village. From there, you can see the airfield pretty good. Would love to get that much of a close look, at least."

Hazard cringed, thinking of his sore feet. However, he had to admit that they'd come this far and that there was no point in stopping now, not with several hours of daylight remaining.

"Okay, Jacob, you crazy bastard, let's roll," the Naval officer announced. "We can rest when we're dead."

"That ain't funny, L T," Lider grumbled.

"Your little piggies getting' sore, Chuck?" Duncan needled.

"Fuck you, squid," Lider spat back.

Lider was the last Marine Raider to accept the Navy men. While he'd warmed up to Hazard, it was partly because they were both from the south and because Hazard had been in the Corps for a number of years. Yet other than that, his attitude shifted from indifference to downright distaste.

"That's Chief squid to you, *boy*," Duncan said dangerously, stepping into Lider's personal space and glaring at him.

"As you were," Hazard growled. "We don't have time for this shit, men. We're a team. In this together, now start *acting* like it. Move out."

The corporal and the chief petty officer held one another's angry glower for a few more heartbeats before they both spun on their heel and started down the road once more. Hazard sighed, and he and Vousa followed.

Long shadows bathed the road as the four men of Able team came to the edge of Palapao. This village, at least, was a true settlement. There were locally styled huts and more substantial houses. There were rows of coconut trees, modest plots of sweet potato fields, taro and papaya. At first glance, it appeared that something like fifty or sixty people lived in Palapao... and they were not alone.

Among the villagers were the clearly distinguishable light beige uniforms of Japanese soldiers. More than a dozen of them. As if this weren't a clear enough indication of how things stood only a few miles inland from the northern coast, a Japanese army transport truck was parked right out in the open near a large communal gathering building.

Even more ominous was the heavy-duty trailer that had obviously been towed by the big truck. The trailer was now unhitched and had support legs lowered to brace it on the ground. Sitting atop the trailer, its twenty-foot-long barrel pointed just east of north, was a five-inch, or in Japanese measurements, 127mm naval gun. With a maximum range of ten miles, the weapon was perfectly targeted and positioned to bombard Lunga Point and the potential landing beaches.

Chapter 22

New Georgia Sound

"Now passing one-one-zero feet!" Frank Nichols, who had resumed his primary duty as diving officer, reported.

"Make turns for four knots, Mug," Williams ordered. "Rig ship for depth charge!"

"Permission to take my usual depth charge station, sir?" Post asked.

"Might as well, Andy," Williams said evenly. "Nice job on bagging those freighters. Pat, would you go back to after battery and take up the DCO spot?"

"Sure thing, Elm," Jarvis said and followed Post down the ladder.

While Jarvis wouldn't be needed as torpedo officer during a depth charging, he was acting XO and Williams would prefer to have him at hand. Especially in a dire situation. Yet the crew needed a damage control officer, too. Somebody to help coordinate retrieving and dealing with the injured as well as casualties to the boat herself.

Besides, Frank Nichols was just under his feet, and the COB was there as well. Williams pulled out a cigarette and lit it, pulling in a hefty drag to help center himself.

Ooooo-eeeee... ooooo-eeeee...

The sound of the destroyer's high-energy, low-frequency echolocation was beginning to reverberate through the hull. It was distant and eerily quiet, yet every man aboard could detect that the sound was growing inexorably louder. The two DDs were heading for where they thought the submarine had fired from, and the submarine was headed at a ninety-degree angle away, but at only two yards per second to her pursuers' twelve.

They would reach where *Bull Shark* had been in less than ninety-seconds, and the submarine would only have travelled less than two hundred yards away by that time. Way too close for comfort.

"Now passing two-zero-zero feet," Nichols said. "How deep do we go, sir?"

Williams knew what the chart said. They'd hit the freighters only a handful of miles off Savo. They *should* have at least a hundred fathoms below their keel.

"Give me a fathometer reading, Frank," Williams said.

Rivers looked at him with a questioning frown. Although the fathometer was a low-energy sonar, it could still be picked up in theory. Williams shrugged. There was a soft dull ping as the fathometer sent a quick sound pulse directly beneath the boat. Nichols then reported the depth to be five-hundred and sixty-two feet.

"Make your depth five hundred then," Williams said. "Rig ship for silent running. Phone talker, pass the word to each compartment."

The bulkhead flappers and hatches had already been closed. Now the men were being instructed to limit themselves to only vital conversation, not to move about the decks unless absolutely necessary and that all noise-making equipment be turned off.

This would mean considerable hardship for the men if the boat was forced to stay down for any length of time. All hydraulic power had been deactivated, thus making it necessary that the planes, rudder and sound heads be managed through sheer muscle power alone. It meant that the refrigeration units were shut down so that the cold room and freezer rooms could not be opened. It also meant that the air conditioning was deactivated, as any of these device's compressors made enough noise to be overheard. Soon the boat would begin to grow warm, and the humidity would rise. If it rose enough, it would make the steel tube a damp and sweaty cauldron that was misery for the men and increased the danger of electrical shorts.

Ooo-eee... ooo-eee...

"They're getting close, sir," Rivers whispered. "Four-hundred yards, bearing two-zero-zero... uh-oh..."

Williams's guts twitched, "What?"

"One's turning to the north, sir..." Rivers said. "Turn rates decreasing on both DDs... estimate twelve knots now."

While that might have seemed like a good thing, it was actually quite bad news for the submarine. The destroyers were slowing to give their sonar crews a better sound profile and because they knew that even at flank speed, a submerged boat could only do nine knots at best. The Japs were going just fast enough to avoid their own tooth shakers and slow enough to hear their victim all the better.

Ooee... Ooee... ooee... bong!

"Oh balls..." Mug Vigliano muttered.

The ship that had turned had found the submarine. Now their sonar beam changed in pitch to a more rapid, high-frequency pinging. A pinging that gonged off the steel hull of the submarine with nerve-wracking accuracy.

"Splashes!" Rivers hissed. "Two... four... six!"

"Now passing three-hundred!" Frank announced just loud enough for Williams to hear.

Overhead, the pinging was nearly drowned out by the rapid swooshing of the destroyer's twin screws as she passed by. There was a terrible quietening as both the sound of the propellors and the sonar beams diminished. A tense and seemingly endless period of waiting while the depth charges plunged into the deep... until they reached the depth at which their hydrostatic pistols would fire and set off the three-hundred-pound charges...

"Where's the other one?" Williams asked.

Rivers had both hands on his headphones, ready to rip them off at the first sign of the ominous clicking that preceded the explosions. He frowned, "Sounds like... bearing one-one-zero, sir."

"No escape to starboard then..." Williams said. "Mug, stand by for hard left rudder when I give—"

Click,click... click—booooom,booom,boooom!

The ocean roared and writhed and seethed around the boat. Concussion waves of enormous force struck the long, lean hull of *Bull Shark*, pushing her back and forth, up and down and throwing men and loose objects around mercilessly. The cork insulation that coated the interior of the pressure hull was shaken loose and flew through compartments like a warm, gray snowstorm. Gauge glasses shattered, light bulbs popped, and human bodies were whiplashed, tossed and battered as two, then another two and finally two more ashcans exploded around the submarine.

"Hard left rudder!" Williams croaked from his position at the bridge ladder. He'd entwined himself in the rungs to keep from being flung about the compartment.

"Think they were set a little high, sir," Rivers said. "But not by much."

"Any sign of a thermal, control?" Williams asked down the open hatch.

"Negative," someone said. Williams thought it might be Janslotter, the new boatswain's mate. "Still isothermal."

"Now passing four-hundred," Nichols intoned. "We're running out of ocean, Skipper."

"Here comes the one that just hit us," Rivers warned. "He's coming in... but... not straight for us, sir. Almost like he's trying to cut us off ahead."

"Where's number two?" Williams asked tersely.

"He's turning as well... bearing two-zero-zero."

The Cactus Navy

"They're herding us," Williams said. "Forcing us to go where they want and cutting off our line of retreat. Least if we don't want to pass under their keels..."

Ping,ping,ping... pong,pong!

Shoo,shoo,shoo,shoo,shoo...

"Oh, Christ all mighty..." Ted Balkley muttered and crossed himself.

"Reverse your turn, Mug!" Williams announced. "All ahead full!"

"Maneuvering answerin' all ahead full... my rudder is hard right, sir!" Vigliano responded tensely but calmly.

Williams was using the sound of the destroyer to mask his own increased screw noise in an attempt to jig under the DD and put some distance between them and the depth charges that would soon follow.

"Splashes!" Rivers snapped. "Another six!"

"Bendix log indicates seven knots, sir," Mug said.

The destroyer's screws passed off the boat's beam, and her pings no longer touched the hull. Everyone aboard was counting. Depth charges sunk at a rate of about eight feet per second. At more than four hundred feet, it would take the depth bombs nearly a minute to reach them, assuming they were set to a depth of four hundred feet. This was, as far as anyone knew, the maximum depth that Japanese charges could be set.

In that same time, the boat would move a hundred and fifty yards from the drop point. However, with the destroyer now passing away, *Bull Shark's* electric motors and reduction gear were making plenty of noise to be tracked by passive listening gear. This left Williams with a terrible choice: maintain speed and get away from the ashcans before they exploded and most certainly be zeroed in on by either destroyer... or slow down and remain silent and take the pounding.

"Midships," he ordered quietly. "All ahead one-third, Mug."

"Here comes the other one," Rivers announced.

"Headed over the first guy's drop point?" Williams asked incredulously.

Even at four hundred feet, half a dozen depth charges could imperil a surface ship passing over when they exploded. Eighteen hundred pounds of TNT created a massive pulse of energy. As water didn't compress to any measurable degree, much of the energy of the explosion's wavefront was forced upward. As it did, a mind-numbing amount of physics came into play, creating pulses of outward energy that throbbed through the sea. This was what truly damaged a submarine. These pulses of seawater acted as battering rams even after the initial explosion. However, once the main force of the concussion reached the surface, it bulged outward, releasing all that energy into the atmosphere. Should a ship be caught in this explosion, it could be damaged or even find itself momentarily heavier than water as the seawater around erupted, and a great area was briefly blasted outward.

"Not exactly..." Rivers clarified. "Bearing indicates she's passing more northwest."

"Cutting us off again," Williams growled.

Six more explosions tore open the sea in a deafening roar. Once more, the ship bucked and rolled like a mad bull. Yet Williams' gambit had worked. The tooth shakers had gone off behind the retreating boat, and the effect, though spectacular, was dramatically reduced.

"Levelling at five-hundred, sir," Nichols said.

"Skipper... the bathythermograph needle is moving," Janslotter said excitedly. "I think there's a thermal right under us."

"Yeah, and so's the bottom..." Williams grumbled. "Mug, come left to course... two-three-zero."

"Steadyin' on two-tree-zero, sir," Vigliano replied.

Hotrod looked up from the DRI and his maneuvering board, "Sir... that's straight for Savo. The island is only five miles ahead now."

"Understood, quartermaster," Williams said, his lunch once more dancing in his belly.

"Advise sir that the fifty-fathom curve is less than two miles ahead of us," Hotrod added tensely.

"Yeah... I got an idea, boys," Williams said.

"Oh, hell..." Balkley groaned but smiled in spite of himself.

For a long minute, there was no sound in the boat. Outside, the sound of two ship's screws churning the sea was audible, but difficult to locate with the unaided ear. This was true of the endless pings from their active sonars. For a time, it seemed to the crew as if all their jinking had finally succeeded in losing their tails. Yet that was not to be.

"Aspect changes on targets!" Rivers suddenly snapped. "I think they figured out where we are, sir... or guessed! One's headed two-five-zero and the other two-eight-zero... bracketing us, sir!"

The pinging began to grow in volume, as did the propellor noise. Within seconds, the powerful sonar beams reached out through the darkness and touched the submarine, gonging off her steel like a death knell.

"Hold on!" Williams shouted, no longer caring about staying silent.

Shoo,shoo,shoo,Shoo,SHOO...

The thundering swoosh of propellors passed by, ahead and astern of the submarine. No one needed to hear Rivers' announcement of splashes. His count of a dozen, however, was certainly teeth-clenching.

"All stop!" Williams ordered suddenly. "Frank, flood negative, flood bow buoyancy, ten degrees down on bow and stern planes!"

"Sir?" Nichols called back in bewilderment. "We're gonna—"

"I know, dammit!" Williams snapped. "Give me a fathometer reading and then carry out my orders, *now!*"

"Bathythermograph is getting more erratic," Janslotter suddenly said. "Depth is... five-four-zero feet."

"We're gonna bottom out?" Hotrod asked, half worried and half approving.

"Keep your fingers crossed," Williams said.

Then the world erupted into chaos. The ship jumped like a popcorn kernel in hot oil. A sleeting storm of insulation flew, bulbs burst by the dozens, plunging each compartment into darkness, men were tossed like rag dolls. Some fetched up against solid bulkheads and received painful but diffused bruises. Some struck hard-edged objects that tore their flesh and caused blood to flow. A few unfortunates were tossed into things that, even in spite of safety coatings, pierced soft flesh, broke bones and in at least two cases, cracked through cranial bones and killed instantly.

Pipe fittings burst in several compartments, spraying cold seawater over the men and their equipment. In the maneuvering room, an improbable series of events caused Chief Harry Brannigan to be tossed from his position at the control cubicle and strike an electrical junction box that had just been struck by a blast of water from an overhead pipe. A tremendous short arced across the chief's body, burning him severely in several places before the circuit breakers tripped. Fortunately, Brannigan didn't even feel the shock as he was hurried into unconsciousness when his head struck the bulkhead.

In the after room, Ensign Andy Post cringed when he heard a grinding and groaning coming from either side of the compartment. His ponderings as to what this might be were interrupted when the ship suddenly seemed to strike a wall. He was flung forward into the compartment hatch where the dogging wheel struck the point of his left shoulder and dislocated it. As he slid to the deck, gasping and groaning in agony, he felt the stern come to rest with a boom.

The boat, moving forward only at a knot or two and at a fifteen-degree down angle, plowed into the sediment of New Georgia Sound bow first. Unfortunately, as no announcement was made that this was the plan, more men were flung forward into hard edges. The stern then settled onto the muddy bottom with a boom that echoed through miles of ocean.

As if to mock Williams, there came another booming sound from the starboard side of the ship. This was followed by a bubbling and gurgling sound. A heavy silence fell as everyone aboard listened to what sounded like the life's blood of their ship bleeding rapidly into the sea beyond the hull.

"The hell's that?" Williams hissed, not really wishing to know.

"Checking sir..." Nichols said. After a minute he appeared in the hatchway. "FBT two-Charlie ruptured, sir. She's venting diesel oil and filling with seawater."

"Fuckin' Exxon marks the spot..." Williams heard someone growl from below.

"Might work in our favor," Williams said. "Big oil slick and no sound from us... they'll think they got us. Let's get some battle lanterns rigged and we'll listen and see what's going on topside. If we're really lucky, the DDs will buzz off and we can start sweeping up."

"And if we're not lucky?" Hotrod asked.

Williams lit another cigarette and sighed, "We're not even going to consider that possibility, Hotrod. We bagged two vital cargo ships headed for Guadalcanal or Tulagi... yeah, we got a spanking for it... but this is our job, people. Think about the big picture."

"All's I can think about right now is that I've been holdin' onto a world-class leak for a good half hour now," Vigliano said, his face a ghastly death's head grin in the gloomy illumination from the equipment indicator lights.

"Always thinkin' with your pecker, Mug," Hotrod quipped.

"What my Aunt Rita always told me," Mug deadpanned.

Williams smiled thinly. His submarine... *Art Turner's* submarine... was jammed into a mud bank over five hundred feet below the Pacific, in nearly total darkness with who knew what injuries to ship and crew and his men could still joke around. No matter what happened, Williams was proud of their spirit and knew that such men could not so easily be defeated.

Chapter 23

Palapao Village – Guadalcanal
– 1940 local time

"What the hell are we doin' here, L T?" Lider hissed almost into Hazard's ear.

For the better part of an hour, the team had hunkered down at the edge of the jungle and spied on the Japanese platoon that moved among the villagers. Here, the rainforest assumed something less of the dense fruity jungle and was more of a blend of tropical and temperate foliage. There were still plenty of birds of paradise spreading their large dewy leaves, tall banana trees, frangipani spreading its pleasing fragrance and ferns. There were also hardwoods, a few pines and other larger trees as well. This meant, among other things, slightly less of the uncounted small creatures of Guadalcanal that loved to bite, sting and suck the blood of human beings.

It was hardly an absence of such life, especially at dusk, when the island's mosquito population rose to greet the night and, like a billion-member vampire coven, sought to prolong their unholy existence on the lifeblood of the living. It was no wonder that malaria, dysentery and other tropical diseases were so predominant.

Thankfully for the men of Baker team, the Marine Corps had

provided for this to a degree. Each man now wore a mosquito net over their heads that attached to their ball caps and to the collars of their BDU camos. Insect repellant, odorless for obvious reasons, had been sprayed on every bit of exposed skin. The Marines had also shown the Navy men how to tuck their trousers into their boots, cinch their belts down tight and the cuffs of the blouses had drawstrings that could be tightened over the wrists. In this way, no creepy-crawlies should be able to get under clothing. Odorless soap was also applied to the boots and trouser cuffs in an attempt to confound freeloading insects' efforts to hitch a ride.

Finally, as a preventative, everyone in the landing party took Quinine and Atabrine each day as a defense against malaria. Chief Hoffman had begun this course several days before *Bull Shark* reached the malodorous jungles of Guadalcanal.

"Our jobs," Hazard said. "Observing."

"Yeah, but we observed already," Duncan said, trying to quietly swat at the endless stream of buzzing skeeters around him. "Shouldn't we go back and report?"

Vousa chuckled. Like the other men, he'd been outfitted in Marine Raider gear. There was simply no way to move around and function on Guadalcanal, even away from the jungles, swamps and rainforests without protective gear. The Melanesian man had a feeling he knew what Hazard wanted to do.

"That gun is pointed right at the airfield," Hazard whispered. "And if the skipper's and Mr. Decker's recommendation is followed, then the primary Marine landing beach is about twenty degrees to the right... again, under that gun's nose. Hell, how do we know the Japs ain't gonna bring up more of 'em? Maybe even position a few along this line of hills? Imagine what these bastards could do on D-Day?"

The implication was clear. Both Lider and Duncan groaned under their breath when they realized what their officer had in mind.

"You want to blow that gun?" Lider hissed incredulously. "Christ... and they say Marines are nuts..."

"We got the satchel charges," Hazard stated, as if this were reasoning enough for doing the insane thing he was contemplating.

"Yeah, and there's at least a half-platoon of Japs who wouldn't take kindly to us usin' 'em, sir," Lider quipped.

"I hate to agree with the corporal," Duncan said. "But sir... for cryin' out loud..."

"All them Japs are wearin' those stupid light tan uniforms," Hazard stated. "Even at night, they stand out like a tattoo on a stripper's ass. Now, us... we got these fancy camouflage jobs. Easy to sneak in, plant a surprise and bug out. Am I right, Jake?"

Vousa turned and eyed the American through his mosquito netting. He had to admire the man's grit and couldn't deny that finally dealing these yellow bastards a shrewd blow pleased him immeasurably.

"We can probably plant a charge easy enough," Vousa said. "The trouble is that once it goes off... all those Nips are going to scramble and come hunting us. We won't be able to simply stroll back up the road pretty as you please."

Hazard nodded, "That's true... but hell, even with the good moon that's risin' we can hide five feet in the jungle, and they'll never even see us."

"Oughten we go back and report and then come back in a day or two, sir?" Lider asked dubiously.

"Might not have the time," Duncan admitted reluctantly.

"Chief's right," Hazard stated. "We don't know exactly when D-Day is... or even when H-Hour might be if we did. For all we know, Watchtower might be gathering offshore this very minute. Nope, I say we blow that gun and *then* hightail it back and report. Sides... from Vungana, they'll see the balloon go up. They'll have some idea of what we've done."

"Yeah, and if we make it back, the captain will have our asses," Lider complained.

"Hey, if you want to stay clear, you can hang back or start back to Vungana now," Hazard said with mild irritation in his voice. "But this is a goddamned war, Chuck. It ain't easy, and it ain't safe. We ain't gonna win it by being cautious all the time. Now I'm gonna blow up that fuckin' gun and anything else I can while we're here. Maybe it's crazy, but we're doin' it. Anybody wants out, say so now. I won't order you in. I'll go alone if I have to."

"Fuck that... sir," Duncan said tersely.

"I'm in," Vousa said.

Lider sighed, "It ain't' like I don't want to smack the Jap around, sir. It's just I'm thinkin' about the big picture. Once we do this, we really stir up the hornets, is all I'm sayin'."

"Oh well," Hazard said. "We're here to *exterminate* the hornets, Corporal. You in or not?"

Lider actually chuckled, "Chance to blow su'em up and kill some Nips? Shit... I'm in."

The men sat in silence for a time, watching the village as the last of twilight faded into black. Just over the jungle, a silvery moon began to peek, casting the scene before Baker team in an ethereal light. The village was quiet, with most of its occupants inside. Many of the Japanese were as well.

Certainly, the officers had retired and a good portion of the twenty or so men that the team had been able to identify. The only people moving about once full darkness had come was a guard who walked a patrol beat along the edge of the road, another near the far side of the village and some crops and a third who stood up on the gun platform.

"How the hell do we blow the gun?" Duncan asked.

"Probably can't with these satchel charges," Hazard said. "Not like we can just toss a few down the barrel. It's a *gun*, after all. But we can frag that trailer. Blast it to smithereens, and the gun's useless. But I'm no demolitions expert either..."

Lider grinned, "The gun provides its own means of destruction, L T. Yeah, we blow the trailer like you said... but we also load a couple of shells into the breech, facing each other. Then we slide a satchel charge down the barrel and..."

The Cactus Navy

"And every Jap in the village opens fire at this racket we're making," Duncan cranked.

"Sounds dangerous," Hazard said.

"Told you this was crazy," Lider added with a soft chuckle.

"What do we do about these guards?" Duncan asked. "Got to take out at least the guy near the road and the one by the gun."

"Leave that to me," Vousa said, shucking his pack and beginning to remove his blouse and trousers.

With admirable stealth and rapidity, the Melanesian officer had shucked his BDUs and replaced them with drab and ragged local clothing. He'd even stowed his cap and mosquito netting. He left the pack lying beside him and hefted his KA-BAR.

"That's all you're taking?" Duncan asked.

Vousa nodded, "All I need... oh..."

He removed a small flask from his pack and opened it. A strong waft of liquor tickled at the men's noses. Vousa poured a small amount on the front of his knit shirt and passed the bottle to Hazard. "One quip nip before we go... little camouflage."

Each man took a drink and passed the flask back to the islander.

"I'm going for the one by the road first," Vousa explained. "Then I'll head for the gun. When you see that one fall, you three come out. I suggest keeping two back for covering fire in case we need it. Take my pack with you. Send one man, I'd say Charlie here since he's the closest to a demo expert. Charlie, you move directly to the gun as quickly as possible with all of the charges. We'll set up the gun, the fuses and run like hell."

"Sounds like a plan," Hazard stated.

"That's generous..." Duncan quipped. "Calling it a *plan*..."

"Ready?" Vousa asked.

"Go," Hazard ordered.

Vousa slipped out of the stand of trees and undergrowth and began walking... lurching was more accurate... down the road along the edge of the village. The others watched as he angled toward the eastern side, melting into the shadows of the trees. In his dark clothing, they could hardly pick Vousa out in the deep gloom.

After a minute or two, he seemed to magically appear almost within arm's reach of the guard. The man was so startled he nearly leapt out of his uniform and quickly brought his rifle up. Vousa said some words that were too soft to make out. The guard replied in a low guttural tone of anger. There was a pause, more words exchanged, and the Japanese soldier seemed to relax.

That's when the Melanesian moved. With a swiftness and deftness that could barely be seen in the dark, he brought up his right hand and slit the Jap's throat before the man even realized he was under attack. Vousa then lowered him to the ground, stripped him of his rifle and ammo belt, and melted into the shadow of a nearby hut.

"Holy cow..." Lider said appreciatively.

"You ready, Chuck?" Hazard asked.

Lider nodded and hefted the three satchel charges they'd brought, "What do you suggest for fuses?"

"Shit... I don't know," Hazard pondered. "The longer, the better, that way we can put some distance between us and the hornet's nest... but if we're spotted, that gives somebody the chance to undo all of our work. I guess you'll have to decide for yourself. Maybe ten minutes?"

Lider nodded and quietly stood along with the other two men. To his surprise, Chief Duncan put a hand on his shoulder and wished him good luck.

Vousa had already made his move. Unlike with the first guard, he didn't use any kind of finesse. He simply moved from shadow to shadow as close as he could and then bolted straight for the Japanese guard. In the man's distraction, he didn't seem to see the sergeant major until it was nearly too late. Yet, at the last minute, the guard whipped around just in time for Vousa to tackle him. They went down wordlessly, disappearing from view behind the corner of the gun trailer.

"Jesus... go, Chuck!" Hazard ordered tersely.

The Cactus Navy

Lider extricated himself from the foliage and then ran like hell. Hazard and the chief followed, with Hazard hefting Vousa's pack. They emerged near the edge of the road, and Hazard set the pack down.

"So, we just stand here and wait?" Duncan asked.

"I hope so," Hazard said. "Damn… should've had Charlie put a charge under the cab of that damned truck, too."

At first, the insane plan seemed like it was going to go off without a hitch. Lider ran as quickly as he could to the gun. His path took him past the truck first, and he stopped to crouch behind it for a moment to both catch his breath and to analyze the situation.

He had three satchel charges consisting of five pounds of dynamite each. They could be initiated by a pull cord or pencil fuse. The pull cord made the charge act not unlike a grenade. Pull, throw and beat feet.

The pencil fuse, on the other hand, gave the user several timed options. The concept was simple: one end of the tube contained a percussion cap that would set off a larger charge. At the other was a small copper section containing a glass vial of acid. Depending on the concentration of the acid, each fuse had a different time delay. When the copper section was crushed, it released the acid, and it would begin to erode a thin wire holding back a spring-loaded striker. When the wire dissolved, the striker was released, igniting the percussion cap and thus the main charge.

Inspired, Lider pulled out a twenty-minute fuse and attached it to one of the satchel charges. He used a small pair of pliers to crush the initiator and then wedged the satchel firmly under the front bumper of the military truck. He then looked around and sprinted to the gun, where Vousa was waiting, crouched over the body of the guard.

"I set a charge under the truck," The Marine whispered. "Ready to do this?"

Vousa grinned, "That I am, mate. What do we do?"

Lider swallowed, "Thankfully, the five-inch gun uses a fifty-pound shell. So we can open the breech and load them in by hand, without using the electrical machinery. My idea is that I set the fuse on a satchel, shove it as far up into the breech as I can, and then we load two shells if there's room. If not, we load in a shell pointed the wrong way. Close the breech and then place the final charge under one of the wheels of the trailer."

"Okay, let's do it," Vousa said. "I'm not sure how much time we've got. Sooner or later, somebody's bound to ask for a report."

"Christ..." Lider grumbled as the two men clambered up onto the trailer.

The gun was very much like the naval version aboard *Bull Shark*, only with a much longer barrel. All of the Raiders had trained on the operation of the guns during the passage, and he knew the gist of how to operate the deadly artillery piece. Certainly, he knew enough to be dangerous.

There were several shells laid out in a locker near the rear of the gun. Lider pointed to it, and Vousa went to open the breech. The cover swung open smoothly, and he had to manually release the tray mechanism and slide it back slowly. He felt around inside, and by the feel of the ridges of the barrel's interior, he knew that only one shell would fit.

He grumbled and set up another ten-minute pencil fuse. The five-pound charge was small, and because it was made of one-pound blocks of TNT, the shape of the bag could be altered. Lider squeezed it down so that it would slide into the barrel and carefully forced it in, being cautious not to detach the fuse.

Suddenly Vousa was there with one of the shells. Together, they carefully laid it on the tray, nose backward and then slid the tray into the gun. To the relief of both men, it went in, and the breech door closed.

"Okay, nine minutes," Lider said as they jumped down to place the final charge. "And I think about fifteen on the truck."

Just as they crouched down by the big, reinforced tires of the trailer, a burst of static and a tinny voice barked out something in

The Cactus Navy

Japanese. Both men met one another's eyes in surprise and fear before they realized that it was coming from the dead guard's two-way radio.

"Shit..." Lider said as he prepared another ten-minute fuse. "Somebody's asking for a check-in."

"We'd better move," Vousa said. "Things may get interesting shortly."

Lider chuffed, "Y'think? One sec... set! Let's beat feet!"

The two men shot to their feet and began to run toward the road. Lider was encumbered still by his thirty-pound pack and Vousa by the two Arisaka rifles and ammo belts he'd snitched. Both men were running at full tilt, the humid night air quickly sapping their stamina.

From behind and to their left, an angry Japanese voice shouted something neither understood. They didn't understand the language, but the *intent* of the shouts was plainly evident.

The jig was up.

Soon more voices began shouting. Japanese men and then native voices of both men and women. Lanterns were lit and flashlights flicked on here and there, and there was the sound of running feet.

'Oh, bloody Christ..." Vousa gasped. "Into the vegetables, Corporal!"

Not far away, Chief Duncan squeezed his eyes shut, "Oh, holy hell... now what?"

"Now we haul... there they are! Chuck, Jake, this way!" Hazard hollered when he saw that the two men were angling toward the edge of the jungle. He knew they wanted to get out of sight quickly, but it would be better if they were together.

Either the two men didn't hear or ignored the order because they didn't change course and quickly vanished into the shadows and the dense foliage. Hazard gritted his teeth, scooped up Vousa's pack and tapped Duncan on his arm and pointed.

The two men ran across the rutted track that was laughably called a road and plunged into the jungle themselves, not more than a hundred feet from where the other two members of Baker team had gone.

Hazard led the way, crashing blindly through thickets of ferns, tangled vines and broad, damp, leafy things. After a moment, he stopped in a relatively clear patch and caught his breath. Duncan stood close by, fumbling a machete from its sling on his pack.

"Where..." the chief started to ask.

"Shhhh..." Hazard implored. "Listen..."

All around them, the sounds of Guadalcanal's night fauna chirped, chittered and screeched. Above this, echoing strangely beyond their impenetrable green walls, Japanese voices shouted orders and questions. Occasionally, a rifle set on automatic would discharge. First one for a second or two, then a bit further away, another, and then yet another along an arc that went from west to north and then east. An arc of men stationed at various points in the village firing outward into the darkness. Randomly sending rounds downrange in the hopes of hitting a phantom.

Over this din, there came to the Navy men's ears a sound of something heavy crunching and crashing through the growth. Every two-seconds or so, a metallic chink or clunk broke through the din. It took the chief a moment to realize what he was hearing.

"Vousa and Lider are hacking their way toward us with a machete," He stated.

"Yeah..." Hazard agreed. He raised his cupped hands to his mouth in an attempt to direct his raised voice. "Chuck... Jake... this way."

A pause in the hacking and then a renewed effort. In another minute or so, two vague man-shaped forms emerged into a thin shaft of pale moonlight. Both men were gasping and gulping damp air.

"You fellas all right?" Hazard asked quietly.

"Oh... we're just... swell..." Lider gulped.

"How long until—" the chief started to ask.

His question was answered rather spectacularly. A thundering explosion tore open the atmosphere, its flash of light so brilliant it penetrated into the dense jungle and lit up the four men for a brief moment. Then a roaring wind howled through the trees, bringing with it the smell of cordite, ozone and screams of pain and terror.

Just as they were recovering from the shock, another explosion boomed out, not quite as large or devastating. Even so, however, it sounded like the end of the world and on every man's face was the wicked smile of victory.

"The gun and trailer," Lider said. "The truck should go up shortly."

"See, Mr. Hazard?" Duncan quipped. "And you just wanted to turn around and go home."

"What was I thinkin'," Hazard laughed.

"Perhaps we should exercise the better part of valor while we can?" Vousa suggested. "While chaos still reigns."

"Now *that* sounds like a good idea," Lider said with a lopsided grin.

Baker team made their way back out to the road and beheld the result of their work. At first glance, which is all they had time for before turning south on the road and running, the gun seemed to be intact. However, the breech and loading mechanism had been completely blasted, the trailer's entire right side obliterated, and the assembly was cocked at a twenty-degree angle. That alone would have made the gun impossible to fire.

The truck was burning, casting a portion of the camp in demonic flickering orange light. By this incandescent glow, the men of the team saw more than a dozen Japanese soldiers running seemingly without rhyme or reason, casting about and shouting amidst a gaggle of villagers doing much the same thing.

"Well..." Hazard said as they jogged away from the scene of the crime. "That got their attention."

Over the screams, shouts and crackling of the burning vehicle rose the unmistakable sound of automatic weapons fire. At least three rifles were pouring out a beehive's worth of deadly lead... and although the men didn't turn to look back, they could hear the lead pellets skittering through the trees and kicking up mud and gravel just behind and to their left.

"Full right rudder!" Duncan said as he angled toward the right side of the road to hopefully put some jungle between themselves and their new friends.

"Think they've seen us?" Lider tossed off sardonically.

"I thought you Americans were here to *help* us with the Naponapo?" Vousa tossed off as the team tried to hug the foliage and increase their speed.

"You're saying this isn't helping?" Duncan puffed.

"*Watashi tachi wa anata wo oitsume anata wo korosu desho yo, Ame-cohs!*" an enraged voice bawled out from the village.

"Well..." Hazard admitted sheepishly, "at least they aren't yelling threatening and hurtful things at the islanders anymore."

"You understood all that gibberish, L T?" Lider asked.

Hazard chuckled, "Nah... but *ame-cohs* is something like round-eyed sons of whores or the equivalent."

"The Japanese *are* a very precise people," Vousa stated.

The four men laughed uproariously as they ran off into the night.

Chapter Twenty-Four

"You're the diligent one, Art," Martin Clemens's voice observed softly from behind Turner.

The submarine captain half-turned and offered Clemens a reserved smile, "Not really, Marty... I'm just..."

"Just worried about your lads," Clemens commiserated. "I savvy, as they say here."

Turner sighed and turned away from the scene before him. It was full dark now, and little could really be observed any longer. Certainly, he could see lights on Tulagi and Savo. He thought he could even see the strike carrier's task group reflecting silvery moonlight. However, he chalked that up to wishful thinking. The landscape below was one dark emptiness in which nothing really moved. There were, perhaps, some pinpricks of firelight in the direction of Lunga Point, but even that was uncertain.

"I'm sorry I didn't greet you when you arrived, Marty," Turner said apologetically. "How was your walk here?"

As soon as the teams had determined that Vungana was clear of Japanese, a runner had been sent back to Vushicoro to inform

Clemens. He and his carriers had trekked through the jungle and had arrived just as the last glow of twilight was vanishing in the west.

"Grueling," Clemens admitted. "Every time I go up that bloody path and see those men carrying those batteries and radio parts... I swear I die a thousand deaths."

Turner chuckled, "I understand. It was no picnic just wearing a ruck. How are Oaks and our Jap prisoner?"

Clemens grinned, "My lads will bring the sergeant up tomorrow if you like. This higher elevation might be good for him. A might cooler and the blasted mosquitos aren't nearly so thick. As for the Nip... we brought him."

Turner was surprised, "You did? So, who's back with Oaks?"

"Your two young lads," Clemens said. "But they'll be all right for a night. I sent Batu back for them."

"In the dark?" Turner asked in surprise.

"He knows his way around this island day or night, mate," Clemens reassured Turner. "By the by... when you'd like to knock off for a bit, Joe has some interesting things to tell you about our prisoner."

"Oh?" Turner asked. "You've been interrogating him?"

"They have, and so have I," a dimly lit figure said as it materialized out of the darkness. Al Decker lit a cigarette and smiled. "He was reticent to talk, as you might imagine... until he got here."

Turner wasn't entirely certain he wanted to know why. He was no fan of the Jap, it was true. Ever since that horrific Sunday morning at Pearl Harbor, Turner had not found it difficult to hate his enemy. Yet it was one thing to see an entire group of people as one sort of faceless golem to be feared and loathed... yet the game was altered when it was one person to another.

Turner was no racist. He couldn't hate an entire ethnicity for the acts of a few. Sure, he could be angry at the Imperial military and their leaders, but he couldn't bring himself to simply and purely hate anyone just because they happened to be Japanese. So, to see a man abused or tortured even, regardless of whether it was necessary or not, discomfited Turner.

It was his conviction, and perhaps it was illusory or even childish, that he was on the side of the good guys. The Japs had attacked them in cold blood. Sure, they had legitimate grievances, at least from their point of view. Yet the brutality that the average Japanese soldier and, to a lesser degree, sailor had already showed in this war was horrifying. Spread out over such a large scale and with so frequent an application... didn't that say something about Japanese character?

The Japanese, like their allies, the Nazis, were fighting for territory. They wanted to acquire and rule over a large portion of the world, no matter who objected. The Allies, and America in particular, wasn't fighting to acquire anything. In fact, they fought to push the Axis powers *out* of what they'd already taken. It was hardly pure altruism, yet it was still a very different and, to Turner's thinking, very admirable goal.

So, in that light, when reports came in of Japanese sailors shooting at the submarines that were trying to rescue them or hideous tortures visited on captured Allied soldiers simply for the pleasure of it, or the rape of captured local women or military nurses... it made hating them all the easier in light of their overall goals. For all that, however, Turner was still not comfortable seeing another man tortured.

He was just about to push these feelings aside and accompany Decker to where the Japanese captain was being held when Clemens' face went ashen, "Blimey!"

Turner whipped around to see what had startled the coastwatcher so, and his own jaw dropped. There, several miles away and lower down toward the shore, a brilliant flash was dying down to an orange fireball. From that distance, it was little more than a candle flame, yet it stood out brilliantly from the darkness of the land.

"What in God's name...?" Turner asked, stepping to the telescope and aiming it at the flames. "I can't quite see... but something is—"

Another flash and then another roiling orange ball of fire. Turner looked back at Clemens for clarification.

Clemens peered through the telescope himself, "I don't know... but something exploded. Twice. Hear the rumble? It is dark down there, but I'd wager that fire is coming from Palapao."

"Oh, holy Jesus..." Decker muttered and began to chuckle.

"What is it?" Clemens asked.

Turner joined in the irreverent laughter, "We sent a team down that way to get a closer look. Hazard, Lider and the chief, along with Mr. Vousa. Off hand, I'd say they discovered something."

"And blew it the Christ up!" Decker said. "Goddamned fools! I hope they make it back..."

"And when they do," Turner said, "we give them a big sloppy kiss and then kick them right up the ass! Well, then... let's go speak to our guest, Al."

Decker led the men into the farthest hut, or the one closest to the entrance to the village. Inside, a kerosene lantern burned brightly and illuminated a scene that made Turner stop in his tracks in shock and revulsion.

Lying on the bamboo floor with his ankles bound together and his arms frapped to his sides was the Japanese army captain they'd acquired several nights earlier. A towel was placed over his face, and Corporal Taggart knelt over him, occasionally pouring water from a small bucket over the rag. Tank Broderick stood by, his knuckles bone-white on his rifle and his face a mask of hardened misery. Joe Dutch stood by as well, looking grave and holding a notebook in his somewhat unsteady hands.

"What in God's name is this?" Turner asked, suddenly angry.

"Interrogation method," Decker explained.

"Yeah, an illegal one if I don't mistake," Turner all but barked.

"Be easy, mate," Clemens said quietly. "This is a bloody war, after all."

"That doesn't make it *right*," Turner said angrily.

"Art," Decker said soothingly, placing a hand on the submarine

The Cactus Navy

commander's knotted shoulder. "This is *their* torture method. This is what the Nip does to our POWs. This is what they do to the Chinese, to locals... to anyone. These are the same people who participated in the Alexandra Hospital massacre. Hear about that? When they took Singapore? The Japs came to this hospital, see. When a British soldier came out with a white flag, the slants fuckin' bayoneted the poor bastard. Then you know what they did? They went into the hospital and bayonetted everyone they could. Including wounded men and doctors... and the nurses, Art. Sound like folks we should give a shit about now?"

Turner worked his jaw in rage. He knew about that and about other incidents, too. Yet he shook his head in disagreement anyway, "Goddamit, Al... that doesn't make it *right*. Two wrongs don't make a right and using another's bad acts as an excuse to do the same is still wrong. Worse. We're supposed to *know* better. We're supposed to *be* better!"

"High sounding words," Decker said coldly. "Wonder if you'd still feel that way if it was your wife the Japs tortured, raped and murdered. If it was your friends who were killed in the Philippines or who were among the Bataan walking dead."

"It can't be that way, Al," Turner said. "It just can't. Taggart, lay off that man. Now. That's an order."

Decker stepped in front of Turner, and his face was set into hard lines, "I'm in command here, Art."

"I don't give a *damn* who's in command," Turner growled, his eyes blazing. "You stop this fucking torture *right now* or so help me Christ, I'll report *you* for a blatant violation of international law."

"Lads, be easy now," Clemens implored. "We're all on the same team, what?"

"Not my goddamned team," Turner said in barely contained fury.

Decker met his gaze and held it for a long time. Finally, he drew in a breath and turned to Taggart, "That's enough, Davie. Let's go."

Decker spun on his heel and stalked out. Taggart withdrew the rag and set the bucket down. He treated Turner to a frown and silently followed his officer out into the night. Clemens scowled and then shrugged.

"You're a good man, Art Turner," Clemens said, patting him on the shoulder. "Maybe too good for this kind of war. Well, I've got to check in with your blokes in Hawaii now."

"God damn, Skipper," Tank said with a broad grin. "I ain't never seen you like that."

Turner suddenly deflated. His righteous anger draining away and leaving in its place uncertainty, "Maybe Marty is right... maybe I don't have what it takes for this shit."

"Don't beat yourself up for being a decent guy, Art," Dutch said gently. "There's no shame in that."

Turner knelt down by the Japanese soldier. The man's... the young man's... face was blanched with fear and his eyes wide as he gasped for air, "Did he even tell us anything, Joe?"

Dutch shook his head, "Name and rank. Captain Yoshi Hinto."

"We already knew that," Turner grumbled.

"He's *Riekusentai*, not army," Dutch stated. "For what that's worth..."

"A Marine?" Turner asked.

"Hai... yes," the Japanese Marine suddenly replied.

"You speak English?" Turner inquired in surprise.

"Yes, I attended college at UC Berkley before the war... class of thirty-seven," Hinto replied in heavily accented English. "I was a civil engineer before the war... before the war with America, that is."

Somehow to Turner's mind this revelation made it all worse. All the more loathsome to torture a man who'd lived among them once. All the more loathsome that this same man would now try to kill a people with whom he'd once been friends. Turner wondered briefly how Yamamoto felt about such things.

"I'm sorry, Captain," Turner said.

"Why you stop them?" Hinto asked.

"I think it's wrong what they were doing," Turner said. "But Mr.

Hinto... I can't guarantee that they won't do it again. That other officer and I are of the same rank, and he *does* have operational authority. Do you understand?"

"Hai..." Hinto replied quietly.

"Maybe if you could tell us something..." Dutch put forward. "Even something insignificant... we could hold them off for a while."

"I cannot betray my people," Hinto replied, almost pleading.

"We're not asking for the password to Hirohito's bathhouse," Turner tried to joke. "Just a little something to give me leverage to keep them from torturing you further. I might even convince my friends that it'd be best to blindfold you and lead you down to a Japanese area to be released. I'm not promising that... just trying to stop this madness."

A long and heavy silence fell. The atmosphere in the little hut was thick and cloying. Strange odors seemed to seep in from the walls and floor. Earth, green things and flop sweat. The smell of fear.

"All right," Turner said, rising to his feet. "Come on Joe. We can't make him talk."

"Howitzers," Hinto whispered so low Turner wasn't entirely sure he'd heard him.

"What?" Dutch asked.

Hinto drew in a shuddering breath, and Turner wasn't certain if the dampness on the young man's face was from the water or his own tears, "A Marine unit is moving six, light field guns to cover a position just east of the airfield. Command believes this is a likely spot for an Allied invasion."

Turner met Dutch's eyes and then looked back at the prisoner, "When?"

Hinto clenched his eyes shut, "Perhaps tomorrow. There is a trail along the northern plains. The beach in question is undeveloped. A large stretch of open ground with only kunai grass. Beyond that, a mixture of palm trees. The beach itself is wide and the approach sandy. I don't know the exact location, only that it is east of Lunga Point and not very far from the Teneru River."

"Thank you, Captain," Turner said. "Rest easy. No one will bother you tonight. I'll see that some food is sent in to you."

"*Arigato...*" he muttered and began to sob.

Turner and Dutch were surprised to find Decker, Clemens and Taggart sitting around the communal fire waiting for them. Tank had followed them out and slung his rifle over his back. On his face, the electrician wore a smug smile.

"Al..." Turner began awkwardly. He had to live and work very closely with Decker and his Marines, and some sort of peace offering must be made.

"How'd you make out, Art?" Decker asked in a tone that was bewilderingly pleasant.

Turner was taken aback, "I... well, he gave me a nugget we may use..."

Decker stood from his seated position and held out a hand, "Art... I owe you an apology."

Both Turner and Dutch were confused. Tank snorted but offered no comment.

Taggart joined his officer and grinned, "Sorry sir... it was necessary."

"Huh?" Dutch asked.

Decker smiled now, "I hoped you'd have exactly the reaction you did, Art. Outrage at the treatment. That you'd defend the prisoner against us. That he'd see us as the bad guys and you as his savior... and be grateful."

"So, it was all a setup?" Turner asked indignantly.

"In a way, sir," Taggart said. "It's a technique the intelligence boys have been working on. Your Mr. Clayton's idea, in fact. The two opposite sentiments jarring the prisoner into lowering his guard."

"In spite of everything I said," Decker added. "I don't like torture either. I can do it if I have to. The Japs *do* commit atrocities seemingly without remorse. At least we can say we feel bad when we give them a dose of their own medicine."

The two men shook hands and the tension dissolved. Turner sat by the fire and gratefully excepted a bowl of canned stew from Marty's cook.

"So, what'd you find out?" Clemens asked.

Turner told them. Decker's eyes glinted with satisfaction.

"I knew he knew somethin'," Taggart stated. "Bein' a Marine and all."

"So let me guess," Tank said as he sat and began to eat. "We're gonna go attack them Japs and their little toy guns, ain't we?"

Turner's face split into a grin that definitely contained a hint of predation, "You bet your sweet little ass, Tank. I may not like torturing Japs… but I'll sure as shit blow 'em all sky high given the chance."

"One might see that as a conflict of ethics, Art," Clemens teased.

"Meh."

Twenty miles away or so, another group of men stood by and witnessed the explosion in the foothills of Guadalcanal. Their reaction was quite different from that of the Americans and their friends.

The executive officer of the strike carrier *Sakai* reacted, to no one's surprise, with volatile anger, "Damn them! Why must these fools plague us!"

Omata Hideki's reaction was somewhat neutral. He was a loyal officer, pleased to serve his emperor and his nation. Yet Hideki was not a hateful man. He couldn't blindly despise his adversaries the way that men like Takashi Sato did. After all, it was his nation that attacked first. One couldn't blame the United States for fighting back.

"It is clear that we are not alone out here," Hideki observed wryly. "Frankly, we *are* at war, commander. We should expect the enemy to shoot back every now and then."

Ryu Osaka smiled at his friend's apt jest.

Sato glared at him as he torched his seemingly umpteenth Golden Bat of the evening. The three men stood on the observation platform around *Sakai's* navigation bridge enjoying a smoke after a late supper.

"Very astute, commander," Sato grumped. "There is a submarine... or *was* prowling about and now Americans have clearly made their way surreptitiously onto Guadalcanal. Not many, based on our scant reports, but they're *there* nonetheless."

Osaka's reaction was difficult to pin down. Like Hideki, he could not hate his foes. In truth, he rather admired them. A few in particular. They were only doing what they must in response to Japanese aggression. Whatever had exploded ashore was no doubt important and was now lost. Lost like the *Fubuki* and her crew that had tried and failed to sink the submarine a few nights ago. Lost like the two freighters carrying vital supplies and equipment to the islands of the New Georgia Sound.

Reports were that the submarine, probably the same one, had been depth-charged to death. The two escorting destroyers, fortunately it was they who'd been carrying additional troops and not the cargo ships, reported sighting an oil slick just before dark.

Osaka wondered if that boat had been the *Bull Shark*. There was no way to know this for sure, as even his communications with Webster Clayton of the OSS were almost entirely one-way. Yet, in his heart, Osaka somehow knew that it was. In his heart, too, he was mildly surprised to discover, he hoped that the venerable boat and her crew had *not* been sunk.

He admired that particular boat and her captain. In spite of the fact that he and Art Turner hadn't met, Osaka felt he knew something of the man by his contact with his officers and crew... some of them at least. Certainly, Thomas Begley had not been a fine example, and Osaka had taken it upon himself to execute the man.

Buried deep in his heart was no small amount of guilt on that account. Outwardly, he had claimed that he'd shot the man because he was an enemy and because he was dishonorable. Yet Osaka knew that he'd also done it out of self-preservation. Begley knew what Osaka was, and Osaka knew without a doubt that not only would Begley have betrayed his own ship and his own nation in exchange for his life, the man would no doubt have sold Osaka's

The Cactus Navy

own secret for as high a price as he would have been able to extract.

"Can we blame them, Sato?" Osaka asked finally. "Omata makes a valid point, after all."

Sato eyed him coldly for a long moment, "Perhaps you'd like to radio them and invite them aboard for tea, eh Osaka?"

"The world is what it is, Commander," Osaka said. "I'm not so blind that I ignore the fact that it was *we* who started this. If I strike a man, surely it is not *honorable* to hate him for striking me back."

Hideki had to school his face. Osaka had a sharp wit, and his barb had certainly gone home. Sato's face flushed with anger.

"They were the ones who strangled our trade and our oil supply!" The XO raged. "So we struck back!"

"Tried to keep us from grabbing up half the islands of the Pacific and to prevent us from being a threat to them," Osaka corrected. "Every coin has two sides, Commander."

"And yet you serve with us," Sato mocked and even offered a condescending bow. "How gracious when you admire them *so much*, Osaka san."

Osaka turned and faced the man, stepping close to him and invading his personal space, "You go too far, commander. I serve my emperor, and more than that, I serve Yamamoto. Loyalty does not require a complete blind faith, as you evidently feel it does. Do not let your rank and position go to your head, Sato. Do not presume to speak to me like this again. For your information, while you stand around and smoke and complain, I have been studying our enemy and their likely activity ashore. I have narrowed down a list of potential sites where what must be a small contingent of them are likely to be stationed. Tomorrow, Omata and I will fly out and closely inspect them... and if I'm proven right, we will attack. It is *wisdom* that wins battles, Sato, not mindless rage. You would do well to remember that."

Osaka turned on his heel and stalked away. Sato scoffed and moved away from Hideki. The pilot only shook his head and

293

followed his friend inside. He'd never seen Osaka assert himself in that fashion before. Aboard *Leviathan,* Osaka had dealt with the arrogant Captain Kajimora with finesse and aplomb. Hideki hadn't suspected that beneath the cool and controlled exterior lay a volcano.

He found that the realization rather pleased him.

Chapter 25

Vushicoro – August 5, 1942
– 0815 local time

"How you feeling this morning, Sarge?" Ted Entwater asked quietly as he and Doug Ingram slipped into the hut where the Marine Raider lay recuperating.

"Useless," Oaks grumbled. "Can't believe I got pegged first day here, and now I'm laid up and trussed up like a damned holiday turkey."

"Well, we've got some good news and some bad news," Ingram said wryly.

"What's the good news?" Oaks inquired hopefully.

"Batu's come back and says Major Decker wants you moved to Vungana," Entwater said.

"Good... least I'll be near some sort of action," Oaks replied. "What's the bad news?"

"That Batu has returned and we're moving you to Vungana," Ingram said. "Probably not gonna be a fun trip, Sarge."

"I could probably walk some," Oaks said. "It's been a couple of days anyway."

"Not just yet," Entwater said. "Clemens's man says you should stay off it at least one more day. And even then, just a quick trip to the latrine, and that's it. We've got carriers and we'll trundle you through the lettuce, don't you worry, Sarge."

"Any word from our people?" Oaks asked.

"Batu returned almost immediately," Ingram replied, "he says that Major Decker and the skipper went up to the village. Lieutenant Hazard took his men down to Palapao to see what was what. He doesn't know anything more, and they took the teleradio and the ham radio yesterday."

Before Oaks could say more, a chorus of Melanesian voices rose outside. Although none of the men knew what they were saying, the frantic sound was not comforting. Even as Batu burst in, the distant but increasing sound of an airplane engine could be heard.

"Naponapo 'e soar become savvy this!" Batu tried to explain, his excitement making his pidgin even harder to follow.

"What the hell...?" Oaks asked.

Entwater and Ingram exchanged glances. Both men unslung their Thompson sub-machine guns and charged them.

"I think he means a Jap plane is coming this way," Entwater said.

"Go check it out," Oaks told them. "But try to stay out of sight."

The two enlisted men, sailor and Marine, ducked out of the hut and toward the edge of the stream that ran along Vushicoro's boundary. The plane was most certainly drawing closer, and villagers were running to and fro, not quite sure what to do.

"Batu, tell them to calm down!" Ingram said, subtly taking the lead. "They'll draw more attention by flipping out like that."

Batu nodded and ran off to shout at various groups and individuals.

"From the east, southeast," Entwater said, pointing.

They couldn't see the plane yet, even though the sound of its engine was very clear over the villagers and the sounds of the rainforest. The two men split up and positioned themselves beneath a pair of teak trees near the center of the village.

"Sounds like a single-engine job," Ingram called to his partner ten yards away.

"Yeah, and low, too," Entwater agreed. "Could be a fighter... but not a seaplane."

Batu had managed to reign in most of the villagers. They began to move about their business in a slower and more deliberate way. It was just in time, too, because seconds later, an Aichi floatplane appeared over the treetops, just skimming the jungle and passed directly over the village at a speed that must have been just above a stall.

"Damn!" Ingram exclaimed. "What was he, fifty feet over the ground?"

"That's weird..." Entwater admitted. "That can't be a normal procedure... that pilot is *looking* for something."

The Raider's guess was certainly borne out when the floatplane banked and made a lazy turn to come back and overfly the village once more. Both military men rotated their position around their trees to keep them between themselves and the line of sight of the aircraft.

"Shit..." Ingram groaned. "This guy knows something, Teddy."

The Aichi soared overhead, its radial engine puttering almost languidly. Rather than flying away and coming back, though, the plane began to bank in a slow orbit around the village.

"I don't like it, Doug," Entwater said.

Ingram gritted his teeth, "Me either, Ted. I think we got only one choice here... we need to take him down."

"With two rifles?" Entwater asked incredulously.

"Two SMGs that fire .45 rounds," Ingram said. "Two of us should be able to knock him down."

"You're nuts!"

"Maybe, but better a live nut than a dead duck!" Ingram said. "Soon as he gets close... you aim for the cockpit; I'll aim for his wings... ready..."

The Aichi was banking low over the stream and continuing to circle clockwise. Ingram held up a fist and shook it at the plane.

"Now!"

Both men stepped out from cover, moved a few paces so that the branches of the trees didn't block their fields of fire, shouldered their weapons and opened up.

The Thompson's range wasn't particularly far, but its punch was undeniable. The big slugs hammered into the fragile fuselage of the IJN floatplane, tearing through the aluminum and hammering into vital machinery. Ingram's rounds tore open the starboard fuel tank, and it began to stream a steady flow of avgas. Entwater's shooting, which was remarkably precise even with the Thompson, sent a line of rounds directly into the engine cowling and then back along the plane's body and into the cockpit. By the time the two men had emptied their magazines, the Aichi's engine had stalled, and the plane was gliding unsteadily toward the jungle at the edge of the village's northeastern perimeter.

"Let's move!" Entwater said, slapping a new mag into his weapon and breaking into a jog. Ingram followed suit, and the two men ran toward where the Japanese plane was crashing into the thick foliage. It crunched and snapped and crackled its way into the dense jungle for nearly a hundred feet before the sheer thickness of the biomass jolted it to a stop.

"Scratch one floater, Sarge!" Entwater shouted as they jogged past Oaks' hut.

The villagers were all chattering and gesticulating wildly. Batu was no longer able to calm them. Instead, he threw up his hands and followed the two Americans as they stomped through the jungle along the swath of broken trees and brush that the Aichi had made as it crashed. The plane lay upright, its starboard wing cocked upward at an odd angle when it struck a lignum vitae tree. Although the stink of aviation fuel was present, there didn't seem to be any fire.

"You go right; I'll go left," Ingram suggested.

Entwater nodded and the two men split up at the aircraft's tail. They held their weapons at the ready and quickly but cautiously made their way to the cockpit doors. Just as Ingram was reaching for the one on his side, it flew open and a man in a naval officer's uniform all but spilled out, flailing and groaning in pain.

The Cactus Navy

Ingram let his weapon fall to hang from its strap and caught the officer before he tumbled headfirst into the bushes. He heaved the man back upward so that he was once again sitting behind the yoke. Ingram was more than a little shocked to realize he *recognized* the Japanese pilot.

"Commander... Osaka?" he asked in utter bewilderment.

The pilot must have struck his head on something because a stream of blood had flowed down from his hairline and onto his collar. His gaze was somewhat unfocused, and he stared at Ingram for a long moment and only blinked in confusion.

"Doug Ingram, sir," the electrician said. "I was in the boarding party aboard *Leviathan*."

Osaka seemed to shake himself loose from his lethargy and pulled a handkerchief from his pocket and pressed it to his head, and then wiped some of the blood away, "Ingram? From *Bull Shark*?"

"Yes sir," Ingram replied, not certain why he was using military courtesy on an enemy.

"Doug, this guy's been hit," Entwater announced from the other side of the plane.

Osaka looked over, and Ingram saw him shudder. The sailor stepped up onto the doorframe to get a better look and saw another officer slumped in his seat. His white uniform was half red on the right side.

"Hang on, Ted," Ingram said and made his way around to the other side of the plane. "Christ... get his belt off... easy now..."

Batu suddenly appeared and looked into the cockpit with interest, "Naponapo 'e needem doctor savvy bang bang good time quick."

"Couldn't have said it better myself," Ingram quipped. "Batu, can you get a couple of men and lash something between two strong bamboo poles?"

Batu nodded, "Savvy stretcher. I go quick!"

The Melanesian darted away again. Ingram was briefly amused by how much energy the young man had even in the heat.

Osaka appeared at the two Americans' sides. He leaned in and inspected the other man's body, "He's been hit in the shoulder and must have struck his head as well... there may be another wound... yes, his calf. We must stop the bleeding."

The Japanese pilot removed a belt, which he wrapped around the second man's leg just below the knee. He then removed his duty blouse and then the undershirt. This he pressed against the bullet wound just below his co-pilot's collarbone.

"Sir..." Ingram began, not quite sure how to proceed or what to do. "Can you tell me... that is..."

"Not now, sailor," Osaka said sternly. "Let us stabilize Omata and then we may talk. If you're off *Bull Shark*, then may I assume some of your crew is here with you? Perhaps an officer?"

"Our captain and two engineers, sir," Ingram said, again uncertain if he should admit anything to the Japanese pilot. He eased his conscience with the knowledge that Osaka was now his prisoner. "Just a small party of men, sir."

"Doug..." Entwater warned softly.

Osaka glanced over at the young Marine and smiled thinly, "I'm your prisoner now, young man. No danger in telling me the truth. Besides... as young Ingram here may or may not know... I'm not exactly your enemy. Come, please assist me in getting Omata out of the plane. Your man is returning."

The three men managed to finagle Omata Hideki's limp form out of the seat and place him on the makeshift stretcher that Batu and another man held at the ready.

"I'll accompany them back to Oaks's hut," Ingram told Entwater. Why don't you have a look in the plane."

Entwater's eyes glinted with interest, "Yeah... good idea."

Sergeant Oaks was nearly beside himself to learn what had happened. When Doug Ingram and a Japanese officer with blood on his collar walked into the hut behind Batu and a stretcher with *another* Japanese officer on it, the Marine could only gape. So many questions were bubbling up in his mind he couldn't speak for a moment.

"Sarge, this is Lieutenant Commander Ryu Osaka," Ingram introduced the thirty-ish man at his side. "And on the stretcher there is Lieutenant Commander Omata Hideki. It's kind of a long story... but we've met."

"What the hell happened out there!?" Oaks finally blurted.

Ingram told him the story of how he and Entwater had shot down the plane. He then briefly recounted how *Bull Shark* had hunted down the Japanese super-sub and how Osaka had been her XO and Hideki her CAG.

"Jesus Christ..." Oaks muttered. "We need to get back to the skipper... and I mean RFN!"

Osaka looked to Ingram for clarification. The young electrician grinned, "Right fucking now... sir."

"I hope we have enough men to guard these guys and the other Jap," Oaks grumbled.

"You will not need them," Osaka said.

Oaks chuckled, "Yeah, I'll bet..."

"Sarge..." Ingram struggled to explain. He didn't know the whole story, but he knew enough. "Commander Osaka... well... he's sort of on our side."

Oaks looked dubious.

"I work with Webster Clayton," Osaka said, casting a furtive glance at his unconscious friend. Oaks noticed. "I have been passing intelligence along when possible."

"Why?" Oaks asked with lidded eyes.

Osaka drew in a long breath, "I'm no traitor, Sergeant. Indeed, I love my homeland... but I do not agree with our leaders' politics or this war. It is foolish. Admiral Yamamoto himself shares this belief, but he is too highly placed to do anything but his duty. However, my feeling is that if I can help bring the war to a close more quickly... then less Japanese must pay the price for Hirohito's and Tojo's lust for power."

Oaks seemed to ponder this for a long moment before a question occurred to him, "It all sounds good, sir... but for the moment, I have one question... well, two, I guess. Why were you so interested in this village, and did you report in?"

Osaka smiled thinly, "I've been calculating the possible locations of a small contingent of Americans that may have come ashore to assist the coastwatchers. I had half-convinced myself that the submarine that's been plaguing us of late was none other than the *Bull Shark*. Evidently, I was correct. Furthermore, I wanted to carefully inspect the villages I thought might verify my suspicions. It's a bit complicated... but if I didn't act definitively, I might have given myself away. Once confirmed, I could pass on erroneous information to some of my fellow officers aboard *Sakai*. As to your second question... no, we did not report. Your ambitious young men gave us far more to think about."

The Melanesian medical practitioner entered then and immediately went to work on Hideki. Oaks ordered Ingram to take Batu and prepare a party to get moving. They needed to double-time it to Vungana.

Although severe, Hideki's injuries weren't life-threatening. The man cleaned the wounds, packed and stitched them, and hooked up an I.V. to Hideki.

"He will do for now," the man told Osaka. "But he needs hospital. Should keep him here for few days."

"Great, now we've got two wounded men..." Oaks grumbled. "Dammit to hell..."

It was then that Entwater rushed into the hut with a big smile on his face, "Sarge! Sarge! The radio equipment aboard the floater is still good. I'd like permission to remove it. I think we and Captain Clemens can use the parts. Also, there's a notebook with Japanese radio freqs and codes!"

Osaka couldn't help but chuckle in spite of everything, "You're welcome, young man."

Oaks had to smile a little as well, "You sure love your work,

The Cactus Navy

Teddy. Good work on bagging that bird, by the way... how long do you need to get the gear out?"

Entwater tapped his chin thoughtfully while he shifted his weight from foot to foot. To Oaks, he seemed like a kid on Christmas morning who had to wait for mom and dad before opening presents.

Finally, the Marine said: "Probably the rest of the day, Sarge."

Oaks sighed, "Okay... well, maybe that works out. Listen Ted... suppose you get the radio gear outta the plane. Can you use it still after that?"

Entwater scoffed at this before recalling himself, "Ahem... sure, I can, Sarge. Alls I need to do is hook it up to one of the plane's batteries."

Oaks nodded, "Okay, good. I'm gonna leave you here when we go to finish that up and to keep an eye on Commander Hideki here. Tomorrow morning, we'll use Mr. Clemens's ham radio to contact you and let you know what's going on and vicey-versy. Then if there's a need, you can get a party of carriers together and get the Commander up to Vungana."

"Aye-aye, Sarge!" Entwater enthused and darted away before Oaks could say any more.

Osaka chuckled, "He's enthusiastic."

Oaks sighed heavily, but there was definitely a fondness in his tone, "He's a bit of a Poindexter. Kind of a tech geek... but a good kid. Well, I guess we'd better be off. Don't know how the hell they're gonna carry me all the way..."

Suinao was the first one to notice the party coming up the path along the ravine. She stood near the edge of the village and barked several times at them, her tail swishing rapidly in anticipation. All the officers and Clemens rushed out of the headman's hut where they'd been gathered around the teleradio. Dutch, Tank and Clemens himself had been growling and swearing over the cantankerous unit and attempting to Frankenstein something together from the various parts Clemens already had and from what the landing party had brought.

"What is it, love?" Clemens inquired casually as he, Dutch, Decker and Turner strolled over to the sheer cliff that all but surrounded them. "Blimey!"

"I'll say!" Dutch added. "Is that... is that a *Japanese* uniform?"

Carefully struggling up the path was a line of men. Most of them were local carriers with boxes, bags and other items balanced in their arms or on their shoulders. Leading the group was Batu, followed closely by Ingram and a Japanese officer in a white tunic. Taking up the rear were a party of four camo-clad men carefully guiding a stretcher between them.

"Is that Baker team?" Turner asked, pointing at the rear of the column.

"I think so," Decker said with a chuckle. "Bringing up Oaks and another Jap prisoner... I sense a story here, Art."

"There's the understatement of the year..." Dutch muttered and chuckled.

"They'll have a time getting your sergeant up the vertical face," Clemens bemoaned.

"Can't we rig something?" Decker asked. "A line or two from a tree?"

Clemens looked doubtful, "I'm sure we could, mate... there is some rope here... but I'm afraid my talents don't lie in that direction."

Turner looked at the coastwatcher and grinned, "Not to fear, Marty. We've got several sailors in our midst."

Decker scoffed and smiled, "*Submarine* sailors, for Chrissakes. What do you fellas know about *knots*?"

"Are you kiddin', Major?" Dutch teased. "I can tie a granny knot so fast it'd make your head spin."

"Show me the line, Marty," Turner said. "I'm a sailor in the literal sense. We'll rig up a boatswain's chair if there's a tree close enough. I don't suppose you have any blocks and tackle?"

Turner and Clemens disappeared, leaving Dutch, Decker and Suinao to watch the procession. After ten minutes or so, they moved over to the top of the vertical wall that gave access to the village.

The Cactus Navy

Clemens had indeed located a pulley, which Turner was currently attaching to the branch of a small but sturdy-looking tree. The tree didn't overhang the wall, unfortunately, but it was close enough that the line angled down at less than a forty-five-degree angle. Turner reeved the three-eighths inch line through the block and secured the bitter end to the trunk of the tree. One of the village boys ran up with a two-foot-long hunk of bamboo log. The wood had been cut for the fire and was at least six inches in diameter and hollow. Turner grinned at the lad, patted him on the head and then fed the other end of his rope through the log.

Everyone in the village, including Suinao, watched raptly as Turner made a large loop and tied a knot. He then had Clemens haul in the slack on the line. Turner sat on his makeshift chair, and Clemens and Decker hauled him up until he swung below the branch.

"See?" Turner joked. "Who's the hero now?"

"Good job, Popeye," Decker quipped. "And just in time, too."

The party carefully picked their way across the access spur that led to the Vungana citadel. The boatswain's chair was used to haul up several of the carriers and their heavy loads. Finally, Oaks, who could walk a bit, was guided across the bridge and into the chair. He was hauled up and over the rim and greeted with smiles and claps on the back. After him came Baker team, looking haggard and in dire need of a rest.

"I sure hope that *somebody* has an explanation for all this?" Turner jibed, looking at the ragtag gaggle of men. His gaze fell on Osaka, and he thought he recognized him but couldn't be sure.

"Oh, we've got plenty to tell you, Skipper," Hazard said, looking at the Japanese pilot in bewilderment. "But I think there's a few stories to go around."

"That's puttin' it lightly," Oaks added, casting a lopsided grin in Doug Ingrim's direction.

"Captain Turner?" the Japanese man asked.

"Yes... do I know you, sir?" Turner inquired.

Osaka smiled, "We haven't met in person, but we did speak to each other in early June. I'm Ryu Osaka."

"Ho-lee-*Christ*..." Dutch breathed.

Decker looked to Turner, and the submarine commander rubbed his temples, "It's getting on to evening, kids... what say we have something to eat and tell some tall tales."

"Bloody hell..." Clemens remarked with a head shake and a lopsided grin. "I don't think my little talk box will hold out long enough to report all of *this*, what?

Chief Duncan chuffed, "You don't know the half of it, sir."

"Neither do you guys," Ingram put in cheerfully.

"Neither do *you* guys," Turner stated.

Chapter 26

Bottom of New Georgia Sound – August 6, 1942

– 0115 local time

Thirty hours.

Bull *Shark* lay on the bottom only a handful of miles off Savo Island, her bow buried almost up to the planes in a drift of mud plowed up by her impact. Her stern planes were jammed in a down-angle orientation, thus preventing the ship from using a stern bell to back herself up and away from the ocean floor.

So far, no progress had been made, and conditions, which had been deteriorating over time, were beginning to do so with greater and greater rapidity. Several clocks were ticking, and something needed to be done soon.

The air in the boat was now more than thirty hours old. In spite of bleeding in oxygen from the emergency air supply and burning oxygen candles in every compartment, the carbon-dioxide levels had risen dramatically. Matches took several swipes to ignite, if they did at all, and the flame seemed to struggle to life, burning indolently for hardly long enough to light a butt. This was made all the more difficult by the fact that the relative humidity in the boat was over ninety percent. The atmosphere in the boat was a saturated woolen blanket that smothered the men in an unbearable swelter.

The low oxygen levels were beginning to tell. Men were advised when not on watch to remain still and quiet. Those on watch felt weary, and their minds became sluggish. Thoughts took an inordinate amount of time to coalesce, and even simple solutions to problems took a monumental effort to resolve.

All that could be done to preserve battery life had been done. Lighting was reduced to the bare minimum in each compartment. Just enough for the men to function. Messages were passed by runners rather than using the internal communications systems. The refrigeration and freezer rooms had been shut down during the attack on the freighters. However, they couldn't simply be left off. The freezer could maintain its frozen food for a good length of time if not opened. The cold room, however, needed to be cooled in order that the vital supplies inside didn't spoil. At the end of each watch, therefore, the refrigeration unit had been turned on long enough to keep the temperature inside below forty-five degrees. Only once while on the bottom was the freezer run. This did, of course, sap the strength of the two Sargo batteries even further.

Meals had also suffered. It was felt that cooking would both create too much heat and use up too much precious oxygen. Elmer Williams was also considering turning out the smoking lamp for good... yet a smoke was just about all the men had at that point.

So they could smoke for the time being. Food was reduced to pastries, freshly brewed coffee at least, and at one point, cold iron rations along with peanut butter and jelly sandwiches.

As if to further twist the knife, the aggressive depth charge attack had left the ship short of nearly a dozen men. Two motor macs from the forward engine room had died from severe head wounds, and their bodies wrapped in canvas and stored in the freezer. Injuries from lacerations to broken bones had kept pharmacist's mate Henry Hoffman busy for most of the previous night. Among the invalids was Paul "Buck" Rogers with a fractured wrist and a possible concussion that left him so dizzy and disoriented that Hoffman had confined him to his rack in the goat locker. Harry Brannigan had to fill in as COB, which meant that Danny Pentakkus was now in charge of the maneuvering room and the boat's crew of juice jerkers. Frank Nichols had been thrown across the control room and had managed, in a bizarre improbability, to strike his Adam's apple against one of the rungs of the conning tower ladder. Not only had he cracked two ribs, but he'd also bruised and enflamed the cartilage of his throat so badly that he couldn't speak except for the occasional grunt. Hoffman said it would pass, but it might take a few days.

It was because of these personnel casualties, among others, therefore, that saw the remaining command crew of the submarine gathered together in the maneuvering room. All three ship's engineers were either off the ship or out of commission. Thankfully, Andy Post, the current communications officer, had started as an assistant engineer. Now he, Williams, Jarvis… who had a bandage wrapped around his left hand where a short circuit had severely burned the back of it … and Pentakkus stood by the now vacant control cubicle. In the dim illumination, the four men's faces looked drawn and haggard. This impression was magnified by the fact that none of them had shaved in nearly two days.

"I've inspected the gear as best as I can," Post was saying. "I've already lined up the valves so that the after-room gang and I can operate the stern planes with local control… but we'll need hydraulics. Human power just doesn't seem to be enough to unjam them. It may be that we *can't* unjam them or that something is bent enough that once broken loose, they should move. I just don't know from inside and down here."

"We certainly can't powah out," Pentakkus said in his Mainer's drawl. "Theya's just not enough juice left in the batries to sustain full powah for more than a few minutes."

"And even if we could," Williams grumbled. "The planes would just shove the ass end of the boat into the muck."

"Ayuh," Pentakkus agreed glumly and sighed. "It's a wicked pissah..."

Jarvis actually snorted with amusement. Williams grinned at him, "What're you gigglin' about over there, Quahog man. He sounds just like you."

"He does not," Jarvis said. "Rhode Island is a completely different kind of New England accent."

"All sounds the same to me," Post joked.

"That's racist," Jarvis said.

Williams grinned, "Okay, okay... it sounds like our only other option is to blow every tank we've got and try and make us so buoyant we break the bottom suction."

"Gotta rememba that we got fuel ballast tank two-chahlie flooded," Pentakkus bemoaned. "Gonna make us all the heaviah."

"Why does it seem we've had this discussion before?" Post asked wearily.

"Cuz we have, kid," Jarvis replied. "But until now, we've been too busy patching leaks and repairing shorts to do much else... as I see though, Elm, we've still got too much water in the bilges. Even if we blow every tank dry, it doesn't seem like enough."

Post nodded, "I've done the calculations. We don't have enough air to blow every tank. The ballast and trim tanks, sure. The variables are okay too... but the safety and negative tanks are full. Hell... almost forgot... the water round torpedo is full in forward as well..."

"And theyas the watah in the bilges as Mista Jahvis says..." Pentakkus added, puffing on a half-burned cigarette. "Them pumps... the drain pump or the trim pump... run them long enough to do the job and we'll lose the batries. They'll suck the goddam juice right out of 'em."

"And there's enough water down there to keep us from rising," Williams concluded bitterly. "At least with the bottom suction holding us down Christ on a fucking *crutch!*"

It was rare for Elmer Williams to use profanity. His midwestern Indiana upbringing had made him a mild-mannered man. However,

The Cactus Navy

with so much riding on his shoulders and the feeling of helplessness that weighed him down, his aplomb was giving way to frustration. He began to pace the compartment, wringing his hands together behind his back in an attempt to think.

If he could just *think*... but what should be a simple puzzle seemed oddly beyond him. *That* idea was steadily pissing him off. There *must* be a solution. There *had* to be! The boat wasn't severely damaged, just low on air and juice.

"Maybe we're lookin' at things from the wrong angle," Jarvis put forward.

"What'dya mean, sir?" Pentakkus asked.

The big man sighed, "I'm not sure, Danny. My brain feels like a bowl of friggin' puddin'... but what I mean, I think... is that we're trying to find a *single* solution to this situation."

A momentary silence fell until Post said: "Complex problems require complex solutions?"

"I thought it was bettah to keep it simple, sweethaht," Pentakkus pointed out.

"Not always," Jarvis said. "Not in this case, apparently."

Williams stopped his pacing and looked thoughtful, "So... what you're saying, Pat... is that rather than trying to find a way out of this... we need to use *all* the ways out of this?"

"If we get topside, then yes, it's all my idea," Jarvis joked. "If not... then it's Danny's."

That drew a laugh from the four men. The laughter and light-heartedness were sorely needed.

"Okay..." Williams said. "So, we need to drain the water, lighten the ship, blow the tanks and potentially force the stern planes out of their downward angle... we've got enough juice in the batteries to do some of this, or all of it for a little while... how much do we have left, Danny?"

"Pilot cells in both indicate twenty-puhcent," Pentakkus said gloomily. "And as you know, sir... the lowah they get, the less juice

311

they can put out. That's sayin' nothin' bout the initial draw from anythin' we turn on."

"Yeah..." Williams said. "Okay, blowing the ballast tanks is easy. That doesn't take any juice. As for the safety and negative tanks... they can be blown, but we don't have enough air for it. They can be pumped out, too, but that takes juice."

"So, what if we blow all that we can with the three grand and six-hundred-pound supply," Jarvis suggested. "We're too deep to use the two-twenty-five."

"Yeah... but we can bleed that into the hull," Post said thoughtfully, his brain seeming to come to life. "Raise the pressure in here so that..."

His train of thought seemed to abandon him for a moment before William's eyes lit up, "So we can hand pump out the negative tank! Dammit, Andy! Why the hell didn't you think of this last night?"

Post grinned and flushed all at once.

Jarvis rubbed his hands together, "We form a bucket brigade. Open up the interior hatch to the negative tank and pour the water in. Then we can hand pump it out or use the electrical pumps to get rid of the water!"

"One more problem is the suction," Pentakkus added. "I think I can get enough juice for all this... but it's gonna be wicked hahd to break us free without the propelliz'."

"One thing at a time, Danny," Williams said. "You start shutting down everything you can. We're already burning candles, so we can get rid of some lights and use battle lanterns, too."

"What about air slugs..." Jarvis suddenly said, as if responding to a question.

The three men looked at him as if he had two heads. Finally, Williams nodded slowly in understanding, "You mean... open the inner doors on the empty torpedo tubes, and then open the outer doors... and the pressure differential will give us a bit of a push?"

"Maybe..." Jarvis said. "Is that crazy?"

"Yeah, that's pretty much nuttier than a pecan log," Post said. "But we've come to expect nothing less on this boat, sir."

Pentakkus' eyes went wide, "Can we even do that? I mean, let's say the pressuh in the tubes is two-twenty-five or close... at this depth, that's just about what it is out theyah... wouldn't that just keep the watah out?"

Jarvis' gleam of triumph faded, "Yeah... no... that's true, too... oh, but wait! The pressure in tubes one through four is already at surface pressure. In fact, maybe less on account of the poppet valves."

"Okay, so we open the outer doors and the water rushes in... but that just makes us all the heavier," Post pondered.

"Yes, but the initial jolt from what... a hundred and twenty cubic feet of water coming in at two-hundred PSI... that might shake the bow loose," Williams opined. "It's just crazy enough to maybe work."

"Ayuh..." Pentakkus considered. "If it's all done togethah..."

"Okay, Danny, you work on your end, Pat, you run forward and talk to Sparky about your outlandish notions, and I'll go and coordinate the draining party. Andy, you standby in the after room. You'll have local hydraulic control over the planes," Williams decided. "The sooner, the better on this. I'd like to get to the surface with some darkness left so we can crank up the growlers and get some juice back into the batteries."

The men separated and moved swiftly through the boat. Now that there was a plan of action, the lethargy of the past few hours seemed to have melted away. This was, of course, simply the effect of adrenaline... yet it was extraordinary what the human body could do when the mind was fully committed.

"Sir, are you fuckin' shittin' me!?" Sparky all but exploded when Jarvis appeared in the compartment and explained his idea.

"Nope," Jarvis replied. "We're gonna return electrical control to the tube doors, and you and your boys are gonna pop those shutters open and fill 'em up."

"You know, sir," Tommy Perkins stated with a smile playing at his lips. "This is the kind of stuff that makes folks aboard think you're a bit off your rocker... with all due respect."

"Bat shit crazy is more like it... sir," Sparky grumbled.

"Yeah, but I'm *very* charmin'," Jarvis replied. He got serious then. "Look, fellas... we got maybe another day's air left. We got water in the bilges, and we got wounded men. I, for one, don't want to sit down here in the mud while who knows what is goin' on upstairs. While our skipper and the landing party face who knows what alone. We're getting' the Christ off this fuckin' mud bank, and that's it. I'm not *asking* for approval. I gave you a goddamned order, Mr. Sparks, and I expect you to goddamned *obey* it."

All the men in the room were deathly silent. Jarvis, perhaps unconsciously, had squared off with Sparky. Both men were large and imposing, with Jarvis having at least three inches on the torpedoman. Most of them had never seen the good-natured and generally jolly Pat Jarvis bow up like this, and it was uncomfortable.

Even Sparks looked somewhat taken aback. Deep down, he felt that the Lieutenant wasn't really challenging him, simply reinforcing the gravity of their situation. However, he also knew when enough words had been spoken and when obedience was required.

"Aye-aye sir," Sparky said smartly. He managed a small smile. "I didn't mean nothin'..."

Jarvis' demeanor visibly relaxed, and he reached out and gave Sparks' shoulder a squeeze, "Hell, I know that, Sparky. It's a crazy idea... everything we do is... but a war is a crazy thing to start with. Stand ready; I imagine the XO will want to coordinate this from control. Send a man up to act as messenger. Also, we're gonna need men for the bucket brigade, too."

Jarvis turned and headed back through the hatch. Perkins treated his boss to a lopsided grin.

"What're you smilin' at, Tommy?" Sparks asked.

"Wasn't sure you two weren't gonna start tossin' biscuits," Perry Wilkes put in.

"Shit..." Sparky drawled. "It weren't nothin'. I like an officer knows he's an officer at times."

"Think Mr. Jarvis was scared to fight Sparky?" Griggs asked and snickered.

"Oh yeah, he looked *real* scared," Jonesy put in and chuckled.

"You two shitbirds think you're awful cute, doncha?" Sparky glowered. "Well then, after you two *volunteer* for the bucket party... you can get your asses back up here to handle the port tubes while Perry and me handle the starboard ones. Sure hope them inner doors don't burst in when you hit them outer door switches, shitheads."

The two young men looked at one another and gulped.

"Activate hydraulic power," Williams said from his position at the ladder to the conning tower. "Phone talker, all compartments, standby to get underway."

The XO could feel the men's fatigue. It oozed through the boat and hung in the thick, humid atmosphere like the fetid stink of a charnel house. The stuffiness of a closed-in space where the oxygen levels had dipped dangerously low mixed with the funk of seventy unwashed human bodies was palpable.

For three hours, the men had toiled from one end of the ship to the other. A line of men from the after room to the control room passed five-gallon buckets of seawater forward from hand to hand and then empty buckets back the same way. Hour after hour they toiled. One forty-pound bucket after another. First, it was dozens, then hundreds, until every man had been forced to kneel on the decks from exhaustion. Every man's lungs heaving as he tried to pull in enough oxygen to fuel the effort of pushing the heartbreakingly substantial buckets up the deck.

Yet they'd done it. Perhaps five hundred times, over ten tons of water, had been passed forward... slightly angled upward thanks to the topography of the bottom, making it all the more tedious... and now the bilges were almost empty. Between hand pumping and activating the drain pump, the ship had been lightened significantly.

"Let's try the ballast tanks now," Williams ordered. "Harry, blow 'em all."

"Wait!" Jarvis said, snapping his fingers in enthusiasm. It was a sort of muted enthusiasm brought on by heavy CO_2 absorption and bone-deep lethargy. "Blow all but the bow buoyancy, the WRT and MBTs one-able and one-baker, Harry."

Brannigan, who was stationed at the three-thousand-pound air manifold and supervising the others, looked at the temporary XO and blinked in confusion, "Sir?"

"Yeah, why not, Pat?" the temporary captain asked.

Jarvis screwed up his face as if it were a physical effort to think clearly, "Because... Christ... because it'll make the stern lighter and it'll rise first... which..."

"Which will lever the boat out of the mud," Brannigan said with a slight smile. "I get it, sir... then we can blow the tubes and..."

"Right," Williams realized. "Okay, do as he says, Harry."

There was a roar as the high-compression manifold system shunted air into the closed ballast tanks. When it had run dry, which didn't take long, the six-hundred-pound system, the main system for blowing ballast, was engaged. There was a noticeable shudder under the men's feet and a light but audible groan, as if the ship herself were mortally tired and loath to move.

It took a moment, but as the groaning increased, the slight downward angle at the stern began to level off as well. It seemed like an eternity, but the bubble indicator above the plane control station slowly began to creep from a stern angle to level and then to a forward angle.

"Phone talker, forward room," Williams ordered. "Tell Sparky to let her rip."

"Forward room, let her rip," the young sailor reported.

Everyone held their breath. For a long moment, the only sound in the ship was the creaking of her steel as her stern rose and pulled at her snugged bow. Then, the entire ship juddered as four reverberating *booms* echoed through the ship. Not until the phone talker reported that the forward room was okay did everyone breathe once again... for what fat lotta good *that* did.

"We're free!" Brannigan exclaimed, pointing at the depth gauge. "five-four-five feet... five-four-zero feet... rising at a foot per second, sir... uh-oh..."

Williams immediately knew what the problem was. With the bow buoyancy, the first set of main ballast tanks and the water round torpedo tank in the forward room full, the bow was heavier than the stern. The ship was rising, but she was also continuing to tilt.

"Blow those tanks," Williams ordered. "Start with the bow buoyancy."

Brannigan turned back to his men at the various manifolds. There was a brief whoosh, and then the sound died rather abruptly.

Rather *too* abruptly.

"Oh, of fuckin' course..." Mug Vigliano cranked from the auxiliary steering station.

"Six-hundred-pound air supply gone, sir," Brannigan reported.

"What's our angle progress?" Jarvis asked, rubbing his temples.

"I'd say... eight degrees per minute, sir," Brannigan said.

"Which means we'll up angle enough to start taking water in through the ballast tank openings before we reach the surface," Williams groaned.

"Anything left in the other supplies?" Jarvis asked.

Brannigan sighed, "Two-twenty-five is empty. All we got is the low-pressure stuff... no good down this far, sir."

"Sir, we still got a down angle on the stern planes," Vigliano suddenly said.

"Yeah, we know, Mug," Jarvis glummed. "Phone talker, alert after room to begin attempting to unjam them."

"No, sir..." Vigliano stated, turning around to face the two officers. "If we still got enough juice in the batteries to run the motors, I can order up a one-third stern bell. Even just for a minute or so."

Williams and Jarvis stared at him and then at each other, their oxygen-famished brains struggling to make the connection. Almost in unison, their eyes widened as they understood.

"Phone talker!" Jarvis said with more enthusiasm. "Maneuvering, control. Engage electric motors. Standby to answer bells."

The acknowledgement was received. Both officers were now clinging to the bridge ladder to keep from sliding forward on the deck.

"All back one-third, helm," Williams said.

The ship vibrated slightly as her four big GE motors kicked on and her propellers began to spin.

"Now passing three-five-zero feet," Brannigan intoned.

The boat began to level off again. A ragged cheer rose up in the control room. It didn't last long, however, as Brannigan broke in.

"Our ascent is slowing," he warned.

"All stop, Mug," Williams ordered.

The boat was nearly level once more and she began to ascend more quickly. However, she also began to tilt forward once again.

"Rocking horse..." Williams muttered.

"Phone talker, maneuvering. How many more times can we pull that off?" Jarvis inquired of the young seaman with the sound-powered telephone hung around his neck.

The minute or so that it took to get an answer taffied into an eternity.

"Control, maneuvering... once more and he says the batteries will be just about bone-dry, sir," The young man gloomed.

"Now passing three-hundred..." Brannigan said.

"Five minutes to the surface," Williams said.

"And five minutes until we start to flood," Jarvis mused. "We might just pull this off, Skipper."

"Won't have the luxury of a pre-surface periscope check, sir," Brannigan warned.

"Doesn't much matter, Chief," Williams replied. "We're going up like it or not. If there is a Jap up there and he blasts us out of the water... well... we're dead either way if we don't go up."

"And there's a fine how do you do," Jarvis said sardonically.

Two minutes passed, and Brannigan announced: "Now passing one-eight-zero feet... gonna need to ring up that stern bell soon, sir."

"Mug, let er' rip," Williams ordered.

Once more the enunciator bells jingled and the ship began to move backward, her forward down angle decreasing. Then, suddenly, the slight vibration of the reduction gears went still. Jarvis and Williams met one another's eyes and frowned.

"Maneuvering says That's all she's got, sir," the phone talker glummed. "Might have just enough to kick on the aux... but no more motors."

"Trim party!" Jarvis and Williams said in almost perfect unison.

"Ogden!" Williams turned to the phone talker. "All compartments! Every man aft! Pronto!"

Men began to file past the control room from forward and from the after compartments; they moved all the way to the maneuvering room. In this way, their sheer weight helped to counterbalance the weight of the water forward. *Bull Shark* levelled off enough so that the precious air in her ballast tanks was not forced out of the open bottoms of the tanks. She breached the surface stern first, shuddered and then bobbed on the calm sea like an old log.

Jarvis was the first up the ladders and hung on the bridge ladder with his hand on the hatch dog. Once he'd gotten the all-clear that the boat's internal pressure had been bled off to something not dangerously above one atmosphere, he threw open the hatch and a rush of gloriously fresh and relatively cool air poured down on him. He drew in the heady elixir, and like magic, his mental sluggishness vanished. The weariness was still there, but his brain fog was rapidly dissipating.

"All clear!" he called down after hauling himself up and scanning the horizon. There wasn't even enough juice left to raise either periscope. "God damn! We're all alone out here on this wonderful night! Ha-ha-HAAAAA!"

All over the boat, hatches were opened, and the heavy, foul air was allowed to vacate in place of fresher. Back in the after-engine room, Fred Swooping Hawk got the word and threw the lever that started the auxiliary generator. The small diesel engine coughed, stuttered and finally began to chug, purring along with a sound that made every man in the compartment whoop with delight.

All through the ship, lights came back on, and ventilation fans began to whir. With the extra generated electricity, the engine snipes were able to actuate the four main GM diesels. Soon the boat was filled with the comforting rumble of her powerful engines. Her systems, including refrigeration, were re-activated and two of her main engines were put on charge duty.

"Holy Christ, Elm tree!" Jarvis said, squeezing his friend's shoulder as they stood on the bridge together. "That was one for the books, huh?

"And *how*, Pat. Now all we've got to do is unstick those stern planes and get the hell outta here," Williams replied. He thumbed the bridge transmitter. "Control, bridge... pass the word for Andy to begin working the planes. Hydraulic and muscle power. At least try and get them level. If he can't, we'll get some men topside to assist somehow."

A moment went by, and then Brannigan's voice said: *"Bridge, control... after room has the word, sir."*

In the after-torpedo room, every available man was stationed at the stern plane gear. Under local control, Post had already engaged the hydraulics and they were pushing as hard as they could. The planes were connected together beneath the platform deck below the tubes and above the drive shafts. There were built-in handholds so that men could lever the connecting axle and angle the planes manually if necessary. Post had every man he could cram into the awkward space heaving like mad, including himself and Walter Murphy.

Men groaned, grunted and cursed as they threw their weight on the obstinate machinery. There was no way to know if the horizontal planes were simply jammed by the concussive force from the depth charge blasts or whether something had actually gotten wedged between them and the hull. It was too dark outside, and the planes were below the waterline.

"Sir... I think it moved!" Smitty gasped.

"Yeah, I thought—" Janslotter began.

There was a hideous screeching. The banshee scream rose to an almost unbearable pitch, and the men were suddenly shoved forward and onto their backs as the planes broke free and quickly shifted from a full dive to a full rise position.

"Yes!" Post hollered.

"Well, I'll be dipped in *shit!*" Murph enthused.

"Okay, everybody outta here," Post ordered. "Murph, let's test them. Swing the planes back to full dive and then to a zero bubble... ready... okay, go..."

The hydraulics once again moved the planes with seeming ease. There was, unfortunately, a mild squeal each time they moved. Post and Murph frowned at each other and then shrugged.

On the bridge, both officers and the three posted lookouts clearly heard the squealing as the planes broke loose. They caught a hint of the squeal afterward, but it was hardly noticeable, especially over the cheering.

"Bridge, control," Brannigan reported. "*After room reports stern planes free and moving as directed. Slight mechanical squeal, though.*"

Williams actually laughed, "Naturally... but at least we're back in business. Chief, put number two on propulsion. Order the helm onto course two-five-zero and all ahead full. Let's get out into the Coral Sea and get the pieces picked up."

"And then what?" Jarvis asked with a wicked gleam in his eyes.

"What, you want *more* of this?" Williams asked.

Jarvis shrugged and lit a cigarette, offering the pack to his friend, "I get bored easy."

Chapter 27

Operation Watchtower – 120 miles W, SW of Guadalcanal
Thursday, August 6, 1942 – 1622 local time

Vice Admiral Frank Jack Fletcher stood on the observation bridge of USS *Saratoga* and considered the dark line of cloud just visible on the horizon off the carrier's starboard bow. In spite of his experiences thus far in the war, he found an appropriate, if not discomforting, symbolism in the ominous dark storm that lay just over the horizon. To him, it was a symbol of how grueling the Watchtower operation was likely to be.

The phalanx of three cruisers that fanned out ahead of *Saratoga* and the new battleship *North Carolina* two miles to her port stood out strangely, even starkly against the fuzzy gray line of the storm that slashed across their angular shapes. Behind the *North Carolina*, the carrier *Wasp* steamed directly in the battleship's foaming wake, albeit two miles astern as well. Directly astern of Fletcher's flagship, the venerable *Enterprise* parted *Saratoga's* own wake exactly in station. To either side of the four big ships were another two cruisers and the final cruiser between and behind the trailing carriers.

An imposing enough force, Fletcher thought, all by ourselves. Yet what trailed in his task force's wake was truly awe-inspiring, if only the first few ships could be seen hull up astern. Admiral Richmond

Kelly Turner's amphibious fleet and their support ships, seventy-two in all, included transports, destroyers, light cruisers and cruisers. One of the largest assembled fleets in history. And what was more impressive still were the nineteen *thousand* Marines who, by that time the next day, would be fighting for their lives on the islands to either side of the Sealark Channel.

For all this force being represented in one place, it made Fletcher uneasy enough to unsettle his stomach at times. Eighty-two ships were not only a massive fighting force... they were a massively tempting target as well. At that very moment, the fleet was no more than a hundred and fifty miles from Tulagi, Gavutu and Florida Islands. There were, at last report, fifteen Japanese seaplanes there. Intelligence reports from Station Hypo and Ultra estimated that the airfield on Guadalcanal would be operational in less than two weeks. And even if they couldn't return, aircraft from distant Rabaul *could* reach Fletcher's fleet and attack. They wouldn't make it back... but a few dozen aircraft lost in comparison to a few dozen *ships* and perhaps a few dozen *thousand* American men was a damned fair bargain.

Exactly the kind of bargain the pragmatic Japanese and the calculating Admiral Yamamoto appreciated. A gamble, in Yamamoto's case, that would pay off *big time.*

It was for this reason, mostly, that Fletcher stood alone on his portion of the exterior bridge and stared at the line of clouds that were surely dumping tons of rain over New Georgia Sound. Those clouds were keeping Japanese planes on the ground... and the water... and preventing them from detecting the irresistible American task force that was steaming toward their destination at twelve knots.

Fletcher had just turned his back to the wind in an attempt to light a cigarette when the carrier's captain, DeWitt Ramsey, approached him with a notebook held in his hand. Fletcher finally got the butt going in spite of the breeze and greeted Ramsey with a questioning look.

"Sir, we've just been contacted by one of our fleet boats," Ramsey stated. "The skipper is asking permission to form up and speak to you, sir."

"Boats?" Fletcher returned in mild surprise. "We don't have any in our task force... and to my knowledge, there isn't an American submarine out here."

The younger captain only shrugged, "I dunno, sir... but they're waiting to speak with you on the radio at your earliest convenience."

"All right... tell them I'll speak to them shortly," Fletcher decided. "Inform them that they may take up station between us and the *Carolina*."

Ramsey turned and strode back into the navigation bridge. Fletcher sighed as he once again turned forward and contemplated his storm. It was a lucky stroke, that bad weather. Maybe a submarine in the area could be as well. She might have information about Jap shipping that would come in handy.

It wasn't that Fletcher was afraid. Far from it. He'd served in the Navy almost since the turn of the century. He'd seen action in the Great War, the Banana Wars and had been in command during the most decisive battles of this war up until now. No, it was that he knew all too well how vulnerable surface ships were to aircraft.

If the Japs could get up a few seaplanes or send a couple of squadrons of Bettys or Vals and a handful of Zeke escorts, they could do severe mischief. Sure, he had three carriers with him... yet Yamamoto had four carriers and even more surface support just two months earlier and look what happened to them?

As if to underscore his concerns, a long, slim dark shape suddenly appeared between two of his vanguard cruisers. One moment there was nothing, and the next, the deadly vessel had emerged from behind one of them, headed nearly straight for *Saratoga*.

Fletcher knew it was one of theirs... yet the visceral reaction to the submarine couldn't be denied. He'd lost his last flagship, *Yorktown*, to a submarine at Midway. The Japanese carrier planes had damaged her, but Captain Buckmaster had managed to get her stabilized again, and the destroyer *Hamman* was lashed alongside for both support and stability. The day after Midway, a Jap sub had somehow managed to get by a huge screen of destroyers and torpedoed *Hamman*. The destroyer's death had further damaged *Yorktown,* and she'd finally succumbed.

Most surface warfare sailors despised submarines. Even their own. Just as there was the black shoe, brown shoe rivalry between a ship's line officers and chiefs and those of the aviation department, so too was there a rivalry between those who sailed upon the sea and those who hunted stealthily below its surface. Sewer rats versus skimmers... or surface pukes.

The submarine hove up a few hundred yards to port of *Saratoga*. Fletcher could see the lookouts in the periscope sheers and the two tiny figures on the boat's tiny bridge. He also saw, with interest, that she had two five-inch deck guns. One forward and one aft of the conning tower. This was unusual but wouldn't be for long. Many of the new *Gato*-class and upcoming *Balao*-class subs would have more than one gun.

What also drew the admiral's eye was the break in the integrity of the submarine's deck. Far aft, it appeared as if some of her decking had been stripped away. Had she been in a battle recently?

No sense in standing on deck and speculating. Fletcher pitched his dead butt over the railing and moved back into the bustling control center of his carrier. Men and officers snapped to attention, but he waved them back to their duties as he strode past and into the radio shack.

The young technician turned to the sound of Fletcher's footsteps, "Would you like me to get *Bull Shark*'s commander on the pipe for you, sir?"

"Yes, please do Saunders," Fletcher said, fiddling with his tie.

The radioman was used to dealing with the high and mighty Vice-admiral by now and was no longer intimidated by his presence. He picked up the handset and spoke into it. There was a pause, and then the young carroty-haired man handed the phone to his admiral.

"Lieutenant Elmer Williams, sir," Saunders informed Fletcher.

"Welcome, Lieutenant... Jack Fletcher. What brings you to our little party this afternoon?"

A soft chuckle, "*A bit of a long story, Admiral. Not one I'd like to share, even over the short-range. If you've got a motor launch, sir, I'd be grateful if you sent her across. I'd be happy to return and report in person... also, we've got a few wounded men here who could use a medical facility better than what we can offer. There's not much better than a carrier's sickbay, sir.*"

Jesus, what the hell happened?

"Of course, Mr. Williams," Fletcher replied. "I'll send a launch to you. I'll order the fleet to reduce to minimum headway to make the transfer of your men easier as well."

"*Thank you, sir, that's very considerate.*"

"Williams... generally subs are commanded by O4 and above..." Fletcher gently prodded.

"*We're no exception, sir. Our skipper, a couple other officers and a few of our men are... on assignment. I'll explain more when I see you, sir.*"

"Very well," Fletcher said. "I look forward to meeting you, Lieutenant. Standby to receive our boat."

The transfer of the wounded went relatively smoothly. Only the most severe cases were sent across. They included Buck Rogers, Frank Nichols and two other men with uncertain internal injuries. Once the men were aboard the small launch, Williams climbed in after them, leaving Pat Jarvis in command. The boat motored across the eight-foot swells and was retrieved by the big carrier even as she and the rest of the fleet ramped back up to cruising speed.

Once Williams had seen his men to sickbay, he was escorted to the flag bridge by a junior yeoman. There he was met by Fletcher, Captain Ramsey and the carrier's intelligence officer.

"Welcome aboard, son," Fletcher said, extending his hand.

"Thank you, sir, it's a real pleasure," Williams beamed.

Introductions were made and coffee poured. The four men

gathered around a big chart table and Fletcher cleared his throat, indicating that Williams should start explaining.

Which he did.

He told them about the Raider team currently on Guadalcanal and how they were to make contact with Martin Clemens and re-supply him and recommend a landing place on the big island. How they'd brought extra radio equipment and how through the use of the ham bands, they were communicating with Hawaii using code.

"Yeah, I've heard that," the intelligence officer, a Lieutenant a year or two older than Williams named Gilbert Blackwood, confirmed. "According to Commander Rochefort, it's one of his staff that's on the box... a WAVE named Turner."

Williams grinned, "No kidding? Well, I'll be... that's our skipper's wife, believe it or not."

"Anvil Art Turner is your skipper?" Ramsey asked, clearly impressed.

"Yes sir, you know him?" Williams answered.

"Never met him... but have heard good things," Ramsey said and looked to Fletcher. "Art Turner was the one that sunk those krauts in the Keys while we were out here mixing it up with Nagumo in May, sir. Took down some Japs during the Midway operation too. Got a reputation as a cool, hard-hitting submariner."

"Good to hear... but what the hell's he doing ashore?" Fletcher asked.

Williams sighed, "It's connected to the OSS, sir. A mister Webster Clayton. This is his operation."

Blackwood groaned but had a smile tugging at his lips. Fletcher cocked an eyebrow, "I know him. He's aggressive too. Damn... I wish Vandegrift and Turner... that's Richmond Turner... were here. No relation are they, Mr. Williams?"

"No sir," Williams said. "I haven't had any contact with the shore since we dropped off our team. Not even with Pearl.

Well... other than sending after-action reports in, of course. So, I don't have any idea if the skipper and his party made contact with Clemens or what's happened since."

"Oh, they have, Lieutenant," Blackwood said ironically. "They've had some... trouble... but nothing too serious. A couple of wounded men, a couple of jap prisoners... this morning's report by Clemens to Townsville was passed on to Pearl and then to us. The team destroyed a five-inch gun that was mounted to cover the airfield and the possible landing beach. An exact landing location was radioed in, based on your skipper's recommendation, I'm told. I'm also told that his prisoners have confessed to a unit of howitzers being moved into position to cover Beach Red. An attempt is going to be made this evening to take them out, too."

"Oh, God all mighty..." Williams breathed.

"It's said Turner is aggressive," Ramsey noted.

"Yes sir..." Williams sighed. "And so is his counterpart, Major Decker."

"Well, I'm glad of it, and I'm sure Admiral Turner will be too," Fletcher said. "The fewer casualties we have getting men ashore, the better. There's not much worse or harder on men than an amphib assault... on the other hand, though, Williams... from the looks of your boat, you aren't exactly shy about mixing it up, either."

Williams blushed slightly, "Well, sir..."

He then told the other officers about the Sakai and how she was prowling the Sealark Channel. He briefly ran over the details of his battle with the *Fubuki* that was guarding the strike carrier task force. After that, he explained how *Bull Shark* had sunk the two freighters and been forced to spend a day and a half on the bottom thanks to their two escorts.

"Christ son!" Fletcher enthused. "Sounds like your skipper's rubbed off on you. Damned fine work. I'd like to buy you a drink... DeWitt?"

Ramsey grinned and stepped aft and through a hatchway that led into a short passage to Fletcher's at-sea cabin. A moment later, the carrier's captain returned with a bottle and four squat glasses. He set them up on the chart table and poured three fingers of something amber into the glasses.

"To Art Turner and the men of *Bull Shark*," Fletcher proposed as he hoisted his Scotch.

Glasses were clinked and sips taken. Williams hooted at the strength of the hooch.

"Lot better'n our depth charge medicine, sir," Williams grinned.

"I hope so, son," Fletcher replied with a chuckle. "That's twenty-year-old Glenfiddich in your hand. Well, is there anything we can do for you, Mr. Williams? Any supplies we can send over? Repair assistance... anything?"

"We're in pretty good shape, sir," Williams admitted. "We've only been at sea for a few weeks. We'll need to put in eventually to have our stern planes looked at... don't suppose you folks could lend us a dozen Mark 14s?"

Ramsey grinned, "Wish we had some to lend you. You're that low already?"

Williams sighed, "Only shoved off with ten. Just what we could put in the tubes to leave room for the Marines and the supplies... and I'm afraid that I'm down to two forward and two aft."

Fletcher grinned, "And you've already earmarked those for that strike carrier, haven't you, Lieutenant?"

Williams flushed again, "Well sir... not unless it's vital. My job is to stay close and ready to assist the captain."

Ramsey chuckled, "Uh-huh. You want that *Sakai*, don't you, Mr. Williams?"

Williams shrugged and flashed a brief smile, "Well sir... my thinking is to head back into the channel by way of the eastern end of Guadalcanal. Then see what's happening there in preparation for your approach."

"We'll be doing an end-around on the western side of the island," Ramsey explained. "Passing Cape Esperance around midnight and then getting on station sometime during the middle watch. Admiral Turner wants to begin putting men ashore at first light."

"Well... *we're* not rounding Guadalcanal," Fletcher clarified. "Turner's amphib force is. We're going to take station not far from here and fly support and bombing sorties."

"If you happen to get there first," Ramsey added. "Admiral Turner would no doubt be grateful if you put those four fish to use, should you have the opportunity. At the very least, if you could radio us and provide an up-to-date report, it would be appreciated."

"Of course, sir," Williams said.

"Oh, Lieutenant..." Blackwood said after polishing off his whiskey, "if there's anything you'd like to pass along to your skipper... I believe Mrs. Turner will be making another ham radio call tonight."

Williams drew in a breath and considered, "Tell him... tell him we're fine, sir."

"I understand, Mr. Williams," Blackwood said, a smile crinkling the corners of his eyes. "And good luck to you, sir."

"That goes for us as well," Fletcher said, extending his hand once more. "Be careful, Lieutenant..."

"Yes sir!" Williams snapped off.

Vungana, Guadalcanal – Sunset

Not only was it raining, but it was foggy as well. Even from their Norman castle-like fortress village, the watchers couldn't see much beyond a half-mile down toward the beach. It was frustrating, as Clemens' radiotelegraph reports of that morning were hot with the implications of an impending operation.

"I still say that beach east of Lunga Point is the best spot," Decker was saying as he, Turner, Clemens and the other officers huddled inside the headman's hut, two kerosene lanterns burning brightly and hotly to help keep some of the humidity from the delicate radio gear.

"That's what I reported earlier," Turner said. "In spite of what the prisoner told us this morning."

"Yeah, but we can't let those Marines come ashore under that howitzer battery, sir," Hazard protested.

"No, we can't," Turner agreed and cast an eye at Decker and then at their sixth guest.

Ryu Osaka sat on a rough-hewn bamboo stool sipping a cup of tea, "No, I agree, Commander."

Clemens looked dubious, "Wizard! We've got the approval of the enemy now."

"I may not exactly be an ally," Osaka said neutrally. "But I am not your enemy, Captain Clemens. At the moment, I am nothing, in fact. I can neither hurt you nor help you now."

Turner frowned and nodded, "A handily placed man in the Combined Fleet is not effective if he's not actually *with* the fleet... so that's yet another issue to consider."

"Eh?" Clemens asked incredulously. "Blimey, Art! You're not suggesting we let this lad toddle off back to his people now? Off with you, then, mind how you go... On his word that he's a right generous sort and wouldn't *dream* of betraying all of us to his superiors?"

"He's proven trustworthy before," Dutch offered.

"Web Clayton thinks highly of him," Turner added.

"Even if he *is* sincere about bringing the war to a close more quickly," Clemens insisted. It stands to reason that he'll do what's in *his* best interest, isn't that so?"

To everyone's surprise, it was Osaka that replied: "You are correct, sir. I'm not fighting for an American victory, as it were. I'm fighting to minimize a Japanese defeat. Too many young men have died, and many more will before this is over."

"More's the pity," Clemens said acidly. Though to his credit, his features wavered, and he seemed to regret his vehemence. He drew in a breath and sighed. "I'd like to believe you, Commander... but I've seen too much brutality already. Like it or no, your people are malicious and sadistic, and it's not going to improve over time, eh?"

Osaka heaved his own sigh of resignation, "I'm afraid that's true, Captain. The army in particular. The navy is... a bit less bloodthirsty... but the Imperial Army... well... all the more reason to end this quickly."

The Cactus Navy

"I'll see what Web Clayton has to say," Turner stated. "I'm not saying we release Osaka and his friend *now*. But maybe we can arrange something *after* the invasion. When what information he has now would no longer be of much use should he blab."

Osaka nodded, "*Hai*... also, there is Omata to consider. He will need a medical facility soon."

"As does my man," Decker said tersely.

Osaka bowed at the shoulders.

"What's of primary importance now," Turner said, looking to Decker for confirmation. "Is taking out that howitzer unit. Tonight."

Decker nodded, "Concur. Based on what we know, Watchtower may very well begin in the next twenty-four to forty-eight hours. We're here and can do something about it."

"And I think we take everybody," Turner said. "Marines and sailors alike... wish Entwater was here. We take Vousa and Batu as well if they want to come. We'll need at least one of them... course, they *both* could use a pair of boots and we're out..."

Clemens sighed and chuckled softly as he pulled his new boots off, "Jacob can have mine. We're about the same size, dash it all."

"You need to take care of your feet, too, Marty," Hazard said wryly.

"Well, I'm not traipsing off into the bush to attack the Nips, am I, Porter...? Again, unfortunately..." Clemens replied with a grin.

"I suggest three fire teams," Decker said. "Me, Porter and Art. Each team will have a Marine and a sailor. Each will have a two-way. That way, we can split up and flank the Japs."

Dutch frowned, "That leaves me back at the ranch again."

Turner eyed his friend for a long moment. Dutch was a submariner and a technical expert at that. He wasn't a soldier... but how to let him down gently and instill a sense of worth.

"I'll need a man or two here," Clemens offered. "Oaks is still not on his feet, and your expertise with comm gear is much appreciated, Joe. Also, we've got prisoners to consider. Both here and at Vushicoro."

"He's right, Joe," Turner said. "And once the Marines come ashore and take the airfield, all of you guys are going to need to join us... and I'm sure that Marty here won't mind having you and Oaks, who should be on his feet by then... to help."

"It won't be right away," Clemens explained. "And it won't be easy. By the time we *know* it's secure, the Japs will too, and they'll do all they can to harass your chaps. Just getting from here to the airfield in a few days might be dangerous... you'll be of great assistance, mate."

"You fellas don't plan on coming back?" Dutch asked Turner worriedly.

Turner shrugged, "I dunno, Joe. If we're right, and maybe we'll find out tonight... tomorrow might be the day. If we're successful at taking out those guns, then our best bet may be to join up with the landing force, as we'll be right there."

Decker nodded, "Probably. Also, based on what Porter and his team found out thanks to Jacob... the villagers in Carambuta might not be our friends. Maybe not in Bumbagoro, either. They may have *already* alerted the Japanese to our presence... if Porter's little fireworks display hadn't done that all on its own."

Hazard grinned, "My momma always said I was incorrigible... how many mortars are there, anyway?"

"Half dozen, according to our Japanese Marine," Joe said. He looked to Osaka.

The commander only shrugged, "I know nothing of this, I'm afraid... but I am not surprised."

"Six howitzers... or whatever the Jap equivalent is," Decker said. "Means at least twenty men to work them and direct them. Then I'd estimate at least a half platoon to provide security. Another twenty men or so."

"At the very least," Osaka put in. "After having that one-hundred-and twenty-seven-millimeter gun destroyed... there may be more men if they can be spared."

"So, four-or five-to-one odds," Hazard stated.

"With surprise on our side," Turner pointed out wryly.

"Well, lads," Clemens said. "I recommend a meal and that you all have yourselves a bit of a cork. We should hear from the lovely Mrs. Turner in a few hours, and then you're apt to have a rather *pressing* evening."

Chapter 28

Honolulu, Hawaii

– 2230 local time

Joan turner had to admit that it had been a pleasant evening. She and Gladys Finnegan had made a huge pot of spaghetti and, between the two of them, had wrangled enough ground beef and pork for at least three meatballs per guest. The guests included the Finnegans, of course, along with their son and daughter, who were Arty and Dotty's ages. The Finnegan kids had returned the day before, and the reunion was rowdy but heartwarming. The Spring Girls had come as well... May Dutch, June Nichols and soon-to-be April Post. Webster Clayton had come to the dinner party as well, partly because of his and Joan's upcoming radio call and partly so that Joe Finnegan wouldn't be outnumbered five to one.

Everyone had shown up at seven, and much to the delight of the kids, Joe Finnegan had wrangled a movie projector, portable screen and a reel of Looney-Tunes from the base along with a print of *The Wizard of Oz*. He had officially earned himself the title of the kids' hero for the night.

The kids had been set up Indian style at the coffee table, and the men had carried the dining room table and chairs into the living room and set everything up so they could all watch the movies while they ate. The kids loved it, and even though things went a bit past their bedtime, it was well worth it. They'd been packed off to bed, the boys sharing Arty's room and the girls Dotty's, and the adults had sat around and shared a few bottles of wine, a few beers and a nice homemade coffee cake brought by June.

"I want to thank you all for this," Clayton said, hoisting his PBR. "Bachelor like me... guy too much married to his work... it's a really nice thing to have a family evening like this."

"Hey, I'm just glad to have another man around to defend me," Finnegan said with a chuckle. "Otherwise, it'd be all knitting and sewing and other junk broads—"

Several throw pillows were put to their evident use and bounced off Finnegan's head to the amusement of everyone.

"I hate to be a wet blanket..." May Dutch began, a bit reserved.

"What's on your mind, honey?" April asked in her southern accent. "As if we don't all know."

May smiled, "Well... it's just... I wonder how the boys are doing out there. How are they tonight?"

"Tomorrow night," Clayton said. "Out in the Solomons; it's tomorrow already."

April chuckled, "Ain't that somethin'? I always forget about that... what do they call it...? The national time line?"

"International date line," June supplied. "Yeah... course the sailors love it because when they come east, I think, they get an extra day's pay."

"I'm sure they're fine," Joan reassured them.

She quickly cast a glance at Clayton. The two of them briefly shared one of those moments of secrecy in which much was communicated. Both of them, and to an extent Joe, knew what was happening in the Solomons. And even Joe Finnegan didn't know exactly when D-Day was for Operation Watchtower, let alone the exact H-Hour for it to begin. Both Joan and Clayton did, and it was partly on their work that the date and time had been established.

The Cactus Navy

"We should hear something soon, ladies," Clayton assured them with a confidence that brought small smiles to their faces. "Once the operation goes into effect... the cat will be out of the bag, and a lot more open communication will be possible."

"You really think everyone is all right, though?" Gladys asked in her boundless nurturing way.

"I do," Clayton said.

Again, he and Joan shared a quick look. They'd both spoken to Joe Dutch the previous night, and they'd been privy to a coded report from *Bull Shark* that had come in earlier in the day. This was one that Joe Finnegan could at least share in. His reassuring smile helped.

"I never thought marrying a Navy man would be like this," May Dutch suddenly admitted, her hands unconsciously wringing the hem of her skirt. "When Joey and I got hitched a year back... there wasn't a war on, you know? Sure, he and Art would put out on the *Tautog* for a month or two... but we never really *worried* about them. Not... not like now."

Joan reached out and took her hand and gave it a squeeze, "I know it's tough sometimes, May. For all of us."

"Yes... but at least you have the kids," June said wistfully. "With Frank getting his degree and then doing special work at GM... and then joining the reserves and being assigned to new construction... we haven't had time to even start *thinking* about a family... well, we haven't talked about it... but I've thought about it."

Gladys sighed, "I guess I'm the lucky one. Sure, Joey might work long hours, sometimes all-nighters, him and Joe Rochefort... but he comes home every day. Oh, April... I hope we're not giving you cold feet, sweetheart..."

April smiled and shook her head, "I knew what I was getting into, girls. I think it's worth it. These guys... our guys... they're *already* war heroes. They've already got good careers ahead of them. Probably all end up admirals, except maybe Franky, who'll muster out after the war and go run some big manufacturing plant or design new cars or whatever. I'm proud to be with a man in uniform, especially now that the world's gone kerflooey."

Joan grinned, "Same here and well said, April."

May sighed, "I know... and your right. It's just there are nights when I wish that damned uniform was hanging in my closet more often."

"I understand, May," Joan told her. "But you'll get through it. We all will. And at least we have each other."

The party broke up then, with the spring girls offering to do dishes, and then everyone saying good night. The Finnegan's left their kids with Joan, as they were already asleep and right next door. After Joe and Gladys said good-night, Clayton shut the front door and regarded Joan.

"You all right?" he asked.

Joan grinned at him, "You're pretty sensitive for a dude."

Clayton had to cover his mouth so his guffaw wouldn't wake the kids, "Occupational hazard, I guess."

Joan sighed as she got him another beer and poured the last of the wine into her glass, "It's the girls... what May and June were saying. They miss their men and are sad and lonely sometimes... and as the skipper's wife, I sort of have to be the rock for them all. But..."

"But they don't realize how sad and lonely you get," Clayton finished. "That you get scared, too."

Joan nodded, "Yeah... and how maybe it might be worse for me, Web. Because unlike them... I'm *inside* the circle now."

Clayton sighed, "Ignorance is bliss? Maybe... and you can always stop, Joanie. Your help with the Midway project was fantastic, as it is now... but if you want out, just say so."

She bit her lower lip and shook her head, "No, Web... no. If Art can go out there and face down Japs and depth charges, I can handle a little math work and playing with a radio, for heaven's sake."

Clayton chuckled, "It's hard being the captain, huh?"

She blinked at him in confusion.

"You're the skipper of the officers' wives club," Clayton said

The Cactus Navy

"Hell, the enlisted wives too, to a lesser degree. They look to you for guidance, leadership and even comfort. You have to show them the brave front... be the rock, as you say. Never letting them see your own fears."

She chuffed, "I guess that's what Arty goes through, isn't it? As the captain?"

Clayton nodded, "And he's damned good at it. Art Turner understands how to command souls, not just bodies. And you know something else, Joan? So does his wife."

"Thanks Web," Joan said, touching his arm. "Now, let's go get on the blower and bullshit these yellow sons of bitches."

"Oh yeah, everybody on this year's roster is doing okay," Joe Dutch was saying over the ham connection. "I think there's a couple of minor injuries on the team... but nothing to worry about."

"*Glad to hear it,*" Joan replied with false cheerfulness. "*So, are you guys going to the big Yankees and Red Sox exhibition game tomorrow? I know you've all been looking forward to it!*"

Turner, Decker, Clemens and Dutch's face all blanched at that. In code, Joan had just told them that D-Day was *tomorrow!* Dutch whistled silently before pressing the talk button.

"Oh god yeah..." he said. "Not sure what time we'll get to the park, though."

"*Better make it early... I heard on the radio that the stadium's gonna start filling up at dawn! Probably a good thing, parking in Manhattan being what it is.*"

Dutch handed the microphone to his captain, who drew in a steadying breath, "Hey there, Mary... how's everything? Everybody doing okay?"

A pause and a wistful voice said: "*We're okay. Kids miss you... the bridge club met tonight... mostly good cheer.*"

Turner thought he understood. The officer's wives and sweethearts were worried, and Joan was their rock, "Good good... tell them all we miss them and... and all my love."

They signed off, and Turner sat for a moment. His heart ached for his little family. His beautiful and cheerful wife, his irrepressible son and his little girl with her mother's bright blue eyes and boundless enthusiasm.

"I'll say it once more... she's champion, mate," Martin Clemens said softly from beside Turner.

The submarine captain drew in a centering breath, "That she is, Marty... that she is... well, we'd better focus on our jobs. From the sound of that call... D-Day is tomorrow morning!"

"Finally..." Clemens breathed. "It's been a long wait, Art, upon my *word*..."

"Just a few more days," Turner reassured him. "Then you can come down with our wounded and prisoners. The Marines will have seized the airfield, and all of this will be just a happy memory."

Clemens laughed, "Righto! Best get this show on the road then, as you lot say."

Decker had already prepared the rucksacks and gotten the men ready to go. Tommy guns and 1911's were oiled and checked over, C and D-rations and extra canteens packed, ammunition doled out, and every man wore a pair of fresh socks and had a spare in his pack.

"All right, listen up!" Decker was addressing the other nine men gathered around the fire. "Our target is a half-dozen or so Jap field guns that have been or are being positioned to cover Beach Red, the Marine landing point east of Lunga Point. My guess is that they're probably infantry guns. Maybe the type ninety-two battalion gun. They're light and only require a horse or two to drag them... though I doubt they've got horses here. Probably using human labor would be my guess. At any rate, each gun will have five or six crew, and they've probably got a half-platoon as security. At least fifty, perhaps as many as seventy men."

Some shuffling of feet and a few mutterings.

"Yeah, that's a lot of Nips against ten of us," Decker continued. "But we've got surprise and the night to help us. That and the gun servers won't be armed, most likely. Now those guns have an effective range of about a mile and a half, so they're probably close enough to

Beach Red to hit the shoreline and the landing craft, which means they're five or six hours' walk from here."

This time the groans were deeper.

"Yeah, that means we hike all goddamned night," Decker went on. "Probably won't be able to engage until dawn. We'll get close and send out one of our scouts to pinpoint their location, and then we'll bivouac a few hundred yards away for a couple of hours to rest. H-Hour is right about sunrise, but in truth, none of our boys is coming ashore for a few hours after that. There'll be an air and sea bombardment before any landing operations, of course. The advantage to us is that by dawn, the Japs will be setting up. They'll either get reports or will see the fleet in position offshore and will be real interested in that."

"Meaning they won't see us come up behind them and bash their fuckin' skulls in, right sir?" Taggart asked.

"Exactly," Decker said. "Now listen up, you bastards... we're assembling into three fire teams. Able team is me and Ingram. Baker team is Captain Turner, Tank and our comedian, Taggart. Charlie team is Mr. Hazard, Lider and the chief. Everybody got that?"

Everybody had that.

"Mr. Vousa and Batu have graciously agreed to come with," Decker went on. "Once we reach our objective, we'll figure out how best to utilize them. Lieutenant Dutch is staying here with Mr. Clemens and the Sarge... and our Jap prisoners. He'll be coordinating communications with the fleet and Teddy back at Vushicoro. Each team will have a two-way, but we probably won't be able to communicate with anybody back here. It is *imperative* that we take out those guns, men. Six of those fuckin' things can do heavy damage to Higgins boats with explosive rounds and tears a shitload of men to shreds with frag rounds. That is *unacceptable*. We're gonna have a bitch of a time enough on this godforsaken island after we take it, so we don't need any of our guys getting blown to bloody rags before they even get to have a coconut. All right. Any questions?"

"Yeah, your team is light a man," Turner said.

"That's not a *question*, Art," Decker chuckled. "But my thinking is that Able and Charlie will be to either side of me, and Doug and I will be directing at first."

"Sir!" Hazard said. "Our party encountered some uncertain locals on our last raid. Suppose they've reported us to the Japanese."

Decker looked at Jacob Vousa, "Sergeant Major?"

"It's possible," the Melanesian officer stated. "I did not like the way the headman behaved when we passed through Carambuta. However... it's dark and that should make things easier."

"It doesn't make any difference," Turner stated. "We've got a job to do, however hard it might be."

Decker grinned, "And that says it all. Final gear checks and let's move out."

Battleship Yamato – Truck Atoll – 1,100 miles from Guadalcanal

Admiral Isuroku Yamamoto once more found himself standing alone in his situation room aboard the mighty battleship. Once more, his battle table was populated with toy ships and little splotches of brown felt all arranged in a diorama-like representation of a particular section of New Georgia Sound. There was large Guadalcanal to the south, Savo Island to the northwest and then to the east a bit, Florida Island, Tulagi, Gavutu and Tanambogo Islands.

There were few ships this time. Not like Midway, where there had been so many the representation seemed almost ridiculous. There were some surface vessels north and west of Savo held in reserve. There was an aircraft carrier and her five escorts east, northeast of Tulagi Island, also held in reserve. There were toy aircraft on the four smaller islands and a handful of pewter soldiers as well. Most especially on the big island.

Yamamoto knew, of course, that somewhere out in the Coral Sea... somewhere close... was an American fleet. What he did not know, and what had been keeping the sleep away for several nights, was how large and in what strength.

Americans had landed on Guadalcanal. Of that, there could be no doubt. IJA and *Riikosentai* troops had encountered them. First five days earlier on the weather coast. Then again that night. In each case, the Americans had defeated the Japanese contingent. However, these contingents had been small patrols and the reports indicated that the American force couldn't be any more than ten or twelve men.

Then several nights later, a large gun emplacement in what had been a coastwatcher's observation point had been attacked and destroyed. Not a critical loss... and it did offer more information than it did cause frustration.

If the Americans were there, and they were attacking positions set up to cover the Lunga Point airfield project... then it followed that this was an advance scouting party for a large-scale assault. There could simply be no other conclusion.

Then his strike carrier group had been accosted by a single American submarine. The boat had succeeded in destroying a *Fubuki*-class destroyer leader. The next day, two supply ships had been torpedoed near Savo Island. Doubtless, the same boat. The escorting ships reported having sunk the submarine, but Yamamoto had his doubts. This combined with the spotty intelligence reports gleaned from partially broken American codes, and the admiral was certain that within twenty-four to seventy-two hours, the United States would invade the islands at the southeastern end of what they called "The Slot."

Yamamoto didn't have to turn at the sound of the hatch to the deck opening to know who it was who'd entered the room. He smiled thinly as he heard the familiar step approach.

"Come to check up on me, Matome?"

Yamamoto's chief of staff, Admiral Matome Ugaki appeared beside his commander and friend, "It is late, sir."

"Yes," Yamamoto said.

"Sleep evades you?"

"As it has for several nights... for the most part, Matome," Yamamoto replied wearily. "There is much weighing on my mind, as you might expect."

Ugaki sighed, "Yes... but wearing yourself to a nub will not solve anything, sir. You must rest. You must allow yourself to recharge."

Yamamoto grunted, "Did Abraham Lincoln rest while fighting to put his country back together? Did Julius Caesar take a vacation while the tribes of Gael plotted against him?"

Ugaki chuckled softly, "Interesting choices... Lincoln aged ten years during his presidency and it all but killed him. As for Caesar... he at least was able to stop fighting in the winter."

"No such luck for me," Yamamoto said wryly. "Have we heard from young Osaka?"

Ugaki shifted uncomfortably, even going so far as to shuffle his feet. Yamamoto knew it was bad news.

"*Sakai* reports that his aircraft was shot down yesterday," Ugaki replied sadly. "There has been no report since."

"They're coming, Matome," Yamamoto said, moving to the other side of the table near the brown blob that represented Guadalcanal and tapping it with the index finger of his damaged hand. The oddness of his two missing fingers somehow adding a note of gravity to the action. "They'll come, and they'll come in force. We are not prepared. Just as before."

Ugaki shook his head, "Sir, you cannot blame yourself for Midway. Nagumo acted stupidly."

Yamamoto laughed harshly, "And yet he still *lives,* and he was placed in command of Third Fleet! Given command over the entire force, including *Shokaku* and *Zuikaku*. Where he got his patronage and how he maintains his favor I do not understand... frankly, I am surprised he didn't commit Seppuku after that *disgrace*."

"It is rumored that he intended to do so... but that Admiral Kusaka stopped him,"

Yamamoto all but spat, "Indeed... Kusaka has a kind heart... and I do not believe for a moment that Nagumo would have carried it through. Playing for sympathy. Make a good show of things... ah, well... now he's once more near the field of play. Third Fleet is out there, Matome, as ineffective as the mighty *Kido Butai* from which it was drawn at Midway. You can see how these things can weigh on the mind."

"War is a difficult business," Ugaki offered.

Yamamoto laughed again, still a bitter sound. "That it *is*, my friend. And it's a business doomed to failure."

"Sir, you cannot believe..." Ugaki trailed off helplessly.

Yamamoto turned to him and locked eyes with his advisor. Ugaki was struck by the intensity in them. Yamamoto's mild and abstemious manner was so disarming until you looked into his eyes and the true power of the intellect and the personality behind them was revealed.

"We had one chance," Yamamoto said. "Had the Pearl Harbor operation been performed *as directed*, we might have had a chance for victory. Not to defeat the Americans, Matome... I believe that is impossible. But we would have crippled them enough to solidify our hold in the territories we acquired. In the years it would have taken them to rebuild their carrier fleet, we could've strengthened our position enough so that a *political* victory could be gained. But no... Nagumo's meekness prevented that. Even my plan to send the *Rabaiasan* to the Panama Canal would only have been a stopgap. It still might have worked, however. Then there was Midway... a well-planned operation that failed utterly... I share some of the blame for that, I'm afraid. I should not have held back the assault fleet... Even so, Nagumo lost four... *four!* Four carriers at Midway! That defeat has, in my opinion, doomed us. The Americans will pour more resources, more ships and more men into the Pacific, and our leaders will commit all of our resources until Japanese dead float bloated and corrupting on a sea of blood."

Matome shivered at the powerfully horrifying imagery and at his commander's black mood. Yet, he couldn't bring himself to disagree. It was still possible that luck would operate in Japan's favor... yet the devastating loss two months earlier was a harsh wake-up call to the people of Japan and one that was impossible to ignore.

"This is a war of attrition, Matome," Yamamoto went on. "The enemy erodes our best while he continues to produce his best. Do you know how the United States Navy treats its pilots, Matome?"

The younger man just shook his head and waited, knowing that the question was rhetorical.

"They remove their flying aces from combat and send them back to the States to train their new pilots," Yamamoto explained. "Bringing their experience and knowledge back so that the next wave of young men goes into the field knowing what to expect and how to fight our superior Zeroes, for example. Do we do this?"

"No sir," Ugaki admitted sourly.

"No, we do *not*," Yamamoto growled. "*We* send our best pilots into combat, over and over and over again until their luck runs out... which it must for everyone. It's simply a matter of statistical probability, Matome. Then we replace our aces with new pilots who have little or no experience! Do you see where this leads us?"

"Yes sir."

Yamamoto sighed wearily, "I have *tried*, Matome, as you know. I've tried to explain this to our superiors. But do they listen? Of course not! We are the Japanese! We are led by a divine Emperor! Victory is our destiny. What *rot*..."

Matome could only stand by and listen. To bear witness to his friend's inner demons. There was no solace he could offer Yamamoto, for like it or not, the Admiral was correct.

Finally, Yamamoto smiled thinly and patted Ugaki on the shoulder, "Fear not, my friend. I am too much a creature of duty to simply roll over and quit. We will fight and fight fiercely. Yet I wonder how our children and grandchildren will see us... but you're correct. Such maunderings will achieve nothing. Let us rest now... for tomorrow, perhaps, we fight. Oh, one more thing, Matome, if you would..."

Yamamoto reached below the table and into one of the

underslung trays there. He brought out a carrier and five destroyer models and set them east, northeast of the Florida Islands.

"If you would do me one small service before retiring," Yamamoto said as he positioned the models. "Have radio order *Sakai* to this position... roughly one-hundred and fifty miles east, northeast of Tulagi."

Ugaki blinked in surprise, "But sir... she's positioned perfectly to intercept the attacking fleet you speak of."

"If I'm right, Matome," Yamamoto replied. "Such a fleet will be comprised of dozens of ships. And I would also expect two carriers at least, possibly three. Large fleet carriers. *Sakai* is a strategic weapon. I will not have her sacrificed now. She will get her chance."

"It shall be as you wish, sir," Ugaki said and hurried out.

Yamamoto lit a cigarette and drew deeply on the bitter tobacco. He smiled to himself as he made his way to his own quarters. If he truly had *his* wish... ah, well... it did no good to think on what was not.

Part Two

Pulling the Trigger

"Enemy troop strength is overwhelming. We pray for enduring fortunes of war" and pledged to fight "to the last man."

— Last Japanese radio message from Tulagi, August 7, 1942

Chapter 29

D-Day – August 7, 1942
– 0600 Guadalcanal time

Elmer Williams stood at the search periscope, his wrists on the handles and his hands dangling negligently over them. He rotated the scope slowly as he scanned the visible horizon, nearly seven miles in radius at radar depth. The sun had yet to rise, but a hint of false dawn was streaking the eastern sky a deep indigo.

"Negative contacts," Williams reported. "Radar, give me a scan with the sugar dog and then two complete sweeps with the sugar jig."

Ted Balkley activated his gear. On his SD air-search radar oscilloscope display, nothing showed. That wasn't really a surprise; it still being dark. Aircraft rarely operated at night unless absolutely necessary. They could fly all right, but landing on a carrier was extremely dangerous.

"No contacts," Balkley reported. "Activating sugar jig..."

Another screen lit up with a display of a local chart. The fuzzy line of the radar sweep appeared over the planned position indicator. Besides this, Balkley had also activated the primary display. The green line across the center remained flat for the first sweep.

However, on the second, there was just the slightest hint of fuzziness. On the PPI, a faint scatter of something edged the western quadrant.

"Something..." Balkley puzzled. "Extreme range, sir. Fourteen-thousand yards bearing two-nine-zero."

"Ships coming up over the hill," Williams opined. "Let's get a little closer and have ourselves a look. That's probably our fleet. No doubt X-ray division off Lunga Point. Mug, all ahead standard. Course two-eight-five."

"Helm is two-eight-five," Mug said as the bells chimed on his enunciator display. "Maneuverin' ansiz all ahead standid."

The diesels growled as they were revved up to provide more electrical power. At a depth of forty feet, *Bull Shark* accelerated to fifteen knots thanks to her snorkel. Should it be the fleet, then the submarine would have to spend the day below the surface as the Japanese would no doubt respond with aircraft. Williams wanted to make sure their batteries were as full as possible.

"And so it begins..." Williams muttered, looking down at his watch. "H-Hour. Boy, are the Japs gonna crap their pants..."

"Their Jap pants," Jarvis added.

Enterprise dive-bomber group VB-6

Lieutenant Harold L. Beule tried to lean forward over the stick of his Dauntless SBD dive-bomber so that he could make sense of the dark landscape below him. There was a little bit of light now, just enough to tell land from sea and sky, but to try and pick out this Jap airfield from ten thousand feet? Unless the Nips were nutty enough to have a couple of lights burning for them, it might be problematic.

"Maybe we oughta drop down to a couple of grand," Beule's bombardier, Petty Officer Thomas "Thumbs" Grindle suggested. "You ain't gonna make heads or tails of that coast by leaning in, Harry."

"Boy, you might be right, Thumbs," Beule grumbled. "Had to get high over them mountains... but we can't come in low like a damned fighter. Gotta *dive* still. Feel like that must be important... says dive right in the description of this here bird, y'know?"

Grindle burst into laughter, "Got me there, Skip."

Beule laughed. "Thumbs, get on the blower and tell the squadron to throttle back to minimum. I think I see the fleet off to our left. They're probably off Koli Point now, so we'll slow down, and it'll give us another couple of minutes for some light."

Beule slowly banked his aircraft toward the west, following the coastline as he did. As with the sunset, sunrise came swiftly in the tropics and in the five minutes more it took the flight to reach the target, Beule was able to distinguish the runway and buildings of the nearly complete airfield below him.

"Goin' for broke!" he said, flexing his hands. "Squad leader to all ships... tallyho!"

Grindle, who was also the radio operator, sent out the word even as Beule shoved his throttle to the stops and pushed his bomber over and began the dive. The big radial engine roared, and the plane quivered as she powered downward at the ground at several times the speed of terminal velocity.

It was inevitably a sphincter-tightening experience for new bomber crews on their first dive. There was something inherently terrifying about purposefully aiming your airplane for the ground and heading almost straight down at over three hundred knots. Many new crews and even some pilots lost their cookies or even pissed their pants.

Luckily, Beule and Grindle were combat veterans, and both men stared intently at the target as it grew larger and closer in their canopy.

"Five thousand feet!" Grindle was hollering over the roar of the engine and scream of the air rushing past the canopy. "Four thousand... three thousand... two thousand... eighteen-hundred... now, Skipper!"

The men felt as if their restraining straps would rip them apart as Beule activated the air brakes, suddenly slowing the plane's descent rate by over sixty percent. As they groaned with the strain, Grindle thumbed his bomb release button, and the big thousand-pound bomb began to whistle away. Beule pulled the plane out of her dive, released the air brakes, and accelerated into a steep powered climb out to sea and over the fleet.

Their payload released, the Dauntless had become far more maneuverable. Although not anywhere close to the nimbleness of a Wildcat and *nowhere* near a Zero, the dive-bomber was built tough, and their course would take the squadron out over the fleet, around to the east and back to *Enterprise* for a reload.

Transport McCawley - 0612

Admiral Richmond Kelly Turner watched from the starboard bridge wing as bright orange fireballs blossomed along the shore to either side of his ship. From his vantage point, he could still see the bombs exploding on Tulagi and the other small islands closer to it, but the bombs that burst on the Japanese airfield at Lunga Point were much closer and far more spectacular. They did seem oddly far away even so. The fifteen transports of X-Ray group were only six miles or so off Beach Red, which was east of Lunga Point. What was stranger still was that he could swear that something was going on in the foothills beyond.

There were flashes of light there. He didn't hear any explosions, at least not from that quarter. The roar of the carrier planes and the thundering of thousand-pound bombs seemed to echo over the entire span of the Sealark Channel, drowning everything in its rumble.

Of course, that would soon be replaced by a racket even more thunderous and even more glorious.

"Sir, radio reports dive bombers have released their payloads and are clearing the area," the messenger of the watch said as he rushed up.

Turner looked at his companion, Major General Alexander Vandegrift and grinned, "Ready for a real show, Alex? Thank you, son. Please tell the radioman to issue the commence fire order. Weapons free on all assault ships. Fire for effect all Watchtower and Cactus targets."

"Aye-aye sir!" the young man exclaimed with barely contained excitement.

Vandegrift beamed, "I like to see a man who loves his work, Rich."

"Ever see a shore bombardment from this many warships?" Turner asked wryly.

"I've seen a shore bombardment time enough," Vandegrift stated. "But nothing on this scale... has anybody?"

"Not in a long time," Turner said as the world around them began to bellow.

Ahead and to port, a cacophony of shattering crashes boomed out as naval guns began to sing their song of destruction. Five-inch, six-inch and the bigger eight-inch guns of the heavy cruisers filled the world with fury. The sheer number of guns and the rate of fire gave one the impression that God himself was playing with the universe's largest Gatling gun.

The partly cloudy sky was alight with flashes, and the targets ashore were awash in smoke and flame. Everyone aboard every ship, whether they could see directly or not, cheered and whooped in excitement.

For the first time in the now eight-month-old Pacific War, the United States and the men of her Navy and Marine Corps were getting some of their own back. No longer were they reeling from a devastating surprise attack. No longer were they scrambling to put together a ragged defense to throw up in front of a crushing Japanese onslaught. No more were they fighting a defensive war. Midway was still fresh in everyone's mind and a magnificent victory... yet it hadn't been an *attack*. America had gotten lucky and had defended herself. Now, though... now... finally, the United States had rolled up her sleeves and, in spite of the hasty preparation of the operation, was coming out of her corner and giving the Jap a taste of his own medicine.

On *McCawley*'s main deck where the Marines were mustered to go down into the LCVPs, known affectionately as Higgins boats, Corporal Marlin "Whitey" Groft of the First Marines found Private Robert Lecky loitering by the rail where the landing craft had been swung out ready to be lowered. The two men weren't in the same platoon but had met on the voyage and become friends, striking up a friendly rivalry as to who could do the best jitterbug.

"Hey Bobby!" Marlin shouted over the din. "How do you like this action, huh!?"

Lecky beamed at his friend, "We're sure givin' them Japs what for, huh Whitey? I ain't *never* seen anything like this! How you feelin'? Was a pretty rough night... any seasickness?"

Groft waved that away, "Nah... I'm four-oh, pal. How about you?"

"Right as rain," Lecky said, staring momentarily at the Higgins boat above them. "Wonder what it'll be like in these jobs, though?"

"Hey, you see that, Bobby?" Groft asked, pointing past the blocky landing craft and at the thin line of land that would be their destination in a few hours.

Lecky leaned out and peered, squinting his eyes, "Nothin's goin' on over there, Whitey... that's Beach Red, I think... but there isn't any report of anything there, far as I know. I don't see what... whoa! Was that an explosion?"

"Looked like it," Groft confirmed. "Just over the horizon, I'd guess. I dunno... it's getting light, so maybe I'm just seeing things."

"Well, we'll know by lunch," Lecky said and lit himself a smoke.

Foothills of Beach Red – thirty minutes earlier

It was just before 0400 when Batu had materialized out of the night and nearly given Art Turner a coronary. The Melanesian was excited and gesticulating wildly. So overcome was he that even Vousa couldn't understand his pidgin until the younger man was calmed down.

"He says he found the enemy," Vousa was finally able to explain. "About a klick to our north and a little east. Six artillery pieces and at least sixty uniformed soldiers. He also says... he also says there were more than that many civilians too. Some islanders and some that looked like the Japanese but not in uniform. They were chained."

"Jesus Christ..." Hazard muttered darkly.

"Pack animals," Decker stated grimly.

"God help us..." Chief Duncan observed. "What kind of people *are* these?"

"Savage and dedicated to their own belief that they have a divine right to what they do," Decker said. "All right then... we know what we're in for. Let's stop here and try to get an hour's rest. Get off our feet, drink some water and try to get some shut-eye. We move out at zero-five-thirty. Don't neglect your feet."

The team had found themselves a bit of a clearing off the path and in an area of jungle that was a bit less rainforest and trending more toward hardwoods and palms. Unfortunately, even concealed, they couldn't risk everyone going to sleep at once, and straws were drawn for guard duty. Lider and Tank had drawn the short straws.

The rest of the men slung their hammocks between trees so that they could sleep off the ground, and to a man passed out the moment they settled in. Tank and Lider stood near the path out of sight, listening intently to the sounds of the tropical night.

"So what's goin' on with you and the chief?" Tank asked after ten minutes of silence.

Lider snorted, "Nothin'."

"Come on, Lider," Tank pressed. "You two bicker like an old married couple. Chief's a good guy. What've you got against him."

Lider sighed, "He ain't a Marine."

"What's that a crime?" Tank jeered.

"You squids got it so soft," Lider complained, suddenly finding an outlet for his grievances. "Comfy racks, good chow... you got no idea what it's like to fight a real war."

Tank chuckled softly, "So I guess your beef is with all of us *squids,* huh? Me, Doug, Mr. Dutch, the skipper... even Mr. Hazard?"

"He was a devil dog," Lider relented.

"Oh, well, how gracious of you, your honor," Tank sneered. "Let me tell you somethin', pal. You leathernecks ain't got the market cornered on hard duty or bravery. Now unlike you, I ain't diminishing what the Marines do. Those kids out there in them ships are about to face some of the hardest shit they ever seen in their lives. But maybe before you judge us *squids,* you oughta walk in our shoes."

Lider scoffed.

"You don't know what it's like, being hundreds of feet down," Tank said and leaned in so he could speak more quietly. "Hundreds of pounds of water pressing on every inch of your boat... the metal groans and creaks and moans as if it's alive. It's deathly quiet, and then, from outside, you hear this clicking sound... then the world goes crazy! The sound of the explosion is so loud it hurts your ears. And it comes from *everywhere,* Chuck... all around you. The ship bucks and rolls and zigs like a baby rattle. Men are tossed around, and the lights go out... and each time you hear a new groan and creak you wonder when the walls will collapse and crush you to death."

Lider's silhouette was stock still. Tank knew he had the younger man's attention now.

"Gettin' crushed if you're lucky," Tank went on ominously. "You know what happens to air when it's suddenly compressed to ten, fifteen or twenty atmospheres? See, Lider, you don't drown when your sub goes to the bottom. You don't get crushed... not right away. Most subs, they can go a lot deeper than they're rated, see. Our own boat went down to eight hundred one time and was intact... so what happens is that when a sub's deep and is suddenly vented to the sea... the air inside compresses. Compressed air heats up. You *burn* Lider. The air is so hot it cooks you. If you're really lucky, the water and the collapse kills you before too long... but it's that last moment that's got to be the worst."

"Jesus Christ..." Lider said in awe.

"And one more thing," Tank said tersely. "Don't forget that the chief, me and all the rest of us sewer rats are *right here* with you and about to assault a superior Jap force. So maybe you might think about knockin' that chip off your shoulder and cuttin' us lowly sailors a break, huh?"

Tank spun on his heel and stomped off a few feet. Lider was left standing alone in the dark, speechless and confused. Inter-service rivalry was one thing. Poking a little fun at each other but all the while respecting all the guys who were your brothers in arms. Maybe Lider had forgotten that last part and allowed good-natured ribbing to devolve into real contempt.

Had he misjudged the Navy? Had he gotten so cynical that he felt he was so much better than them? Lider didn't know and didn't want to think about it. But he would have to work with the chief. No matter what, the mission had to come first.

Tank and Lider had been relieved by Decker and Turner forty-five minutes later. The two officers admitted to one another that the small amount of sleep had probably made them feel worse. Their feet were sore and now swollen after having rested for a time. Yet they'd changed their socks, choked down a D-ration chocolate bar and a pack of crackers and let Tank and Lider get what rest they could.

At five-thirty in the morning, the men split up into Able, Baker and Charlie teams. Batu went with Hazard and Vousa with Turner. Decker stated that his team, Alpha, would be the center, Turner's team the left flank and Hazard's the right. They'd work into position to cover the Japanese firing line as best they could, reconnoiter the situation and then decide on their attack.

Moving through the jungle was hard enough at night. Now, the teams had to split up and move silently... or as silently as circumstances would allow. They'd rested only a kilometer from the Japanese position, yet it had taken the entire thirty minutes before dawn for them to work into position. Close enough to see without being seen.

Thankfully, the Japanese were confident in their situation. They had sixty soldiers, ten to a gun. Half of these were there to watch the other half as they worked their pieces. Additionally, they had their human workhorses chained together behind the center of the line of guns to act as both a shield and as a potential early warning system should anyone be foolish enough to make a try at them.

There was, in fact, a group of men foolish enough to make a try for them. They'd worked into place behind the line of artillery and hunkered down in the vegetation waiting for their moment.

The line of howitzer-like field guns was arranged over a fifty-yard area on the crest of a low hill that overlooked Beach Red. The elevation gave the Japanese enough height to see across the lower hills and open plains of kunai grass to the shoreline just over a mile away. There were some palms and other trees on the crest of the hill that gave the guns some concealment. Each Type 92 piece poked out between a pair of trees like cannons in the embrasures of an old fort. In three of the trees, men had climbed up and settled themselves in with binoculars to act as spotters, one man to a pair of guns.

"Well set up," Decker whispered to Ingram, who crouched beside him. They, too, were on a slight rise that gave enough height to see over the tops of the cluster of civilians directly before and below them.

"What do we do about those folks, sir?" Ingram asked quietly, nodding at the five dozen shadows that sat hunched over fifteen yards away.

Now that the eastern sky was just beginning to lighten, the dark shapes of the men and guns were beginning to take on some washed-out details. The Japanese were easy enough to pick out in their pale uniforms. This was especially true for the four officers with their red sash belts and their swords. Yet even in the gloomy light of pre-sunrise, the misery of the chained people was obvious, just in the way that they hunched over themselves with their heads lolling and their almost statue-like stillness gave definition to their plight.

"I don't know, Doug," Decker said. "We try not to hurt them, of course... guess we'll see."

Before Decker could expound further, the men paused to listen as a distant humming began. At first, they were worried that somebody somewhere had disturbed a big wasp's nest and the angry insects were coming to exact their revenge.

Yet the sound grew too loud and too fast. Even as the teams realized what they were, the roar of aircraft engines soared overhead and passed, headed toward Lunga Point. The distant sound of multiple whistles suddenly became rolls of tremendous thunderclaps that literally shook the earth under their feet.

The chained people began to move about then, some trying to rise, some chattering away in pidgin, and some crying out in fear. Harsh Japanese was now being shouted back and forth along the firing line as officers and sergeants managed their suddenly frightened men. One of the gun captains, one nearest the left side of the line, actually fired off his weapon. The field gun barked, its moderately high-pitched shriek seeming strange amidst the loud low rumble of the bombs.

"We should go now, sir!" Ingrim hissed. "While they're distracted!"

Decker held up his hand, "Easy, Doug... not yet. These are just the previews; we wait for the main show. Radio to Baker and Charlie teams hold position. Just a few more minutes..."

Ingram, who was in charge of the two-way field radio, brought the bulky unit to his lips and spoke softly into it. There was a series of crackles and two barely audible acknowledgements.

"Baker team roger," Taggart said into his radio fifty yards to Decker's left. He leaned in closer to Turner. "What is he waiting for, do you think, sir?"

Turner grinned at the younger man, "You tell me, Davie, he's your boss... I'd guess the naval bombardment, though. This is just the carrier portion of the assault to get the japs nervous. But out there, somewhere, are probably a few dozen cruisers and destroyers about to open up with the big guns. Gonna be a helluva light show."

"Think we're far enough back, sir?" Tank asked dubiously.

Turner shrugged, "I sure hope so, Tank... Word might have reached the fleet that there's a couple of field guns here. But if so, then they also know that *we're* here and that we're gonna take these jokers out. Hope that keeps their gun directors off us."

"That's reassuring," Tank said sarcastically.

A hundred yards to their right, Charlie team was getting ants in the pants as well. Literally, as it turned out.

"Goddammit!" Duncan growled. "I think we're near a red ant hill... shit! Son of a..."

Hazard tried not to laugh as he waved Duncan around to Lider's left. The chief somehow managed to crab-walk to his left, all the while keeping quiet and swatting at a couple of fire ants that had found their way up his boots.

"Can't wait to be shot of this fuckin' place..." Duncan grumbled. "Fuckin' ants... fuckin' centipedes... fuckin' spiders could carry off a child or a small woman... fuckin' leeches... fuckin' man-eating lizards..."

"Jesus, Chief," Lider cranked. "What part of keeping your trap shut on account of we're surrounded by Japs don't you get already?"

"I ain't *never* gonna complain about the noise in the engine rooms again..." Duncan grumbled as he settled in. "So let's attack these slopes already and get outta this fruit city!"

"At ease, Chief," Hazard managed to say evenly and without cracking up, though it took an effort. "We gotta wait for just the right time."

"I'm gonna scrag me a bucket load of these yellow shits," Duncan growled. "And I swear to the sweet living baby Christ in a playpen, sir... we're keepin' at least one of these slants so I can stake his yellow heinie down to one of these goddamned fire ant hills and see how he likes it."

The Cactus Navy

Even Lider had to stifle a snicker. Whatever he might think of the Navy in general, Lider had to admit that the sailors who'd come ashore were tough men. The chief, although he grumbled about the bugs, was as steadfast as any gunnery sergeant Lider had ever known.

"What do you think the signal will be?" Lider asked Hazard.

The sky was now light nearly to the western horizon, although the sun had yet to make its appearance. After the bombings at the airstrip the Japanese officers had managed to get their men settled down and refocused. Even the far-left gun crew had been hollered at and re-organized. After all, their part in the battle wouldn't come until the landings started.

A sense of calm had just settled over the enemy troops and prisoners. The dive bombers had all vectored out over the sound and the world, at least for a moment, seemed still once more.

That's when the fleet opened fire. Bright flashes from out to sea were quickly followed by an earth-shattering wave of atmosphere-blasting fury that trampled even the frantic shrieks of jungle birds and monkeys.

Although the explosive shells of even an eight-inch gun were nothing compared to the thousand-pound bombs dropped by the Dauntlesses... there were a *shitload* of them. Four miles offshore, the booming of the guns rattled like automatic weapons fire. Seconds later, the shore to the west roared and rumbled as dozens, then hundreds of shells burst on the ground and in the air above. It was nothing short of glorious

Hazard was about to shout, he'd have to in order to be heard, that this might qualify as a signal when Duncan's radio crackled with static and the tinny voice of Major Al Decker removed any doubt. The three men had to huddle together to hear the Marine officer over the din, but his words were unmistakable and welcome.

"*Light 'em up!*"

Chapter Thirty

Tank's grenade sailed high and true, landing nearly at the foot of the far-left gun and exploding among the men packed there. There were screams of pain, shouts of alarm and an eruption of gunfire. Even with dozens of Arisaka rifles discharging close at hand, they could barely keep pace with the din of the naval bombardment.

"Bursts!" Taggart advised as the three men moved apart and began inching forward through the brush. "Pick your targets and conserve ammo!"

Although he wasn't in charge and younger than the other two men, he was a seasoned Marine Raider. His training and combat indoctrination were valuable. Turner didn't think to contravene Taggart's directives because he was right.

Turner shouldered his Thompson and began to squeeze off bursts as he moved forward. At first, it was like shooting fish in a barrel. Tank's first grenade had taken down four men, and the other six were still trying to regain their wits. Turner's first two bursts took down two soldiers. Tank and Taggart took down three more before the final man, the gun captain most likely, dove behind his piece and began returning fire.

By that time, however, the crew of the next gun twenty yards down the line had moved to what cover they could find and were also joining the defense. Unfortunately for them, only six of the ten men per gun had a weapon. Still, from behind their piece and the trees, the Japanese were doing a fine job of halting Baker team's progress.

"I'd sure love to hit that ordnance crate!" Tank shouted.

"Won't do you any good, Tank!" Taggart called from a few feet away and behind a teak tree. "They're hardened against small arms fire and grenades!"

"Figures!" Tank shouted. "I'm goin' for it anyways! Cover me!"

"Goddammit, Tank!" Turner barked as he and Taggart emptied their magazines in the direction of gun number two.

The burly electrician was snaking his way along the ground, using the cover of the underbrush and tree trunks to conceal himself. The problem would be that from the edge of the trees to the guns was something of a lane of open ground five or ten yards wide before the next line of trees through which the guns poked. He'd have to cross that open ground without any concealment.

"Is he out of his mind, sir?" Taggart asked incredulously.

"Aren't we all?" Turner shot back, ejecting his magazine and quickly seating home another. "We gotta get that one behind the gun!"

"I'll get him, sir; you give Nutsy Fagan there covering fire!" Taggart called.

He moved into position as best he could and sighted along his barrel at the carriage of the field gun where its one remaining crewman must appear. Turner set his weapon to full auto and waited. The half-dozen soldiers at the next gun seemed to pause as well, probably wondering why the firing had ceased. Tank was nearly out of cover now. Turner and Taggart saw the man gather his legs up under him in preparation for a lunge across the twenty feet of open ground that lay between him and the large munitions box.

"Go, Tank!" Turner shouted as he rose to his knees and leaned out from behind his tree's trunk. He aimed for the next gun and squeezed the trigger, sending a full magazine's worth of .45 rounds downrange in seconds. He swept his barrel back and forth in a limited arc, forcing the six armed men there to stay low. Tank half-ran, half crawled like a land crab toward the six-foot-long, two-foot-high iron box that contained the three-inch howitzer shells. As expected, the last crewman tried to take advantage of this and leaned out with his sidearm rather than his rifle and aimed for Tank. Before he could pull the trigger, however, a large hole appeared in his forehead, and the back of the man's skull exploded outward in a nauseating bloom of blood, bone and brain.

"Out!" Turner shouted as once again he changed magazines.

The problem was that each of them only had six. Turner had already gone through two, Taggart one and Tank one.

"Don't blow it yet!" Turner called to Tank. "Use it as cover for now! Davie, can you work your way further down the line toward number two? I'll keep plinking from here until you get into a better flank position."

"Aye-aye, sir!" Taggart said and began belly crawling further into the brush.

Turner was impressed. For most of the time he'd known Taggart, he'd seemed like a typical loud-mouthed sort of jarhead. Yet Taggart could not only shoot and stay a cool cucumber in combat, but he also had a good head on his shoulders, too. The submarine captain would have to remember to talk him up to Decker... if any of them survived.

Due to the terrain at their end of the line, Charlie team was at something of a disadvantage. From their cover to gun six was over thirty yards. Easy shots, but daunting to cover in person and not an easy throw for grenades. Lider's first attempt landed five yards short of the group of men. The grenade exploded, and one of the men went down with a wound in his leg, but the other nine were able to scramble behind what cover the ammo box, gun and trees afforded.

"Shit!" Lider cursed as he and Hazard began to fire off single rounds from their Thompson's.

"Lemme give 'er a go!" Chief Duncan said.

He was a tall and rangy man, trending toward lean. However, he had unusually long arms that had proven more than once to be enormously strong. Duncan pulled the pin on a grenade, cocked his arm and flung the pineapple for all he was worth.

Not only did the grenade sail across the intervening distance between the Americans and the gun, it actually sailed over the gun and landed in front of the barrel... and exploded *behind* several of the Japanese soldiers there. The crack of the grenade going off was joined by screams of agony as three men were peppered with razor-sharp iron shards.

"God *damn!*" Lider said in awe. "You oughta try out for the Tigers with that arm, Chief!"

"What, and miss all this?" Duncan asked as he prepared to toss another grenade.

Both Hazard and Lider noticed that the next gun down, number five, had taken a keen interest in them as well. Those men, the soldiers anyway, had also moved to positions of cover and were firing in the general direction of Charlie team's position. It was somewhat random, as they had yet to home in on the exact location.

Duncan tossed his grenade and, once again, his distance was good and his aim true. The explosive landed amidst another group of Japanese soldiers and blew several men into gory rag dolls. The remaining five broke and ran west toward the dubious safety of their friends.

By then, Duncan had gotten his own Thompson into action, and the three Americans took down several of the fleeing Japanese before they could get more than a few yards.

"Think we could blow that gun?" Duncan asked as he and the others moved five yards away from their original position.

"Ammo box is made of heavy metal," Lider explained. "Not even a grenade would puncture it. But if one of us could get over there, we could open the lid and drop in a grenade. Best thing would be to load the gun, drop a pineapple down the barrel, shove a bunch of rocks and dirt and shit in and then fire the gun. Overpressure would blow out the breach."

"And kill the man who fires it," Hazard said.

"Maybe not," Lider explained. "If you could attach a line to the trigger mechanism and set it off from the side, out of the way of the blast… you should be okay."

"*Should* be?" Duncan inquired archly.

"I'm willing to give it a shot," Lider said. "Got some twine in my pack."

"Chief, you think you could hit that next gun with a pineapple from here?" Hazard asked, leaning around his tree and squeezing off a burst in the direction of the said gun.

"It's about fifty or even sixty yards, sir…" Duncan said. "That's pretty damned far, even for me."

"Even if you drop short, it might be enough," Lider explained. "Fatality range is about four or five yards, and injury range is about twelve or so… but that don't matter if I read Mr. Hazard right."

"Distraction," Hazard said. "You throw a grenade, and when it goes off, Chuck here hauls ass."

"Sounds crazy to me," Duncan said as he received Lider's two grenades. "You sure about this, Lider?"

The half dozen armed Japanese by gun five poured a fusillade of rounds in their direction. The 7.7mm lead projectiles whispered through the trees and bushes like horizontal raindrops, passing barely over the men's heads.

"Can't be worse than this," the Marine said grimly.

"Their firing discipline is poor," Hazard said. "All firing at once like that… wait until they fire again, Chief and then let er' fly."

"Okay…" Duncan said, pulling the pin on a grenade and squeezing the handle. "After they quit, you three give me a couple of bursts of cover…"

Once more, half a dozen Arisaka rifles crackled. This time,

however, the Japanese Marines were using their heads. They fired short bursts in four-man salvos. Two men held back while four fired, and then the next two men held back and so on. In this way, they could keep up a much longer stream of fire and keep the Americans pinned down. The Japanese didn't yet know how many there were, only that they were now under attack from three points on their firing line.

However, Vousa had been working his way west, away from the other three and opening up his firing angle. When he was ten yards to Hazard's left, he rose to his knees behind a deadfall that had once been a lignum vitae tree and opened up on the *Riekusentai* from closer to their flank. He took down two of them before the remaining four had the good sense to throw themselves behind whatever cover they could.

In the meantime, Duncan hurled his grenade toward them. It fell short, but only by about five yards. The grenade burst in a flash of smoke, fire and metal shards that peppered the gun and anyone or anything exposed.

Lider bolted across the open ground and dove to the dirt behind the ammo box. Unfortunately, one of the gun's crew had not run earlier. He'd been hiding behind the trunk of a large palm whose base was surrounded by a large hibiscus bush.

The man leapt up from behind his hiding spot, bayonet affixed to his rifle and lunged for Lider, roaring *Banzai* as he did so. Lider, who was lying prone behind the ammo box, had nowhere to go. The best he could do was to roll onto his side and throw up his rifle to try and ward off the charge.

Duncan, without even thinking twice, jumped to his feet and sprinted across the open ground. Hazard shouted a string of curses and followed suit. The Japanese soldier's face was a mask of fury as he drove his blade toward Lider's belly. The Marine swung his rifle and kicked up his right leg as the blade reached him. He did fend the blow off, but not entirely. He'd only managed to deflect the bayonet so that it missed ripping out his guts and instead plunged into his hamstring, the razor-sharp blade sliding completely through the muscle and out the other side.

"God *damn* you!" Lider bellowed in rage and pain just as Duncan reached the two men. The tall submarine chief petty officer bowled into the smaller Japanese man, hurling him back and off his feet. The two collapsed into a heap as Duncan began reigning powerful blows down on the shocked Marine. Hazard appeared beside him and fired into the Asian man's head, ending the struggle forever.

In the meantime, the other soldiers at gun five had popped up to shoot at the Americans as they ran across the open ground. However, either they'd forgotten about the fourth man to their right or simply ignored him. Because as they rose to fire, a metal object flew through the air and directly into their midst. Even as it exploded, another fusillade of heavy caliber rounds tore into them. The grenade and the fire took down the four men in short order.

"Chuck!" Hazard said, kneeling beside the now supine Lider and examining his bloody trouser leg. "Hang on, buddy… who's got the first-aid kit?"

"Jacob does," Duncan said, kneeling beside the men and peering over the lip of the box.

A moment later, Vousa slid to the dirt beside the Americans, "Gun five's crew is down… oh, bloody hell!"

"Get the kit," Hazard snapped even as he reached for Vousa's pack.

The Melanesian protectorate officer slid out of his pack, "Can you help him?"

Hazard began cutting Lider's BDU trouser leg, "I think so. It looks like the blade went straight through the ham. Depends on the bleeding… how you doing, Chuck?"

"Swell…" Lider groaned. "Little yellow fucker… thanks, Chief… I guess I owe ya'."

Duncan grinned, "First round at the Goonieville Lodge or at Paula Poanas is on you, Chuck."

"Deal," Lider said, reaching out his left hand. Duncan shook it. "Maybe I was too hard on you squids... you're not all bad."

"Nope," Duncan replied. "We're bad... but it ain't a blowout."

"You say that gun's out of commission?" Hazard asked Vousa, nodding at the next howitzer in the line. He was opening the first-aid kit and rummaging.

"The men are dead or have run," Vousa said. "The next guns down the line are occupied by Able and Baker."

"Okay..." Hazard decided. "You and the chief go and do what Chuck suggested. Blow the gun. Then get back here... I've got an idea on what we can do for this one."

"You two be all right, sir?" Duncan asked with evident concern.

"We're just ducky, Chief, now get the lead out, already!" Hazard ordered and smiled.

Decker hadn't initiated combat from his position when the others had. He knew that once all hell broke loose at either end of the artillery line, the Japanese in the center would be distracted and focused to either end. However, the officers were also located in Decker's section, and they would be less likely to overreact.

Based on the uniforms, the artillery unit was a mixture of *Yahohei*, or army field artillery personnel and *Riekusentai*, the Marines. There would be a lot of Marines on Guadalcanal, Decker decided, as the project to build the airfield was the IJN's baby. No doubt the army would show up eventually, but the Japanese Marines were every bit as tough and fierce as American Marines were.

Another issue that Decker had was the gaggle of civilians between himself and the guns. He couldn't just rush forward. He'd have to work around them, and that small amount of time could be deadly for his team, and the poor bastard's chained together.

Fierce fighting was breaking out to the left and the right. For the moment at least, the twenty men at guns three and four were staying by their pieces, gathering around between the two guns in order to stay out of the line of any stray fire, of course. The officers were shouting at the men and at each other, pointing and gesticulating wildly. Finally, two of the four officers joined their gun and security teams and began organizing them into firing lines.

"What do we do about those people, sir?" Doug Ingram asked, pointing at the human pack mules.

Decker sighed, "Not sure, Doug..."

"Can't we release them, sir?"

Decker frowned. They *did* have some basic tools in their packs. Pliers, screwdrivers, wrenches and a pair of heavy dikes... if the chains could be cut, the people would no doubt run in every direction. That could be both a blessing and a curse.

To Able team's left, from the far end of the firing line, a tremendous explosion shook the ground and trees around them. A blast wave wooshed past, carrying with it loose dirt, leaves and grass. The first gun had exploded in a spectacular thunderclap that had felled two trees that were to either side of it.

"Jesus Christ!" Ingram gulped.

That set the Japs into another tizzy. It also caused the prisoners to burst into an uproar. They shouted, screamed and cried out in several languages, writhing and jerking in every direction at once, their chains rattling and succeeding only in making themselves more uncomfortable.

"Shit... let's go, Doug!" Decker decided quickly.

Ingram didn't even have time to ask why before the Marine Raider commander leapt to his feet, broke from cover and lunged down the gentle slope from the top of the rise. Without a second thought, the young submariner ran after him. Decker led Ingram right into the middle of the chained prisoners. None of the Japanese seemed to notice, but Ingram had his Thompson shouldered and was scanning for targets over the heads of the mass of humanity before him.

It took an almost laughable few moments before the mixture of Korean and Melanesian slave workers became aware of the two

Americans shoving into their midst. They began to chatter again in confusion and fear, not certain what to do.

"It's one long chain that threads through these leg irons, sir," Ingram said, pointing at the feet of one man. "If we could cut it..."

"Do any of you speak English?" Decker asked as people simultaneously pressed in on the Americans and tried to back away. "Savvy English?"

Someone did, it seemed. A rather pretty Guadalcanal islander in her mid-twenties blinked at him with large brown eyes, "I savvy sometime belonga... 'e come 'e savvy noombo muchly bring things and stuff Clemens."

"I think that means yes, sir," Ingram quipped wryly. "Kinda..."

Decker knelt down at her feet and slipped out of his pack. The entire time he was digging through it to find the tools, he felt an odd prickly sensation between his shoulder blades. As if any second, he and Ingram would be spotted by a Jap and a 7.5mm round or a bayonet would strike there.

Decker found the heavy-duty angled cutting pliers known as dikes and yanked them out, showing them to the woman, "We free you. Savvy? You go free from Naponapo."

Her liquid brown eyes went wide with fright, "No! 'e make muchly hurtem'..."

"Oh geez...!" Ingram bemoaned. "They're afraid of being set free... God all mighty..."

"Well, too bad," Decker said, placing the cutting blade on one of the chain links and bearing down. The chain was heavy, perhaps each link three-quarters of an inch wide and twice that long. It reminded him of an anchor chain that you'd use on a boat around forty feet long. The sharp dykes didn't break the link at first, he had to scissor them and squeeze with all his might.

"Sir, I think we're getting some unwanted attention..." Ingram warned.

"Almost got it..." Decker groaned. "Fuck me... ha!"

The link snapped, and he pulled on the chain and opened the cut link enough to break the chain apart. People all around had been watching, and they knew enough that they'd been freed. They all began to yank on the chain. At first, they were working against one another until finally, an older Korean man who'd been chained next to the young woman bent down and pulled the cut end of the chain through his shackle. He turned and began to do the same for the person next to him.

"Oh, shit!" Ingram quailed. "I think we're in trouble, sir!" Uhm... *run!*"

Although the shouted suggestion was meant for Decker, it was almost as if all sixty prisoners suddenly learned to speak English and had heeded the warning. People began to break and run as their feet were freed, dividing into two groups that went east and west. Some stumbled over one another, either in haste or because they had yet to yank the chain from their leg irons. Yet within a second or two of cutting the chain, the two Americans found themselves exposed and alone. Decker shoved the dikes back into his pack and blinked in surprise.

"Let's go, sir!" Ingram urged as he began to fire.

Decker slid the straps of his pack over his back and leapt to his feet, shocked to see the wide-eyed Melanesian girl gawking at him. He cursed aloud, grabbed her hand and yanked her along as he turned to run after the group of fifteen or twenty former prisoners that were bolting in the general direction of Charlie team and up the small rise north of the artillery line.

Decker was rather stunned and confused when what felt like a mule kicked him in the back. A sharp lance of pain and, what was even more strange, a small fountain of blood that ejected from his left breast pocket. In the next instant, he found himself stumbling, his knees suddenly becoming gelatinous and drawing in a breath became a substantial effort... as if he was struggling to pull air through a pillowcase.

The Marine officer stumbled and pitched forward, hardly able to reach out a hand to break his fall. He was on his hands and knees, gasping and gulping for air. Somebody was riding on his back... a big, fat bastard by the weight of him... where was his gun? Why couldn't he get a breath, for Christ's sake...? Was it getting darker...?

There were sounds all around him. The rat-tat-tat-tat of machine guns... the screams of humanity in anger and fear... sounds of disturbed jungle life squawking in protest. There was the underlying sound of distant thunder that seemed to go on and on... and on...

Someone was kneeling beside him now. A small but sturdy body was pressing under his right armpit. The small person, who couldn't have been much more than half his size, heaved him up onto his feet and supported him as they stumbled forward. Decker's vision was tunneled down, and all he could see was a grassy and shrub-covered hill. He stumbled, lurched and almost fell, but the form at his side kept him going. Whoever it was possessed surprising strength for their size.

Another voice now, from his left. It sounded familiar and seemed to be saying something... but he couldn't understand it. There was a roaring in his ears. It was like being beneath a waterfall... God, if he could just catch his breath...

The ground leveled, and there were trees. Suddenly, there were more people around. More hands on him. His pack was slid off, and then hands... many hands... grabbed hold of his arms and legs, and Decker suddenly found himself looking up at the blue sky. He had the oddest sensation of floating, hovering above the ground and yet moving over it.

He was lowered. Hands did things to him, touched him in odd places. The sky grew black, and the sounds became one melodious stream of white noise. Something shook him... and then again... blackness... and suddenly the sky was there, and a face blotted out the color. A face he knew... or thought he did.

"Take it easy, Al," the face said in a strong voice that filled Decker with relief. It was reassuring. It cared, and it also said, without saying, that it would handle things. "Just lie still now. You're gonna be all right."

"Art..." Decker asked.

"Yeah," Turner said, squeezing the man's shoulder. "Just lie easy, Al. We got 'em. Mission accomplished."

"Good job..." Decker said, smiled, and then the world went dark again and stayed that way.

Chapter 31

USS Bull Shark
– Eastern New Georgia Sound

It was exhilarating and yet oddly eerie to hear the thunderclap of hundreds of naval guns from below the surface of the sea. The reverberating booms of gunnery traveled the eight miles or so to the stationary *Bull Shark*, thrumming through her steel hull and rattling dishes, equipment in its shock-absorbing mountings and shivered up the men's legs and into their torsos.

Williams, Jarvis, Harry Brannigan, the acting COB, along with Ralph "Hotrod" Hernandez, the senior quartermaster, huddled together around the master gyrocompass chart table examining the slot. Pencil marks had been made in Sealark Channel to show where the invasion fleet was, as well as another set of marks a hundred miles south of Guadalcanal to illustrate Fletcher's carrier support task force.

"The question is," Williams was saying. "Is where will the Japs come from? When they get their act together and are forced to react to this... where will their attack originate?"

"Plus, where's that little carrier," Brannigan said. "Our fleet is right where they *were* for several days, right? So, where'd they toodle off to and how come they ain't attackin' now?"

"Yeah, that's been bothering me all morning," Williams admitted.

"The first thing they'll do is send planes from Rabaul," Jarvis opined. "They have to. That's their closest operational base now that we've shown up and blasted the seaplanes to rubble. Maybe *Sakai* will send her planes in, too... but they've got to come in from Rabaul. At least Bougainville, as it's a little closer and intelligence has it, there's a friggin' airstrip there too."

Williams groaned, "Geez... but that's over five-hundred miles. Maybe the Betties and Vals can make that round trip... but Zeroes?"

"Thus, the Bougainville option," Jarvis said. "It's close enough. As for the carrier... I dunno, Skipper. She's one carrier, and a strike carrier at that. What's she got? Twenty, thirty planes, maybe? They'd never survive the ack-ack from the fleet or the CAP from Fletcher's three carriers, for Christ's sake."

"Yeah, but the Japs don't know we got three carriers," Hotrod stated.

"Sure they do," Williams admitted. "Or they'll *guess* we do. Yamamoto is a crafty old bird. He'll never just assume we sent seventy ships to the slot without air cover. Not after Midway and the battle right around here a month before that."

"So Rabaul sends some planes," Brannigan mused. "Maybe does a little damage... but they'll send the ships in after dark. When the planes ain't flyin', right sir?"

Williams nodded, "I think so, Chief. And they'll come in between Savo and the Florida Islands, like they always do."

"Or maybe that strike carrier comes in with her escorts at night, too," Jarvis said. "Or maybe she waits until the shooting's over and the ships are underway again. Then she comes in and picks them off or attacks our boys on the islands."

"Either way... from *where* does she come?" Williams asked.

The four men fell silent. After a while, Hotrod tapped an area of the chart to the northeast of Florida Island.

"If she's cooling her heels, she'll be out here," Hernandez said. "A hundred miles or more. She wouldn't dare come close now, as we've said. So, she steams up here and hides maybe even two hundred miles away. She can cover that distance in six hours. But she's so far out of the stadium nobody even thinks to look for her."

Jarvis nodded and smiled thinly, "Then at sunset, say, or maybe even after midnight, she comes in to within a hundred miles of Sealark Channel. She's still out in no man's land where nobody thinks to look. She can send in her birds and do heavy damage to our new captures and then zip away with nobody knowin' the better."

"So, we go after her?" Brannigan asked. "Head out that way and see if she's lurking out there as Hotrod suggests?"

Williams frowned and tapped his chin thoughtfully, "But what about the fleet?"

"What about 'em?" Jarvis asked. "What the hell can we do with four pickles on board? Our invasion force has a large number of surface warships already. If the Japs come, it's gonna be a ship-to-ship action, I'd think."

"And we're just not armed enough to do a whole lot of good," Williams finished the thought. "But we *could* intercept *Sakai* before she can do too much harm... all right, XO, plot us a course so that we're traveling northeast in the carrier's most likely line of egress and return. We'll stay submerged for the rest of the day... gonna be way too many birds up there for comfort."

Florida Island – 0715

"So, how do we get outta this thing?" Private Russel Miller asked from his seat on the foremost bench.

"Over the side," Coxswain Gordon Kelly tossed off. "These Higgins jobs are s'posed to have ramps that fold down in the bow... but the big wigs are savin' them fancy jobs for the big to-do in Africa. Stuck *us* with the economy model."

"So we gotta swim?" Miller asked incredulously. "With forty pounds of gear?"

"Well, you jump in first and let us know how it is, Russ," Corporal Pete Scoggins jibed, lightly punching Miller on his arm.

The rest of the Marines in the boat laughed, releasing some of their tension. For all of them, even their L T, this was a first. An amphibious landing on a hostile shore and every man crammed into the swaying wooden LCVP was secretly scared shitless.

"Lookin' pretty quiet over there, Gordo," the boat's engineer said from beside the coxswain as he stood and scanned the approaching beach. "Thought there'd be hordes of Nips tryin' to pump us fulla lead."

"Yeah, hah?" Kelly said in his thick Boston. "Looks wicked quiet over there, dude... Well, either way, it's gonna be a pissa... everybody hang on, I'm gonna run her onto the beach here..."

The thirty-six-foot-long Higgins landing craft slowed down from nine knots to four. Just enough speed to nose her blunt bow onto the bottom sand and keep her relatively stationary while the Marines bailed out. The propellor in the rear of the craft was cowled by a sort of protective cylinder that kept it from being damaged and allowed the craft to nose right up into two feet of shallows.

Russel Miller, being on the portside and having little choice, stood and leapt over the gunwale and into the water. For some reason, he expected to plunge down into a warm tropical bath that would close over his head. He was a little surprised to find that the remnants of the surf was only up to his knees. He grinned and sloshed ashore, ludicrously bending almost double as if that would somehow keep hundreds of machine-gun bullets from tearing him to shreds.

Miller was even more surprised when he walked right up to the high tide line without a shot being fired or hearing even one Jap shout in alarm. For a brief moment, Miller realized that he was the first American Marine to come ashore in all of the Watchtower forces... and absolutely *nothing* had happened.

"S'matter kid, Lieutenant Beaushard asked wryly as he and the rest of the platoon tromped up onto the beach. "Disappointed you ain't caught a round yet?"

Miller smiled sheepishly and watched as several more boats nosed ashore in the light surf. Soon there were dozens of them, and hundreds of Marines lined up on the beach, their jungle pattern utilities standing out starkly on the light golden sands.

"It's just... not what I expected, sir," Miller admitted.

Beaushard sighed, "Well, we did bomb the beejeebers outta the place. But I got a feeling we're not getting off easy yet... all right! Form up, men! This island needs a thorough sweepin' out, and we're the broom!"

A chorus of hoo-rahs echoed along the line, and the United States Marine Corps began to march inland.

Tulagi – 0800

Several miles away from Florida Island, Colonel Merritt "Red Mike" Edson stood at the stern of his own Higgins boat and watched as the heavily wooded and hilly island of Tulagi drew closer. The aircraft carrier sorties had long since stopped, although fighters still wheeled overhead as an improvised combat air patrol for the fleet. The shore bombardment had stopped too, its tremendous rolling thunder suddenly ceasing and leaving an odd stillness by comparison that even now, more than an hour later, still seemed unnatural.

Edson studied the shoreline toward which the fleet of thirty Higgins boats drove. Tulagi was Operation Watchtower's primary objective... although, since the discovery of the airfield on Guadalcanal, that line had blurred somewhat. It had been the capital of the British Solomon Islands Protectorate and had a large, natural deep-water lagoon that was a perfect harbor for ships and to act as a seaplane base. Of course, the Japanese being the shrewd operators they were, did not keep all of their eggs in one basket.

That's why they split their seaplane unit and operated some from nearby Gavutu, the adjoining Tanambogo and even had a few at Florida Island. Of course, the air raids and naval gunnery had made short work of them. All fifteen Kawa Nishi birds had been pulverized. So, for the most part, the other three islands were now simply a mopping-up exercise. To root out and eliminate the Japanese personnel that remained there.

Tulagi, however, was another story. It had extensive facilities and a power station. Before the war, the Brits had operated a hospital, government facilities, a harbor, small hotel, and there was even a golf course on the island. There were, it was rumored, a thousand Japanese soldiers there now as well.

Tulagi had another prominent feature, a feature that now dominated the shoreline the Raiders were approaching. Along the coast of the island, a little way in from the dune, was a long ridge of limestone and coral. This ridge was nothing less than a giant block of Swiss cheese. Full of inter-connecting caves that made perfect hidey holes and were, it was reported, stuffed to the gills with Japs. Edson knew that securing that ridge would probably occupy the vast majority of the fighting... and exact the highest toll in men.

Edson was nearly thrown off his feet when the landing craft suddenly ground to a halt on what sounded like rough bottom. The coxswain cursed and turned back to him.

"Sir, these damned reefs are too shallow!" the young man said, a Lucky Strike clenched in his teeth. "From the looks of it, this is about as close as we're gonna get."

"Well, you're aground, so that means it's only what... two feet deep?" Edson asked, making his way forward.

"Aye, sir... but then the reef drops off ahead there, see?" The coxswain replied. "Might be four or five feet deep until it rises again."

"Well..." Edson sighed. "Guess that means we're getting wet. Off packs! Hold 'em over your heads, boys! Let's *move out!* Tojo's busy, and he doesn't want to wait on us all day!"

The men began to pile out of the Higgins and were doing so all along the reef. They were anywhere from thirty to one-hundred yards offshore, and the going was slow, as many Marines were up to their armpits and holding their rucks over their heads to keep them dry.

The Cactus Navy

At first, it seemed as if there was nobody stirring ashore. There were no shots nor any sign of movement. However, it was a short-lived illusion that was brutally shattered when at several points along the ridge, machine guns began to rattle out in throaty, staccato anger.

Luckily the Higgins boats, although in no way armored and their wooden hulls no safety against incoming fire, were at least armed. They all had a pair of .30 caliber light machine guns, and every boat along the line began firing into the dunes and the hills beyond. It was nearly impossible for them to find exact targets, but by laying down steady arcs of suppressive fire, they did dramatically reduce the Japanese onslaught.

Marines began to reach the shore and ran up to the high-tide line, opening their entrenching tools and going to work like mad digging low trenches for them to hunker down in and set up to return fire. First in ones and twos, then in groups of four and six men and finally by the dozens, more than two-thousand Marines swarmed the beaches with the rattling of machine guns all around and the raindrop sound of rounds striking the sand and the surf. It was inevitable, no matter how effective the covering fire, however, that the more men crowded the shore, the more likely the body count would begin to mount.

Brigadier General William Rupertus sloshed ashore a hundred yards down the line a minute before Edson himself did. The two officers waved at one another as they hunched over to join their men under what little cover they had. Rupertus even managed to smile at Edson, pointing to his helmet and the loose pieces of fabric glued to it in order to reduce the gleam from the metal.

Edson's jaw clenched as he made it up the beach and past the bodies. There were at least two dozen that he could see. Men who'd been hit by heavy caliber machine gun rounds and practically torn in two. Men whose guts had spilled onto the beach and who lay face-down in a swath of vermillion horror.

The seasoned general shivered just a little. No one could fully understand what a raid like this was until he lived it. People watched war movies and saw heroic deeds of bravery and sacrifice... yet they didn't know about the almost overpowering smell of a battle. The coppery tang of blood that hung heavily in the humid air. The pervasive chemical odor of cordite and, of course... the stench of dead men's *shit*. The movies didn't explain how men's bowels emptied when they ceased to live. Hollywood didn't know how when young men were scared, sometimes they pissed their pants. The American public didn't realize just what a truly nauseating cocktail was the stink of fear, vomit and bloody feces... a reek that could get so thick in battle that a man would *taste* it days later.

Already, in just a few minutes, Edson's Marine Raiders had lost over one percent of their men... and this was only the beginning.

Guadalcanal - Behind Beach Red

Art Turner had been nothing less than astonished. After Tank had gotten close to the first gun, Batu had run out to join him as Turner and Taggart laid down suppressive fire. The two of them had pushed the ammo crate beneath the carriage of the gun, or as much as they could, and had left the lid open. Tank had shouted something, and then he and Batu had turned to run.

As they neared the tree line, Batu had spun, yanked the pin from a grenade and threw it with admirable precision.

"Fuckin' run!" Tank shouted as he barreled into the trees.

"Jesus Christ!" Taggart squawked.

"You crazy son of a bitch, Tank!" Turner shouted as he too turned to scramble through the tangles of ferns and vines and who knew what until all four men dove behind what cover they could find and...

A roar that outdid all that went before shook the earth around them, causing leaves to fall and a wave of heated air to hammer through the foliage. So strong was the blast that the low-pressure after the shockwave passed actually sucked the air from his lungs.

When the dust settled, the men picked themselves up, spluttering and coughing and turned back to see what they'd wrought. The gun

The Cactus Navy

had been dismounted. The carriage was a wreck and the field piece itself had been blown fifteen feet away and its barrel lay almost vertical, the open nose buried deep enough in the dirt to keep it standing. The two palms that had been to either side of the gun now lay on their sides like two dead soldiers.

"Jesus Christ," Taggart repeated, coughing out dust. "You sailors all this nuts?"

Tank made a show of dusting himself off, "Now there's nothin' wrong with blowin' stuff up, Davie. Kinda puts a smile on your face, don't it?"

From further down the line, another rumbling explosion drew their attention. This one wasn't nearly as spectacular, but it had a similar effect. It took out another gun and further threw the Japs into a shit fit.

What happened next, however, was even more astonishing. Although they couldn't see from their position, Baker team figured out that Able team must have freed the sixty-odd, chained workers. An enormous uproar of screams and cries of fear rose as a large group of people seemed to break apart.

However, as Turner and his men gathered their wits and got back into some kind of formation in order to move forward, they were surprised to see that rather than fleeing in every direction, the workers suddenly stopped and began to *attack* the Japanese!

Still dazed, the Japanese artillery crews and their Marine escorts took far too much time to get it together, and the workers took advantage. The groups of former prisoners suddenly began shouting in rage and fell upon the soldiers, beating and scratching and dragging them down. Many of the men seized rifles and turned them on the soldiers, cutting them down with bullets and savage bayonet thrusts wherever they could. It was astounding, and Turner stared agape as the soldiers began to run, abandoning their posts and fleeing for their lives before the tsunami of murderous fury they'd created.

In battle, as in nature, however, to flee is to invite pursuit. The Koreans and Guadalcanalers ran them down and slaughtered every single Japanese to a man. They exacted some measure of penance for whatever had been done to them by their former tormentors.

"Holy cow!" Tank whooped as Able team began to walk down the line of guns toward the center of the fracas.

They saw that a small group of workers was moving up the low incline behind the firing line and made their way to them. There they found half a dozen of them carrying Al Decker. Doug Ingram walked beside them, looking pale and worried. When he saw his skipper, Ingram began waving his arms and shouting for Turner.

"What happened?" Turner asked as he and his men joined the procession.

"The Major took one in the back," Ingram said worriedly and pointed.

Turner could see a large red splotch on Decker's chest, and there was clearly a hole in his blouse near the left breast pocket. His innards twitched at the sight and at the sound of Decker's labored wheezes.

"Sucking chest wound, sir," Taggart said. "Missed the heart, thank God, but..."

"We'll do what we can for him," Turner said with a confidence he did not feel. "We'll pack the wound, and when our boys come ashore, which should be any minute now, we'll see about getting him aboard one of the transports."

Ingram was startled when his field radio broke out in a burst of static. The unit was squealing and chirping with overlapping transmissions that at first made no sense.

"The Marines have hit Florida Island and Tulagi," Ingram reported. "And the carriers are keeping a CAP over the slot, sir. From what I could hear, landing operations have begun for Beach Red. The Marines should be coming ashore soon."

Through the now meandering crowd of captive workers came Charlie team, rushing through the press. Chief Duncan had one of his long arms around Chuck Lider's back and seemed to be supporting the man. On his other side, Porter Hazard held his elbow.

Jacob Vousa was moving among the prisoners speaking to them and asking questions.

"You all right, Corporal?" Turner asked Lider.

"Goddamned Jap stuck me in the leg," Lider groaned. His eyes grew wide at the sight of the islanders setting Decker down on a makeshift bed of fern branches.

"Chest wound," Turner said. "We're gonna do what we can. Doug reports Cactus landing forces are on the way. I'm hoping we can get him on an LCVP and out to a ship with good hospital facilities."

"What now, sir?" Hazard asked Turner.

The submarine captain looked over his men and sighed. They'd now lost three of their five Marines. Lider was partially mobile, at least, but based on the bloody towel tied around his thigh, he would probably need a doctor, too. Decker was in serious danger, and Oaks, while perhaps nearly on his feet, was ten miles away.

"Now we finish what we started," Turner said. "How'd you guys blow number six?"

"Loaded the gun," Lider explained as Duncan and Hazard eased him into a sitting position. "Taped the handle down on a pineapple, pulled the pin and dropped it down the barrel. Then we shoved some dirt and gravel and leaves and junk down it."

"Then we tied a bit of twine to the trigger mechanism and moved off as far as we could and fired the gun," Duncan finished.

"Over pressurized the breach, sir," Lider continued. "Blew out the breach loading gear. Gun's useless... what the heck did you guys do?"

Taggart snorted, grinned and pointed at Tank, "Sherman the Tank over here put the munitions box under the gun and Batu tossed a grenade into it. Damn near blew up half the island!"

"Subtlety is not my strong suit," Tank admitted proudly. "Besides... I wanted to see a ka-boom... there was supposed to be an Earth-shattering ka-boom..."

"Well, let's finish the job," Turner said. "Tank, Chief, Taggart, you guys think you can spike the rest of the guns without killing us all or destroying the earth?"

Taggart frowned and looked at Decker.

"He'll be all right for now, Davie," the captain said kindly. "We'll do what we can for him. But I need those guns taken out *before* our troops hit the beach. Don't want them thinking they're under attack."

Taggart drew in a deep breath of resignation, "Aye-aye sir."

Turner turned and looked to the north. From their position on the low ridge above the guns, they could see the shoreline just over a mile away. The line of palms and hardwoods broke and became a wide plain of kunai grass. Beyond that, dotting the azure blue sea, were dozens of dark shapes on the horizon. The transports of Operation Watchtower. And between them and the shore, tiny dots began to take shape. Dozens of them. The Higgins boats that would deliver fourteen thousand Marines and hundreds of tons of supplies were beginning what would be the first of many round trips to the shores of Guadalcanal.

Chapter 32

Beach Red, Guadalcanal
- 0919

Lieutenant William H. White couldn't take his eyes off the beach. It just didn't seem right to him... this long, gently sloping strand of golden-white sand with a grass-covered dune and swaying palm trees behind that. The swell had subsided overnight, and the low waves appeared to glide across the turquoise waters and then lightly foam as they caressed the long beach.

Where were the Japs? Where were the machine gun nests and shore guns blasting men and boats into bloody pulp and matchwood? This was more like coming ashore at a tropical resort than a damned *invasion*.

"You okay, sir?" Private Robert Lecky inquired from beside White.

The young lieutenant, only a few years older than most of his men, gathered himself and smiled at Lecky, "Just wondering where the action is, Lecky. How about you? This ride in started out a little bumpy... you doin' all right?"

Lecky chuckled, 'Oh, I'm right as rain, sir. Didn't even feel a twinge of seasickness or anything. Am lookin' forward to plantin' my boots on solid ground for a bit, though."

Lecky's wish was soon granted. White's boat and the rest of the first wave slid their bows into the shallows at nearly the same moment, and over a thousand men of the Fifth Marines sloshed ashore, their reliable but outdated Springfield 1903 rifles at the ready. Two lines formed, the rear to provide covering fire as the front ranks began to dash up the beach and the dune. The men ran inland nearly a hundred yards, every step an agony of tension as each man wondered when the shooting would begin. Who would be the first to fall under an enfilade of Jap machine gunfire? When would their flesh be torn open and apart by cigar-sized rounds from heavy weapons? How many precious seconds of life remained to these young men before it would be brutally ripped away from them...?

...and yet...

Even as the first wave began to hurriedly dig foxholes, the bizarre peacefulness of the landscape took on a strangeness that they couldn't fully appreciate. As lines of trenches were dug, the rear guard moved up and exchanged places, taking up entrenching tools while the first wave took a break from the exhausting labor and shouldering *their* rifles.

After about a half-hour of this, however, it became clear that there was to be no attack. No Japanese machine guns or artillery... no charging Nips ran for them with gleaming bayonets and shrieks of "*Banzai!*" on their lips. The only sign that the island even *might* be occupied were a handful of pillars of smoke that seemed to be rising from the trees a mile inland.

"This is just too strange," White said as he inspected the initial entrenchments and gathered his men. "Where *is* everybody?"

"I don't know sir," Lecky said, returning from a sweep along the line of coconut palms with a half-husked nut in his hands. "But least we got plenty of snacks!"

Gunnery Sergeant Willis Blethwengler strode up and saluted White, "Initial perimeter secure, sir. I've sent out fire teams from first and third platoon to do a deeper sweep... Lecky, what the hell are you doin'?"

The Cactus Navy

Lecky had managed to clear away enough coir to get to the nut. He used his combat knife to punch out the eyes and dig a larger drinking hole. He then tipped the nut back and drained a healthy mouthful of the cool and refreshing coconut milk.

"What if the Japs done poisoned all these nuts lyin' around here?" Blethwengler groused. "Are you simple, or what?"

White couldn't help but laugh, "Hell, Gunny... it's probably all right."

"Yeah, Gunny," Lecky said, wiping his mouth. "Hotter'n hell's half-acre out here. Sides... how could them Japs inject poison into all these here nuts lyin' around?"

"All right, wiseass," Blethwengler grumped. "You can join second platoon on *their* next sweep, since you're so refreshed and all."

"Yeah, just watch out for crocs and tarantulas and killer parrots, Bobby!" Whitey Groft tossed off as he passed the group.

"All right, you jarheads," White said, "let's get crackin'. First Marines are due on the next run, and we gotta get to hill twenty-six before dark. Fortify it and make ready to pounce on the Japs."

It was on the next deep sweep that Robert Lecky's squad ran across something interesting and rather shocking. As they climbed up past the fields of kunai grass toward an area of level ground, they thought they saw signs of human activity. A couple of palm trees were knocked over, and what looked like field artillery pieces were strewn about as if flung down by a giant petulant child. As they cautiously drew near, they discovered that a large cluster of people was gathered on a small ridge above what was left of the guns. From the midst of these people, some of whom were Asians and some islanders, strode two men in what looked like dirty Marine Corps issue utilities. One was a tall, lean man with broad shoulders and dark blonde hair showing from beneath his camouflaged ball cap cover. The other man was shorter and a bit younger.

Both men were clearly American. They were smiling and their rifles slung across their backs. The leader of the squad, a second looey fresh from OCS, stepped forward.

395

"Identify yourselves," he ordered sternly but not menacingly.

"Boy, are we glad to see you fellas!" the tall man said with an irrepressible grin lighting up his face. "I'm Lieutenant Commander Art Turner. Captain of SS-333 USS *Bull Shark*. This is Corporal Dave Taggart, First Marine Raiders. And who might you be, sir?"

There were surprised mutterings from the officer's eight men. They matched his own bewilderment, "Uhm... a submarine commander... what... uhm... I'm Second Lieutenant Luther Wilcox, sir, Fifth Marines. We just landed at Beach Red less than two hours ago."

"Yeah, we saw that, sir," Taggart stated.

"You guys do this?" Wilcox waved an arm at the destroyed line of guns.

Turner nodded, "They were setting up to give you guys a hard time. Couple of nights ago, we blew a five-inch in Palapao, a village a little inland from here."

"We were sent in a few nights ago to make contact with and re-supply Captain Martin Clemens, the lead coastwatcher here," Taggart added.

"And to make recommendations and reports to command," Turner said, tapping his chest. "It's been... interesting. Listen, Lieutenant, we've got wounded men. Two of my Marines, including the unit CO, are wounded and need a hospital ship or the fleet's best medical facilities. I've got more men inland with Captain Clemens as well, including another wounded man and a couple of prisoners."

"Our sergeant was wounded a few nights ago," Taggart added. "We think he's okay... but being looked at by a real doc wouldn't hurt. Any chance we can get them sent out, L T?"

Wilcox was beginning to look far out of his depth. His smooth boyish face was clearly distressed. To his credit, however, he seemed to gather himself and nodded, "I'm sure something can be arranged, sir... but what about your... uhm... your friends there?"

"They were the pack mules for this artillery train," Turner explained. "Korean forced labor and locals, as far as I can tell. Two of

The Cactus Navy

my men are islanders and with the Protectorate. They'd all like to stay with us until such time as Lunga Point is secure. Certainly, the Koreans. The islanders will no doubt want to return to their villages."

"I'm afraid this is all getting way above my pay grade, Commander," Wilcox said. "Lecky! This is Private Robert Lecky, sir. He'll escort you back to Beach Red. By now the First Marines should be landing and General Vandegrift himself might already be ashore. Either way, sir, you'll be able to speak to somebody with more authority than me. I'm sure we can get you and your people squared away."

"Thank you, Lieutenant," Turner said, shaking the young man's hand.

Wilcox and his party continued on their way on their assigned patrol route. Lecky, a seemingly exuberant wide-eyed young man, stared around him in wonder. All along the line of what was left of the guns, dozens of Japanese bodies lay strewn about where they'd died. Some with bullet holes, some with their throats cut, some with their skulls bashed in... but all equally dead.

"This musta been quite the hullabaloo, sir," Lecky said in awe. "I didn't know submariners did this kind of work."

Turner chuffed, "Me either, son. War makes strange bedfellows and asks for even stranger deeds."

"Sir!" Porter Hazard suddenly appeared at turner's side. "Permission to return to Vungana and inform our team there that they can come down?"

"I'm not sure it's quite safe yet, Porter," Turner stated. "After all, the Marines are still landing and off-loading supplies yet."

"Yes, sir, but by the time we get back there and get everything squared away to move, it'll be another day or maybe two at best," Hazard said. "I think we owe it to them to let them know what's going on, sir. And Marty and I can arrange to get Entwater and Commander Hideki from Vushicoro and at least to Vungana and wait for the word to come down."

"As if Marty doesn't already know what's up down here," Turner mused. "Very well, Porter, if you think you don't mind a hike. Take Davie and Batu with you for security."

"I'd like to stay with you and the Major, sir, if it's all the same," Taggart said.

"Okay, I'll take Batu," Hazard said. "Now that the troops have landed, sir, we should be able to make direct contact tonight."

Turner reached out and took hold of the man's shoulder, "Be careful, Porter. This little dust-up here may have alerted the Japs and stirred them up. You remember what Jake said about some of these villagers... why don't you take him with you as well."

Hazard nodded, "Aye-aye sir. Good luck to you, too, sir."

Turner watched as Hazard and Taggart went back to the gathering of Americans and former slaves. He drew in a centering breath, trying to shake an odd feeling that he could only identify as dread.

"Very well, Lecky, let's get this goat fuck underway."

The slot, approaching Sealark Channel – 1010

Lieutenant Saburo Sakai was only twenty-five years old and already one of the most experienced of Japan's flying aces. He could lay claim to fifty-eight enemy aircraft shot down and was such a master of the A6M Zero that his plane was almost an extension of his own soul.

Sakai, who secretly liked to believe that the new strike carrier currently in the Solomon Islands was named after him, was an unusual young man. He was an odd blend of good-humor and easy-going nature. Always wore a smile and always had a kind word for his ground crews. Yet, he was entirely ruthless. In combat, he killed without a second thought or mercy. In spite of this, however, he did not hate his enemy, as so many did. He admired and even felt for them, especially fellow aviators whom he'd shot down... but they *were* his and his empire's enemies and thus received no quarter.

At 0800 that morning, word had come from the great Yamamoto himself that the naval base at Rabaul launch a strike force to attack the American fleet at Guadalcanal. The admiral did not dare send in ships, not in broad daylight and with several aircraft carriers lurking somewhere in the Coral Sea.

The difficulty, of course, was that the distance from New Britain, on which the town and base of Rabaul were located, to the attack zone and back was a thousand kilometers. Add in even a few minutes of operations over the area while the bombers dropped their payloads, and it quickly became clear that fuel was going to be an issue.

Sakai and his fellow pilots, those in the Zeroes at any rate, were instructed to return to a new airstrip that had recently been laid out on the southern end of Bougainville. This would cut the trip a little short and should allow the fighters to stay with the dive-bombers and ground-bombers, what the Americans called Vals and Betties. The Zeroes would be supplied with drop tanks and should have enough fuel to escort the bombers down the slot, cover them while they attacked the American fleet and then escort the bombers out of the Sealark Channel and back to Bougainville.

As Sakai and his flight soared high over New Georgia Sound, and as the huge American invasion fleet hove into view, he began to wonder just who'd planned this mission and exactly what was going through their minds.

The American fleet was *enormous!* There were transports gathered near Tulagi and the other close islands, as well as even more near the northern coast of Guadalcanal. There were yet more transports in between, no doubt waiting their turn to get close to shore and deliver more men and supplies. Protecting these ships were dozens of gray warships. Destroyers, light cruisers and heavy cruisers as well. They were arranged in picket lines around the transports, their anti-aircraft batteries ready to defend the fleet.

Sakai didn't see any carriers, but he was not surprised by that. Carrier warfare was conducted from long distances. The American flat tops were probably a hundred miles to the south, launching and recovering flights of fighters every few hours. No doubt there would be a few dozen Wildcats orbiting Sealark Channel already.

Sakai confirmed this as his flight drew closer. Tiny black dots began to appear in the skies over the waters between Savo, Guadalcanal and Tulagi. The Grumman F4F Wildcat, the Americans' staple carrier fighters, were waiting for Sakai and his bombers.

He was not daunted by this. The Mitsubishi Zero was superior to the American counterpart in almost every conceivable way. The "Zeke," as the Yankees sometimes called them, could climb faster, turn quicker and had greater overall speed. They were lighter and nimbler and could literally outfly any airplane in the world. For all this, though, Sakai also knew of his aircraft's weaknesses and the Wildcat's few but significant advantages.

By now, after two major carrier engagements with the United States, Japan knew quite a bit about the Wildcat. They knew, for example, that the fighter had self-sealing fuel tanks. The Zero, on the other hand, if hit in its tanks, could and often would go up like a blow torch. The Wildcat was better armored, which made it heavier and less maneuverable but did protect the plane and allow it to keep fighting even after multiple hits. Finally, the Wildcat was outfitted with four wing-mounted .50 caliber Browning M2 machine guns with four-hundred and fifty rounds each. The Zero had only two heavy 20mm cannons in her wings, and two smaller 7.62mm engine cowling mounted guns. Although the fuselage-mounted guns had five hundred rounds apiece, the 20mm had but sixty each. This gave the Wildcat an overall advantage in firepower. Finally, the American plane could fly over twenty-five hundred meters higher than the Zero.

Understanding these things allowed Sakai to understand how his enemy operated. It allowed him to make the best use of his nimble aircraft's advantages and exploit his enemy's weaknesses.

"Flight leader to attack units one and two," Sakai said over his radio. "Enemy fighters sighted. Proceed to engage. Attack unit three, escort bombers on surface attack run. Weapons free."

With that pronouncement, Sakai throttled up to full power and vectored in toward the oncoming Wildcats. There were quite a number of them, perhaps more American planes than Zeroes. They appeared to have come from the south, which was what Sakai suspected all along. Probably two fighter squadrons from two fleet carriers so far.

The sky began to fill with the roar of radial engines as Sakai's Nakajima screamed into full power and the larger Pratt and Whitney engines of the Wildcats did the same. Sakai had to admit that for bulkier and slightly slower airplanes, the Wildcats were quite graceful. He'd never faced the Grumman before and was about to receive some very hard-won data on the plane.

Ahead and slightly above him, a pair of Wildcats were angling in toward the Japanese bombers. The two planes were perhaps a hundred meters apart, and Sakai smiled as he vectored his plane toward the closer of the two. He rose toward the Americans, who were five hundred meters above him and angled for a shot. As he locked in, Sakai caught movement out of the corner of his eye. The second Wildcat had snapped over and was barreling right for him, angry red tracers reaching out for his bird!

Sakai swore, snapped his Zero into a wing-over dive and circled away from his target. The second Wildcat roared past, and Sakai hauled his ship around to get on the attacker's tail, only to see the *first* F4F coming for him! Was this a new tactic of the Americans?

Over his radio, Sakai could hear the group's overall leader, Lieutenant Commander Tadashi Nakajima, cursing and ranting in rage, "...damn! Damn these Ame-coh spawn of whores!"

What Sakai and the rest of his fighter pilots did not know was that this was indeed a new and proven tactic. Seasoned fighter pilot Jimmy Thatch, who'd been at the battle of the Coral Sea and Midway, had developed the tactic a year earlier, and it was colloquially known as the "Thatch Weave."

Essentially, in order to compensate for the Zeke's greater speed and maneuverability, a pair of Wildcats would fly in formation. Sometimes two pairs as well. One plane would play the Judas goat.

When the Zero angled in on its intended victim, the victim would turn toward his wingman, who would also turn toward the victim plane as well. In this way, the slower Wildcats would use the Zero's own approach against him. Letting the Japanese pilot set himself up for an attack.

After passing the first two Wildcats, Sakai spotted a lone aircraft angling toward him. Now, this was more like it. A one-on-one dog fight that the bulkier American could never hope to win. The ace had to admit that the Americans were certainly bulldogs. In spite of their disadvantages, they leapt into a fight with vigor.

Lieutenant James "Pug" Southerland was thinking something very similar as he watched the white airplane with the meatballs painted on her wings arc in toward him. He was thinking that it was no wonder the Japs were so aggressive when they had birds like the Zeke to fly. He also briefly thought that he himself might be out of his gourd for going after the bird with such gusto.

Sakai had only a second to react to the other pilot's aggressive run. He snapped out a burst from his nose cannons. To his surprise, the Wildcat snap-rolled to the right, losing altitude and banking into a tight turn. In shock, Sakai watched as the American completed his evasive maneuver and came at him again, this time from below, climbing toward Sakai's belly.

The Japanese ace was stunned. He'd never seen any enemy plane react that quickly or gracefully. Perhaps the intelligence on the Grumman was inaccurate…? The man was using his own favorite strategy, too… that of coming up for a belly shot.

Sakai snapped his own plane over, diving and rolling into an inverted loop that put him below and behind the Wildcat. His thumb twitching over the trigger, Sakai lined up and fired… only to see his tracers cut through empty air!

The Wildcat was climbing, nosing over into an inverted loop of his own. Just after the apex of the loop, the American snapped his bird over and rolled into an attack, sending heavy rounds sizzling past Sakai's canopy far too close for comfort.

The Cactus Navy

"Jesus Christ!" Southerland swore as he heaved his plane into maneuvers even he didn't know she was capable of. "Who the hell *is* this guy?"

The fight went on for what seemed like a long time until finally, Sakai succeeded in positioning himself below Southerland's port quarter and let fly with his heavy guns. The 20mm rounds tore into the port wing root and aileron. The Grumman was finished, no longer able to maneuver the way she had before.

Sakai knew he'd finally won. He could take his time now and destroy the plane at his leisure. He switched from the heavy machine guns to the lighter, rose and poured in several bursts... but the plane still flew. Thinking he'd missed, Sakai moved in closer and squeezed his trigger. He must have pumped four or five hundred rounds into the Grumman, but the obstinate American plane still flew! The ace was once more astonished. How could this be? Any Zero taking that kind of punishment would have been a flaming ball of death long before.

Sakai moved in so close that he felt that he could actually reach out and touch the other aircraft. He was amazed to see that the plane's tailfin and rudder were hardly more than a tattered rag. Truly this was an admirable aircraft. Sakai switched back to his 20mm guns and prepared to fire, but when he saw the Wildcat's canopy slide open, he held back. The American pilot was bailing out, and Sakai wasn't about to kill the man while he did so. Not after such a skilled duel.

The American extracted himself from the cockpit, waved at Sakai and leapt off the wing, plummeting down toward the light blue waters at the shore of Guadalcanal. Sakai saw the man's chute open and then smiled and squeezed his trigger, shredding more of the F4F and sending the airplane into a death spiral.

Just as Sakai was searching for another target, a lone American Douglas SBD Dauntless dive-bomber came roaring at him from over Guadalcanal. This was truly perplexing, as the Dauntless was *not* a fighter. Although nimbler without its payload and admittedly rugged, the Dauntless was even less a match for the Zero than the Wildcat. Still, the pilot managed to put a round through Sakai's canopy uncomfortably close to his head. The ace admired his opponent's grit even as he flung his bird up and over, corkscrewing around the banking dive bomber and moving into position to fire. Sakai's rounds tore into the SBD, killing the rear seater and shredding the plane's fuel lines. Black smoke began to billow from the plane's oil manifold as her pilot bailed out and sank toward the ground.

His adrenaline pumping, Sakai caught sight of a flight of eight fighters far off over Tulagi. Once more he throttled up and vectored in, covering the distance in just over two minutes. He angled in from slightly below, lining his cannon sights up on one of the trailing aircraft. He frowned as he got closer. Something wasn't quite right. The planes weren't Wildcats. They were differently shaped and a bit longer... they were torpedo bombers! From the profile, Sakai guessed they were the new Avengers that were to replace the older Devastators. From his remembered briefing material, he knew that these aircraft also had tail gunners... tail gunners that were already lining up on him!

Having moved in too close to break off now, Sakai said a quick prayer and opened fire.

Although he may have hit one or two, the combined fire of the Avenger's guns smashed into Sakai's Zero... and the pilot himself. Sakai heard thumps and shattering glass, felt as if someone had clubbed him in the head with an iron pipe, and the world went black. Even as he lost consciousness, Sakai knew he had finally run out of luck and at least could die a warrior...

...and then consciousness returned. Sakai found himself in an inverted dive only a thousand meters above the sea. Stunned, confused and aware of an agonizing headache and that he could not see out of his right eye, the half-conscious pilot pulled his airplane into level flight. Gingerly, he reached up and touched his face and head. His face was covered in blood, and several shards of glass were sticking out of his cheek. There must be more in his eye as well. He

The Cactus Navy

then felt up along his bloody hairline and found a *hole* in his skull! A crease that oozed blood and made him nauseous just to realize that a machine gun round must have struck him a glancing blow.

Once more the world went black...

...and once more, the pilot woke and had to recover his airplane. This was no easy task, as Sakai discovered that his left arm and leg didn't seem to respond to commands. For an oddly tranquil moment, he peered down at the toy-sized ships spread out below him. Perhaps... just perhaps, he could ram one of them and die as a Samurai. Taking out several of the enemy in the process. As cool air washed over his devastated head, however, Sakai regained a portion of his wits and knew that his duty lay elsewhere.

He flew back to Rabaul, a trip that took more than four hours of agony and wavering between consciousness and grayouts that threatened to end his life. After circling the runway, Sakai just succeeded in not crashing his Zero and taxiing to a stop.

Concerned ground crews helped the wounded pilot out of his plane. By this time, at least, his paralyzed limbs were somewhat restored, and he could stand with assistance.

"Sir!" a petty officer implored. "We must take you to a surgeon *immediately!*"

"No..." Sakai croaked. "I must report... one of you drive me to headquarters..."

The young ground crew looked at Sakai's plane and at the man in undisguised awe. His reputation as a flying ace and a Samurai warrior, a man who truly lived by the Bushido code, was already legendary... but *this!*

"Please sir," the petty officer pleaded. "Your injuries..."

"No!" Sakai insisted. "It is my duty."

The petty officer pulled in a breath and nodded, "*Hai*. It will be my honor to accompany you, sir."

The young man drove Sakai to the administration building and held his arm as the pilot shakily walked into the air group commander's office. The man, a seasoned pilot himself in his early forties, looked up at the unannounced visit. The rebuke he was about to deliver for the interruption died before it could leave his mouth when he saw Sakai barely managing to stand there before him.

"My God!" the man said, leaping to his feet. "Why is this pilot not in the hospital, petty officer!?"

"I insisted, sir," Sakai said. "The attack in the Sealark Channel did not succeed as well as we might have hoped. I believe we took down a number of American planes... but to my knowledge, only two ships were hit and only damaged sir, I... I..."

This time when the world went dark, the young pilot would stay out for quite a long time. He would recover but would not fly again for several years. Yet that he *would* fly again after such trauma was a testament to his willpower.

Chapter Thirty-Three

"Where the hell is everybody, Whitey?" Lecky asked a slightly older and beamier Marine corporal after he'd led Turner's party across a large field of coconut palms that stood in oddly straight lines. They'd been planted as part of a copra plantation, no doubt.

At the edge of the plantation, where the rows and rows of palms gave way to more kunai grass, a company's worth of Marines appeared to be fortifying a mostly open hill. There were already tents, a partially completed rampart piled up from the earth that had once been in the trenches outside the encampment. Several Deuce and a Half trucks and several Jeeps were moving between the now very crowded landing area of Beach Red and the hill.

The corporal, who identified himself as Groft, smiled. "You'll love this, Bobby... and something you should know as well sir... so this here hill, marked as hill twenty-six on our map, is supposed to overlook the airstrip."

Turner looked out over what landscape he could see to the west and there most certainly was no airstrip, "Aren't we still a mile or so from the Teneru River?"

Groft nodded, "Yes sir. And we're *eight* miles from the damned airstrip... pardon me sir... so First Marines have moved on and are currently castrameting... that's setting up camp, sir... along the riverbank near Alligator Creek."

"I know what castrametation is, Corporal," Turner said with an arched brow.

Groft cleared his throat, "Ahem... yes sir. Anyway, General Vandegrift went on with First. They've decided to grab the airbase tomorrow."

"Who's in charge here, Corporal?" Turner asked. "Or better yet, at the beach? I've got wounded that need immediate shipboard medical attention."

It took some time and some doing. Finally, Turner was able to arrange to get Lider and Decker out on a Higgins boat to the *McCawley*. His slave brigade was turned over to an officer at the hill twenty-six camp, and then he led Tank, Duncan, Ingram and Taggart to the First Marine camp at Alligator Creek.

Turner was led into Vandegrift's tent after he'd seen that his men were given something hearty to eat for a change. The submarine captain was a bit surprised by the fact that an officer of Vandegrift's reputation and stature would be residing in such a makeshift forward encampment. He was even more surprised when the remarkably fit older man seemed to read his mind.

"So, Turner, you're asking yourself what in the hell is this big, muckity-muck general doing out here in the middle of banana land instead of back aboard the *McCawley*, right?"

Turner's mouth dropped open, "I... uhm... well, sir... yes, as a matter of fact."

Vandegrift sat in a canvas chair adjacent to the one he'd offered Turner and began to fill a pipe. The man had an undeniable air of competence and toughness about him that, rather than intimidating Turner, made him feel at ease.

"I could ask you the same question, Art... may I call you Art?"

"Of course, sir."

"Good...." Vandegrift said, puffing. "What the hell is a decorated sub driver who is, at last report, up for *more* medals in addition to his Navy Cross... doing out here?"

"More medals sir?" Turner asked and then recollected himself. "I go where I'm needed sir."

Vandegrift smiled, "I know. I was at the meeting where your friend and mine, Webster Clayton, recommended *Bull Shark* to deliver Major Decker and his team. Anvil Art Turner goes ashore with the Raiders... God all mighty... I'd be prepared to pin another Navy Cross on that uniform, son. Maybe a silver star and a presidential citation as well. Jesus H... you're in command what... six months and you've already got a laundry list of kills. That's to say nothing of what your XO is doing out there... and then you pull this crazy stunt."

Turner grinned and reached into his BDU blouse breast pocket only to discover it was empty, "Dammit... as I said, sir, I go where I'm asked."

Vandegrift chuckled, "And I'm glad for it. Was your good word that recommended Beach Red, I understand. Oh, here..."

Vandegrift pulled a pack of Marlboros from his own utility breast pocket. "Drop yours in battle, or what?"

Turner sighed, "Lately it seems I can't keep the damned things within five yards of me... thank you, sir."

"How about Clemens and the rest of your people?"

"I've sent a team back to make direct contact," Turner explained as he lit up. "I've got a couple of Japanese Naval officers as prisoners... one wounded. I'm at something of a stand as to their disposition, however."

"How so?"

"One of them is a... well, I don't' know what to call him... a sort of mole, I guess?" Turner explained. "Clayton has been in contact with him. A Lieutenant Commander Ryu Osaka. He's in tight with Yamamoto and is out here as an observer from a strike carrier."

"The *Sakai*," Vandegrift said. "Interesting... so what's the problem?"

"Well sir... if we just take him back to Pearl or Brisbane, or what have you... he's no longer any good to us."

Vandegrift nodded in understanding, "But if he gets back to his people... he can still work on our behalf."

"Exactly. He's not a turncoat... just a guy who's not too thrilled with the Hirohito and Tojo duo. He's helping us to prevent more Japanese losses. He feels, and says Yamamoto does as well, that they can't win."

Vandegrift pondered that for a long moment, "So you want to get these officers back to their friends somehow."

"Yes sir."

"How?"

"That I don't know yet, sir... I suppose we may have to wait for an opportunity. Simply calling Rabaul and asking them to come pick up their boys is out... have to play it by ear."

"Well, we'll be moving to the airfield tomorrow, whether the Jap likes it or not," Vandegrift said. "But I don't think this is gonna be an easy op. So far, it's been a cakewalk here... but the yellow sons of bitches are fighting tooth and nail across the channel. And I believe that Japan is going to send reinforcements to this island. I don't want to be a pessimist... but I think we're in for a hellacious time keeping what we've got here. Point is... I think an opportunity to return your friends to their countrymen may crop up sooner or later. Has to."

Turner nodded, and his head suddenly felt like it weighed twenty pounds. A wave of fatigue struck, breaking upon the shores of his mind and adding many pounds to the weight of his eyelids as well.

"For now, though," Vandegrift said, getting to his feet. "You and your boys ought to rest a bit. You look done in."

"It's been a long night, sir."

"A long few days before that, too, I'll bet," Vandegrift said. "My clerk will set you up. Welcome to the party, Commander... and thank you for your service so far."

"Thank you, sir," Turner said, shaking the offered hand.

Turner was shown to an olive drab framed tent in which several cots had been set out. He sat on one and slipped off his boots, intending to simply lie down for a few minutes and relax. However, the long night, the draining heat and the fighting had given his system other notions.

He hardly had time to lay his head on the pillow before he sunk down into a deep slumber.

Vungana – later that day

The sun was nearly touching the sea off toward Savo Island. Joe Dutch stood by the telescope and looked out over the vast expanse of the Sealark Channel and the fleet of toy ships that bobbed there. When the sun had risen and Clemens and his people had awakened to see the huge fleet, cheers and whoops of joy had gone up, even among the villagers.

Dutch helped Phil Oaks to get out of his cot and hobble out to the telescope mount. His shoulder was still tender and made it hard to use his left arm. His leg was also painful but could support him for short stints of time. The sergeant had gazed out over the scene that was laid out before and below them like a hungry man entering a banquet hall.

"My God..." he said, a grin nearly splitting his face. "Ain't that a gorgeous sight, L T?"

"It sure is, Phil," Dutch said. "And it means that all the shit we've gone through over the past week has been worth it. The Navy and Marine Corps have arrived ... and *how!*"

"Blimey that's a sight for sore eyes, lads," Marty Clemens said, joining them with Ryu Osaka in tow. "I can't tell you how long we've been waiting to see this."

Dutch turned to the Japanese naval officer and regarded him. Osaka's face was neutral, betraying nothing. Dutch sensed, although he thought that he was only projecting, that Osaka was both pleased and saddened by the sight.

"Impressive," the IJN officer said finally.

"How's Mr. Hideki?" Dutch asked.

A party of carriers had been sent back to Vungana before dawn to retrieve Entwater and Hideki. The young Marine had brought with him additional radio parts scavenged from the plane. The Japanese officer was semi-conscious and, although stable, clearly needed a doctor.

It was felt by Dutch and Clemens that, in spite of the rugged terrain and harrowing journey, Hideki would be better off at Vungana. With everyone together, moving again down to the Lunga Point airfield when the time came would be simpler.

"He's weak but conscious," Osaka said.

"My lad is keeping an eye on him," Clemens said. "Along with our *Riekusentai* guest. No worries, eh?"

"This will be... bloody," Osaka stated quietly.

Oaks cocked an eyebrow at Osaka but nodded in agreement.

"Why do you say that, Commander?" Dutch asked.

Osaka drew in a long breath and sighed, "This invasion cannot be allowed to stand. The Imperial Navy is afraid of nothing. They will attack. The *Riekusentai*... our Marines... will come. The army will come. I fear your men are in for many months of brutal fighting. Planes will attack by day, and the IJN will rule the sound by night."

"With all that out there?" Dutch asked, waving a hand to the north. "And who knows how many carriers south of us?"

"Yes... but this is temporary," Osaka said. "Soon, the transports and their escorts will depart. Your carriers will be needed elsewhere. The Marines you land will have to complete the airbase and fend for themselves, for the most part, I think. I believe you'll be victorious... but it will not come easily."

"He's right," Oaks said. "If we've learned anything in this war, it's that the Jap is tenacious."

Osaka chuffed, "He certainly is."

The Cactus Navy

"When do you think they'll come?" Dutch had asked.

"Tonight... or tomorrow night at the latest," Osaka predicted.

His prediction had been born out before noon. Japanese planes from the northwest flew in and were engaged by Americans who vectored in from over Guadalcanal's mountains. Even in the daytime, the sky was afire with tracer rounds and the roar of engines and the booms of explosions.

This on the heels of the bombings and naval bombardments.

Across the sound, smoke rose from Tulagi, Gavutu, Tanambogo and Florida Island as the ground fighting there became fierce. The Japanese personnel were outnumbered six to one, yet they dug in and fought with almost supernatural resolve.

Now darkness was falling, and the aircraft from both sides were retiring for the night. Yet, according to Osaka, the IJN warships would come in after dark, using their advantages of superior equipment and experience to go after the invasion fleet. Clemens and the remaining landing party members at Vungana would have front-row seats for what was bound to be a ferocious naval engagement.

Michael, Clemens' cook, ran out of the headman's hut. He was grinning and waving his arms excitedly.

"What's he on about?" Oaks asked.

"Savvy radio 'e say you come, you talky talky right now!" Michael said, his usually decent English descending into pidgin due to his enthusiasm.

"All right, Michael, all right," Clemens said, patting the young man on his shoulder and bending down to scratch and pet Suinao as well. The little black dog had taken her cue from Michael and was equally excited. She could always be found with the cook at mealtimes. "Let's remember our dignity. Perhaps you'd like to come along, Joe?"

Dutch nodded, "Be right back. Don't run off, boys."

"Ha-ha," Oaks said wryly.

Clemens ham radio set was on, and a crackle of static quietly played on the speaker. He picked up the microphone and gave his call letters, "Who's calling, please?"

"It's Turner," came the familiar and welcome voice of the submarine captain. Dutch and Marty grinned at one another. *"How are you boys faring up there?"*

"We're well, mate," Clemens said. "We saw the little show you put on, at least the end results. Can I assume that you've met with the tourists and are safe?"

A laugh, *"Roger that, Marty. First and Fifth Marines are here. A little delayed in getting to the resort... but we're four-oh. Has Porter arrived yet?"*

Clemens and Dutch looked at each other. Clemens replied: "No... we've gotten no new visitors all day. Are they due to return?"

There was a short pause, and then Turner came back a little less jovially, *"Affirmative... he, Batu and Jacob started back for you around ten-hundred... I'd think they'd have arrived by now... been nine hours."*

"It is twelve or thirteen miles," Clemens replied reassuringly.

A grunt, *"yeah... and they might have stopped to rest a while. Was a long night... hmm... do you think you could send out a scout, Marty?"*

"Wilco, Art," Clemens replied. "Try not to fret, however. As you say, they might have hunkered down early and decided to complete the journey in the morning. How'd you fare overall?"

Turner related the story and the casualty report. Both Dutch and Clemens groaned at the news that both Lider and Decker had to be evacced. Turner also asked them to put their heads into the problem of how to get Osaka and Hideki back to the Japs in a way that wouldn't raise suspicion.

"Put it to Shadow," Turner suggested.

"You trust him, Art?" Dutch asked.

"I think so, Joe... I trust my instincts. And Web trusts him too... I think Shadow is sincere in his beliefs, and we need a man like that."

They signed off and went back outside to eat their evening meal. Clemens asked two of his men to pack a light ruck and scout out the potential return route of Hazard's party at least as far as Bumbagoro.

The Cactus Navy

Then the five unlikely companions... an American submarine engineer, a British officer, a Marine Raider sergeant, a Marine Raider PFC and a Japanese naval officer stood on the edge of Vungana's precipice and watched the last of twilight vanish over the slot. There was a palpable tension in the air... an expectation that something would happen.

Although the night of August 7/8 would pass peacefully... it was but the calm before the storm.

Seventy-five miles to the north, northeast, just outside the boundaries of the Solomon Islands' waters, a long and deadly black shape parted the waters as it rose from the depths. All around her slender hull, the dinoflagellate cells of plankton erupted in bright flashes of light, causing a temporary foaming glow around the boat. This reaction was a defense mechanism to ward off predators and resulted in some of the most beautiful nighttime scenes at sea.

And the submarine, whose powerful diesels now rumbled to life, was indeed a predator. The most dangerous predator to swim below the surface of the sea, and she was ravenous. Not for schools of fish or a fat seal... no, this *Bull Shark* had a craving for steel.

"Ship rigged for surface," Andy Post said to Pat Jarvis as the acting XO climbed up the ladder to the conning tower. "Lookouts ready."

"Very well," Jarvis said, waiting for Hotrod Hernandez to crack the bridge hatch.

The boat's ventilation system was able to bleed off most of the internal pressure, but after a long dive, it was still a good idea to crack the hatch and bleed off any extra. Hernandez turned the dogging wheel, and a temporary wind was created as the internal pressure of the boat equalized with that of the atmosphere.

"Begin air accumulation," Jarvis told Post. "Messenger of the watch, inform the skipper we're rigged for surface. Lookouts to station."

Five men went up the ladder, Jarvis being the first. He and Hernandez took up their positions on the tiny bridge while the three lookouts scrambled up the periscope sheers and into their perches. The torpedo officer scanned the dark horizon with his powerful binoculars. He wasn't surprised to see nothing, especially since the moon had yet to rise.

"Bridge, control," Post's voice called over the speaker. "*Number one and two on charge, three and four on propulsion. Maneuvering standing by to answer all bells.*"

"Very well," Jarvis said. "Okay, Hotrod, let's get this show on the road."

"Helm, bridge," Hotrod spoke into the transmitter now. "All ahead full. Course zero-zero-zero. Make turns for ten knots."

After the acknowledgement, Jarvis ordered an SJ sweep on PPI. With the boat on the surface, the radar masts were at their full height and could see the uppermost works of large ships from as far away as eighteen miles.

"*Bridge, radar,*" Ted Balkley's tinny voice filtered up to them. "*Negative contact at this time.*"

"Very well," Jarvis said as he pulled out a pack of cigarettes and offered one to Hernandez, "Might be a long night, Hotrod. Pretty boring."

"My father, *señor*, is a wise man," Hernandez replied in an over-the-top Mexican drawl. "He always said that after a hard day of toiling in the fields, a man should always take time to be grateful... to kiss his wife, play his guitar and laugh with his friends at the cantina."

"Your dad is a farmer?" Jarvis asked.

"He is an accountant, *señor* Jarvis."

Jarvis threw back his head and roared with laughter, "You're such an *asshole*, Ralph!"

"*Si...*"

Chapter 34

D-Day+1 August 8, 1942 – 0800

USS Bull Shark – 130 miles northeast of the Florida Islands

"Pressure in the boat," Frank Nichols reported. "Green board."

"Very well," Elmer Williams replied. "Open main ballast vents. Flood safety, flood negative. Helm, all ahead two-thirds, planes fifteen degrees down."

Bull Shark's main ballast tank vents opened, and geysers of seawater erupted as from below, the sea pushed up and into the tanks and forced the air inside out. The submarine drove herself forward, her speed falling from ten knots to six as she was now running only on battery power. With nearly a thousand tons of water weighing her down and making her negatively buoyant, the big boat broke the surface suction and plunged down into the azure-blue of the Pacific.

"Forty-five feet," Nichols reported.

"Close main vents," Williams ordered. "Blow negative to the mark. Proceed to six-five feet."

Bull Shark had pushed the envelope that morning. Rather than diving at first light, she'd stayed on the surface, using her diesels to continue her zig-zag search pattern. In truth, she could use the snorkel to continue to do this even at periscope depth. However, the feather line from the thick device would make her easy to spot from the air... and as the boat was hunting an aircraft *carrier*, it was thought this was a bad idea.

"Periscope depth," Nichols said somewhat more subdued; the concept of having water over one's head had that effect on most submariners.

In Nichol's case, his subdued tone was also due in part to the fact that his throat was still sore from his injury several days earlier. Both he and Rogers had been checked out by *Saratoga's* chief medical officer, given what treatment was possible and sent back to the submarine after Williams' meeting with Fletcher. Rest and time was the primary prescription.

"How's our trim?" Williams asked.

"Good trim," Nichols said. "Bow planes rigged and a two-degree up bubble on stern planes."

"Very well," Williams said. "Quartermaster of the watch, proceed on Mr. Jarvis' search pattern."

"Aye-aye sir," Paul "Buck" Rogers replied.

He'd finally recovered from his head injury enough to resume his duties. Although the COB looked a bit pale and wan, he seemed able to stay on his feet. "Proceeding on zero-zero-zero... Bendix log indicates six knots."

"Bring us down to four, Chief," Williams said. "Gotta keep these batteries going all day."

The work of the control room proceeded quietly and almost casually. The bow and stern planesmen sat on their bench, Frank Nichols standing behind them watching the gauges. The manifold men stood by the various air controls, occasionally being directed by Nichols to adjust the trim tanks, Buck Rogers stood at the master gyro table with Williams carefully plotting the ship's position against the penciled in pattern that Pat Jarvis had come up with to try and find the *Sakai*. And up in the conning tower, Wendel Freeman sat at the helm with his eyes on the rudder angle indicator and the gyrocompass repeater, making occasional adjustments to the submarine's course. Behind him, Chet Rivers sat at his sonar gear with his headphones over his ears, diligently spinning the JP and the JK sound heads in an attempt to detect the slightest hint of mechanical sound out in the vast ocean.

Just before 0900, Henrie Martin and Bill Borshowski entered the control room from the after-battery compartment carrying a tray of bacon and egg sandwiches and a coffee service.

"Thought you boys might could use sometin' in dem bellies," Martin announced in his Cajun drawl. "Huntin' dem Jap work up an appetite, I gar-run-tee."

Borshowski shook his head and chuckled. In his own heavy Chicago accent, he added: "I keep tryin' to tell this crazy Cajun he's gotta make more Kielbasa, Chicago dahgs, maybe some deep-dish pizza and some honest to Christ Chicago-style bar-bee-qued baby backs, hah?"

"Sounds like a heavy breakfast," Rogers quipped as he took a sandwich and a cup of coffee.

Martin laughed, "Got youself anudda of dem sammich, Chief. Need to put some meat back on dem bone, you hear?"

Rogers grinned and took a second sandwich. He bit into one and whistled, "Whew! Put some cayenne in this, Henrie?"

Martin grinned, "Good for ya'."

Nichols took a bite and laughed. He cleared his throat a few times and partially rasped, "It's good, but damn, Henrie... we've only got so many heads on this tub!"

"0900 sir," Freeman called down from the conning tower.

"Very well," Williams said. "Planes, zero-four-zero feet. Ted, standby on radar sweeps. Sugar dog first and then switch to the jig."

"Aye-aye, sir," Balkley's disembodied voice floated down from above. After the boat reached radar depth, the air search radar was activated. There was a moment's pause and then another.

"Something, Ted?" Williams prodded.

"Uhm... maybe, sir..." Balkley supplied. "Very faint contact... range indeterminant."

"Switch to the sugar jig," Williams said, setting his plate and cup down on the gyro table and going up the ladder until his head poked above the combing of the hatchway.

Balkley switched gear and did a complete sweep with the more powerful surface-search radar, "Bingo! Distant contact bearing three-two-six... range eighteen-thousand yards... moving fast, possible aircraft, sir."

"Track him," Williams said. "Has he seen our masts?"

Balkley switched from the standard display to the planned position indicator. He made a note on a piece of scratch paper. "I don't think so, sir... seems to be headed one-one-five... speed one-five-five knots. Should be visible on the scope, sir."

"Boatswain, take a look with number one," Williams ordered.

Martin Janslotter, the boatswain's mate, was on periscope watch. He activated the search scope and snapped the handles down, "Okay... scanning from bow to port... got him, sir! Low-flying or distant aircraft... looks like a seaplane.

big boy, too. Four engines. And I'm pretty sure it ain't one of ours, sir."

"Where's he going?" Williams wondered, a gleam in his eye. "Nothing out that way for a long, long way... is that bird flying straight, Ted?"

Balkley checked his readouts again, "Yes sir, course is steady on one-one-five."

Williams grinned and rubbed his hands together, "I think we just got a break, fellas. Down scope, secure the radar. Helm, come right to course one-one-five. Periscope depth, Frank."

There could be very few reasons why a seaplane was flying out to sea toward no particular destination. She *might* be searching for Fletcher's carrier task force. She *might* be doing a long easterly sweep outside the Guadalcanal combat zone for approaching Allied shipping... or she might, just *might*, be headed to rendezvous with a strike carrier task force of her own.

"Sir?" Frank Nichols broke into Williams' thoughts.

The Cactus Navy

"Yeah, Frank?"

Nichols looked a bit uncomfortable. There was obviously something on his mind and he was reluctant to bring it up. Andy Post, who had been working in the radio shack handling that morning's fox broadcast as well as the latest coded directives, stepped out and up to the other two officers. He too, looked as if something were on his mind.

"Can we speak to you a moment, sir?" Nichols asked.

"Okay, Frank, Andy... step over here," Williams replied, moving into the forward passageway in officer's country. "What's on your minds, fellas?"

Post cleared his throat, and Nichols pushed his rimless specs higher up on the bridge of his nose, "Ahem... Sir..."

"For Christ's sake, Frank, drop the sir for the moment and just talk to me," Williams urged, not unkindly.

"Elmer... why are we going after this carrier?" Nichols finally asked. "We've got four fish... ahem... two in each room... that's hardly enough to sink her, let alone deal with her escorts."

"Us against six ships, sir..." Post reluctantly added. "Isn't that... well... suicide?"

In truth, Williams had pondered that very thought more than once. The fact that he was actively pursuing the *Sakai* was something of a surprise even to him. Had he really come that far? Had the young new XO who'd been assigned to the as-yet-unfinished *Bull Shark* back in January really become so daring?

He wasn't sure he had an answer for himself or his officers. He might say something like, what would Anvil Art Turner do... but that was a bit ridiculous. It intimated that he, Williams, was on Turner's level, and he didn't believe that to be true. It also opened him up to the same criticism from the men.

"Honestly..." the XO began. "I'm not entirely sure. Yes, I could argue that *Sakai* is a threat to our Marines on Guadalcanal and the other islands... but if I'm totally honest... it sort of feels personal. She's sort of... I don't know... waving a red cape in our faces if you see what I mean."

"Elmer, we went after two freighters and nearly got creamed," Nichols reminded him. "Now you're taking us with an almost empty load of pickles up against a *fleet*. It seems more than a little reckless. Ahem... dammit... like maybe somebody else should handle this one."

"What would the skipper say, do you think?" Williams asked.

Post chuckled softly, "Probably that with four fish, he could get *Sakai* and three of her escorts, but..."

"But I'm no Anvil Art," Williams admitted.

The two other men glanced at each other and then back at Williams. Nichols looked a bit sheepish, "We're not saying that exactly, Elm... just..."

"It's okay, guys," Williams stated. "I don't walk around here with delusions of grandeur. But if our skipper is anything, and if he's taught *me* anything... it's that we're at *war*. It's not safe, it's not easy, and it *is* reckless. You've got to push till it gives... and then push some more. That's how we're gonna beat the Jap. They're dedicated to the point of religious fervor. They fight and die for their emperor. You don't beat people like that by being cautious. We've got to be... *I've* got to be... aggressive. To know an opportunity when I see one and exploit it. This is Art Turner's boat, and that's what he would do, so by God, it's what we're gonna do."

Post couldn't help but grin. Even Nichols, who was a bit more conservative, smiled at the sentiment.

"You've got our support, sir," Nichols said.

"Always have, Elm," Post added.

"Thank you, fellas, ... I never doubted it," Williams said, shaking both of their hands. "Now let's get to work, huh?"

The two men ducked aft and back into the control room. Williams was about to follow when a hand fell lightly on his shoulder. He jumped a bit, surprised to find Pat Jarvis' handsome features smiling at him.

"Well said, Elm tree,"

Williams grinned at his friend, "Thanks, Pat. I'm sure if they asked you, you'd have just told them cuz I said so."

Jarvis chuckled, "Nah... I'd have said pretty much the same thing. Art Turner is a friendly, soft-spoken, easy-going guy. Has no problem joking with our crew or with them joking with him. He understands men and how to motivate them. Yet, you and I both know there's a lionheart in there. He's one of the toughest bastards I know, and he makes it look easy."

Williams scoffed, "So do you, Pat. You don't fear anything. Nothing daunts you... me, well..."

"Don't sell yourself short, Elmer," Jarvis said quietly. "You've come a long way, and you've got a head for this business. Sides—" Jarvis treated Williams to a toothy grin "—you screw up too much and I'll clean up after ya'."

"I hate you, Pat," Williams laughed and punched the torpedo officer in the shoulder.

"I know you do, pal... I know you do. Now let's go get us a Jap flattop!"

Guadalcanal – Lunga Point Airfield

"Where the hell is everybody?" Turner asked as he rode onto the nearly completed airstrip in General Vandegrift's Jeep.

"Think they must have bugged out yesterday, sir," the gunnery sergeant driving the vehicle stated. "Probably saw all the ships out there and high-tailed it for the hills."

"More likely than not," Vandegrift said from the front passenger seat. "What do you think, Colonel?"

Beside Turner in the rear seat, a barrel-chested Marine in his mid-forties nodded grimly, "I agree sir. Although I wouldn't be surprised if we get some voluntary prisoners once they see we've captured the place and how many of us there are."

"I'd also not be shocked if, once the next air raid begins, the remaining Japanese troops come after us," Turner opined. "Use the distraction as a chance to at least take a few of us out, wouldn't you say, Colonel Puller?"

Lieutenant Colonel Lewis B. Puller smiled thinly, "Good thought, Commander. And my friends call me Chesty."

"My god..." Vandegrift muttered. "Look at this place! The Japs sure did a helluva job setting it up for us, huh?"

The four men laughed as the Gunny drove them across the airfield, where a full battalion of Marines was already inspecting and cataloging the base's resources as well as setting up perimeter defenses. There were few Allied vehicles on Guadalcanal as yet. Admiral Turner's cargo ships were still unloading as quickly as possible, and there were already logistics problems on the beach. Most of the Marines had to march from Beach Red the entire eight miles to the airfield.

Now they were toiling in the late morning sun. Scrambling to solidify control over what they'd come to secure. Even now, reports were coming in via radio of another Japanese bombing raid from Rabaul. Soon the men on the ground would most likely be under attack from the air.

The logistics of unloading all the transports and the men, vehicles and supplies they carried was becoming a nightmare. There simply weren't enough landing craft to do the job quickly, and Turner had already heard reports of the Navy and Marine Corps bickering over who was supposed to do what. The Navy felt that it had done its part by getting the invasion force to the theater but that once the LCVPs hit the beach, it was the Marines' job to hump their own gear. The Marine Corps was trying to secure their position and felt that the Navy ought to spare sailors to act as stevedores in order to move things along. It was by no means a bitter conflict, but it made the submarine Commander uneasy, and it irritated him. The Jap was the enemy, not your own services.

The airfield *was* impressive, though. The thirty-six-hundred-foot runway was nearly completed. There was a nearly complete airdrome with six hangars and blast pens, compressor shops for charging torpedo engines, a medical clinic and a refrigeration plant. As the Gunny drove, the officers took note that a large power station had also been nearly completed. There was even a small, narrow-gauge service railroad, machine and repair shops, wooden barracks, roads, bridges and even a wharf that would certainly come in handy for unloading the fleet's supplies once the base was secure. One interesting feature was the very Japanese-style administration building. It was new and reminded Turner of an Asian pagoda.

"Our boys are already finding treasures galore," Puller stated. "The tent city between Cacoom and the Lunga River is loaded with soap, razors and all sorts of toiletries just left behind. I've heard reports of large caches of beer, sake and rice..."

"Plus, the vehicles, sir," the Gunny added. "Construction equipment, trucks, cars and a bunch of bicycles."

"Sounds like this is our MO from now on," Vandegrift joked. "Let the Japs fix everything up nice, and then we come in and yank the rug out from under 'em."

The field radio in Vandegrift's lap suddenly crackled to life, *"General, this is Major Landry... we've secured the radio station and have her up and running on battery power."*

Vandegrift thumbed the talk switch, "Very good, major. Once the power station is up and running, we should be able to keep you in business full time."

"Yes sir..." the man said hesitantly. *"But... well, when we activated the set, it was already on a certain frequency... and... well, sir, this is weird..."*

"What is it, son?" Vandegrift asked with just a hint of impatience in his voice. As the operational commander of all Marine forces, Vandegrift was already extremely busy and about to become more so.

"Sir... do you have a Commander Art Turner with you by chance?"

Puller cocked an eyebrow at Turner. Vandegrift half-turned in his seat and did the same. Turner only shrugged.

"As a matter of fact, I do, Major," the general replied. "Why?"

A sigh, "*General... there's a Japanese naval officer asking to speak to him.*"

"What the hell...?" Turner muttered.

"We're on the way," Vandegrift answered. "Tell your mystery caller to hold the line. Out."

"You're a popular guy, Captain," Puller said wryly.

"Lucky me," Turner cranked.

The General dropped Turner at the small radio station after exacting a promise to be briefed later. The submariner entered the small building and was pleasantly surprised to find Sherman "Tank" Broderick and Doug Ingram working with the Marines. After inquiring, Turner was told that Chief Duncan and Taggart were on the power station detail.

"You've got a call, Commander," Major Landry said wryly.

"Who the hell is it?" Turner asked irritably. He had a bad feeling about this, although he couldn't quite have explained why at the time.

"Doesn't say, Commander... just asked for you."

"Very well... put him on then," Turner said, stepping up next to the short and wiry Marine officer. He took the offered handset. "Turner."

A crackle of static and then a man with a moderate Japanese accent said: "*Good morning, Captain. Congratulations on your temporary victory. You and your Marine friends should savor it while it lasts, however, because your elation will be short-lived.*"

Turner sighed. He was in no mood for theatrics, "I don't have time for this... who the hell are you and what the hell do you want?"

"*I am your opponent... your nemesis. I am the man who will sink your pathetic submarine. I am the man who will destroy you personally, Turner... in short, I am the man in control of your destiny.*"

Turner laughed humorlessly, "Big talk. High-flying words for a coward who makes threats over a radio link. Again, I ask you... who the hell are you, and what the *fuck* do you want?"

There were smiles and chuckles from the Marines and the two

The Cactus Navy

sailors. There was an unmistakable hardness and no-shit tone to Turner's voice. The Japanese man laughed snidely.

"*My name is Commander Takashi Sato. I am the executive officer of the carrier* Sakai. *As I said, Turner, I am your new worst enemy. For the moment, however, before our battle of wills and personal conflict begins... I would like to propose a gentlemanly exchange. A matter of honor, if you will, to show that while I will destroy you and everything you care for... I do respect you as a worthy adversary.*"

"Who the hell is this clown?" Turner asked no one in particular. "Guy sounds like something out of a bad movie... Commander, I don't know what bee you've got in your bonnet... and I don't care. And before I tell you to go pound sand, I will ask you exactly what this exchange is. What do you want of me?"

Another laugh, "*Do you play chess, Arthur? I do and enjoy the game immeasurably. You already have two of my... let's call them knights, shall we? And I have one of yours. You are currently holding Lieutenant Commanders Ryu Osaka and Omata Hideki in your custody. I want them back. Admiral Yamamoto wants them back. In exchange, I offer you one of your pieces in good faith.*"

A pause and then a weary sounding Porter Hazard's voice spoke from the ether, "*Sir? Sir, that really you?*".

Turner's stomach lurched, and his blood boiled in a simultaneous and very unpleasant mixture of fear and loathing. He'd heard plenty of horrifying stories of what the Japanese did to their prisoners. The mental images of what they might be doing to his officer were deeply disturbing.

"How are you, Porter?" Turner asked. "How's the rest of the team?"

A long pause, "*Batu's ... dead, sir. Jake was right... one of those villages sold us out. We walked into an ambush. They got me and took out Batu... I'm sorry, sir.*"

Turner gripped the handset so hard he heard it crack, "It's all right, Lieutenant... what about Vousa?"

"*We were ahead, and he was scouting. I called out to him to run* when we were jumped... but the damned fool stuck with us. The Japs caught him and me... but let him go."

"Why?"

"To deliver a message to you, sir... and to show you how to find us..."

"Are you all right?"

"I've been better... but hangin' in there, sir."

"Well, you stay strong; we'll get you out of there, pal," Turner said encouragingly. "Put what's his nuts back on."

"*It's simple, Commander,*" Sato was back again. "*You deliver Osaka and Hideki to the location that your island nigger will show you by this time tomorrow morning. I don't have to tell you what happens if you fail.*"

"Son of a bitch..." Turner growled. "And then I suppose you put a bullet between my eyes, too, right? Betray your little bargain and kill me, my officer and whoever else I bring?"

A boisterous and eerie laugh, "*You do me much disservice, Arthur. No, no... I am looking forward to our game. If all I wanted was to simply kill more Americans, then I can do so. I could kill your man now and leave Osaka and Hideki to their fates. I don't care much for them anyway... but the chance to match skills and wits with a contemporary? One who's already proven himself a worthy adversary? This is more than just doing one's duty, Arthur. This is the chance of a lifetime! You bested Klaus Brechman. You defeated Kajimora and his super-submarine... now it is my turn. I want a clean, fresh board. All of my pieces and all of yours. Then and only then can we truly enjoy the penultimate game!*"

"Fuckin' *looney*-tunes..." Tank muttered. The radio conversation was easy to overhear.

Turner wanted to reach through the radio waves and strangle the arrogant, maniacal bastard. However, he had little choice in what he could do or say at the moment.

"Deal," he finally answered.

"*Excellent! I shall see you tomorrow so that we might each see one* another's face. To look one's enemy in the eye is to truly understand him, Arthur. We shall bow to one another and then engage in honorable combat! One samurai to another, eh?"

"Yeah, yeah," Turner scoffed in blithe dismissal. "You just hold your end up, Sato. You take care of my man. You feed him, you treat him right and treat his wounds, if any."

"*Do not fear, I shall be the consummate gentle—*"

Turner reached out and snapped the set off and tossed the handset on the desk, "Goddamned lousy arrogant son of a..."

"Are you seriously going out there to get your man, Captain?" Landry asked.

"You bet your ass," Turner said and set his jaw.

"Ballsy... damned ballsy..." the Marine said in admiration.

"They don't call him Anvil Art for nothin'," Tank said. "Just the mention of his name makes the yellow man quake in his goat-boots."

"Yeah," Turner said and smiled crookedly. "Especially when I bring my own personal Tank with me."

"Aww, *nuts*..." Broderick moaned but smiled despite himself.

Chapter 35

USS Bull Shark 1940

"All stop."

Dick Vigliano replied to Jarvis' order and waited expectantly. Jarvis turned to Chet Rivers at the sound gear and nodded. After two minutes, Rivers looked back at the acting Exec.

"No passive contacts," Rivers said quietly.

"Very well," Jarvis replied. "Mug, all ahead one-third. Teddy, raise the search scope."

The thicker search periscope with its superior optics rose until the head was hardly more than a foot above water. Jarvis peered through expecting to see the last glimmers of twilight in the west. Strangely, though, he did a complete rotation and saw nothing. Absolutely nothing.

"Awful dark up there... Teddy handoff to Chet. Standby on both radars. Diving officer, make your depth zero-four-zero feet."

Again the acknowledgements and the boat tilted slightly up by the bow. Now Jarvis' scope head was high enough that he should be able to see anything on the surface of the sea out to about seven miles. Yet still, the eyepiece was as black as the inside of a cow.

"Hmmm..." Jarvis mused. "Let 'er rip, Ted."

"No contacts on sugar dog... switching to surface scan..." Balkley reported tonelessly. "Negative contacts on sugar jig, sir. Free and clear up there."

"Very well," Jarvis said. "Down scope. Surface the boat. Manifold stations shunt excess pressure into the blowers. Lookouts to the conning tower. Rig conning and control for red. Messenger of the watch, alert the skipper we're floating the boat."

The surfacing alarm blared three times, and all around the men, the roar of high-pressure air blowing the water from the ballast tanks filled the boat. The lighting in the tower and below switched to a blood-red hue that would allow the men to adapt their night vision before going topside. Again the boat tilted upward and then settled on the surface, her pressure hull air being bled into the air accumulation system to mostly equalize the pressure that always builds up in a submarine, even on a routine dive.

"Mug, turn the wheel over to your relief. You're with me as quartermaster of the watch," Jarvis ordered.

"Aye-aye, sir," Vigliano replied and then called down for a relief helmsman.

They then climbed the ladder to the bridge hatch and turned the dogging wheel. A hiss and a rush of air created a temporary breeze as the boat's internal pressure lowered down to the normal fourteen pounds per square inch at sea level. Mug opened the hatch, and then he, Jarvis and the three lookouts raced up the ladder and into the warm but clammy night. It was Fred Swooping Hawk who solved the mystery first.

"Like pea soup out here, sir," he said as he passed to climb up the sheers.

"Of course..." Jarvis muttered wryly. "Sea fog... might come in handy this evening."

The phenomenon commonly known as sea fog is an advection that occurs when warm air above cooler water condenses. Wave and wind action stirs up the surface and throws salt particles into the air, which then act as condensation nuclei. The dense fog can be hundreds of feet thick or so close to the surface that sailors going up a mast can see over the top.

It has the disadvantage of rendering vision all but useless, especially at night. However, *Bull Shark* was equipped with two radar systems that were in no way affected by fog.

Jarvis thumbed the bridge transmitter, "Radar, bridge... give me an automatic sugar jig sweep on PPI."

Mug held up a small, red-filtered flashlight and aimed the beam at his maneuvering board. He made a small mark with a grease pencil and nodded to himself, "We should be coming up on a course change, sir. Gonna need to turn to one-five-five here shortly."

Jarvis sighed and smacked his lips, "Christ, bet you could bring a hot pretzel up here and it'd salt itself... yeah, that's my figuring too, Mug. Would be nice to be able to take a lunar... but the dead reckoning indicator will have to do."

"*Bridge, radar... no contacts,*" Balkley said with evident disappointment.

"Very well," Jarvis sighed. "Okay, Mug, let's get her on the growlers and top up the Sargos."

He knew how the men felt. When they'd spotted the seaplane that morning and had followed its course submerged, they hoped that the fifty miles or so they'd traveled would have brought them into sight of their quarry. They were now nearly two hundred miles from Guadalcanal and the Sealark Channel. Out in the middle of nowhere hunting for ghosts.

"Helm, bridge," Mug ordered. "Alert maneuvering to answer bells on main engines. One and two on charge, three and four on propulsion with an eighty, ninety split. All ahead standid'. Right standid' rudduh, steady up on course one-five-five."

Jarvis chuckled, "You like sayin' standid', don't ya', Mug?"

The New Yorker chuckled, "For a guy who's from the Ocean State and sounds not too different, you got no room to break my shoes, sir."

"I'm not makin' fun, Mug," Jarvis implored. "Now, don't go and get all upset... would a nice kiss help?"

Vigliano guffawed, "Anybody ever tell you that you was a few slices short of a loaf?"

"Nope," Jarvis said, breathing deeply. "Not anybody wanted a promotion, at least."

Both men were silent for a moment, along with the lookouts above and behind them. Normally the men in the perch would chin wag about sports, movies, dames or was Tyrone Power, Alan Ladd or Clark Gable better to play them in the movie. That night, though, with visibility down to zero, all the men topside were deeply quiet, as if tiptoeing through a cemetery at the witching hour.

That's why when the bridge speaker crackled to life, it made both Jarvis and Vigliano jump. Both men hoped the other hadn't seen.

"*Bridge, radar!*" Balkley sounded excited. "*Quarter-hour sweep revealed something, sir!*"

"What?" Jarvis pressed.

"*Faint signal... dispersed... I think maybe I picked up signal bleed from an air search set, Mr. Jarvis!*"

Both men on the bridge exchanged wide-eyed glances and quick smiles, only barely visible to one another due to the hellish glow from the open bridge hatch. Each one looking satanical in his predatory glee.

"Good work, Ted," Jarvis replied. "Can you home in yet?"

A pause, "*Negative... but if I had to guess, I'd say the source was between three-zero-zero and zero-one-oh relative, sir.*"

Jarvis' faint smile now grew into a shark-toothed grin, "Got you! Got that sonama bitch! Mug, let's see if we can't help Teddy out. Put us on a one-three-zero... and JOOD?"

Another pause, and then Harry Brannigan, acting chief of the watch and junior officer of the watch, replied from his station in control, "*Here, sir.*"

"Harry, sound general quarters. Battle stations torpedo!" Jarvis said and barely managed not to laugh maniacally.

The Cactus Navy

Inside the boat, the fourteen-tone gong of the general quarters alarm blared. It's oddly church-like bells calling every man aboard to his battle station. Even on the bridge, the men could hear the chief electrician's mate's voice echoing on the 1MC public address.

"*All hands! All hands! General quarters, general quarters! All sections, battle stations torpedo! This is not a drill, repeat, this is not a drill. The smoking lamp is out!*"

"Pfft!" Jarvis scoffed. "Try and get a butt lit up here, why doncha?"

Minutes passed once more in silence. The heavy fog did strange things to the sound of the engines. It seemed to box everything in, shrinking the world around them. It was easy to imagine that rather than being out on a vast open expanse of sea, the submarine was gliding through a cavern beneath some mountain as if in a Jules Verne novel.

"You think we've found our friends?" Elmer Williams' soft voice said as he popped up through the bridge hatch.

"We're about to find out, Skipper," Jarvis said, glancing at his watch in the red beam of a flashlight. He thumbed the transmitter button. "Radar, bridge... sweep on sugar jig."

The three men waited tensely for the report. In the periscope sheers, the three lookouts listened keenly as well. With the fog so thick and the night so dark, they couldn't see anything anyway.

"*Bridge, radar... multiple contacts bearing zero-one-five,*" Balkley's voice said almost reverently. "*Range thirty-thousand yards.*"

"We got you now, Tojo..." Jarvis muttered. "How many, Ted?"

A pause, "*Uncertain exactly, sir... but at least three. One is certainly larger than the rest.*"

Jarvis turned to Williams, "Here you go, Elm. We've found them, I'm sure of it. You have the deck... Skipper."

Williams grinned up at his friend, "That's a negative, XO. I'll be assistant approach officer. The attack is yours. Bout time you busted your cherry anyway."

Jarvis chuckled, "I'm the guy on the TDC, remember, Elm tree?

Y'know... the guy that *shoots* the damned fish? And what do you mean bust my cherry? What kinda talk is that for a nice, Christian, mid-western boy?"

There were chuckles from above as well. Williams grinned, "Well, now you're gonna be the guy who cons the attack, Patty m'lad. Don't worry, I've got a reasonably smart monkey to work the computer for you! And as for me being a nice, sweet Indiana boy... I still am... but you've been a terrible influence on me. Just wait till my mom finds out."

Boisterous laughter followed the XO down the hatch. Jarvis laughed and shook his head as he thumbed the box again, "Control, bridge. Phone talker, alert both rooms to load their fish. Depth will be six feet, speed high. Target is the carrier."

Earlier that day, Jarvis and Williams had agreed that it would be a good time to routine their four remaining torpedoes. Since four was all they had, they *had* to work properly. Not to mention that pulling and reloading was good drill for the pickle gangs.

It was because of this, therefore, that Walter "Sparky" Sparks was standing in the middle of his room barking and bawling his men out.

"Come on, you lazy bastards!" he entreated. "You ain't had to do shit this whole fuckin' cruise. Now we got a big fat juicy carrier just waitin' out there to be fucked, and what're y'all doin'? My granny could load a goddamned torpedo faster'n that, and she's seventy-six years old!"

"You sure got a big mouth, Sparky!" Bob Jones tossed off as he and Griggs hauled on the tailing tackle, or taggle, to heave number sixteen into tube one.

"He uses all that hot air to help charge the impulse manifold," Eugene Parker added from the other side of the room where he and Perry Wilkes were adjusting the rollers for number sixteen before hauling it into tube two.

"You a fuckin' smartass now, *Eugene?*" Sparks growled.

"Aye-aye Sparky!" Parker replied snappily, getting a laugh from the rest of the men.

The Cactus Navy

"Well, seems like a fuckin' genius Einstein such as yourself would put them big mouth muscles to work and speed his sorry ass up," Sparky chastised, although, as usual, his eyes gleamed with the love for his job. "On account of your team is behind Jonesy over here and you got the third man in charge of the room workin' with ya'."

"Our fish is heavier," Wilkes popped off.

"Shit Perry," Tommy Perkins, who was standing between the tubes ready to set depth and speed spindles. "We all seen you coming out of the shower... when you bother to take one that is... and your fish ain't no heavier than anybody else's."

"Not what your sister says," Wilkes grunted as he and Parker hauled on the taggle, and his team chortled and whooped.

"You assholes just let me know when it's in," Sparky said, paused and then: "Now *that's* what Tommy's sister says!"

The room erupted into grunting laughs as the men hauled the torpedoes into the breaches.

"Hey, Murph..." Marty Janslotter said as he set up the rollers on number nine. "You gonna give us a hand with this or just sit back there with your thumb wedged?"

"Rank has its privileges, Marty," Murph said, leaning against the portside stack of bunks and puffing languidly on a Pall Mall.

"Well, I'm the boatswain, for Christ's sake," Janslotter replied.

"Yeah, on a submarine," Smitty jeered. "Real fuckin' backbreaker *that* must be!"

The men snickered as the taggle was rigged. Electrician's mate Paul Baxter and fireman Horris Eckhart were on loan to the after room for reload duty. They began to heave on the lines, which squealed through the blocks that made up the tailing rigging. Their torpedo began to slide across the rollers and into the tube.

"You guys just bore me," Murph said. "Been a dull cruise so far and I'm hopin' we get some action."

"Boring?" Eckhart asked in his funny Wisconsin accent. "We already bagged two freighters and a Jap tin can, doncha know!"

He pronounced it bayged.

"Three ships," Murph scoffed. "We still got four fish aboard. I'm just hopin' we get to use 'em all and get at least one more, that strike carrier. I hear we'll be headed to Brisbane after on account of its closer... you know what them Australian broads will do to you fellas when they see this boat come into port with a broom strapped to the sheers?"

Baxter grinned, "No, Murph... what'll they do?"

"Lemme tell ya'," Murph expounded. "Lotta Aussies been called up for this war. Remember, the Brits and the Aussies have been fightin' for longer'n we have. Not a lot of single men in Aus. Kinda the opposite of Pearl, y'know?"

"Yeah," Janslotter quipped. "Like fifty to one dudes to dames. Man can't get laid there for love or money."

"Well, money," Smitty added. "Three bucks gets you three minutes with a girl in one of them boogie houses on Hotel Street."

"Shit, that's a bargain for you, Jack," Baxter added. "Two for one, huh?"

Uproarious laughter and even a friendly punch or two. The torpedoes were loaded, impulse air flasks charged, outer doors opened, and the ready fire levers thrown. Both torpedo rooms were ready to fight.

"What's our play gonna be, Pat?" Williams's head asked from behind Jarvis and Vigliano's feet.

"That flattop's got radar," Vigliano stated.

"Yeah, air search," Jarvis noted. "But we're getting' close... probably gonna have to dive. Clear the bridge!"

The lookouts scrambled down from their platform and vanished down the hatch. Mug went down, followed by Jarvis, who pulled the release lanyard and the big hatch swung down over his head. Vigliano dogged it and took his place at the chart desk. He was still acting quartermaster and would backstop the plotting party in the control room.

"All stop," Jarvis ordered. "Phone talker, maneuvering. Stand by to answer bells on batteries. Dive, dive, dive!"

AOOGA! AOOGA!

"Rig out dive planes, close main induction," Jarvis ordered.

"Green Christmas tree!" Frank Nichols said from below. "Pressure in the boat."

"Open MBT vents," Jarvis said. "Flood safety, flood negative. Make your depth zero-six-five feet, diving officer. Helm, all ahead two-thirds."

Bull Shark's main ballast tanks and in-hull buoyancy compensation tanks filled with seawater, and she slid smoothly below the surface. She was now truly what her name implied her to be. An undersea predator homing in on her prey. Her teeth, four Mark 14 torpedoes loaded with nearly seven-hundred pounds of high-explosive torpex each, were sharp and ready to tear into the steel flesh of her victim.

"Sound, what've you got?" Jarvis asked after receiving word that the boat was at periscope depth and had good trim.

"Not much, sir," Rivers replied in confusion. "Not even with the rock crushers shut down... I think there might be a faint machinery signature sixteen-thousand yards off. Same bearing as radar's... zero-one-five."

"Might be sitting idle," Williams opined as he leaned against the bridge ladder and lit a cigarette.

Jarvis nodded, "That'd explain the low signature. Auxiliary machinery running... but on three ships? That's odd, isn't it?"

"They're Japs, Mr. Jarvis," Vigliano joked. "Most of their shit is odd."

"Yeah, they eat raw fish... blegh!" Ted Balkley, the periscope assistant now that his radars were underwater, said.

"Yeah, but they do got them girls that walk on your back... *ay chihuahua!*" Hotrod called up from beneath their feet, accompanied by chuckles and snickers.

"We're doomed..." Williams muttered and smiled.

"Well, let's nose up and sniff 'em out," Jarvis said. "Helm, right rudder. Course one-five-zero."

"Sir, my helm is right... steadying up on one-five-oh," Freeman said.

"Plotting party," Jarvis announced. "We're still working on the radar contacts. Until we get a good sound bearing. And our targets are stationary it looks like... should be fish in a barrel."

"I wonder..." Williams muttered, rubbing his chin.

Jarvis looked at him and raised his eyebrows in a question.

"Wonder if that submarine is still with them," Williams pondered.

Jarvis nodded, "Yeah, she could be on the surface or below them like a watchdog. Still though... why are they just sitting out here almost two-hundred miles from the slot? It doesn't make any sense..."

"Who knows?" Williams asked. "Frankly, even if we did know, there's not a hell of a lot we can do about it. We've got our target, and that's what we've got to focus on."

Bull Shark slipped quietly through the sea at five knots. After nearly an hour, Rivers's sound gear was definitely picking up machinery signatures. He thought he detected three ships, but he couldn't be sure.

"All stop," Jarvis ordered. "Up scope... okay... still like pea soup up there, dammit... down scope."

"What're you thinking, Pat?" Williams asked.

Jarvis lit a cigarette for himself and pulled in a deep drag, "As I see it, we've got two choices, Elmer. We wait until the fog clears and hit them on the surface... or we go active so that Chet can get accurate bearings and counts."

"You mean send out a big announcement that there's a submarine within six-thousand yards?" Williams asked incredulously.

"Least we'll have somethin' to shoot at," Jarvis stated. "If we're successful no matter what, once our fish explode, the Japs will know we're here."

"What about creeping up at periscope depth until we can see them in the scope?" Vigliano asked.

"With the vis what it is out here, Mug..." Jarvis considered.

The Cactus Navy

"They'd hear our reduction gearing before we could see them, I think. Nope. It's either we get the ball rollin' or wait until they start moving."

"And you're not patient enough for that?" Williams teased.

Jarvis grinned, "It's a virtue, but it's not an infinite supply. I say we get to within fifteen hundred yards and then bawl them out."

"Oh Jesus Christ..." somebody muttered from the control room. The acoustics were such that even soft words reached the conning tower above.

"Risky, Pat," Williams said.

Jarvis drew on his pill again and shrugged, "I keep hearin' rumors about some kinda war goin' on someplace... and war is risky business."

"Where'd you hear that nonsense?" Williams asked lightly, playing along with Jarvis' attempt to make light of the danger.

"Heard it on the radio," the torpedo officer replied. "Tokyo Rose said so."

"Oh, then it *must* be true," Frank Nichols chimed in from the diving station.

A round of subdued but authentic laughter filled both compartments. Williams drew in a breath and sighed.

"It's your show, XO."

"Helm, all ahead one-third," Jarvis ordered. "Chet, keep your ears peeled."

The boat once again moved through the black waters, stalking ever closer to her still and quiet prey. After nearly half an hour, Rivers pulled off one of his headphone cups and turned to Jarvis.

"I think we're close, sir... possibly within fifteen hundred yards."

"Diving officer, twenty-degree down bubble. Make your depth one-zero-zero feet," Jarvis ordered as he squared his shoulders and prepared himself to give his next order. The next words out of his mouth would commit the submarine to the battle and might earn them all medals or might consign them to a watery tomb. He cleared his throat, "Chet... light 'em up."

Chapter Thirty-Six

The navigation bridge of the IJN strike carrier *Sakai* was strangely quiet. The men at their stations did not chat with one another. The officers on the deck stood around the plotting table and silently pondered the charts. Having nothing to report, the radarman and the sonarman at the after stations simply monitored their equipment in silence. The helmsmen forward in the pilothouse area sat still at his wheel and engine enunciators. There was little for anyone to do with the ship sitting idle on the sea.

Captain Kenji Igawa sipped at a lukewarm cup of tea and looked at his Seiko wristwatch for what must be the hundredth time since the sun had set. Not that there had been much of a sunset, not with the damp woolen surface fog settling in at dusk.

He, like all the senior officers of his now three-ship task force, knew that sometime at or after midnight, Vice-admiral Gunichi Mikawa would be leading a task force of cruisers and destroyers into the Sealark Channel to attack the American invasion fleet. Miraculously, according to the last report at least, Mikawa's fleet had not yet been detected. The plan was for them to come down the slot and then move out of it to the south and circle around Savo Island from the west and southwest. Upon reaching this destination, Igawa would be notified to begin his run toward Guadalcanal at flank speed. It was hypothesized that his carrier would be within sixty to eighty miles of the American fleet by dawn. He would then send a full strike and then send his task force southeast to rendezvous with his airplanes.

It was hoped that Mikawa's attack, followed up by a bombing run from *Sakai,* would not only destroy or disable a significant portion of Admiral Turner's fleet but that it would demoralize the Americans on the sea and on the land. This would soften them up for a major strike later on by the mobile fleet.

Igawa would have preferred to get closer to the Florida Islands and wait patiently there rather than being so far away. However, it was represented to him by Yamamoto himself that there were other dangers than American surface ships and aircraft. It was hardly a point to argue, Igawa had to admit. Just a few days earlier, an American submarine had sunk one of his escorts.

Yet not long after that, it was reported that this boat had been depth-charged into oblivion after assaulting a supply mission in the slot. This could not be confirmed, and Yamamoto felt that either the submarine could have survived or that another might have taken her place.

Thus, Igawa's new strike carrier was relegated to sitting idle in the open ocean with but two destroyers. At least they were of the newer *Asashio*-class... but still. Then again, his ship, built on a converted cruiser hull, was fast and nimble and equipped very much as a destroyer would be. She did have sonar, air search radar and even twenty depth charges. She was armored below the waterline and had a twenty-plane airwing to boot.

Igawa didn't like sitting idle. He was of the mindset that idle hands did evil's work. His ship and her task force were designed to fight, not sit twiddling their collective thumbs.

The surge of fear at the sudden disruption of the funereal calm that hung over his ship like the fog surprised Igawa, therefore. It was due more to surprise than anything, he told himself, quickly pushing down the nervousness and embracing the notion that something was finally happening.

It slowly dawned on the crew as well, and their alteration from placidity to urgent concern was fascinatingly in time with the signal that danger was near. One moment they were quiet and still, and the next, a high-pitched moan began to echo through the hull. It took several seconds for the true nature of the sound to register. By then, the whine had grown loud and was accompanied by an audible gong as the powerful beam of sound struck the hull.

"Active pinging!" the sonarman suddenly bleated in alarm... as if everyone within a mile hadn't already discerned that for themselves.

For the moment, Igawa was glad Sato had left the ship on an errand earlier that day. He didn't relish the way the man chewed the heads off sailors for the smallest infraction, "Localize, sonar. Maintain yourself."

"Possible submarine, bearing zero-two-zero, range one-four-five-zero meters," the sonar operator stated.

"So," Igawa pondered. "We meet again, Yankee? Are you the wolf who hounded me before? Or are you a new dog searching for his next whipping... Arawi, have the radioman send to the task force - Initiate search procedure blue."

Goro Arawi, acting executive officer, stopped in his tracks and looked back at the captain, "Sir, that is a wide-scale search pattern... our adversary is much closer."

"I'm aware of that, *Yakuin*," Igawa said gently. "I wish to confound them. Proceed, please."

"*Hai*."

"Surface contacts!" Rivers reported. "Three surface contacts bearing zero-zero-zero... oh... four contacts, sir... although one appears to be nearly on top of the other. Assess submerged submarine at about our depth."

"Designate targets as Able through Dog," Jarvis ordered. "The carrier is Able; the sub is Dog."

"Aye-aye," Rivers, Vigliano and the plotting party called out almost in unison.

"Baker and Charlie are underway," Rivers was saying. "Screw noise, spinning to high power... sounds like they're moving off in opposite directions."

"Probably a search pattern," Williams opined.

"Able is stationary... no, wait... slow, heavy screw noise," Rivers was listening intently and trying to discern the variety of sounds he was hearing. "I think... think she's making sternway, sir... or pointed northwest."

"How about Dog?" Jarvis asked.

"Can't tell," the sonarman replied. "She's not moving, though."

"Hmm..." the torpedo officer stroked his jaw in thought. "Can you get a heading for Able?"

"It appears she's moving... zero-four-zero, sir."

"Throwing down her gauntlet," Jarvis muttered.

"Daring us to come after her," Williams agreed. "Opening the range so we'll have to follow."

"Speed, Chet?" Jarvis asked.

"Turn rate is two knots, sir."

"We're gonna give him *exactly* what he wants," Jarvis decided. "Just not how he wants it. Diving officer, make your depth six hundred feet. Smartly. Helm, make turns for four knots."

There was a long pause, and then Nichols' disembodied voice said, "Pat... after that pounding we took off Savo..."

"Understood," Jarvis said, meeting Williams' gaze. "We may not need to go that deep. Find me a halocline. Chet...re-establish range to all targets. Single ping on active."

Rivers turned and blanched as he eyed Jarvis and then Williams.

"Mr. Jarvis has the con," Williams said simply.

"Single ping, aye..." Rivers announced.

The boat rang with the powerful super-sonic blast of raw decibels.

"That must be confusing the hell out of the Japs," Vigliano said with an irreverent chuckle.

"Got new range and bearings," Rivers announced. "Able bears three-five-zero, range fourteen hundred yards... Baker bears three-two-five, range twelve hundred, heading... two-seven-oh. Charlie bears zero-one-zero range sixteen hundred heading zero-nine zero."

"And the sub?" Jarvis asked.

"Still sitting there," Rivers said. "Range now one-one-five-zero yards... I don't know the depth, but I'd guess periscope depth for them."

"The wildcard..." Jarvis stated.

"Now passing one-five-zero feet," Nichols called.

"High-energy pinging," Rivers reported. "From Baker and Charlie. Able is quiet, even though we know she's got echolocation capability."

"And the submarine just sits there nice and quiet..." Balkley muttered.

The boat was tilted forward significantly. Jarvis had to put a hand on the periscope barrel to keep from slipping. Nichols was certainly taking them down smartly. The advantage was that they'd find a thermal layer more quickly... but the hull popping sounds would be easier for the Japanese to hear.

Bull Shark began to compress. The pressure of the sea seeking a way inside the metal tube that violated her depths. Popping, creaking and even groaning as the boat's steel skin and frames strained to maintain her shape and integrity.

"Now passing two-five-zero feet," Nichols called.

"Ease off on your planes," Jarvis ordered. "Fifteen degree down angle. Rig for silent running."

Williams dropped down and took up his position on the plotting party. At the master gyrocompass table, Hernandez, Andy Post and Chief yeoman Clancy Weiss worked together on the complex plot. Every few minutes Rivers would provide updated bearings, and the men would plot them out.

Whenever there was a complex problem like this, the yeoman was called in. Although his responsibilities were primarily that of the ship's clerk, Weiss was a genius with math. He could do in his head what many men had to use slide rules and even an adding machine for.

"What's he up to, sir?" Post asked quietly, jerking a thumb upward to indicate Jarvis.

"I think he's planning to beat the Japs at their own game," Williams said. "We've all had our turn; now it's his."

"He's smart enough to do it," Weiss stated.

"And *loco* enough, as well," Hotrod added with a grin.

Williams chuckled softly, "If there was ever a guy who's a *Bull Shark* at heart, it's Pat. I think he and the skipper have a lot in common. Little bit different styles, but Pat's fearless, confident and has the brains to do all of this in his head. He won't' let us down... but don't be surprised if the shit hits the fan soon."

"Ahem..." said Jarvis's disembodied voice from above. "You know I can hear you guys, right?"

"Now passing three-five-zero feet," Nichols called out and smiled at the other men. Behind him at the manifold stations, Buck Rogers grinned as well and gave a thumbs up. He then grinned wider and pointed at the small device mounted over the chart table.

The bathythermograph was a simple device that compared ocean temperatures outside the hull. It registered this data by tracing a stylus across a smoked card. When the ocean was isothermal, or the same temperature at all of the sensors, the stylus would simply trace a flat line.

However, the salt content of the ocean wasn't always the same. Different salinity levels altered the density of the water and its temperature. When that temperature began to change, the stylus began to zig-zag across the card, as it was doing now.

"Thermal!" Williams announced.

"Now passing four hundred feet," Nichols said, glancing upward at a particularly loud metallic snap.

The Cactus Navy

"Depth hold," Jarvis said. "Helm, come left to course zero-four-zero. Plot, assuming that Able hasn't altered course or speed, where would she be now?"

"Course zero-four-zero," Freeman announced a moment later.

"Pat, she's potentially bearing three-five-five, range nine-hundred yards," Williams announced.

"Elmer, can you run the TDC?" Jarvis asked.

"Oh, holy Christ..." Post muttered, "he's gonna shoot blind..."

"From four-hundred feet..." Weiss muttered with a head shake.

"Is that even possible?" Nichols asked.

"I heard of it being done below a hundred," the COB said.

"Tube doors are already open," Post added dubiously. "So, I guess..."

Williams went up the ladder and took Jarvis' usual position at the torpedo data computer. He activated the machine and began cranking known values into it.

"Phone talker, forward room," Jarvis said. "Order of torpedoes is one, two. Set depth on all weapons to six feet. Speed low. Elmer, this is a blind shot, so maybe a three-six degree spread."

"Pat... we don't have weapons to waste," Williams warned.

Jarvis sighed, "No... but we can't very well go up into that hornet's nest with only four either. I've got a plan, XO."

Mutterings and groans in the tower and below, but they were ironic and contained admiration.

"Set," Williams said.

Jarvis drew in a breath, "Fire one... fire two. Helm. Come left to course three-five-zero."

"Fish running hot, straight and normal," Rivers said. "Losing bearings fast, though... they've climbed out of the layer."

"Now we wait..." Jarvis muttered and crossed his fingers.

"He's out there," Igawa said to Arawi. "He's out there lurking right now... Sonar, send to I-123. Tell them to begin active echolocation."

"What of us, sir?" Arawi asked.

Igawa narrowed his eyes, "No... not yet, *Yakuin*.... We must draw him out, this American..."

"Sir, I-123 acknowledges," the sonar tech said from behind the two officers. "Beginning high-energy echolocation... sir... sir! Torpedoes in the water!"

The sonarman switched from headphones to the loudspeaker, and everyone on the bridge heard the high-pitched scream of steam-driven torpedoes. Igawa turned to him, "Where!?"

"Incoming torpedo, starboard bow!" A lookout on the observation deck screeched.

"Helm! All back emergency!" Igawa snapped. "Right full rudder!"

The ship's powerful steam turbines whined as more steam was shunted into them. Behind the bridge, partially buried in the island structure, the smokestack began to pour out greater amounts of exhaust as the carrier accelerated.

Sakai began to move faster, and her bow slowly turned to port as her stern turned to starboard, beginning a long arc that would draw her away from the onrushing torpedo. Igawa and Arawi ran outside and to the forward railing. Although the fog was lifting ever so slightly, it was still hard to see much more than what was beyond the square bow of the strike carrier. Yet out of the gloom, a ghostly finger of bluish light was visible. It grew longer and longer, reaching out inexorably for *Sakai's* nose.

"Will we clear?" Arawi wondered aloud as he watched with wide and fearful eyes.

"Yes...*yes!*" Igawa shouted in triumph. "It's running just ahead of us! Strange, though... does it not seem slow?"

Arawi was just pondering this obvious oddity as he watched the bubble wake disappear, blocked by the overhang of the forward flight deck and then reappear, tracking at an acute angle away from the ship.

"Another! Captain!" the same terrified young man shouted from the starboard side of the deck.

Both senior officers saw another ghoulish line of phosphorescent light materialize out of the blanket of darkness. Arawi's heart leapt into his throat as he mentally calculated the angles.

"Sound collision!" Igawa roared into the open hatch to the bridge. "*Now!*"

This time, the carrier would not avoid the torpedo. It had been fired at a slightly different angle, an angle that put it right in line with *Sakai's* middle.

There was a horrifying moment of tension as everyone on the bridge waited for the inevitable. It was almost a relief when it finally came... almost.

The ship shuddered violently, heeling to port at more than fifteen degrees. The collision alarm screamed, its long wailing cry sounding almost as if the ship herself were howling in agony.

Men were tossed off their feet and out of their chairs. Loose objects slid to the deck and shattered. Electrical shorts sparked off fires in the lower decks, and a secondary rumble sent shivers through the ship's frames.

"Damage report!" Igawa roared. "Phone talker!"

A young man with a sound-powered telephone was trying to make sense of the dozens of reports crisscrossing over the open circuit. He swallowed and looked at his captain with a face that was sweaty and ashen.

"Torpedo impact in fire room number one," he said almost breathlessly. "Fire in oil bunker number three... watertight hatches secure... flooding in fire room number one. Fortunate... it's helping to subdue the fire. Engineers on scene now, sir... they are making an inspection and organizing rescue parties... Lieutenant Nogata reports he believes that things are under control. We still have motive and electrical power from portside boilers."

"Helm, all ahead two-thirds," Igawa snapped angrily. "Port your helm... so, our American adversary has proven himself clever, Arawi. He has drawn first blood."

We're not out of the race yet, sir," Arawi said hopefully.

"No... our *Sakai* can still run, but she *is* limping," Igawa said. "Radio... all escorts, find that ship and sink her!"

"A hit!" Rivers exclaimed, raising his fists in triumph. "Got that son of a bee, sir!"

"That's some good silence there, Chet," Jarvis teased.

Rivers blushed, "Sorry sir... uhm... one fish struck. Thought I heard some flooding, but the carrier's three screws are still active. Sounds like she's turning, but the salt layer is making anything definitive hard to detect."

"Maybe *Sakai* is moving off," Williams said. "Pat... only one thing we can do."

Jarvis grinned, "Concur, Skipper... helm, all ahead two-thirds. Diving officer give me a ten-degree up bubble. Phone talker, alert the after room to stand by. We're gonna make another try for the carrier. I got another plan!"

"What about the DDs and the sub?" Andy Post asked from below.

"Low value targets," Williams replied. "That carrier is priority number one. Even with two destroyers up there, if we can kick the carrier out of the game, we've won. We also know there's a halocline at four-hundred so we can evade."

"Now passing four hundred feet..." Nichols stated.

"Still in the layer," Buck Rogers said.

"Echo ranging," Rivers announced. "Scattered and low-freq... but it's out there."

"Good," Jarvis said. "It'll give us an idea of where our dance partners are."

"Now passing three-eight-zero feet," Nichols reported.

"Bathythermograph is going flat," Rogers warned. "We're leaving the layer, sir."

Everyone aboard could hear it now. The eerie and thankfully distant low-energy sonar sweeps meant to locate a submerged boat. The low-energy sweep produced a longer waveform. Although less effective at homing in on an object and returning data, it increased the odds of detecting something that could then be pinpointed with higher-energy and higher-frequency pings.

Ooooo-eeeee... ooooo-eeeee...

"Don't know which is which anymore," Rivers said quietly. "But I think the source off our port beam is Baker, and the one off our starboard quarter is Charlie... light, fast screws, too... Baker is two-thousand yards, Charlie is twenty-one hundred yards..."

"Where's Able?" Jarvis asked tersely.

"Now passing three-five-zero," Nichols said.

"Hold your depth," Jarvis ordered.

"Detecting slow, heavy screws bearing zero-five-zero, range two-one-five-zero," Rivers said. "Nobody near us at all, sir."

"What's the speed on the carrier?" Williams inquired.

Rivers began pumping his fist up and down as he listened to the turn rates. There were a lot of sounds in the environment, and only a well-seasoned sonarman could tell them apart. Jarvis wished Joe Dutch were aboard as well. He and Rivers had the best ears of any sonar operators Jarvis had ever known. Dutch was simply blessed, and Rivers was quite an accomplished piano player, which probably helped to tune his ears.

"I think she's making six knots, sir," Rivers finally reported. "Headed... holy cow, sir! She's headed three-three-zero!"

"Plot?" Jarvis asked.

They knew what he wanted to know. After a moment, Hotrod Hernandez spoke, "She'll cross our bow at six hundred yards, sir."

"Active ping—" Rivers was cut off by a high-pitched whine that grew loud and then gonged off the hull.

"God *dammit!*" Jarvis cranked. "From where?"

"Almost dead astern... five-hundred yards," Rivers said.

"The sub," Williams pronounced.

"Aspect changes on Baker and Charlie!" Rivers declared. "Increased screw noise! They're headed for us!"

"Any other ideas?" Vigliano asked. "Now would be a good time, sir."

"What about a bubble?" Nichols called up from below. "I put a bubble into one of the tanks with the vents open."

"And it goes topside and gives our position away..." Jarvis said as he pondered. It wasn't a criticism; he was thinking through the problem.

"They've already got a position from that ping, possibly," Rivers said.

"What about a trail of bubbles like... like Hansel and Gretel?" Post added.

Jarvis and Williams' eyes met, and both widened. Jarvis snapped his fingers, "Yeah! But in the *opposite* direction! Wendel, hard right rudder, all back two-thirds. Frank, open vents in bow buoyancy and MBT number seven. Standby."

The torpedo officer watched the gyrocompass repeater until it read zero-three-zero. He could tell that the ship's forward way had been checked and she was moving backwards.

"Meet her!" Jarvis said.

"Here comes Baker! Charlie is incoming too, eight-hundred yards and closing fast!" Rivers announced.

Even from nearly half a mile, the churning of the destroyer's screws began to reach the submariners. It was faint at first but grew in intensity, sounding very much like doomsday.

Shoom, shoom, shoom, shoom...

"What're you waiting for?" Post asked from below.

Williams smiled a death's head grin, "Ashcans. Rig for depth charge!"

Another active ping, and it was joined by high frequency ranging from the DDs as well. Throughout the boat, compartment flappers were shut, and watertight doors dogged down.

Ping, ping, ping...

Shoom, shoom, shoom...

The roar of propellors was so loud the men had to raise their voices to be heard, even three-hundred and fifty feet below.

The Cactus Navy

"Splashes!" Rivers said. "Two... four... eight! Jesus... an even dozen! Both ships dropped and are crossing overhead!"

Silence... tension... and then the clicks...

Wham! Wham! WHAM, WHAM!

Bull Shark bucked and rolled and heaved. The underwater rodeo ride tossed loose objects and threw men off their feet. Gray snow drifted about compartments as cork insulation was shaken loose. Light bulbs exploded, and men cried out in fear and pain as tiny shards of glass scoured them, or they struck hard and unyielding objects with yielding flesh.

"Now Frank, blow the bow tank!" Jarvis shouted, barely managing to cling to the periscope barrel. "Wendel, all ahead full!"

"Holy Christ!" Vigliano said, his eyes wide and not from the bleeding cut on his forehead. "I think I know what you're doin', Mr. Jarvis!"

"Well shit, I hope so, Mug... you're the Goddamned quartermaster!" Jarvis guffawed. "Frank, blow number seven and close the vents! Hard dive! Get us back below the layer, fast!"

Outside *Bull Shark,* the echo-ranging continued, and the screws faded away. After a moment, however, they began to grow louder again. The boat angled down by the bow and drove herself toward the crushing depths in an attempt to escape.

"Quick, Chet, get me a last bearing on that carrier!" Jarvis said.

"Zero-four-niner," Rivers replied. "Still making six knots, still holding her heading."

"Phone talker, after room," Jarvis said. "Set depth on both fish to six feet. Order of tubes is seven, eight. Speed high this time!"

"Now passing four hundred feet!" Nichols shouted.

"Here comes the layer, sir!" The COB reported.

Boom! Boom,boom,boom... Boom!

From astern, several more tooth shakers exploded, the sound muffled somewhat by distance and the ocean layers. The boat was still rocked, but it seemed almost gentle as compared to what had gone before.

"Bada bing!" Vigliano laughed. "Them little yellow stronzos fell for it!"

"Chet?" Jarvis barked.

"Zero-six-five," Rivers responded. "Losing him, sir..."

"Mug? Elmer?" Jarvis inquired.

The men knew what he wanted to know. Williams was cranking numbers into the TDC, and Mug was doing a lot of figuring on his maneuvering board. He had the IsWas on the chart desk as well.

"He should pass astern of us at three hundred yards or so," Chief Weiss called up from below. He was the first to finish the calculation.

Williams was cranking that data in as well. What Jarvis wanted to know was when to fire and at what angle. Currently, *Bull Shark* was moving at nearly a perpendicular angle to *Sakai's* course. The carrier would pass astern of the submarine and continue on, opening the gyro angle that the two stern torpedoes would have to be fired at to hit her.

Another problem was that the torpedoes needed to run four-hundred-and-fifty yards before the impellor built into the weapon would arm the exploder mechanism. Fire too soon, and the torpedoes wouldn't arm. Fire too late, and the carrier would have time to evade, or the gyro angle would open too far, and the torpedoes couldn't be aimed without altering the ship's course.

"Helm, come right ten degrees," Jarvis called. "Frank, hold us at four-fifty."

The salt layer was scattering the sound above. Echo-ranging could no longer be heard, but the thrum of the larger ship's screws could. Although the temperature variation was distorting the sound.

"Okay, I've got a solution, Pat," Williams said. "I'm leading the fish a little and giving them a two-degree spread."

"Aye-aye, Skipper!" Jarvis said. "You have fire control."

"Ten-seconds..." Williams counted. "Five... firing seven... firing eight!"

"Helm, right standard rudder," Jarvis said calmly. It was done now. All torpedoes had been fired and whatever happened,

happened. "Decrease to all ahead two-thirds. Smoke 'em if ya got 'em, fellas."

"Fish running true..." Rivers said. "Rising through the layer now..."

"How long?" Jarvis asked.

"Fifteen-seconds," Williams said, leaning back in the torpedo officer's chair and stretching. "Getting hot down here."

"Ten..." Vigliano counted, peering at his watch. "Five... zero... minus five..."

Nothing. The torpedoes would have struck the *Sakai* by then if they were going to. After another thirty-seconds, it was clear they'd missed.

"Was a good try, Pat," Williams said. "You did tag him once, though. Once we get outta here and go topside, we can radio in *Sakai's* position and maybe Admiral Fletcher can take her out after sunup."

Jarvis sighed and sparked a cigarette, "So much for losing my virginity, huh? Elmer bagged a ship... Frank bagged a ship... Andy bagged a ship... but good ole Patty he ain't bagged a God—"

From far off, a distorted but unmistakable *thwack, boom* resonated through the sea. Even through the thermal layer, the sound found its way to the submarine's flesh and mechanical ears.

"Was that *Sakai*?" Jarvis asked in surprise.

Vigliano frowned at his board and shook his head. "No way, that fish ran a thousand yards past her bearing..."

Post stuck his head up through the hatch, "It's rough... but based on the courses and bearings from Able and Baker, you might have gotten one of them, sir."

"Get us up above the layer, then Andy," Jarvis said. "See if we can hear somethin'."

The submarine once more nosed upward, planing up through the dark ocean as she headed south and out of the combat area. Another distant clap of thunder, and then another.

"I'd swear that was a boiler going up," Rivers said, cupping his headphones.

"Now passing three-eight-zero," Nichols called.

"I'm getting contacts again," Rivers said. "Fast, light screws bearing one-two-five, range two-six-zero-zero... slow, heavy screws bearing one-six-zero, range two-one-five-five... that's all, sir. No, wait... I hear breaking up sounds."

Rivers switched to the loudspeaker, and everyone in the conning tower and the control room listened. There was the distant whisper of propellors churning water but overlaid was a terrible groaning and screeching that tore at every sailor's heart. It was the sound of a ship in the final and violent throws of her death.

Every man fixated on what was most likely the sound one of the destroyers plowed her way toward the abyss ten thousand feet below. Her hull, which had broken in two, plummeted through the water column, twisting and bending and scraping as the pressure built and deformed her steel. Several times, low thumps joined the groans as pockets of air were exposed and blasted outward.

"My God..." Jarvis said softly. "Poor devils."

"There you go, Pat," Williams said quietly, jerking his thumb at Rivers to turn off the sound. "Welcome to the club."

Jarvis smiled, "Feels both wonderful and terrible. So... can we go home now?"

Chapter 37

Guadalcanal
– August 9, 1942

The sun was barely peeking over the western horizon when the full implications of the previous night were realized. Although Martin Clemens and his coastwatchers, including Joe Dutch, Phil Oaks and the Japanese prisoners, hadn't seen anything on the night of the seventh... the night of the eighth to the ninth had been an entirely different story.

A storm had come in over Sealark Channel near midnight and had settled near Savo Island. The men were jolted from sleep when one of the islanders who was posted as lookout began shouting excitedly. Everyone rushed outside in the wee hours of the morning and in a misty drizzle to witness a spectacular battle.

Off toward Savo, an uncertain number of ships were engaged. Naval guns boomed and thundered; their roars carried far inland to the village of Vungana. Star shells exploded and soared over the sound, providing tantalizing glimpses of perspective-shrunken surface warships maneuvering and fighting one another.

For hours, it seemed, guns boomed, and shells exploded. The flashes of naval artillery and star shells hanging high over the combat area cast coruscating ripples of light on the underside of the storm clouds. At times the sky itself seemed to be aflame in a hellish light. More than once, huge fireballs erupted into the sky, momentarily painting the sea a goldish-crimson and illuminating a mortally wounded ship.

It wasn't until the first radio messages came in at dawn that the true implications of the battle and the true tactical situation around Sealark Channel became clear. The Japanese strike force, led by admiral Gunichi Mikawa had slipped right past the two picket destroyers positioned west of Savo. They'd surprised the cruisers and destroyers positioned between Savo and Guadalcanal and Florida Island and had fallen upon them and wrought a terrible vengeance.

The Australian heavy cruiser HMAS *Canberra* had been badly damaged and finally had to be scuttled. The American heavy cruisers *Astoria*, *Quincy* and *Vincennes* had been sunk as well. The heavy cruiser *Chicago* had been badly damaged, as had several other ships. More than one destroyer had been sent to the bottom in a vain attempt to do their duty. There were other casualties as well, not the least of which was the reported deaths of more than a thousand sailors.

Truly horrifying were the reports of men in the water being taken by sharks. The waters around Savo teemed with sharks, and they had become accustomed to dining on human flesh. The islanders, like many people who lived on small landmasses, needed an efficient way to dispose of their dead. So, they floated them out to sea after death, where they were consumed by predators. And those same predators had taken full advantage of the worst American naval loss of the war thus far.

This was hardly the only bad news. It seemed that Admiral Fletcher, worried about the safety of his air group with so many Japanese warships and planes in the area, had decided to leave the vicinity under the premise that his task force was running low on fuel. Further, this had alarmed Admiral Turner, who decided to pull his fleet out of Sealark Channel by sunup. General Vandegrift had talked him into a delay. It was only because Admiral Mikawa hadn't pressed his advantage and come after the transports did Turner agree to a few more precious hours.

The Marines on Guadalcanal and the other islands were alarmed by this. Even as of the morning of the ninth, less than half the supplies and equipment had been unloaded. Turner's ships had worked through the night to do so, but there simply wasn't enough time or manpower to accomplish the monumental task in less than the four days he'd planned for. So, before the sun set on this new day, the twenty-thousand Marines would be left with no air cover and no supply ships. They'd be alone, with only a few days of food to sustain them until something could be arranged. At least at Lunga Point the Japanese had abandoned enough food to allow the Marines on Guadalcanal to stretch things out for a few weeks, provided they cut meals down to twice per day.

And among all of this bad news and chaos, Lieutenant Commander Art Turner seethed and fretted over Porter Hazard. Jacob Vousa had made it back to the airfield shortly before dawn and had been allowed to sleep for a few hours before Turner debriefed him.

As the sun rose, Turner and Vousa sat sipping coffee together outside the Pagoda. They dined on a breakfast of canned bacon and eggs and some local fruit.

"How'd you get away?" Turner asked the islander.

Vousa chuffed angrily, "They allowed it. The Japanese officer provided me with instructions and told me to get back to you with his message."

"He spoke to me on the radio," Turner said. "He's out of his goddamned mind."

Vousa was troubled. He didn't like being set free after seeing young Entwater killed and Hazard taken prisoner. His deep-rooted feelings of guilt were etched into his face.

"Jake, you can't blame yourself," Turner said. "And you and I are gonna get him back."

"I would be wary, Commander," Vousa said.

Turner chuffed, "Yeah, no shit... but what choice do I have?"

After that, the two men gathered what was left of the landing party. The captain had explained the situation and asked for volunteers. To his surprise, every man stepped up, even Doug Ingram.

"We've got four sailors, one Marine Raider and a protectorate officer," Turner stated a bit glumly. "Against the entire Guadalcanal Jap force."

"Piece of cake," Duncan had quipped.

"Sir... we'd better run this by the General," Taggart had suggested. "He might not like us dashing off half-cocked like this."

At first, Vandegrift had not been open to the idea. The man was, unfortunately, furious and overburdened and had not reacted well to Turner placing one more thing on his plate.

"Goddammit, Commander!" the General had raved. "This is hardly the time for a fuckin' walk through the woods!"

"With all due respect, sir," Turner had said as he stood rigidly at attention. "Lieutenant Hazard deserves better than to be left to the Japs."

Vandegrift's brow had knitted ominously, "Let me tell you something, son. We just suffered a devastating blow last night... hell this morning! Boats are still pickin' up men outta the water... or what's left of them. That Goddamned Fletcher fucked off, leaving us no air cover. And now *Turner*... Christ, save me from Turners... is leaving and taking most of our supplies with him. I got Japs to the east and west, we got a Jap fleet somewhere in the slot, I heard a report that another goddamned Jap air attack is on the way from Bougainville, too! But that's not enough shit in my shit sandwich, no! Now *you* waltz into my office and claim that you're traipsing off into the jungle, risking more American lives to retrieve a single man on account of some nutty Nip officer challenged you to a duel! Does that about sum it up, *Mr.* Turner?"

The submarine captain had flushed crimson and cleared his throat, "Uhm... aye sir."

The Cactus Navy

Vandegrift glared at Turner for several very long seconds before he seemed to relent a little. He sighed heavily, "Christ knows, Art, that you and your men did a helluva thing coming ashore and getting with Marty Clemens. The success of our landing thus far is in no small part thanks to you and your boys. Not a man among you who won't get a medal for it..."

"Including Porter Hazard, sir," Turner pressed. "And I'd like to see him pin it on, not have it shipped to his family."

"Yeah..." Vandegrift said, suddenly soft and sad. "Wouldn't we all... but dammit, Art! You're risking half a dozen lives to save one. And *one* of those lives is a highly decorated, well-seasoned submarine commander. Not one man in ten thousand can do what you do, son. The Navy's invested a great deal in you and hopes to get an even greater return during this damned war. You don't piss that away on some half-assed gung-ho rescue mission."

"Sir..."

Vandegrift threw up his hands, "If I *ordered* you not to go, would you disobey me?"

Turner flinched and shifted from one foot to another, "No sir."

Vandegrift's eyes seemed to drill straight into Turner's soul. After a moment he nodded, "Very well. Permission granted, Commander. But I'm telling you now, if you think I'm eating your ass off, wait until you get to Brisbane and old Uncle Charlie gets ahold of you... You take only your men, understand me? I can't spare even a squad right now on such foolishness. You're a guest here, so if you and your sailors and Corporal Taggart want to do this thing... then on your head be it."

"Aye-aye, sir!" Turner said, snapping to attention.

"Dismissed," Vandegrift growled.

Turner had spun on his heel and opened the door. Just before he closed it, Vandegrift called out his name.

"Sir?"

The older man glowered for a moment and then smiled thinly, "God go with you, son. Good luck."

It was four hours later, as the sun was high overhead and turning the rainforest into a sweltering steaming misery that Turner's band of merry men made contact with Joe Dutch and his group. They met on the rough road that led to Palapao from Bumbagoro. The village of Bumbagoro, which had once boasted nearly forty people, was strangely empty. Something bad had happened there, as half the huts were burned to the ground and there were ominous dark splotches scattered about the houses.

Dutch had come with Oaks, Osaka and Hideki. Hideki was mobile but needed the support of Osaka. Oaks was doing all right on his own but did make use of a thick gnarled walking stick.

Ted Entwater had elected to stay behind. He would assist Clemens with his gear, as well as assist with watching over Captain Hinto until such time as Clemens was ready to come down to Lunga Point.

"What happened?" Oaks asked after the handshaking was over.

"The Japs got Porter's team," Turner explained. "They took out Batu and forced Vousa here to find me. There's some crazy Japanese officer who thinks that he and I are in some sort of deadly game of wits or whatever."

Osaka's eyes narrowed, "Is this man called Sato?"

Turner nodded, "You know him, Commander?"

Osaka laughed humorlessly, "I do. He's the executive officer of *Sakai*. An unpleasant man who struck Omata and I as being filled with hate."

"Your assessment was correct," Turner said and looked at Hideki. "Are you all right, commander?"

Hideki blinked and smiled but just shook his head.

"Omata does not speak English," Osaka explained. He spoke to his friend briefly in their language and then looked back to Turner. "He says he is doing all right and thanks you for your concern."

"Commander..." Turner began, trying to find a way to explain.

"There is no need, sir," Osaka said. "I understand the situation. Sato is offering to exchange your man for us."

The Cactus Navy

"That sort of works out in our favor," Dutch said.

"*Hai*... perhaps," Osaka admitted. "But I warn you, Captain... be wary of this man. I would not trust him."

Turner scoffed, "Yeah, no sh... you're correct, Commander. I don't. Yet, I have no choice. We're to bring you to Palapao. I suppose we should get going... unless Hideki or you, Sarge, would like to rest awhile?"

"I'm good," Oaks said. "The sooner we get there, the sooner we get Mr. Hazard back... and the sooner I can start paying back the Japs for what they've done."

He cast a quick look at Osaka. Turner thought it might contain just a hint of apology.

"I understand, Sergeant," Osaka said.

"All right, here's how we're gonna play it," Turner said. "Me, Dutch and the two guest officers will approach the village. Corporal Taggart and Tank will be our guard. Oaks, Doug, Chief and Jake, you stay behind and concealed, ready to back us up. If the balloon goes up, you start blastin'."

"That exposes all of our most valuable assets, sir," Oaks warned.

"Nah, I'm hangin' back," Duncan quipped and grinned.

"Unavoidable, Sarge," Turner stated. "Sato expects to see me and his officers. I hate to ask you to stick with me, Joe... but you do know some Japanese."

"As do I, sir," Oaks reminded Turner.

"Yeah, but you're wounded," Turner said. "Joe?"

"I'm in," Dutch said without hesitation.

"All right then, let's move out," Turner said. "We get Porter and get back to the airfield. I've got a nice chewing out coming from command, it seems, and don't want to miss *that*."

Everyone chuckled and broke up. The backup team stayed a hundred yards behind Turner, and after hiking through the sweltering jungle for another two hours, they came to the bend in the road that opened to reveal the village of Palapao.

"Christ..." Dutch muttered as he surveyed the scene.

"You should've seen it up close," Taggart quipped.

The remains of the five-inch naval gun still sat where it had been. The trailer had been blasted to bits and the gun had toppled over onto its side. A blackened, half-demolished husk was all that remained of the six-wheeled truck that had delivered the gun. The land around the machinery was scorched, and at least two huts had been reduced to charred piles of rubble by the explosions.

Standing outside the communal hut, as casual as if they were waiting for a table at a sushi house, were half a dozen Japanese Marines and one naval officer resplendent in his stiff-collared white uniform. He was a beefy man. Large for a Japanese national, although still half a head shorter than Turner. The man's large round face split into a grin when he saw the Americans walk into view. He even waved jauntily as they approached.

Turner and his men had their Thompson sub-machine guns held at the ready. Interestingly, the *Riekusentai* held their Arisaka rifles at port arms but not even close to a ready fire position.

"As you see, Commander," Sato said as Turner approached to within a dozen paces. "I too have security... but they are not taking an aggressive stance."

"I suppose I should be grateful, Commander?" Turner asked acidly.

"I told you, this is a matter of honor," Sato said, sketching a bow. "My word that this exchange would be a simple and straightforward matter."

"Uh-huh."

"Good afternoon, Osaka san," Sato addressed himself to his countrymen. "I trust you are well? As is Commander Hideki... mostly."

Osaka nodded, "We have not been mistreated."

"That is fortunate," Sato said, grinning wickedly.

"Where is my officer?" Turner demanded.

"Just there," Sato said, pointing to a stand of trees behind one of

The Cactus Navy

the huts. "He is alive and waiting for you. As promised, I tended to his wounds and fed him."

"Then bring him out," Turner demanded.

Sato laughed, "No, I'll leave that chore to you. I'm aware that you have a second team behind you, Arthur. A bold but predictable move. Very good, our game begins. I have no wish to be ambushed. My men and I will escort the commanders to our aircraft and be on our way. What happens once we're gone... well, that's between your forces and ours here. I am just a sailor, after all. I want nothing to do with this land warfare foolishness."

"No deal," Turner said. "You bring out Lt. Hazard right now, or none of you leave."

Sato laughed, a deep and self-satisfied belly laugh, "Treachery? I think not, Captain. Observe."

From out of the vegetable fields to the north, men in pale khaki began to appear. First four, then eight, then twenty and then fifty. An entire Imperial Army platoon. They quickly formed into two ranks, with the front-rank kneeling. Fifty Arisaka rifles swung up and took aim. The soldiers were two-hundred yards away, but that was more than close enough to hit their targets.

"Treachery indeed," Turner spat.

"They will not harm you if you do not make any aggressive moves," Sato said. "Their instructions are to guard our retreat, see that you recover your man and not to interfere as you make your way back to Lunga Point."

Turner could see rage briefly flash over Osaka's face. The man quickly schooled himself into stoic resolve, however. He couldn't afford to protest, even using honor as a premise without raising suspicion.

"Then go," Turner growled, "and remember that we have a score to settle, Commander."

Sato laughed again, "Oh, believe me, my worthy opponent, it is not something easily forgotten. Good afternoon... and let our game begin."

Sato, Osaka and Hideki moved away behind the huts, surrounded by their guard of Marines. For a long moment, the four American men simply stood in the clearing, gazing at the platoon of soldiers staring back at them. When would the hammer fall? When would the betrayal be revealed...? When would they be mowed down?

"They aren't firing," Tank said quietly, as if even speaking the concept aloud would make it so.

Turner saw that Sato's party was at least as far away as the soldiers, headed for a river and a big seaplane that had landed on it, evidently. Nothing seemed to move for a long moment.

"Let's go get Porter," Turner said, a growing sense of dread curdling his stomach.

Something was wrong. Something was in the works; he could feel it. The entire scenario simply *reeked* of a setup.

The three men moved behind the huts, momentarily out of sight of the Jap platoon. They rounded one hut and approached the small stand of palms. Porter Hazard was indeed there.

The Japanese had crucified him.

Hazard hung suspended between two palm trees, his own palms nailed to the trunks, and his feet lashed to each one as well. His BDUs were coated in dried blood, and his head lolled limply from his sagging body.

"You bastard..." Turner could barely manage to whisper, so overpowering was his fury.

A red mist of rage descended on him. Nothing else existed then. Just pure, primal rage that felt as real and alive as he did. The world lost its definition. He could hear nothing, didn't feel the heat nor the light breeze. Only his own heartbeat thundered in his eardrums as his vision tunneled. The only sensation was his anger... and the hard steel and wood of his weapon.

"Sato!" Turner screamed as he spun and brought the weapon to his shoulder. "You mother-*FUCKER!*"

The stifling afternoon was ripped open by the clatter of the automatic weapon expelling its .45 caliber shells downrange in the direction of Sato's party. They were by then almost three hundred yards away. Too far for the Thompson to be truly accurate.

Turner's weapon began to click as it dry fired, but he couldn't release the trigger. Finally, Tank shook him and broke him free of his spell of rage.

"Sir! Sir!" the electrician's mate was shouting. "He's alive!"

Whatever Turner might have said was cut short by the crackle of fifty rifles going off almost at once. The army had joined the fray, or so it seemed. In the next instant, though, nothing happened.

The three men were behind several huts and not in the direct line of fire of the IJA. Perhaps they were shifting position and that was just an opening salvo?

Turner didn't care. He sprinted over to where Taggart was using pliers to pull the thick nail from Hazard's right palm, "Help me, Tank! Support his weight!"

Taggart yanked out the nail and did the same to the other hand. Turner bent and began untying the knots from the man's left ankle while Taggart did the other. Soon they had Hazard lying on the ground, gasping for air, his face a tortured mask of agony.

"Jesus God all mighty..." Tank breathed, his horror at what the Japanese had done so powerful that tears sprang into his eyes. "You hang in there, sir... you're gonna be all right..."

Turner hoped that was true. Aside from having spikes driven through his hands, the submarine officer had been stabbed repeatedly with bayonets. The Japanese had been careful about not making any of the wounds fatal by themselves. Several in the meaty muscles of Hazard's thigh, a bicep, the muscle of a shoulder, a foot... but taken together along with the beating they'd obviously given him... his right eye was swollen shut, his lower lip split and bleeding, and the left side of his face swollen and purple with bruising... he was in danger of losing his life.

"We gotta get him outta here," Turner said, his enormous wrath having drained away to be replaced by fear for his officer and friend. "That son of a bitch... why aren't the Japs shooting anymore?"

The village erupted into gunfire again. Yet something was odd. It wasn't coming from the north this time... but from the east, from the road.

"Don't tell me Oaks is firing on a whole fuckin' platoon!" Taggart gulped in disbelief.

"Nah... that's way too many weapons..." Tank said in confusion. "And ain't that a fifty-cal?"

He was right. Dozens of rifles were firing, and over them, a heavy machine gun was chattering away. There was firing from the north now, along with shouts in Japanese and high-pitched shrieks of agony. The three men looked at one another in astonishment.

"No time to worry now; let's get Hazard outta here," Turner said.

"Sir..." Hazard croaked, his unswollen eye cracking and gazing at Turner.

"I'm here, Porter, just hang on, buddy," Turner said, reaching an arm under Hazard's back and under his buttocks. "Come on, Tank. Taggart, you cover us best you can."

"Aye-aye," the Marine said, shouldering his weapon and leading the way out of the stand of trees and east.

The fighting grew in intensity for a moment and then seemed to die off. As Turner and his men stumbled out of the relative cover of the huts, casting about for some way out of the village without being gunned down, they stopped in their tracks, their mouths gaping open.

Two Deuce and a Half trucks were parked on the road along with a Jeep. Mounted to the Jeep and being manned by a Marine in camo was a .50 caliber machine gun. A platoon of Marines lined the road, their Springfield rifles trained on what was left of the IJA platoon. Standing near the leading truck was Oaks and his party, along with two Marines Turner had met the previous day.

"Over here, sir!" Private Robert Lecky called out.

"With all due respect, Commander, get the lead out already!" Whitey Groft called from beside him. "Who knows how many more of these monkeys are out here?"

"Thank the living Christ!" Tank huffed as he and Turner side-

The Cactus Navy

stepped across the open ground with their burden. "The fuckin' Marines!"

"Hoo-rah!" Turner exalted.

"Thought the General wasn't sendin' anybody!" Taggart exclaimed in disbelief.

"Don't look a gift horse in the mouth, Davie!" Tank declared and laughed out loud.

"Captain..." Hazard croaked out in obvious agony.

"Yeah, Porter, yeah... we'll have you with a doc in a jiffy; just hang in there," Turner encouraged.

"Yeah... that's all fine and great... but I could really use a cold beer, sir..."

The three men with Hazard laughed uproariously with the release of their tension and terror.

"You got it, Port," Turner said. "I'll even spring for a joy girl. Show her your purple heart; she'll love it."

Hazard coughed up blood but managed a pain-filled chuckle, "Oh... I'll show her somethin' purple, sir..."

They were met by cheering Marines and a medical corpsman. The navy corpsman began to examine Hazard but was stopped by Groft.

"Not now, Doc, get him into the truck," the corporal said. "The general'll be mighty peeved we don't bring back what he sent us out for."

"Damn sir!" Lecky observed as he glanced Turner and his party over. "They call us *Marines* crazy."

"You're the ones that came out here," Dutch said wryly. "Coulda stayed back safe and sound at the airfield and waited for the Japs to bomb you."

"Boring," Lecky said and lit a smoke.

Epilogue
Brisbane, Australia
– August 13, 1942

"Permission to come aboard, sir," Rear admiral Charles Lockwood said as he stood at attention near the end of the gangplank.

"Granted, sir, you're welcome," Art Turner said, still feeling odd in his clean service khakis after so long in dirty BDUs.

Lockwood cut an impressive figure standing on the brow with the hilly city of Brisbane rising beyond the submarine tender and Morton Bay to his left. He saluted the colors aft and then stepped up and extended his hand.

"So, you're Anvil Art Turner," Lockwood said. "Damned glad to make your acquaintance, sir."

"Thank you, Admiral. Likewise," Turner replied. "And welcome aboard *Bull Shark*. Would you like to take a turn through the boat, sir?"

"I would, Captain," Lockwood said. "And then I'd like to meet with your officers in the wardroom. Let's make room for the boys to deliver your mail and some goodies for the lads."

Bull Shark was tethered outboard of two other submarines, with

– August 13, 1942

the huge submarine tender herself moored to one of the quays at the naval facility. The relief crews were following behind the admiral carrying crates of fresh fruit, ice cream and sacks of mail. *Bull Shark's* crew, under the watchful eye of Buck Rogers, waited and fidgeted on the boat's wooden decks... or what was left of them... to enjoy their arrival in port. They'd enjoy the fresh supplies before being dismissed for R and R.

Turner led Lockwood down the forward hatch into the torpedo room and then all the way to the after room and back to the forward battery compartment. There, they stepped into the wardroom where Elmer Williams and Pat Jarvis sat sipping coffee.

"I have to say I'm impressed, Captain," Lockwood said. "Your boat is as spit and polish as any inspecting flag officer could wish. You'd be amazed at some of the disasters that pull in here."

"Thank you, sir," Turner said. "I owe it all to a top-notch set of officers and men."

ComSubSoWesPac nodded as he accepted a cup of coffee from Eddie Carlson and sat down, "All right, gents, I'm a busy man and I like to cut to the meat of any matter. First of all... Captain Turner. Would you mind explaining to me just what in the exact *hell* you thought you were doing, going to meet a Japanese officer with only eight men?"

"It's all in my report, sir," Turner said stiffly. Now he was in for it. "And after all, Admiral... we'd already been doing reckless things for nearly a week."

"Are you being flip with me, son?" Lockwood asked in a hard tone and with narrowed eyes.

"No sir," Turner replied neutrally. "But our mission was already dangerous. And I couldn't leave my man out there, sir."

Lockwood studied Turner for a long moment before the hard-set lines of his face softened and he permitted himself a small smile, "Anvil Art Turner... Jesus H. Christ... when Bob English and I talked about the kind of submariners and captains we needed to fight this

Epilogue

war... we should've made you the mold, Captain. And you obviously rubbed off on your officers. Barely a week on station off Guadalcanal and you boys bagged two destroyers and a pair of heavy freighters. Over twenty-thousand tons of shipping and with only four fish! Ha-ha-ha-ha! I sure as hell can't ride you too hard for that. You're what we need in this war, gents. The Jap knows how to fight, and he's damned good at war. We're behind in many ways, and it's men that know how to push the envelope that're going to bridge the gap and send our enemy backpedaling all the way to Honshu."

Williams's and Jarvis's stony expressions eased into smiles of pleasure and relief. Turner's did as well.

"Now I'm not here to blow smoke up your asses," Lockwood went on and then chuckled. "Well, not entirely. The Watchtower mission has just begun, and it's going to be a heller. Your job isn't done there, Captain... nor any of you. I'm sorry to say that your crew isn't going to get much liberty this time out. Give you all a couple of days while the relief crew loads you up and slaps on some patches. But with Fletcher and Turner both bugging out, our Marines are sitting out there in the eastern Solomons with their green butts hanging out. It can't be allowed. We'll talk more about this in seventy-two hours, Captain. I've got something planned, and I think *Bull Shark* is just what I need. Now then, there is something else that I've been asked to do both by Bob English and by Admiral Nimitz himself. We'll handle that before you shove off."

"Sir?" Turner asked.

"The boat's getting another unit citation," Lockwood stated. "I've got Silver Stars for all of your officers. For this mission and the last. An additional Bronze Star for Williams here, and one for Hazard, too. How is he, by the way?"

Turner sighed, "In bad shape, sir. We couldn't risk moving him, so we left him at the medical clinic at Lunga Point. Admiral Turner's doc fixed him up before they pulled out."

Lockwood sighed, "Brave man. Got some medals for a handful of

– August 13, 1942

your men, too, Captain. And no, I didn't leave you out. You're getting a Silver Star to go with that Navy Cross of yours. General Vandegrift has also requested that you receive the Navy and Marine Corps Medal for your performance."

Turner flushed, "Sir... I... that is... thank you, sir. The awards for my men are honestly reward enough for me."

Lockwood grinned. Like Turner, he'd been a submarine captain. He knew what a good crew meant to a commanding officer, and he nodded in knowing approval.

"This has been a hard year," Lockwood said more solemnly.

"Hard for the Fleet. Hard for the country. We've taken a lot of hits and have barely managed to hold our own. And the hell of it is, 1942 isn't even over yet. But thanks to you men, and thanks to Major Decker and his Raiders... and to the ongoing efforts of our Marines in the Solomons... we've finally been able to hit back. To throw a solid punch into Hirohito's *guts*, gentlemen. He got himself a draw in the Coral Sea. He struck out at Midway... and now he and his bucktoothed lackey Tojo know that America can and will hit back and hit back *hard*. We've got more men lining up to serve and more boats coming off the stocks every week or two. And it's young, aggressive go-getters like you boys that're gonna spearhead the Navy's push right up to Tokyo Bay. Exec, you get your repair and replenishment list to the tender asap. I'll make sure it's gun-decked through. You fellas go enjoy your three days off. Have a few beers, catch a show... and watch out for those Australian ladies. They're so eager for men you might lose half your crew! Then get back aboard because I'm sending you right back into the lion's den."

"Aye-aye, sir," Turner said, and all the men stood.

Lockwood shook their hands and he showed himself back up on deck. After he'd gone, Nichols, Post and Dutch filed into the wardroom with expectant looks on their faces.

"Well, it's official," Jarvis said. "We've gone and screwed up in reverse."

Epilogue

"Huh?" Post asked.

Williams smiled, "We're so good that Uncle Charlie is sending us back out to get our butts handed to us again."

"It's not all that bad, guys," Turner said wryly. "We do get three whole days to kick up our heels."

"Three?" Post asked a little irritably. "Most boats get two weeks, sir."

"Most boats stay on patrol for two months," Jarvis pointed out wryly. "Our patrols, so far, have been short."

"New mission?" Nichols asked. "Think it'll be another one of Mr. Clayton's crazy notions?"

That drew groans from the officers and even Carlson.

"Who knows?" Turner asked. "From the sound of it, though, we're headed back to the Solomons. I, for one, am glad. We've got a missing man in this wardroom, and after what he's gone through, I want him back."

That got a round of here-here's.

"All right, gents, it's shore leave time," Turner said. "Go enjoy yourselves."

"What about you, Skipper?" Williams asked.

Turner smiled, "Oh, I'm gonna join you. First round of drinks at the O-club is on me. But first... I'm gonna write a letter to Joanie."

The men filed out, with Pat Jarvis lagging behind long enough to treat Turner to a smile and a squeeze on the shoulder. Almost as soon as the big torpedo officer had vanished through the baize curtain, Paul Rogers stepped in.

"Buck, how the hell are ya'?" Turner asked. "How's the noggin?"

"Been on duty since before you came aboard, sir," Rogers said.

"I know... just wanted to check in as your buddy Art and not as the CO."

Rogers grinned, "I'm as sound in the mind as you are, Skipper."

"Well, then we're doomed," Turner said and then got serious for a moment. "Just between us chickens, Paul... how'd the crew do this

– August 13, 1942

time out? How are they feeling? I wasn't here for some of the hijinks..."

"They did great," Rogers said. "Even with missing officers and men and casualties... including me... the boys really stepped up. As for how they feel, Art... they're beyond proud. As far as they're concerned, they work for a legend. You goin' ashore only made it a bigger one."

"Oh, hell..." Turner demurred at that.

"Don't worry, they know you're human too," Rogers said. "That sort of makes it even better. You're this larger-than-life war hero that's something right off the silver screen... and yet they know the real you, too. Warts and all. We're a family, sir. And you're the fun dad."

Turner laughed, "Good... thanks, Buck."

"If it's any consolation, there's a rumor goin' round that you and the other officers are gonna be in Life magazine. That Tregaskis guy interviewed you before we left, and there's other scuttlebutt along that line."

Turner chuffed, "They can do better than me. Now Elmer... and Pat, too. They'd make great stories."

Rogers chuckled and shook his head, "America needs war heroes, Art. Just be thankful you're not being sent stateside to sell war bonds."

Turner laughed and shook his head, "No, they're being kind to me and putting us all back in Tojo's crosshairs again! All right, COB, get your sorry ass topside and go tie one on. I've got a letter to write."

"Tell Joanie I send my love, sir."

Turner sat at the table with a sheet of lined paper before him and suddenly realized he didn't know what to say. How did one summarize so much in so few words? How to communicate all that he felt in simple pen?

There wasn't really even a need. Joan still had the ham radio set that Clayton had installed in their home... he *could* just talk to her. Yet, he felt something was needed. He felt that he needed to put something down on paper for her and for his children.

478

Epilogue

Inspiration came, and he began to write. The words poured out of him, and the feelings that expressed themselves onto the page were true and right.

He finished and sat back, blinking away tears and smiled, "In short, gang... I love you."

A Word from the Author

Phew! Was that a roller coaster ride or what? I sincerely hope, as I always do, that I've brought you a few hours of entertainment. A few groans, a rolled eye or two and a couple of laughs.

Writing this series is, I'll admit, a lot of hard work. Yet, it's also incredibly rewarding. As often as I color outside the lines… that is to take poetic license with history… I do labor to utilize as much historical truth as I can. For the truth is, especially when it comes to this war, incredible enough on its own. The bravery, sacrifice and Herculean efforts of the greatest generation cannot be exalted enough. There is a great deal of reading and research that I do for these novels, and I hope that what comes as a result has been satisfying for you as well.

As you can tell, we're already set up for book #4. To be honest, the invasion of Guadalcanal and Tulagi was so important, and so much happened that I could've literally written an entire novel just around August 6 – 9. And there is so much more to come! We just can't move the *Bull Shark* on to other pastures yet, as Hirohito and his men have a great deal more planned for the Solomons.

If you've enjoyed this book, I urge you to visit Amazon or Audible and give it a review. Your comments and thought are always welcome… even the poopy ones. For example, in *Leviathan Rising*, it was pointed out *after* the damned book was published that both I and my editor missed the fact that I was using the word ordinance rather than ordnance when talking about bang-bangs! I've fixed it since, but it just goes to show you that even a sour puss, like a clock, can be right as much as twice a day!

Oh, and I've been informed by Mike Roll, my editor, that I did it again 3 times in this one, too...! But that was because I was writing it when I got the review and missed changing ordinance a couple of times... so my bacon has been saved!

I'd also like to urge you to visit my website and join my free email list. You'll receive a free novella from another of my series, Scott Jarvis, Private Investigator – a case that involves diving for Spanish gold, no less. Also, I occasionally send out a newsletter with information and goodies about once a month, so you won't be bombarded with junk.

www.scottwcook.com

Warmest regards,
Scott W. Cook
Storyteller, amateur historian and crackpot

Other books by the Author...

Scott Jarvis Private Investigator

A thus far 11 book series that follows a cop turned P.I. in Florida whose cases range the state from Orlando to the Keys, from Tampa Bay to Miami. Follow Jarvis as he faces down mafia bosses, dirty FBI agents, Central American warlords, corporate raiders and even comes in contact, in an indirect way, with the men of **USS** *Bull Shark!* Oh, and if you see a coincidence between Scott Jarvis and Pat Jarvis... you're not wrong. They're related.

Catherine Cook Sea Adventures

It's the great age of sail when heroes like Hornblower, Aubrey, Lewrie and Nelson sail the seas in their battle against revolutionary France and Emperor Napoleon Bonaparte. A young woman, bred to the sea in the tradition of her grandfather, the famous James Cook, finds herself thrust into a struggle against Britain's enemies and in command of a frigate. A unique take on a fascinating historical period filled with adventure and courageous deeds. Cannons thunder and steel clashes in this 2 book and growing series.

Printed in Great Britain
by Amazon